THE
GIRLFRIEND

THE GIRLFRIEND

Michelle Frances

KENSINGTON BOOKS
http://www.kensingtonbooks.com

KENSINGTON BOOKS are published by

Kensington Publishing Corp.
119 West 40th Street
New York, NY 10018

All Kensington titles, imprints, and distributed lines are available at special quantity discounts for bulk purchases for sales promotion, premiums, fund-raising, educational, or institutional use. Special book excerpts or customized printings can also be created to fit specific needs. For details, write or phone the office of the Kensington Special Sales Manager: Attn. Special Sales Department. Kensington Publishing Corp., 119 West 40th Street, New York, NY 10018. Phone: 1-800-221-2647.

Library of Congress Card Catalogue Number: 2017951257

Kensington and the K logo Reg. U.S. Pat. & TM Off.

ISBN-13: 978-1-4967-1246-2
ISBN-10: 1-4967-1246-3
First Kensington Hardcover Edition: February 2018

ISBN-13: 978-1-4967-1248-6
ISBN-10: 1-4967-1248-X
First Kensington Electronic Edition: February 2018

10 9 8 7 6 5 4 3 2 1

Printed in the United States of America

THE
GIRLFRIEND

PROLOGUE

Monday, March 2

I LOVE MY SON. THAT WAS ALL THAT COUNTED. IT DIDN'T MATTER THAT she was about to do something heinous. An opportunity had been granted to her, a beacon of light through the devastating last few months, and Laura knew she had to take that opportunity. She'd agonized over it for hours; but now that the decision was final, she felt a wave of terror at what she had to say. The words that were going to break her into pieces. This was the first time. She briefly considered rehearsing it, but the words—the word—wouldn't form properly in her head. Her instinct was to bat it away violently.

Crossing to the sink in the en suite bathroom, just off the private room at the hospital, she looked at herself in the mirror hanging above. A brief check that her soul was still intact through her worn blue eyes reassured her further. No flashing green irises, no demon-like pinhole pupils. She looked more tired though, and she was shocked to see how much she'd aged. There were more lines around her eyes and mouth. There was also a sadness, a haunting despair that she had desperately tried to keep at bay with this new expensive hospital, the best doctors she could find, and brittle hope. For a moment, she forgot what she was about to do and thought only about what was soon to happen.

The heartbreak was a physical force that made her double over, clutching the sink. After a few seconds, she stood. Nothing had changed.

Cherry was back today. Laura had checked and the flights from Mexico usually arrived at Heathrow early in the morning. She looked at her watch. Maybe she'd be back in her flat in Tooting by now.

A lump formed in her throat as she held her phone, but she swallowed hard. She had to get this right. *Any mother would do the same,* she reminded herself again and again, a mantra to get her through it.

She dialed the number carefully. She went cold, then clammy, in alternative waves, buffeted around by her agony. Her life was soon to end. The life that had meaning. Holding the phone with two hands, trying to stop their shaking, she waited for the rings in her ear to be terminated.

1

Nine months earlier, Saturday, June 7

*L*AURA HAD A GOOD FEELING ABOUT TODAY. A DELICIOUS START-OF-the-summer sensation had embraced her the minute she opened her eyes. She was up and dressed before it was even seven-thirty on an already-hot Saturday in June. Walking along the landing to Daniel's bedroom, she listened for sounds of him stirring, but the room that they kept clean and welcoming while he was at medical school was silent. He was still asleep, hardly surprising, seeing as he'd come home long after she'd gone to bed the last couple of nights. Daniel had been home from university for two whole days now, but she'd not yet seen him. Work was at a pressure point and she left early in the mornings and he was out when she came home. Catching up with old friends, no doubt. She was envious of those conversations, hungry for information. She wanted to hear everything, soak it all up, enjoy the excitement she felt for him just starting out in his professional life, and relish the summer with him before he went off to do his hospital training. Today was their day, no last-minute urgent changes to the drama series she was producing for ITV that kept her in an edit suite until nine o'clock at night, no meetings, just a day together, mother and son.

She opened the door a crack, the smile ready on her face. The room was flooded with sunlight, the curtains wide and the bed made. She stopped there for a moment, confused, then realized he must have gone down to make breakfast. Glad that he was already up and about like her, she hurried excitedly down the stairs of her Kensington house and burst into the kitchen. It was empty. She looked around, a little lost, a pang of anxiety fluttering through her. Then she saw a piece of notepaper on the counter. Scrawled on it was a message: *In the basement. Will be HUNGRY!* She smiled. He knew she hated it to be called the basement; the word rang with a false modesty. It was a huge addition that went vertical, instead of horizontal, and had cost her husband a fortune. Still, it was no worse than what he called it. Howard had wanted a "den," he'd said, and she'd almost laughed at the absurd understatement, except that she knew he wanted his den in order to get away from her. He'd suggested it quite casually one night and said it would be useful, somewhere for "either of them to get a little space," and she'd struggled to hold back the astonishment and hurt. They hardly saw each other anyway; he was always at the office or golf or tucked away in his study. He'd then employed some very skilled and expensive builders who had dug out the earth beneath their house and filled it with a game room, a wine cellar, a garage, and a swimming pool. The neighbors had been upset with all the noise, the conveyor belts of rubble spewing out of the ground, and the general disruptive blot on the landscape. She'd been left to apologize, but at least it had been temporary and nothing like the steel magnate's four-story subterranean bunker down the road, which had caused his neighbors' front pillars to crack.

Taking the elevator down to the pool, she waited for the hum of the motors to stop and then stepped into a twilight of lapis lazuli blue. Cutting a frothy swathe through the sublit water was Daniel; as usual, the sight of him made her heart soar. She walked to the top of the deep end just as he was finishing his length and knelt down to the water's edge.

He caught sight of her and stopped, water pouring off his strong shoulders as he hoisted himself effortlessly out of the water and threw his arms around her. She squealed in admonishment, as he knew she would do, grinning and holding her tight; and then unable to resist, she hugged him back.

Feeling the wet seep through, she pushed him away and brushed at the dark patches on her yellow shift dress.

"That was not funny," she said, smiling.

"Just giving my old mum a hug."

"Less of the 'old.'" In Laura's head, she was still twenty-five and often looked at other women, fascinated by their encroaching middle age before realizing she was the same generation. It amused her that she was stuck in some sort of age amnesia; amused her still further when a look in the mirror confirmed that although she looked good for her age, she most definitely was not twenty-five.

"Come on, all the boys fancy you, and you know it."

She smiled. It was true she enjoyed the flirtatious company of Daniel's friends, the way they came around and leaned lazily on her breakfast bar, addressing her as "Mrs. C" and telling her how good her French toast was. It had been a while since she'd seen them.

"How are Will and Jonny?"

"Don't know." Daniel started to dry himself with one of the plush towels that Mrs. Moore changed three times a week, regardless of whether or not anyone had used them.

"But didn't you see them yesterday?"

"They work," he said flippantly, disappearing around the side of a carved wooden screen, "already out there changing the world."

"In insurance? And I'm aware they work, I was talking about the evenings. Where have you been, then, the last couple of nights, if not with the boys?"

There was a silence from behind the screen and Laura didn't see that Daniel was smiling, a secret smile of reflection. He'd meant to keep it to himself for a bit longer, but suddenly felt the urge to tell someone. Little by little, he would let out some, not all, of the details, enjoying reliving them as he did so.

"Hey!" he said as Laura poked her head round.

She stood, arms crossed, waiting for him to answer her question. "You're perfectly decent." She watched fondly as he pulled on shorts and a T-shirt, proud that her genes had produced such a good-looking young man. Of course, Howard had had a part in it, but their son took after his mother in looks. Same height, same thick, wavy blond hair, and strong bone structure. Instead of giving her the answer he knew she wanted, he smiled cheekily as he made his way to the elevator.

She took a sharp intake of breath. "Don't you push that button."

"Are you coming?"

Laura followed and pretend-pinched his earlobe. "I'm going to get it out of you."

The lift started to rise. "Ow! Can I take you for brunch?"

She lifted her eyebrows. "It requires an announcement?"

The doors opened and he took her hand and led her out and through the hall into the expansive oak-and-granite kitchen. "Just want to treat my mum."

"You old charmer. But before we go, give me a clue. I couldn't stand the anticipation." She stood firm.

He poured himself a voluminous glass of juice from the fridge. "I've been looking for an apartment. You know, for when I start the hospital training program."

She sighed. "You're sure I can't persuade you to move back home?"

"Ah, Mum . . . apart from the holidays, and not all of those, I haven't lived at home for five years." It wasn't that Daniel led a louche social life, he just enjoyed his privacy as any twenty-three-year-old male would, and didn't want to spend the next two years living under his childhood roof, basement pool or not.

"Okay, okay. So, apartment hunting. At night?"

He grinned. "Just meeting with the agent."

It took a moment and then it clicked. "A girl?"

"She's very thorough. Knows exactly what I like."

"A girl!"

"You say it like I've never dated before."

"But this one's special," she said decisively.

"How do you know?"

"Well, you've seen her the last two nights, haven't you?"

"Yes . . ."

"And only just met! Come on, spill. What's her name?"

He was amused by her enthusiasm. "Cherry."

"A fruit! Short season, select."

"What?"

"Exotic?"

"She's got dark hair. . . ." He held up a palm, shook his head. "I can't believe I'm saying this."

Laura clutched his hand. "No, don't stop, really. I want to hear all about her. Where's she from?"

"Tooting."

"She *is* exotic! Sorry! I was joking. I'll be serious now." Laura kissed his hand contritely. "How old is she?"

"Twenty-four."

"And she's a real estate agent?"

"Yes. Well, she's training at the moment. She's only recently started."

"And she works here in Kensington?"

"She wanted to sell nice houses." He heaved himself up onto the work surface. "She learned about the area by pretending to be moving here. Went to see twenty-seven flats with other agencies before going for the job. Found she could talk about the properties and the likely clientele with aplomb." He laughed. "That's what I call enterprise. And then . . . quite audaciously, made up a résumé. Or at least embellished it. Made herself sound like the 'right kind of girl.'"

Laura smiled, although she was a little taken aback by Cherry's behavior. Which was silly as she had nothing to do with her work and wasn't her employer. She tapped Daniel's knee with the back of her hand. "Come on, I thought you were taking me out."

He jumped down and held out a crooked elbow. "It will be my pleasure." He wanted to treat his mum, look after her, be the son that he knew she, somewhat embarrassingly, liked to show off. They'd sit in the brasserie and she'd bask in their mutual good humor, and he knew he'd enjoy himself too. He always made time for them to be together, especially ever since he'd been aware that the relationship between his parents had little warmth. There wasn't even much in the way of companionship. His father was rarely around, as his job as partner at a large accounting firm kept him fully occupied; Daniel wanted to make up for some of the loneliness that he knew his mum felt. It had been a while since he'd seen her, which added to the guilt, the prickly discomfort of another secret. He hadn't yet told her he was cutting their day short. He was seeing Cherry again tonight.

2

Two days earlier

MAYBE HAVING THE BEST OF EVERYTHING WHEN HE WAS A CHILD meant that he never yearned for anything, at least nothing that money could buy. Daniel had been bought a superb education and was clever—a fortunate combination that meant he liked school and school liked him. He'd shown a particular aptitude for science, which had delighted his parents and professors, particularly when he'd been invited to study medicine at Cambridge. To complement his academic cultivation, he'd had the holidays that were considered necessary: He'd learned to ski, to dive, and to appraise the world. He'd done all of this with an enjoyment and interest that had reassured and pleased his parents; but despite being lavished with everything a boy could want, Daniel had somehow managed to remain unspoiled. His response to the Great Wall of China was one of genuine wonder, and he was grateful for the comfort of the first-class flight home. However, when he'd arrived at Heathrow, he'd jumped on the tube rather than call his father's driver to come and pick him up. His laid-back attitude extended to clothes and he grew perversely attached to items that had long since passed their best. Once, he'd retrieved a pair of briefs from the trash that Mrs. Moore had thrown out on one of his trips home from university. He'd then hidden them, holes and all, in the side pocket of his holdall. Those briefs were old friends and he would not be parted from them.

And so it was that he set foot in a real estate agency on one of the most expensive roads in London that represented some of the most exclusive properties, while he was dressed in a faded T-shirt and a pair of cargo shorts with holes where the seams met at the pockets.

"I need a flat," he said, smiling to the hesitant girl who politely approached him as he came in the door.

"To buy or rent?"

"Buy." And he was directed to the back where a dark head was bent forward over a large, gleaming wooden desk, scrutinizing some papers.

"Can I help you?" When she looked up and smiled her client-welcoming smile, he felt himself respond in kind. Suddenly the job of flat hunting seemed a whole lot more pleasant. She had a cap of straight raven hair, which danced as it moved around her face.

"I'm looking for a flat."

Her eyes were dark too, deep pools with fathomless depths. In them, he caught the mental calculations as she subtly took in his frayed shorts and T-shirt.

"How many bedrooms? Did you have a particular location in mind?"

"Two bedrooms," he decided instantly, thinking the second would be useful as a study. He hadn't had much time to think about what he needed as he'd driven back from Cambridge early that morning. Wandering around his parents' house, he'd been aware of the likely pressure from his mother to stay if he became too comfortable. It was best to start the ball rolling straight away; it wouldn't be fair to let her get her hopes up.

"And location?" Once again, he detected suspicion about what he was doing here. No streets around Kensington and Chelsea were cheap, but some were prohibitively expensive. He knew he didn't look the sort to have a couple of million to spend. Which in theory, he didn't.

"Cherry Laine?"

Her face smiled tightly. Irritated, but trying to remain professional. "There's no such street in the area."

"God no, I wasn't winding you up." He pointed to her nameplate, black letters on brass background, and smiled. "You should be in an agency in a village in the Cotswolds or something."

She stared at him long and hard, then turned her iPad to face him. "Depending on your price category, we have four properties that match what you're looking for. This one is just two minutes from Knightsbridge station—"

"I'll go and see it."

She paused and tapped her screen. "Okay. This next one—"

"I'll see that too."

"But I haven't even told you about it."

He enjoyed watching her uncertainty about how to take him. No doubt, most people who came in here were stuffed with the importance of how a property should be, how it should rightfully fit their needs. They probably put great energy and effort into finding the perfect place, something that seemed to Daniel a colossal waste of time. The quicker he got it settled, the better. "And the others."

"In a hurry?"

"I should imagine for the price, they're all pretty nice? How much are they, anyway?"

"These particular properties range from between two and a half and four million—"

"Wow!"

"And, yes, they're exceptional—"

"There you are then. I need somewhere to live and I'm sure I'd be extremely fortunate to live in any of those you've selected. So, shall we go and take a look?"

Her hands fluttered over the screen. "I need to make appointments."

"Later today then?" He smiled. "I'm sure I'll be your easiest client. I'll have one picked by teatime. It is you showing me around, isn't it?"

She flicked her eyes across him, reassuring herself she hadn't just encountered a psycho. "Yes," she said firmly, "it is."

This time, he was smarter, she noticed. Since he'd walked into her office this morning, he'd changed into a pair of navy chinos and a light blue shirt. So far, he'd followed her obediently around the first-floor apartment with little comment. She waved a hand toward the ground. "As you can see, there are wooden floors throughout, and one of the benefits of this property is, of course, the hallway."

He gazed up and down. "What's so special about it?"

"It's not so much that it's special. It's the fact it's there."

He thought: In what world was a hallway considered a perk when you were paying two and a half million pounds? He didn't want to offend her by saying this, and, after all, he was guilty by association. He was the one looking around it.

"And this is the living room," she said, indicating the room through a doorway.

He peered in. "Nice sofa. Yellow."

"Lemon," she corrected. "Of course, these furnishings will be removed on sale. The owner has left them to present the property."

"So, it's vacant?"

"Yes. And there's no chain."

"Did the owner not want the sofa at his or her new place?"

Bemused, she looked at him. "I should imagine . . ."

"What?"

"They bought new."

He smiled, then followed her down the covetable hallway, glancing down to see if there was anything he might be missing, but decided to concentrate on Cherry instead. He liked the way she walked, with purpose, as if she cared about where she was going and the reason for getting there. He had a feeling she might extend this determination to other parts of her life, and he found himself wanting to know more about what they might be. Just then, she turned and caught him staring at her. She stopped and folded her arms.

"The kitchen is in there." She pointed and it was obvious he was meant to go first.

"Sorry, I wasn't staring at your bum."

She raised her eyebrows at his outspokenness. "Are you really interested in this flat?" As much as there was a certain charm about this man, she couldn't bear time wasters. And she had a pretty good eye for spotting them, having been one herself, although that was justified as it was a means to an end.

"Yes," he said quickly, wanting to reassure her. "I'll take it!"

"But we haven't seen the others."

"This is the cheapest of the ones you have available, right?"

"Yes."

"Why pay more? Even this seems . . ."

"Yes?"

"Obscene?"

She looked at him.

"Sorry, I just find it a little . . . offensive. All this money. For one flat."

"But you want to buy it?"

"Yes, please. And I'd like to buy the furniture too. If it's for sale." In fact, Daniel had been told in no uncertain terms by his father that renting was not an option. It was considered a complete waste of money—his father's money, really, as Daniel had a trust fund. If the flat passed his father's scrutiny, it would become a family investment. "Anyway, one flat's much the same as another, isn't it?"

Cherry opened her mouth to speak.

"Of course, it's not! No, no, sorry . . . Consider me very ignorant. But . . . I was just thinking . . . there are better things we could be doing with our time."

She braced herself, knowing what was coming next.

"Are you free tonight by any chance? Could I take you out for supper?"

Cherry always found it amusing the way rich people called it "supper," as if they'd never quite left boarding school. At least, it gave her a little more confidence that he actually might be able to afford the flat he'd just so casually declared he'd have. This was actually her last appointment of the day; they were supposed to have seen the others the following morning. All she needed to do was return the keys to the office and the evening was hers. She thought about her plans, a ride home on a sweaty tube that delivered other workers to various parts of South London that diminished in salubrity as the seats were emptied. She always felt left behind, the poor relation by the time they reached Tooting Broadway, but at least, she thought with a shudder, she wasn't quite at the end of the line. Then it was a quick stop in Sainsbury's to get something to eat before returning to her tiny flat with no hallway. She'd hang up her precious suit with the others, the most valuable things she owned, and then no doubt would spend the evening studying property on the Internet and wondering just when she might be able to get out of there. She looked up at her client. She liked him, liked his devil-may-care attitude. It made a change from those who turned a property down because the bathroom fittings were chrome and not brass, and were offended when the seller wouldn't change them before closing. Why not go out for supper with this man, she thought. It was, after all, the reason she'd worked so hard to get a job in this part of town in the first place.

3

*L*AURA SAT IN HER USUAL SEAT, AT A RIGHT ANGLE TO HER HUSBAND, and picked at her grilled-chicken salad. All the windows in their large, airy dining room were open, but it still felt oppressive. She'd spent a languorous afternoon in the garden. Daniel had been sprawled out on a lounger, she under the giant umbrella. He would answer her questions, with eyes closed against the sun, laughing at her enthusiasm to know everything about Cherry; she was taking full advantage of the fact he couldn't see her drink him in. Then, just when she'd stood to go and start cooking, he'd opened his eyes and sat up, with an awkward look on his face.

"I meant to say . . ."

She turned back, a smile on her face.

"I sort of promised Cherry . . . It's a concert. In the park . . . I'm sorry, I know I said I'd stay home with you and Dad. . . ."

She quickly swallowed her disappointment and brushed off his apologies, telling him to go and enjoy himself.

Laura looked down the length of the empty gleaming formal table that seated ten, with just her and Howard clutching the end as if they were on a sinking ship, and suddenly felt an overwhelming irritation with it and the bizarre way in which they sat, following some dead ritual for so long neither of them questioned it.

She turned her gaze to him. He didn't seem bothered by the table, the heat, the fact they'd stopped talking to each other. He was reading the day's *Telegraph,* with his glasses pushed up onto his forehead, while filling his mouth with salad and new potatoes. He'd been out all afternoon—she was used to that—but now he was back and she wanted to talk. She heard the chink of his knife on the china plate, the Mozart playing in the background, and her voice intruding sounded alien.

"Anything interesting?"

He didn't look up. "Just the golf."

The golf. She felt a twitch of hurt. That was one of the few things he still got excited about. That, and Marianne, of course. She never knew which he was really doing. He'd always tell her it was the golf, every Saturday, Sunday, and some weekday afternoons too, when he could get out of the office. However, she knew— knew by the way he came back a little happier, a private happiness he kept within himself—which days he'd seen her. It wasn't that it was a surprise; that had come twenty years ago when she'd first discovered the affair. Mrs. Moore had gone through his pockets before taking the suits to the dry cleaners and left the receipts on the kitchen worktop. She'd seen them at breakfast, after Howard had already left for work, and Laura knew in absolute certainty she'd not received those flowers, nor had she been taken to lunch the previous Saturday. He denied it at first, of course, but she knew, and eventually he angrily admitted it—as if it was her fault.

"All right, it's true. Are you happy now?"

It was the wrong choice of words. Of course, she wasn't happy, her world had just imploded, and then she discovered it had been going on for two years and he was in love with Marianne. She was married, too, though, had young children, and wasn't prepared to split up the family. Laura considered leaving him—she had some money, so she would've been all right—but there was Daniel to think about. And Howard, in an emotional outburst, said he didn't want to leave his son, who was barely out of toddlerhood, so he promised to finish it and she took him back. But things changed. Howard was miserable for weeks, working late and hardly saying a word, and the irony was that he never saw Daniel anyway. They fell into a pattern. He went to work and she brought up their son. Laura was used to loneliness. Her childhood had been an endless string of nannies as her mother went to parties and her father was at work. She was an only child—it had been too inconvenient for her parents to have any more. Laura had longed for a relationship with her mother, but it never came, and both her parents were now long dead. Determined that Daniel wouldn't feel as abandoned as she had, she buried the hurt over Howard's affair into positive things for her son: clubs, holidays, friends. Their relationship grew strong and Howard started to feel left out. He found it even harder to be at home and worked even longer hours and the resentment grew. Because he felt sidelined, he became crueler to Laura, criticized her parenting when Daniel cried on the weekends at this man whom he didn't recognize, who picked him up.

Then one evening, after Daniel had started university, Laura was at home while Howard went out for a drink.

"Just someone from the club," he said.

It had harpooned her unexpectedly, when she was filling the kettle with water, a sudden, swift plunge to the heart and she dumped the kettle in the sink while she fought to breathe again. For she suddenly knew who someone from the club was. Marianne was back, now that their respective children had grown. And then she remembered he'd been out with someone from the club the week before. Before that, she couldn't remember and panicked while she wracked her brain. After the revelation had subsided, she felt exhausted, beaten; she knew it was because those two were still in love. Gradually "golf" had spread to whole weekends and she saw him less and less. Occasionally she considered whether she should ask him for a divorce, but it didn't seem to matter so much anymore. Even though she knew Howard was the cause of the loneliness, facing up to it, breaking them apart, would only make the wound open and raw. She'd always preferred to concentrate on other things. Daniel had been at the center of her life for so long, and now she was secretly thrilled with the notion that he'd found someone special, someone she might be able to be friends with.

"Daniel's out again tonight."

"I assumed as much."

"That's the third night in a row."

He still hadn't looked up from the paper and let out a small laugh. "He's a grown man."

She suppressed her frustration. "Yes, of course. He's with a girl."

Finally Howard looked at her. "Good for him."

She smiled. "I think he's smitten. They only met three days ago. And he's seen her every night since."

"What's your point?"

"Oh, come on, Howard. Don't you want to know who this girl is who's swept him off his feet?"

"You obviously do."

"Maybe I'll text him."

"Don't you dare," he whip-cracked.

Hurt, she paused, with the fork midway to her mouth. "I'm *joking*."

"Leave him alone. Just because for the first time in his life, you don't know every detail. Don't interfere."

"I'm not interfering," she said quietly, and suddenly wanted to leave the room. She put her napkin down on the table and got up. She was about to take her plate to the kitchen when—

"You're obsessive"—it was sudden, blunt—"possessive."

She stopped dead.

Neither of them said anything for a moment; then he got up from the table and left.

Laura stood there, her plate in her hand. Tears pricked at her eyes, not just at the shock of the accusation, but because of the look he'd given her as he left. It was a look of deep resentment. She sat for a moment, and then as if to stop his words settling on her somehow, she stood again quickly and walked into the kitchen. She knew better than to follow him; he'd gone to the den and, anyway, she didn't feel like confronting him, wasn't in the mood for an argument.

The plate clattered on the counter and then the anger and indignation at what he'd said came out. He was the one who had made himself absent all those years. What did he know about the mammoth job of bringing up a child? The all-encompassing care when they were tiny, the lack of sleep, the wiping of cheeks, hands, bums, tables, high chairs, wipe, wipe, wipe. The inability to go to the bathroom by yourself, the absolute knowledge that one hug from you would soothe the bumps and bruises, and those hugs had to be always available. The constant reverse psychology/humor/diversion tactics required to get through an average day with a toddler. He'd never had to deal with, or suffer, the heartrending tears when they didn't want to go to nursery school or try to work out why, when their four-year-old reasoning couldn't explain they found it difficult to have the confidence to make friends. He hadn't had to make the decisions over sports, clubs, and parties, or work out how to strike the balance between encouraging independence, without making their son feel he was unsupported, or solve the night terrors after the sudden death of his grandfather from a heart attack. What did he know about any of this? She felt a rage at his appalling shortsightedness; and then with a glass of wine, the anger subsided. Nobody knew any of this, nobody but a mother.

She picked up her wine and found her book by the fridge and took them into the darkening garden. The jasmine was beautifully pungent, its hundreds of tiny white starlike flowers just breaking out now that June had arrived. She lit the citronella candles and soon the moths came to investigate. As she sat in the swing seat, she let her mind drift. It was funny thinking back—it had been practically just the two of them for years, and now Daniel was on the verge of moving out permanently. She was suddenly reminded of something he used to say when he was three. He'd pretend to be a puppy and bound around her.

"Woof!" he'd say. "Do you like him?"

"He's gorgeous."

"You can keep him if you want."

"Can I?"

"You can keep him forever." And he'd throw his arms around her neck tightly.

The cat came mewing pitifully, his tail like a toilet brush, and she saw a fox sniffing around the large opaque window in the middle of the lawn that formed part of the ceiling of the subterranean pool room. Moses jumped onto her lap and stood there, still meowing and waiting for salvation. She'd originally gotten him for Daniel when her son was nine, to teach him about looking after pets. He was a small silver-gray Burmese and she'd ended up growing quite fond of him. Picking up a small stone, she threw it in the direction of the fox; she disliked them, was wary of their capabilities and lack of boundaries. Recently she'd heard a distraught, incredulous woman call into a radio breakfast show talking about how a fox had brazenly walked in through the open back door and climbed into her baby's cot in the middle of the day. She shuddered. If that had been Daniel when he was small, she would have probably smashed the fox's head against the patio. Three nights in a row, she thought with a smile. Who sees someone three nights in a row right off? What did this girl have that was so special?

As she mused about Cherry, she thought about another girl, a girl a tiny bit older than Daniel. Rose was Laura's firstborn. She'd been the perfect baby, eating and sleeping right on schedule from day one. Which was why it had been so unusual when at only a few days old, Laura had had difficulty waking her to nurse. When it happened again three hours later, Laura was worried enough to take her to the doctor. He took one look at her and she was rushed to hospital. She was diagnosed with group B streptococcus, contracted from undetected bacteria in the birth canal. After twenty-four hours, the doctors told them Rose was going to die, and two hours later she did, in Laura's arms. She was exactly seven days old.

The guilt had almost broken her, and their marriage. Laura was consumed with the thought of whether Rose would have survived if she'd gone to the doctors when she'd slept through her first feeding. The thing that saved them both was her getting pregnant again. Ten months later, when Daniel was born, Laura had vowed to whichever presence might be listening that she'd devote her life to this tiny creature and never let anything happen to him. And in return, could he be kept safe?

The cat lowered itself onto her soft thighs, half-closing his eyes in relief at the fox's disappearance and Laura stroked his fur. He watched the demented moths with occasional darting eyes, but was either too lazy or tired to actually do anything about them. As Laura swung gently in the seat, she thought fondly of this girl she'd not yet met, this girl who was the same age her own daughter would have been.

4

Saturday, June 7

*I*N HER LIFE, CHERRY HAD NEVER BEEN ON THREE DATES, ONE NIGHT after the other. They headed into Hyde Park, past the golden Albert Memorial and across the Serpentine; Daniel was carrying a picnic hamper backpack, while she held the blanket. It was hot against her body and she moved it, trying to have as little contact with it as possible. The blazing heat of the day had subsided into a Mediterranean-like evening. It was still light, and would be for at least another four hours, and the park was full of people filled with a spontaneous holiday-like zest and optimism.

Cherry was starting to enjoy herself. They'd gotten past the first couple of dates, with their potential for awkwardness and bouts of extreme politeness, and invisible ties had started to form. She knew he was extremely focused on becoming a cardiologist, liked cycling and white-water rafting, and wrote using his left hand, but ate with his right. He knew she liked strawberries, but not strawberry jam, her father had died when she was young, and she'd lived in a flat with her mum, whom she'd rarely seen because her mum had had to work.

She'd kept to herself that the flat was in a run-down part of Croydon, in the midst of streets that were constantly littered with debris: empty beer cans, discarded soft furnishings and general detritus, unidentifiable sodden rags that looked as if they still contained something misshapen inside their dirtied casings. There was little money when Cherry was growing up, even less so when her father had died. He'd been so stupid, so selfish, as to not have life insurance. Her mother had had to increase her hours at the monolithic superstore on the edge of the town just to keep their tiny flat, and Cherry found her material world shrinking from low-budget fashion to hand-me-downs, no vacations except the occasional day trip to the beach, and embarrassments at school. No money for a copy of the annual photo when all her friends were crowded round, giggling over who stood next to whom in the yearbook picture, while Cherry stood aside, excluded and self-conscious. She had hated being poor. No, Cherry kept all this to herself and said something vague about coming from Surrey, which Croydon used to be part of, albeit many hundreds of years ago. More information changed hands and with familiarity came warmth, and gentle teasing reinforced those tender bonds. They'd also had their first kiss, a not unpleasant experience; in fact, Cherry knew she found Daniel extremely attractive.

They reached the fenced-off arena where tonight's concert was to take place. Daniel handed over the tickets he'd miraculously managed to get hold of at such short notice and they were in. They followed the throngs to the grassy seating area and she let Daniel choose a place that had a good view of the stage. He laid out the blanket and she sat down, stretching her long, lightly tanned legs out in front of her. She noticed that quite a few people had brought portable chairs and was faintly aggrieved that they didn't have the same. She suspected after a few hours her backside would feel the hard ground beneath it, but then the London Symphony Orchestra started to warm up and she made an effort to put it out of her mind.

"I used to come here every year when I was young," said Daniel. "We'd walk over, bringing tea with us. It was Mum's way of educating me in classical music."

So this was his local park. It was a far cry from what she'd grown up with: the careworn bleak collection of paint-peeling apparatus that had always harbored a few lifeless teenagers, like mold you couldn't quite get rid of. Cherry had never been to a classical concert before, although she made a point of listening to Classic FM every now and then. She thought she'd carefully test him out with this news.

"First time for me. With classical anyway."

He batted her statement away. "Trust me, you missed nothing before now. At least, I never really appreciated it when I was younger. Early twenties is the perfect time to enjoy classical—it says so in the Scriptures."

She smiled, pleased with the way that went. It seemed she was not to be judged for cultural holes in her upbringing, which made her relax a little. Should she ever make a faux pas or misunderstand something, it hopefully wouldn't put him off her.

"So this means then," she said, accepting the chilled glass of Chablis in the obligatory plastic glass that he poured for her, "that we are at our peak."

"The entire Proms lineup beckons. What are you doing the first Friday in July?"

She thought quickly as to what he could be referring to and remembered what she'd heard on the radio. It was the very first concert—the start of the BBC Proms annual eight weeks of classical music.

"Standing in the Royal Albert Hall, waving a Union Jack?"

"It's a date," he said, laughing, and they looked at each other, both glad they'd banked something for the future, and each had been as keen as the other. Then the music started to play and she watched the violinists bow fiercely in unison, each musician pouring his heart into the score. Goose bumps appeared on her arms and she turned and smiled at him in a way that made him catch his breath.

"I wish I had a talent like that," she whispered admiringly before turning her face back to the stage.

Daniel sneaked little glances at her while she was watching the orchestra. He loved how there was something refreshing about her newness to things. Old girlfriends, sisters of his friends from school, had been hard to surprise, and some even harder to please. He'd often felt jaded just by being in their company. Cherry, although far from gauche, hadn't been hothoused since a toddler and he found he could enjoy a classical concert that he'd experienced many times before, just by being there with her. He suddenly felt an urge to share even more with her: galleries, concerts, trips to the coast, maybe even a holiday abroad. There and then, the summer took on a new promise.

As Mozart's symphony lifted her and dropped her back down again, Cherry sensed she was being watched and she let him. She enjoyed the attention and it was nice to have it from someone of quality, something that had only happened once before in her life.

It had been six months since she'd last seen Nicolas Brandon, but his face was as clear as if he sat in front of her right now. She'd persuaded an old school acquaintance to go out for a drink (on the pretext of wanting to catch up), only the place she chose was a small, discreet, upmarket cocktail bar some way from both of their homes. She walked in, her friend exclaiming in loud admiration behind her at the surroundings, and there he was, as she knew he would be. She opened her purse and took out some money.

"Do you mind getting these? I'm going to the loo."

Her friend went to the bar and Cherry walked toward Nicolas. When she was only a couple of yards away, he looked up and the startled, embarrassed look on his face both gratified and pained her. He was the eldest son of a telecommunications mogul and was in his last year of a master's in economics at Oxford as a precursor to the training he'd get at his father's side; eventually he was destined to take over the family business. He'd grown up on the Webb Estate, a gated residential conservation area housing multimillion-pound mansions in the very southern part of Croydon, where the hundred-year-old "rules" included a banning on the wearing of shorts and hanging out washing in the garden.

She saw him glance around as if he was pretending he hadn't

noticed her, but there was no way on earth she was going to let him escape. She advanced right up to his table until he had no option but to acknowledge her.

"Hi," he said, feigning surprise.

"Hi yourself. Didn't think I'd see you here."

"Michaelmas break. We finished last week."

She knew this because she'd looked up the dates for the Christmas holidays on the university's website.

"So, er . . . you still come here?" he said.

It had been their place, one that he'd brought her to on their first date, and she remembered the times they'd held hands across the table and made plans for when he left to go back to university. She was going to change her shifts so that she no longer worked weekends at the restaurant where they'd met and instead visit him at Oxford. It hadn't struck her at the time that all the plans had been to his benefit more than hers.

"Last time probably. I'm moving."

"Oh yes? Where to?"

"Kensington." It wasn't strictly true, but there was enough truth in it.

"Oh?" A tiny, disbelieving smile crossed his face, as if she'd gotten confused about where and what Kensington actually was.

"What, you don't think I'm good enough?"

He frowned and looked away. "It's not like that."

"No? I remember you saying your parents had certain demands on you, things you said weren't your ideas, but you had no choice if you ever wanted a chance to take over your father's business."

She looked up as a girl, a beautiful silken blonde, approached the table from the direction of the restrooms, a look of consternation on her face. Cherry stood stock-still, her heart hammering. He hadn't wasted any time. This was the kind of girl his parents would approve of: a girl with money, a good background, good connections.

"Is everything okay?" she said suspiciously, looking from one to the other.

"Fine," said Nicolas quickly.

"Here you go, one apple martini," said her friend, thrusting a glass at her. She saw Nicolas look up. It was a drink he'd introduced her to and she immediately wished she hadn't ordered it. She turned sharply and walked away and heard the blond girl sit down and ask hushed questions about who she was. When she got to the bar, she looked back and saw them huddled. He was trying to persuade her to drink up so they could leave; and all of a sudden, Cherry didn't want to be the one left behind. She threw back her drink, grabbed her friend's hand, and announced they were going.

It wasn't how she'd planned it. She'd wanted him to be impressed, wonder if he'd made a huge mistake dumping her at the end of the summer, maybe even realize he wanted her back. For Cherry had always believed Nicolas would rescue her. Pluck her from the celebrity chef's restaurant chain where she worked. A dead-end mistake of a job that she should never have had.

She'd been destined for better things. Incredibly bright at school, she was too much for the overstretched teachers who'd just given her more work and let her get on with it. When she'd left with five top-grade A Levels, she was completely broke. University was out of the question. She just couldn't afford it. It wasn't just the cost and the debt; Cherry had an urge to escape from her poverty-ridden lifestyle. She wanted to do the most simple of things, like learn to drive, move away from home, start to create a life for herself. But her generation was entering a future that had very little to offer. Unemployment for the under-twenty-fives was at an all-time high, and they certainly had no hope of buying a home. Instead *their* long-term financial burden would be paying off the nation's debt.

In desperation, she'd disappeared on a working vacation to Australia with her meager savings from a Saturday job, thinking that there would be opportunities there, that she would try a number of different jobs and someone would notice her cleverness, her potential, but she soon realized it was a treadmill of fruit picking and waiting tables. Worse, she'd felt poor. She wasn't meant for backpacking. So she'd come back and the only job she'd been able to get was as a hostess at the restaurant. A step above waiting tables. What was supposed to be temporary had slipped one year into the next and she'd watched, incensed, as the graduates in the training programs got fast-tracked to managerial positions and bigger paychecks. People her own age who were less smart than she was, but who had been able to afford university, apparently received automatic kudos.

Just when she was at her lowest, Nicolas had come along and her world opened up again. Being with him made her feel good, feel special, like she belonged. Her brain reengaged as they debated how to fix the economy and youth unemployment. He gave her a taste of what life with money was like and she had held her head high in the fancy restaurants and been a natural at picking out a good wine. Then it all ended abruptly one Saturday evening when instead of picking her up as planned, Nicolas had phoned to tell her his parents wanted him to concentrate on university and they felt she was a "distraction." They were forcing him to choose between her and a role at the family business and he couldn't put her through an uncertain future, which he might well have if he wasn't gifted a job with his father. The breakup devastated her. All the time that she'd been honest about her humble upbringing, the inadequate school, the working-class family, it had been a bitter mistake. She realized by the way he'd cast her aside that she wasn't going to find her opportunities being who she was. So Cherry decided she would reinvent herself. Then she would immerse herself in the world in which she aspired to belong. Only this time, she wasn't going to tell anyone where she came from.

All through her school years, Cherry had had one loyal ally, an ally that fought side by side with her to put her in a better place: books or, more commonly, the Internet. It was extraordinary what you could learn. She'd read avidly, one link pulling her to another until before she knew it, she'd woven an intricate web of self-acquired knowledge. Added to this were day-to-day world affairs from the *Guardian*, where she'd absorbed the language of the erudite journalists and carefully eliminated any last trace of

Croydon from her voice. When she'd gone for the interview at Highsmith and Brown real estate agency, she'd felt reassuringly well-armed. With a few embellishments on her résumé, the research from her false persona as a Chelsea-ite, along with that web of knowledge she'd worked so hard to create, she landed the job.

It had been five months since she'd joined, almost to the day. She knew because she'd seen the date approaching in her diary, marked with a red circle that was placed there as a target—or maybe a warning—and so far the only male attention she'd had, had come from the window cleaner.

"All right, love?" he said as she changed the sales details in the window and she stiffened before checking whether anyone had taken any notice. He continued to cast glances at her as he swooped his squeegee in arcs over the window and she fumed with humiliation. Why couldn't he chat up one of the other girls? Abigail or Emily. She felt he could see through all she'd built up and recognized a kindred working-class spirit. She was horrified that his attention might expose her.

"Talk to me again and I'll have you fired for hitting on me," she said, then turned her back.

Other than that, they were married, gay, coming in with their girlfriends, or so far up their own arses that they didn't notice her.

But all that was behind her now—finally her luck had changed.

As the orchestra got up for the interval, Daniel turned to her.

"What do you think?"

She was suddenly filled with a heart-soaring happiness. Here she was on a glorious summer evening at a classical concert with a man who seemed intent on making sure she had a good time.

"It's fantastic."

She looked around and sensed she could spot those with money; the girls were made up of a disproportionate number of blondes, their hair effortlessly honeyed and falling in long waves that they tossed from side to side, knowing it would fall coquet-

tishly back over their eyes. The boys were tanned and their ex-
pensively casual shirts fell outside shorts that were slung low over
buttocks. The same as the boys back (she never said "home")
where her mother lived, but the difference between here and her
part of Croydon was the cost of the underpants. She felt a sense of
fierce pride that she could hold her head up amongst them. She
was no different from these people; in fact, she was probably
smarter, and the fact she'd made it so far proved that she was capable. It just went to show what you could achieve if you thought
about it and put some effort into it. For the first time in a long
time, she felt she was creating some real distance from her upbringing.

"Can you play anything?" she asked.

"I was forced to learn the piano until I was fifteen."

" 'Forced'?"

"Actually, it wasn't that bad." He looked at her and felt he
could say it. "My teacher's daughter, who was three years older
than me, used to sunbathe in the garden in full view of the double doors from the music room."

She laughed and thought: *It's good that he can be relaxed enough to
tell me these things.* Cherry genuinely didn't mind hearing them.
She knew men hated high-maintenance women, and she would
save the jealous outbursts for when they had purpose, to bring
him into touch with how much she cared. It was one of those
cards worth saving.

"You?"

Cherry had already decided not to lie too much about her
background if it could be helped. Lies had a nasty habit of catching up to you. Still, this friendship was at a fledgling stage and
there was no need to weigh it down with the dreary truth that
there hadn't been the room for a piano, even if there had been
the money. There was barely room for the sickly cream leather
sofa her mother had saved months for, eyeing it in a DFS discount
store until the sales started. It had built-in reclining seats, something Cherry found diabolically tasteless.

"I wasn't really the musical type. Languages were my thing.
French especially."

"Fluent?"

"*Oui.*"

"Any others?"

"Spanish."

"Impressed."

"And Italian."

"Really?"

She shrugged modestly. "They're all very similar. You just have to think about it."

"You must have been good at school."

"I was. Except they only did French."

"So, how . . . ?"

"Taught myself. Downloaded courses."

"Wow!" He looked at her with renewed admiration. "Wow! I could have done with you on my Grand Tour."

"You had a Grand Tour?"

"My mother's idea. It was great, we took the Orient Express as far as we could—her idea again—then trained across Europe. I got to see some amazing places."

Cherry, who had only been abroad once, to Australia, was taken with the idea of a long sojourn through Europe's best cities, but they didn't have time to talk anymore as the orchestra started warming up again so they rearranged themselves to face the stage. Cherry sat with her arms around her knees and watched avidly, wondering how long it would take to learn to play an instrument at such a level and if she might start learning. There were probably lessons online. After a while, Daniel put his arm loosely around her right thigh and she felt a thrill at the possessiveness, this first touch of its kind. Then she leaned against him and they exchanged small intimate smiles every so often.

"It seems early," said Daniel as they walked back across the park after the concert had finished.

It was still light, the evening was long and inviting, and both had their minds on what was going to happen next. Neither wanted to go home yet.

"Do you fancy a drink?" asked Cherry, looking dubiously at the packed trendy bars, where people were spilling out onto the streets.

"We're a bit laden," said Daniel, indicating the picnic ware.

"You want to take that back?"

"And have my mum insist on meeting you?" He smiled at her. "As much as I'd like that, she'll have to wait."

Cherry's heart jumped with delight. Daniel was already thinking about introducing her to his mother! She thought about it and decided that they already had another date in the bag, and if they woke up together, there was the very strong possibility they'd spend all of tomorrow together too. She could make him wait until he moved into the apartment he'd just had an offer accepted on, but that was still a few weeks away. She felt that was too long.

"I've got a nice bottle of Sancerre in the fridge."

He smiled. "Thank God one of us has got their own place."

He made it sound as if her situation were the preferable one, even though he was in the multimillion-pound house. When he'd told her where he lived, she knew exactly how much it was worth; then she'd Google Earthed it, homing in to see as much detail as possible until the picture had blurred.

They smiled at each other, each knowing the path they'd just taken. He took her hand, and held it all the way to the tube, just like they were a couple.

5

*L*AURA SAT IN THE LARGE RECEPTION AREA AT ITV TOWERS, GRATE-
ful for the air-conditioning. She'd come a long way since she'd
worked there in her early twenties as a script editor in the drama
department. It was the same time Howard had swept her off her
feet and she'd given it all up when Rose, then Daniel had arrived.
It was only when Daniel reached his teens that she suddenly
found she had time on her hands and so had tentatively tested
the commissioning waters with an idea for a new drama she had.
Some of her old contemporaries were now running the drama
departments at the channels and after a few "remember me?"
e-mails (the industry was incestuously small), she got those first
important meetings, then sold the idea. Seven years later and she
had a small but thriving company and was, she thought, respected
in the industry. Admittedly, the BAFTA win had been some years
ago now, but everyone knew how arbitrary and how fashion-
dependent these things were. At the moment, a comedienne who'd
also branched out in drama was at the top of everyone's wish list
and every proposal with her name on it got green-lit, and, it was
hoped, would go on to win prizes. In two years' time, it would be
someone else.

She checked her iPhone for messages. Daniel had not come

home Saturday night as she'd suspected; as Sunday had stretched on, she'd become ever more aware of his continuing absence. She'd made him lunch, but had to put it in the fridge, and then she'd sort of drifted around the house, waiting for him to return, looking forward to seeing him, and getting more and more restless the later he became. By five o'clock, it suddenly occurred to her that he might not come back that night either, and she laughed at herself and at the sensation she had of being stood up. She gave herself a stern talking-to, and went to bed, having not seen either of her immediate family all day, as Howard had gone to golf.

Her name was called and she stood as the PA to the Commissioning Editor of Drama came to take her up in the elevator to the eighth floor, where she sat in a small meeting room with Hercule Poirot on the window.

"Laura!" cried Alison as if she was welcoming a long-lost friend. They kissed each other on both cheeks. Alison always spoke in inflated tones of optimism and energy, and Laura generally found it best to respond in kind.

"How've you been?" gushed Alison, taking a seat on one of the plastic chairs. Laura sat opposite.

"Good!"

"Well, we're *thrilled* with ep one." Alison also littered her sentences with extravagant adjectives: superb, extraordinary, fantastic, were also to be found often, prowling around like ninjas waiting to attack in a showy display of power.

Laura took an inner sigh of relief, but it was a bittersweet pill. She'd done the last-minute changes to the final scene as Alison had "suggested," after having her argument that the lovers wouldn't have left without saying good-bye to the jilted best friend swept aside in Alison's trademark passive-aggressive way.

"I don't know, I just don't *believe* it, do you?" she had said, and Laura had thought, *Yes, I do, as did you, presumably, when you read the script six months ago.* She tried to persuade Alison otherwise, but had hit a brick wall. Laura knew that if she wanted a second series, or any other commission with ITV in the near future, she'd have to not be "difficult" and do as she was being asked. The director, naturally upset at the last-minute major change to his work, was comforted with the promise of two episodes on the hoped-for next series.

"The ending really works for me now. I saw it this morning and I was . . ." Alison clutched her bosom in theatrical agony. The young PA silently brought in two cups of tea and left them on the glass table before leaving again. Laura said "thank you," while Alison pulled a face that threatened to break into tears.

"I'm glad it works for you." She knew, as did everyone in the business, that Alison needed a hit badly. Her recent run of new dramas had failed to make the expected viewing figures; and when this happened, people got fidgety. Nobody in TV liked to be around failure, and the finger of blame was already starting to seek out a victim. Alison had a particular talent for dodging its trajectory, but even she was arming herself with reinforcements. Her ego, being what it was, thought that she had just saved a *good* drama and turned it into a *mind-blowing* drama.

"I've spoken to Sean and he wants to know what else Cavendish Pictures might be able to do for us."

There was her reward, and this time the relief was sweeter. Times had been hard for the independent-production industry the last couple of years and Laura needed a new commission. Sean was the Head of Drama and had the power to green-light. The fact he wanted to work with her again was very good news indeed.

"Do you have anything you wanted to chat to us about?"

Laura thought about her ideas slate. There were a couple of new ones that she had already earmarked to pitch to ITV. "Yes."

"Fantastic! Can you send over some treatments?"

"Of course."

"And we'd like to set a meet, just the three of us."

"Great." Laura pulled out her iPhone as Alison did the same. Tap, tap, stroke.

"He's rather busy until next month, so shall we say the eighteenth of July?"

"Here?"

"We'll take you to lunch."

"Lovely! Look forward to it."

That settled, Alison pushed her phone aside. All the news had been delivered and the meeting came to a natural close. More kisses and an exchange of "fantastic working with you" and Laura made her way back onto the street. She glanced at her watch—almost three o'clock. She decided not to trek all the way back to her Covent Garden office. It was too hot—the heat wave had been in the news this morning and it was 90 degrees in London. The afternoons were always the worst, when the dust and the fumes seemed to envelop you and stick to your skin. Instead she called her PA to say she'd be working from home for the rest of the day. Hailing a black cab, she jumped in.

Once they hit Kensington, the traffic was as usual snarled with the school run and her driver took a short cut down Gloucester Road. Laura had been running through her mind all the projects she could pitch to Alison and Sean and had been unaware of her route until now. She looked out the window and, seeing where she was, sat up in her seat. There it was, on the corner of Old Brompton Road, blue-and-brown signage. It came closer and closer to them; and then just a few yards before they got there, she called through the glass.

"You can drop me off here, thanks."

She paid and waited for the cab to drive off and then made her way along the pavement to Highsmith and Brown.

Laura stood, not quite in front of the windows, and looked in at an angle, pretending to check the photos of exclusive properties displayed in front, but really trying to see the personnel in the office behind. A combination of the reflections on the window, her position, and the fact she was still wearing her sunglasses made it difficult to see anything. In the end, she gave up, lifted her glasses onto her head, moved to the right, and stared in. They were all busy, which gave her more opportunity to try to work out which one Cherry was, but then she didn't have to, as it was obvious. She was stunning.

Cropped, lustrous dark brown hair that showed off her beauti-fully structured face. And a body that would make men weep. Laura watched for a moment, taken aback by how beautiful she was. No wonder Daniel was smitten. She was pleased for him, but . . . No "but." She could see how someone could be so besot-ted. She smiled. She was *pleased*. Cherry attended to a customer and Laura saw her face light up, youthful, determined; the sheer force of life in her was intimidating. Laura quickly looked away. She suddenly felt embarrassed at having been spying and smiled a foolish smile to herself. She walked on, but the image of Cherry came with her.

Laura turned down a residential street, leaving the bustle be-hind. As she passed the stuccoed white houses, gleaming in the sun, flanked by evenly spaced trees with their generous shade, she found herself wondering what Cherry was like. What were twenty-four-year-old girls like these days? What would Rose have been like if she'd lived? Then she knew what she wanted to do. She set her shoulders determinedly back and made her way home.

"Why don't you invite her for supper?"

"What?"

Laura had come back to her house to find Daniel home, but sleeping. Now they were all seated around the large table for din-ner, and the three of them seemed to tip it back down and keep it afloat. Neither she nor Howard had mentioned Saturday night's little scene, but enough time had passed for it to have drifted away from them. Neither brought it up.

"Your mother's dying to know more about her."

Laura ignored him. She noticed he didn't ever read the paper when Daniel was home.

"We want to meet her! Don't *we*, Howard?"

"Sure," deadpanned Howard.

Daniel laughed. "Already? I've not even been seeing her a week."

"It's not me putting the pressure on," said Howard.

Laura resisted the urge to huff. "Howard, if you want to see

your son this summer, I would recommend a little more enthusiasm. He's already blown us off once, remember."

"Am I in trouble over that?" asked Daniel.

"Terrible trouble," said Laura. "And I have a feeling you might
be seeing a lot more of Cherry this summer, and so before you
both disappear into some"—she sighed wistfully—"blissful bubble, it would be nice to meet her."

Daniel nodded. "You make a good point."

"Call her now."

"Now? What's the rush?"

"I need to be able to plan. Why don't we say Thursday? Six-
thirty?"

Laura wasn't entirely sure why she was pushing it so much. She
knew she was unlikely to see Daniel as much as she'd hoped over
the summer. As much as she'd been looking forward to it, she was
accepting of the circumstances. Grown sons have their own agendas. But something made her want to get to know Cherry before
they disappeared.

Daniel was on the phone. He covered the mouthpiece. "She
can't do Thursday. . . ."

Laura thought quickly. "Friday, then?"

This was passed down the line and seemed to hit success. "Call
you again later," Daniel said softly, then hung up.

"She'd love to come."

Laura smiled. She was surprised by how much she was looking
forward to it.

6

*E*VERY TIME CHERRY WENT TO VISIT HER MOTHER, SHE RESOLVED that this time she would be different. She would be open, friendly, relaxed. She would talk to her without snapping and without feeling panicked, trapped by all the things that reminded her of her penniless childhood. It wasn't her mum's fault that they'd had no money all those years, but as soon as she was let into the small two-bedroom flat, it seemed to suck out all her good intentions. The large-screen TV too big for the room; the fluffy rug in the middle of the living-room floor; the horrible tilting sofa; the oversized tin of second-rate chocolates on the side, open for guests. Cherry knew that Wendy, her mum, valued these little perks from the supermarket. She always had firsthand knowledge of all the deals; she said they'd saved her a fortune over the years. Cherry hated supermarkets and hated their "deals" even more. The trash they encouraged you to buy and fill your house with. The markets bled people of every bit of their deficient wages they could trick them out of, dressing the deals up as some comradely arm about the shoulders: *"We're on your side, we know how you feel, times are tough."* But all the time, they were piling up huge profits. At an average of £10 each, her mum's DVD collection was worth two grand. Correction—it had *cost* two grand, it was probably worth a couple of hundred quid, if that. It frustrated Cherry that her mum never stopped to work it out.

"But that's a classic," Wendy had said at the new addition of *The King's Speech.*

"It's a piece of plastic in your living room. How often do you even watch it?"

Owning a classic didn't make you more of a film buff, didn't mean that you were erudite or give you an eye for quality. It made you a mug, especially when you could watch the same movie on TV or borrow it from the library. It didn't ever occur to Cherry that her mum might actually enjoy watching the DVDs, might even be grateful for them as she spent most evenings when she wasn't working alone. She'd never found someone that lasted after Cherry's father had died.

She kissed her mum chastely, trying to avoid the usual bear hug and lipstick brand on her cheek.

"Mum!"

"Sorry, it's just that I hardly ever see you these days."

It was true and Cherry, awkward, evaded answering. "How are you?"

"Fine. Can I get you a drink? Glass of wine, seeing as we're celebrating?"

Cherry knew that her mum would only have white, and that it would be sweet, something she detested, but she didn't want to upset her. So Cherry made some excuse about not starting too early, saying she'd have tea instead. She followed Wendy into the kitchen, where her mum made a cup of tea in a mug with Daniel Craig's face on it. No neck, just his disembodied, handsome face with its craggy smile staring out, floating on a background of white china. It looked surreal. As her mother filled the kettle, Cherry took a moment to appraise her. She'd dyed her hair again—it was a different color every time Cherry saw her, as if she was working her way through the L'Oreal brunette spectrum. (Eighty-three there were in total, her mum had said once, finding out this nugget of information from the supplier's catalogue.) Underneath that, it was gray, but the color had once been the same lustrous brown-black as Cherry's. She'd inherited the best of both of her parents' looks, with the odd gene thrown in from a grandparent in a collection of random good luck that could never have been predicted.

Wendy led her into the living room. "You can have the tilter if you want."

"No, it's fine, you have it." Cherry quickly sat down at the opposite side of the sofa, remembering the time she'd been made to sit in the tilting seat to satisfy her mother's excitement and had been thrust back like she was at the dentist's, and had felt every bit as helpless.

"I'm thinking of painting that wall red." Wendy pointed her mug at the wall that was the backdrop to the massive TV. "Like a statement."

"A statement of what?" Cherry hadn't meant to let the irritation creep in, but here it was already.

"I don't know. Why do you always have to be so . . ." She was going to say "critical," but bit her tongue. Not today. They both looked into their mugs of tea, vowing to do better.

The TV was on mute, a game show. Cherry hated all game shows for the single reason that the members of the public always ended up unwittingly humiliating themselves by looking cheap or ridiculous in their carefully chosen TV outfits. She also couldn't stand how thick everyone was. Teachers not knowing the capital of Canada. It was pathetic.

"How's work?" said Cherry.

"Oh, you should have seen the queues on Saturday. We sold out of every one of the disposable BBQs and I *told* them we'd need more."

"They should listen to you."

"Yes, they should," said Wendy, pleased.

"How long have you been there now?"

"Well, I started when you was just two, as we needed the money," Wendy began, and Cherry, who'd heard this story before, found herself just waiting for the punch line. "It was only meant to be part-time and I started at checkout, worked my way up. Took on more days when your dad passed. I was reliable, you see, and a hard worker. None of this needing to disappear to take the dog to the vet or what-have-you. Anyway, it'll be twenty-three years this September." Wendy smiled proudly, lost for a minute in her own achievement. Cherry could think of nothing worse than being stuck in a mammoth warehouse full of people pushing around huge wire baskets on wheels; she secretly thought that becoming a section manager after twenty-three years didn't sound like that much of a promotion. Surely, you'd be heading up the entire region or something by then; but thinking about it all depressed her, so she stopped.

"The good things come to those who work hard, see. That's when you get the promotions and stuff."

"How's Holly?"

"Not happy. Her daughter went to an *X Factor* audition, but had a really hard time. They slated her apparently. Holly got really upset about it." Wendy leaned forward and patted her knee. "Never mind about all that. What about you? I still can't believe my daughter's gotten herself a proper job now! There's always money in property," she said sagely, although this was a general perception that Wendy had latched onto rather than personal knowledge.

At last, Cherry could smile, although she wouldn't be going into any detail. "Good, really good, in fact. I'm enjoying it a lot at the moment."

"Well, that's great. I always knew you'd do all right. You was the smart one of the family. So, what do you do then? Sell posh houses?"

"Yes, mostly. A few rentals."

"Bet they go for a bit up there, don't they? How much would it cost me to rent my flat up in la-la land?"

"Well, it wouldn't look like this exactly, but for the floor space, about three grand."

"Three grand a month!"

"A week."

Wendy's face was so gobsmacked, so dumbfounded, that Cherry

started to giggle. She couldn't help it. She wasn't being malicious or making fun of her, but with her mum's jaw dropped and held in some sort of freeze frame, it just looked funny.

Wendy slowly closed her mouth. "Jeez, Louise!" And then, aware of how she must have looked, she started to laugh too. For a short while, when each looked at the other, it just made them laugh more. It was a rare moment, the two of them getting on, sharing a joke. Pleased with the way they seemed to have hit on a safe topic, Wendy suddenly got an idea. "Hey, me shifts change next week. I get Tuesdays off. Maybe I could come and see you, take you for lunch?"

Cherry thought quickly and pulled a face. "I only get half an hour."

"That's illegal!"

"It's fine—"

"No, you're entitled to an hour. It's the law. You should speak to your boss about that."

"Leave it, Mum."

"No—"

"Mum please!"

Wendy was silenced. For a moment. "Are they paying you properly?"

"Mum!"

"You was never that good with money, always frittering it away."

Cherry choked on her tea, actually splattering some on the cream leather sofa.

"Don't look at me like that. You blew your savings on a trip to Australia."

"A working vacation. A cultural experience." She looked around for something to wipe off the tea and found a box of tissues, Kleenex Collection, with a photograph of water lilies on the front. It was designed to appeal to homemakers who thought it important to make tissues part of their decor. For a moment, she hesitated, not wanting to take one, as if it was a sweet offered by a witch who'd trap you in her lair once you'd tasted it. She was reminded that if she ever lost her job, this flat was where she'd have to return. The bleakness of it all frightened her.

"You could have invested it," continued Wendy. "Premium bonds or something."

"Mum, premium bonds pay you no interest."

"No, but they're better odds than the lottery."

Cherry gritted her teeth and decided not to point out the obvious. Instead she said: "What would you do? If you won?"

"Go on a big trip. I'd take Holly. She could do with a bit of cheering up."

"Would you move?"

"There's them nice new houses that they've built next to the River Wandle."

Cherry made a sound of exasperation. "Mum, you could leave Croydon, you know."

"Never. Born here. It's in me blood. No better place as far as I'm concerned."

This declaration made Cherry fidgety again and anxious to speed the evening along. To think she could've been at the Cavendishes' beautiful house tonight. She had desperately wanted to accept Laura's dinner invitation, but she knew that canceling the visit to her mother was just too complicated. It would only have prolonged the agony, anyway, as she would've had to have found another date.

Cherry had already invented something she had to get away for—meeting a couple of friends for drinks—and had told her mum on the phone before she'd even arrived. She surreptitiously checked her watch. She could start making sounds in about ten minutes. Croydon was so far out, it could legitimately take ages to get anywhere else in London. In actual fact, she was going home to figure out what to wear the next day—an outfit that had to cover the evening too. Something that would be suitable for "supper" with Mr. and Mrs. Cavendish. ("Supper" didn't sound so bad now.) Daniel had said not to worry about what she wore, but, of course, that was ridiculous.

"Anyway, maybe I'd win enough to buy one of them big mansions on that Webb Estate."

Cherry stiffened.

"You ever hear from Nicolas?" Wendy said, feigning nonchalance.

"No."

"I suppose it's to be expected." She sounded reassured, as if her suspicions had been proven right, and it made Cherry bridle.

"What do you mean?"

"You know, he was a bit different, wasn't he?"

"Different how?" she said dangerously.

"Well," stated Wendy nervously, "the rich have a different life. Not something we really know about." Wendy patted Cherry's hand, meaning to be consoling, to dismiss him and welcome her back to their mutually supportive club, but Cherry recoiled inwardly. She was consumed with anger and pride. Even her own mother thought he was out of her league. It was so *wrong*, so utterly ridiculous, to believe that you couldn't be with someone else, that they were better than you because they had money.

"You're not upset, are you?"

"No."

"Only . . ."

"What?"

"You might not have seen this." Wendy pushed across the local paper and opened it up to the local wedding section. Nicolas's face smiled out at her; next to it was the blonde from the bar in a tiara and white gown. They radiated togetherness. Cherry went rigid and she forced herself not to show any emotion other than indifference. She looked at the photo for signs that he was thinking of her instead, that the marriage to—she read the name, Gabriella Clara Butler Oswald—was something he'd been pressured into, something he had to endure if he was to stand a chance of taking over his father's business. She thought she might have caught a glimpse of strain in his smile but then that could've just been a reaction to the relentless greed of the wedding camera, shot after shot. She pushed the paper back. "Good luck to them." It was said in a tone that meant the subject was closed.

"Do you want to check your room, see if there's anything else you need to take back with you? I've sorted through all your old toys from when you was little."

Cherry did not. She already had everything she wanted from this flat and the thought of taking any part of her childhood into her new life felt like the worst kind of contamination. "I can't, Mum, I'm going to meet some friends. Maybe next time, eh?" And with that, she stood. "I need to get going actually, got to get back into London."

Wendy covered her disappointment and stood too. "Ah, well, thanks for coming out all this way, love. I do appreciate it."

There was a brief silence during which neither of them said anything and then Cherry smiled brightly. "Right," she said, and made her way to the door.

She let her mum kiss her on the cheek and then found a small box pressed into her hand.

"Happy birthday," said Wendy, beaming, expectant, and Cherry could tell it was something she'd been dying to give to her. It was wrapped in doodled flowery paper, the kind that looked as if it was designed by a four-year-old and came under the category of "cute." The right thing to do would have been to open it there and then, but Cherry couldn't face pretending not to be disappointed. She put it in her bag.

"All the best, love," said Wendy, with a catch in her voice.

It was agony. Cherry knew her mother was aware she couldn't wait to get away, but she quickly pushed the realization away, pretending not to notice Wendy's look of hurt. Her chest was tight with guilt; she hated being there, hated what she became when she was there. "Thanks, Mum."

She escaped and hurried back to East Croydon station. With every step, the guilt grew. She got out her phone and sent a soul-clearing text, something jolly and lighthearted about how nice it had been to see her. Once she'd gotten a cheerful reply, she felt the pain in her chest ease, and gradually the train and then the tube transported her back home.

It only took half an hour to get to Tooting and the evening was still warm. She poured herself a glass of wine left over from the weekend with Daniel and went out into the tiny courtyard garden. It was only three steps wide and six steps long and she could see St. George's hospital chimneys from beyond the fence and the row of Victorian flats that ran parallel to hers, but it was a little piece of outside. A fox slipped quickly and silently into a hole it had dug under her fence and disappeared into the neighbor's garden. She sipped her wine and watched it go, impressed with the creature's ability to make a home anywhere in London. She'd heard a radio show a few weeks back where people from places like Barnes and Chelsea were phoning in to complain about the foxes coming into their houses. Tooting had been as close as she could get to the capital's center, rising rental prices acting as a thicket of thorns to keep her from going any farther.

This made her think about what she was going to wear the next day, and galvanized, she took her wine inside to the bedroom. Opening up her wardrobe doors, she scanned her clothes critically. It was going to be another hot day, so something that wouldn't look creased and shabby after working in the office. She decided on a tailored sleeveless silk shirt and navy pencil skirt. She made a space for the chosen items in the middle of the wardrobe by pushing everything else to the sides and then hung them together. She looked at them, satisfied for a moment, before closing the door. She went back into the garden and thought excitedly about the next day and how much she was looking forward to meeting Daniel's parents. Felt a warmth toward Laura for inviting her over, and so soon in her and Daniel's relationship. It was something that had never happened the entire time she was seeing Nicolas. She imagined them hitting it off right away and a wave of pleasure washed over her as she saw herself fitting in. Daniel was so easygoing and she had a feeling that his parents would be her type of people.

It was only much later, when she went to bed that night, she remembered the present. It was the latest iPhone and Cherry knew it was her mother's attempt to understand her, buy her something that she thought the younger generation might like. She also knew the cost would have been a sacrifice for her mum. It seemed so sad somehow and, anyway, she already had one. The guilt flared up again and she discarded the gift in a drawer and lay back on the pillows and sighed. How her mother fit into her future, she didn't know.

7

Friday, June 13

THE CAVENDISH HOUSE WAS ONLY A TEN-MINUTE WALK FROM THE AIR-conditioning of the office, but Cherry was hot and bothered. Even in early evening, it was 80 degrees and she quickly and subtly checked her armpits for damp patches. Other than a tiny five-pence-shaped dot under the right arm, thankfully, she'd escaped.

Cherry was nervous. She wanted to be liked. She looked at the bunch of tiger lilies in her hand, artfully arranged in brown paper with twine, tied like a corset's stays, and wondered again if they were too much. There seemed to be a lot of them and they were, well, big. They should be, she thought wryly, they'd cost her sixty quid. And then again, lilies were big. She counted the stems: seven. Surely, that wasn't over the top? She swapped hands so they didn't get too sweaty and decided it was too late to do anything about them now. The important thing was she wouldn't show up empty-handed. She turned into the Cavendishes' street and, checking her watch, realized with a flicker of apprehension that she was going to be early. Oh, God, she didn't want to look too desperate or anything. Quickly she turned down another side street, which, if she followed it around, would bring her to the other end of the road she was in now. She walked along, pretending to be a little bit lost in case there was anyone around who might know the people she was going to see and a story of her wandering around came out in some later casual conversation. The idea of it made her cringe with embarrassment.

She turned back into the top end of the Cavendishes' road, checking her watch and matching her pace so that she reached the iron gate of number 38 at exactly six-thirty. She walked across the checkerboard of immaculate black-and-white tiles to the large, imposing black front door and rang the bell. It wasn't long before it was thrown open, a warm, wide welcome from Daniel. He took her hand and kissed her fully, but quickly, on the mouth.

"Hi. They're dying to meet you," he whispered in her ear as a sort of preemptive warning, and then she heard two sets of footsteps approaching.

Mr. Cavendish was first, a large, broad-shouldered man who was used to striding into rooms without any fear of who might be in them. He wore a short-sleeved shirt tucked into shorts, an odd mix of semiformal and casual, and she felt pinned down by the full beam of his—not unkind—eyes. He grasped her free hand with more force than was necessary in a confident, brisk male way, and if she was honest, it hurt.

"Dad, this is Cherry."

"Howard," he said, introducing himself. "Nice to meet you."

"Great to meet you, Howard."

He let go of her hand and it tingled as the bones realigned and the blood rushed back. Then it was Laura's turn. To Cherry's surprise and secret delight, the other woman took her hand and, after looking at her in some sort of charmed way, drew her closer and kissed her on each cheek.

"Lovely to meet you, Cherry."

"You too." She handed over the bouquet. "These are for you."

Laura took them with a look of genuine pleasure, and Cherry was glad she'd paid so much for them.

"Oh, they are absolutely beautiful. Thank you."

Cherry couldn't quite believe that this glamorous woman was probably the same age as her own mother. They couldn't look more different. Laura was tall, statuesque, and a shimmering blonde.

Her cream silk blouse and wide-legged caramel trousers draped over her frame as if they were privileged to do so; the whole effect was one of a burnished gold goddess.

"I love your top," she found herself gushing, and had to try to suppress the flush that rose up her cheeks.

"Likewise," said Laura. "That color is amazing on you."

The flush went higher. Cherry felt as though she'd forced Laura to say something nice in return and she stood there, dumb and smiling and wishing fiercely she had been a little more sophisticated.

"Time for a drink," said Howard, and he led the way into what Cherry knew would be only one of the reception rooms. She sat on the edge of a long gray sofa and, thankfully, Daniel took the seat next to her. Laura was a few steps behind and must have put the flowers down somewhere as her hands were free. She couldn't have put them in a vase that quickly and Cherry found herself feeling slighted. Were her flowers lying bruised on a shelf somewhere?

Get a grip, she told herself sternly, *she's hardly going to disappear for ten minutes arranging flowers when you've only just gotten here. The flowers will be fine.*

"Aperitif?" said Howard.

"Yes, please."

"Bellini?" However, he was already pouring one and handed it to her. She tried not to let the bubbles go up her nose as she had a sip.

"You've been working today?" asked Howard as he continued to serve the drinks.

"Yes, at Highsmith and Brown."

Laura took a glass from her husband and glided into the armchair opposite her. "Daniel said. Do you enjoy it?"

"Yes, very much."

"How long have you been there?"

"Not long." She didn't elaborate, and in the pocket of silence, she moved her glass to the other hand. She knew she had to relax, but she was so anxious to make a good impression, her mind was working overtime trying to remember what she did and didn't want to say. She was in danger of coming across as rude.

"What did you do before?" asked Howard.

"I was in the hospitality industry."

Both of Daniel's parents smiled with what Cherry took to be polite interest. She felt another blush threatening. It was obvious they knew that she'd said this as a cover for working in a restaurant. Feeling foolish, she spoke quickly. "Before that, I was in Australia. I was, um . . . I wanted to take some time off after my . . . exams."

"Which university were you at?" said Howard.

She inwardly cringed. "Er . . . I didn't . . . but I did do my A Levels."

What is the matter with me? Trying to justify myself, like a child.

"So you came back and decided to start a career, learn on the job. Very commendable," said Laura, "especially with the cost of university these days."

Cherry smiled and nodded along. She knew Laura was covering for her. She self-consciously swapped her glass back into the other hand and wondered what to say to change the subject.

Daniel pulled her from the sofa. "Come on, let me show you around. You can give us your professional opinion."

She followed him out of the room, feeling like she'd failed the first test. They were barely through the door when Daniel pinched her bum. She only just managed to suppress a squeal and poked him in the arm in admonishment, but, in fact, the intimacy had cheered her.

"The hallway," he said. "As you can see, we have one."

"And very beautiful it is too," said Cherry, aware that his parents could probably hear everything they were saying. And it was: a gleaming parquet floor led to two large curved white and wood staircases, one going up, one down. A Turkish rug was placed in front of the marble fireplace, which was flanked by a large armchair, and Cherry wondered if anyone actually sat there.

"You don't need to worry so much. They like you," Daniel said in lowered tones, but Cherry gave him a warning look. She'd heard Laura come in behind them.

"I'm just going to finish the soufflé," she said, and headed into the kitchen.

"We won't go in there, don't want to disturb the chef." Instead he led her up the staircase. As they got to the next floor, they didn't stop: "This is Mum's room," and he continued upward, as Cherry noted how a whole floor could be dedicated to one person's bedroom and probably huge bathroom and dressing room. She also noted that Mr. and Mrs. Cavendish didn't appear to sleep together. At the next floor, Daniel led her into one of the bedrooms. "My room," he said. "Well, it's not really, not anymore. But this was the room I had when I was growing up." It held a solid oak king-sized bed, a wardrobe, and a desk, but what set it apart was that it was a photographic homage to the man who stood beside her. Photos covered every wall, every surface: Daniel at Machu Picchu, Easter Island, the pyramids. A range of extreme sports: mountain climbing, skiing, white-water rafting in the Grand Canyon. Pictures of the Grand Tour. There were trophies, cups for rugby, cricket, and tennis. Each one was dust free and gleaming. It was a visual representation of his boyhood and all he'd had access to.

"Wow, quite an achiever."

"Nothing to do with me. Well, I did run about a bit. . . . I mean it's Mum who insists on putting them up."

"She must be very proud."

Cherry moved over to the window and picked up a photo of Daniel cycling in the Pyrenees. Someone, presumably Laura, had marked this on the mounting, along with the date. As she put it back down, she looked out the window and her eye was drawn to a bluish-tinged rectangle, about three meters by two, in the middle of the lawn. It looked like glass.

"What's that?"

He came up behind her. "The window. For the pool."

Cherry turned, wide-eyed. "You have a swimming pool under there? Underground?"

"Yep. Starts under the garden, goes farther under the house. And off that, under the front of the house, a cellar and a room where Dad likes to hang out, watch movies. And next layer down, small garage. Fancy a dip?"

Cherry stared at the window, tried to imagine what it was like. "Haven't brought my suit."

"Doesn't matter." Daniel started to kiss the back of her neck, but she squirmed.

"Your mother's downstairs," she hissed.

"Yes," he said, continuing to kiss her.

She pushed him away. "I want to make a good impression. Don't make me look ruffled."

"You look absolutely beautiful tonight. Fancy a quickie?"

"Absolutely not."

A bell rang. He groaned. "My mother has other ideas."

"Tell me that wasn't a summons?"

"It's a large house. She had to call me to the table somehow. What am I going to do about this?" He indicated his groin, which was bulging against the fly of his shorts.

"Think of me naked all through dinner."

"You are such a tease." But he loved it, and she knew it. Holding her hand, Daniel led her back down the stairs and they met with Laura in the hallway. She was carrying a tray with four steaming ramekins. "Sorry if I cut the tour short, but this will go flat."

Daniel dropped her hand as he went to take the tray from his mother. It gave her an irrational sense of abandonment and the nerves swiftly kicked in again.

Dinner was served in the dining hall, where the table was boarded by the largest number of passengers for some time. Cherry was opposite Howard, Daniel his mother. Everything shone with purpose: the cutlery, the glasses, even the dinnerware, a white set with watercolor flowers painted around the edge. A large modern oil hung from the wall, nearly the entire length of the room, a statement that was as confidently expensive as the rest of the house.

"Ta-da!" said Daniel as he placed the tray of soufflés on the table.

Cherry immediately got a whiff of an unmistakable fishy scent. Crab. She balked. She'd had a bad experience with one of her mum's discounted purchases at the outer limit of its sell-by date and had spent most of the night throwing up in the bathroom. The smell was making her feel nauseous, but she resolved to get through it. A dish was placed in front of her, a fluffy pillow of soufflé just waiting for her to break through its peaked surface. She waited as long as she could, until everyone had been served and had taken their first bite. Then she picked up the small fork, thinking it might load less on it than the spoon, and tentatively tried it. It was all she could do not to gag. Cherry wondered miserably how she was going to get through the course without being sick or offending her hostess. She stopped for a sip of wine, then slowly forked up another mouthful, but Laura noticed she was struggling.

"Is everything okay?"

Cherry considered bluffing, but caved in. "I'm sorry. I don't like crab."

"Oh, my goodness, don't eat it."

"Sorry . . . ," repeated Cherry, embarrassed. "It makes me feel . . . unwell."

Daniel clapped his hand on his head. "It's my fault. Sorry, Cherry. Mum asked me to check. I completely forgot." He looked contrite. "I thought it would be okay."

"I'm so sorry," said Laura, standing and taking away her plate.

"Poor you," said Howard.

Laura went to take the plate into the kitchen. "Moses can have it."

"The cat," explained Daniel.

"Well, I thought it was delicious," said Howard, scraping the last from his dish as Laura reappeared.

"Very nice, Mum," said Daniel.

"Glad you liked it." She ate her own portion and looked regretful. "Sorry, Cherry."

She was being kind, but Cherry was mortified. She heard her

stomach rumble and pulled the muscles in quickly so it wouldn't be noticed.

"And you're hungry!" said Howard. "Can we get her anything else?"

"I'm fine, honestly."

"Are you sure?" continued Laura. "I feel like I just tried to poison you or something! Some melon? Or I think we have a bit of pate in the fridge."

"I was ill on mussels once," said Howard, "never been able to face them since."

Cherry wished they'd all shut up about it. Daniel put a comforting hand on her leg under the table.

"Thanks, Dad, don't think we need any reminders of that one."

A mewing sound came from the kitchen. Laura stood. "Moses," she called, "are you still hungry?"

"Always have a pet," said Howard. "Green garbage cans. Although, I am more of a dog man, myself."

"Why didn't we get one, then?" asked Daniel.

"Your mother wouldn't have it. Reminded her of the cocker spaniel she had as a child."

"He was run over," said Laura. "It devastated me. I had nightmares for weeks."

"Shame," said Daniel. "I like dogs."

The cat mewed loudly and came prancing in, then rubbed himself against Laura's legs. "Don't listen to him!" she said. "You're our favorite."

Cherry looked at the animal with immense dislike. It was irrational, she knew, but even the cat was conspiring against her. Everyone but Cherry liked the bloody soufflé. Why couldn't she be a soufflé-liking person like these people?

"Fillet steak and sauteed potatoes for the main course?" said Laura tentatively to Cherry. "Is that okay . . . ?"

Cherry gave an overly compensatory smile. "Sounds great."

"What's for dessert, Mum?" asked Daniel.

"I wondered when you'd get to that." Laura smiled. "Presumably, you know all about Daniel's addiction to chocolate, Cherry?"

Cherry smiled again, a big beam to match the conversation. She didn't.

"I have to hide it when he's home," said Laura.

Oh, do you! Ha-ha-ha, thought Cherry.

"You'll be pleased to know it's . . . chocolate-and-pistachio marquise."

Daniel threw an arm around his mum. "You star!"

Cherry didn't know what a "marquise" was.

"Is that okay?" Laura asked her.

"Yes, lovely," said Cherry.

"I must be crazy to move out," said Daniel, and Cherry got a little flutter of anxiety. She looked up and, with relief, saw he was joking. It was obvious they got on well though, he and Laura. Extremely well.

It was an alien concept to her, being close to your mother, and their easy banter threw her off balance. She imagined having that level of closeness with her own mum and instantly cringed with revulsion. It hadn't always been like that. They'd been close when she was young. As a child, she'd adored Wendy, in fact; but then as she'd gotten older, she'd become embarrassed of her, this mother who worked in the supermarket and whose world was so small.

It was made worse by Wendy being so nice. She was like a puppy, always running around after her, wanting to be part of her life. It made Cherry guilty and she sometimes thought that if Wendy would just slap her across the face and tell her how bad her behavior was, it would make everything so much easier. Thoughts of Wendy put Cherry in an even darker mood. She tried to shrug them off, enjoy the steak and what turned out to be a posh chocolate mousse.

"So, when *do* I get my den back?" asked Howard, topping up everyone's wine.

Daniel laughed. "Yesterday," he explained, "Dad came down to use the pool. There was plenty of room for both of us," he said to his father.

"Your stroke is all over the place. More water out of that pool than in."

"You just didn't want to get shown up."

"I've been perfectly used to you not being here. Cherry, it's a shame you couldn't keep him entertained last night as well."

"Cherry had other plans," said Daniel.

"Yes," said Cherry.

They all looked at her. She'd said very little during dinner, too nervous, too self-conscious to really contribute, and it felt odd to be the center of attention. She hadn't intended the one-word answer to sound so mysterious, but now, she suddenly realized, it actually worked out quite well.

"Anything nice?" asked Laura.

She made herself look embarrassed to have to be saying it, as if she didn't want to make a big deal. "It was my birthday. I spent the evening with my mother."

Daniel sat back in his chair in surprise. "You never told me!" He took her face in both his hands and kissed her. "Happy birthday!"

She smiled modestly. "Thank you."

"How lovely!" exclaimed Laura. "Many happy returns for yesterday."

Cherry was pleased with everyone's reaction. Now she couldn't be accused of letting Daniel know in advance so as to secure an expensive present, but she secretly knew that his inevitable guilt at missing her big day would probably procure something even better. Howard had already been to the kitchen and was coming in clutching a bottle of champagne and four glasses, which he held upside down by the stems. Pleased, Cherry noticed that it was Veuve Clicquot rosé.

"This calls for a celebration," said Howard. He gave everyone a glass of pretty pink fizz and lifted his own. "To Cherry!"

"To Cherry," said Daniel and Laura, and for the first time that evening, she felt a part of everything.

"So, what did you get up to with your mum?" asked Laura.

The bubble evaporated. Cherry felt on the spot. She could hardly talk about a strained hour in the pokey flat, avoiding the tilting sofa, and thinking of excuses to leave. Everyone was looking at her expectantly, smiling. "Not much."

She watched Laura's face become puzzled before she covered again. "Well, sometimes it's nice to have a quiet one."

Cherry churned inside with misery. At that moment, she felt a gulf apart from everyone else in the room, including Daniel. She had a sudden overwhelming need to get away, to catch her breath and work out what had gone so wrong with this evening she'd been looking forward to so much.

She stood. "I'm just going to go . . ."

Laura indicated the way out into the hall. "First door on the left."

Cherry locked the door behind her and sank down onto the floor. Why couldn't she fit in? Her mother's words of the night before rang in her ears: *The rich have a different life. Not something we really know about.*

Was she right? So far, the evening had been a horrible collection of tense, awkward moments. Nothing like she'd envisaged. She'd imagined herself falling into a warm friendship with Laura, finding some common ground early on, maybe sharing a joke or two, perhaps even going into the kitchen to help Laura with the supper. Cherry had even dreamed of Laura as a motherly substitute, taking her under her stylish wing and being the kind of mother she wished she had. She burned with embarrassment at her girlish fantasy. Somehow she had spent the evening feeling inferior, unworthy of these people. Humiliation turned to resentment and she angrily flushed the toilet and ran the taps, just in case anyone was listening. She just wanted to go home, and the disappointment and sense of failure were crushing. How was she ever going to escape her life if she couldn't even hold a conversation with someone over a certain salary bracket?

She took a breath and then opened the bathroom door. The hallway was empty. Making her way back into the dining room, she saw everyone had left the table. Howard had disappeared, and Laura and Daniel had their backs to her and were peering over a laptop. Laura had an affectionate arm over Daniel's shoulders and Cherry stared. The draped arm felt like a barrier to her, stopping her from coming in.

"She's found you somewhere wonderful," said Laura.

They were looking at photos of the flat. What was she, the staff, the hired agent, only useful to find property for her son? Even as she thought this, Cherry knew it was unreasonable, but she didn't care. She walked over and joined them. Then she deliberately put her arm on Daniel's lower back and started to caress it. He turned to her and smiled. On Laura's face, she caught a look of surprise and felt her quickly take her own arm away.

"It is nice, isn't it?" said Cherry. Keeping her eyes on the screen, she smiled inwardly, a sense of satisfaction creeping over her as she kept her hand possessively in place.

8

*T*HE KITCHEN WAS FULL OF POSTDINNER DEBRIS; PLATES, GLASSES, and pans were stacked by the sink, the culinary wreckage from the evening. The dishwasher had long finished its gurgling with the first load that she'd filled some hours before, but Laura couldn't face the rest. It could wait for Mrs. Moore in the morning. She sat on her swing seat in the garden, pushing herself against the ground with her foot, pondering the evening. She had seemed nice enough, Daniel's girlfriend, although quiet. Laura supposed she was nervous, but it had been hard to engage her in conversation. . . . In fact, she'd practically clammed up when they'd mentioned her birthday with her mother. And then there was that odd thing she'd done, at the end of the evening. With her hand. It was almost as though she was claiming Daniel, wanting to score a point? No . . . that was silly, and Laura felt bad for thinking it. The girl was probably just nervous as hell, poor thing. Soon after, Daniel had offered to take her home, and Laura had known they were itching to get away, and she smiled, knowing they needed time for themselves. Daniel had driven her back to Tooting, and as he'd left, he made it clear she shouldn't wait up. Once they'd gone, Howard retreated again to his study. Even Moses had gone out for a night prowl and now she was left with her thoughts.

The wind coursed through the trees at the end of the garden and she shivered. The temperature had dropped for the first time in a week. Laura realized she was cold and went back inside, closing up the bifold doors behind her.

Lying in bed, she tried to sleep, but felt restless. The curtains billowed in the buffeting wind; then there was a crack of thunder. Finally the storm that they had been waiting for was breaking. The rain started, and in a matter of seconds, it was hammering against the window, in some disjointed torrential rhythm as the wind blew it bullyingly about. Laura got up, and as she went to close the window, she saw a flash of lightning against the sky. It lit up the garden and the large opaque ground window glistened wet in the rain. Then she heard a faint mew. The next flash illuminated Moses outside the bifold doors, waiting to be let in.

"Oh, Moses," she said exasperatedly, but quickly went downstairs. As she opened the doors, he scuttled inside, gratefully rubbing his thanks against her legs. She stood for a moment and watched the storm, but then a flurry of rain blew into her face and she shut the door. She looked around for Moses, but he had gone for a late supper, so she left him and went back upstairs to bed.

She lay staring at the ceiling; through the plaster was Howard in his study, engrossed in work one floor above her. She thought about how sad it was that they didn't really talk anymore. She turned over on her side and instead thought of Cherry. She resolved to do something for her. Something to make her feel comfortable; perhaps she'd take her out somewhere. Yes, that would be nice. She switched off her light and the room plummeted into darkness. She tried to block out the storm battling at the window and at some point must have succeeded, for she drifted off to sleep.

9

*T*HE FOLLOWING MORNING WAS FRESH, WITH A SOFT BLUE SKY. THE streets had been washed by the rain, but were now dry in the morning sun. As Laura stepped out of her front door, she saw Daniel's open-topped Mercedes turn at the corner and make its way down toward the house. She went to the gate and waved as they came closer: Cherry was in the passenger seat.

"Hello, you two."

They pulled up outside the house and Daniel gave Cherry a lingering kiss. Then he jumped out and, to Laura's surprise, Cherry swung her legs over and shifted into the driver's seat.

"Thanks again for a lovely evening, Laura," called Cherry with a smile that didn't seem to have any of the anxiety she'd displayed the previous evening. Then she drove off quickly, with a squeal of tires.

Laura was taken aback. "What's she doing?"

"Going to work."

"But . . . but that's your car."

"I've loaned it to her today. We were late getting up," he explained, "and I didn't want her to get into trouble at work." He smiled to himself; now that Cherry had discovered sex properly, she found she loved it, much to his delight.

"Oh, right." Laura, if she admitted it, felt a little put-out. She'd bought Daniel the car for his twenty-first birthday. It had been a special gift, one that she'd thought about for ages beforehand and had chosen carefully.

"That's okay, isn't it?"

"Of course! How do you know she's a good driver?"

Daniel laughed. "Oh, Mum, don't worry. I think she'll be fine. Although that was a bit of a racing start," he said, watching as Cherry did another wheel spin as she turned out of the other end of the street.

"Well, it's nice that you have such a trusting relationship."

"Thanks again, Mum. For all the effort you put in last night. Fantastic steak."

"My pleasure."

"So, what did you think?"

"Hmm?"

"Do you like her?"

"Very much."

"She was nervous."

"I thought as much. No need to be. Long-term, this one, is she?"

"Hope so," he said, and made to go inside. "Do you fancy a coffee?"

"Love to, but I've already got a date. Bit of shopping, then meeting Isabella for lunch."

Daniel kissed Laura on the cheek. "Sounds good. Send her my best."

"I will." She waved to Daniel as he closed the door; then she set off in the direction of the main junction where she'd pick up a cab to take her to the King's Road.

"Love it," said Isabella, "it'll do very nicely for an office meeting."

Laura lowered the striped shirt.

"I'm sorry, darling. It's nice, it truly is, but where has all the fun gone?" Isabella asked.

"It is fun."

Isabella pulled a face.

"Okay, *this* is fun," said Laura, plucking at her blue sleeveless dress.

"Yes . . . ," said Isabella, unconvincingly, looking kittenish in an emerald halter neck that set off her glossy red hair, "but what I mean is, when was the last time you bought something for a social occasion?"

Laura was silent. They'd come to their favorite restaurant, a small select French place just off the King's Road. They'd been coming for years and the waiters knew their preferred table and which special of the day they'd most likely enjoy. Secrets had been exchanged here, promises sworn on, and confessions frequently applauded. They had been friends for twenty-five years and told each other everything.

"You see?" she said, waggling a finger.

"Howard and I don't go out anymore."

Isabella put her hand on Laura's. "No, well, he's too busy with that trollop. Why do you put up with it?"

Laura folded her shirt and put it back in the stiff designer bag, not answering immediately.

"Divorce him."

"No. Anyway, that's just what he'd want."

Isabella sighed, knowing the conversation had been had many times before. "What else, then?"

"What do you mean?"

"Other evening entertainment."

Laura was aware she didn't really have any. "Bridge night?"

"Doesn't count."

"By the time I've finished work, I'm exhausted. Friday night I just want to stay in."

"Well, there's a reason to give it all up." Isabella couldn't quite understand why she worked—it wasn't for the money; Laura loved what she did. It gave her a sense of identity and achievement, the fact she was successful in such a competitive, cutthroat industry. And most of all, it was hers. Her company had been a friend to her when Daniel was away studying and Howard was away at golf. She couldn't think of giving it up.

She smiled at Isabella. "I wouldn't know what to do with myself."

"Oh, trust me, darling, you soon would." She leaned forward mischievously. "Anyway, don't you miss it?"

Laura laughed, but Isabella was not to be put off and waited for her answer.

"Oh, I don't know, I suppose so."

"I know the perfect man. I'll set you up. Nothing too obvious. You can come to dinner, there'll be a group of us and I'll sit him next to you."

"Who is it?"

"You don't know him. He's a colleague of Richard's."

To Laura, the thought of small talk with a stranger was as enticing as a visit to the dentist. "No thanks. Anyway, that would just make me as bad as Howard."

"Oh, come on."

"No, honestly. Anyway," she said tantalizingly, "it's not me going for romance at the moment. . . ."

Isabella leaned in. "Who?"

"He's completely smitten. This could even be the real thing. . . ."

Izzy clapped her hands in delight. "Not Daniel?"

Laura nodded.

"What! Does this mean our great plans have been thwarted?"

"Completely blown away." Their children had played together ever since they were babies. Brigitte and Daniel had waved rattles at each other as they lay on blankets, while she and Isabella had attended whatever postnatal class, playgroup, or personal-training session they were up to that week. They had always joked their children would marry.

"We met her last night," said Laura.

"What's her name?"

"Cherry."

"Is that her real name?"

"Less of the sarcasm. She's very nice."

"Does she work?"

"She's a real estate agent. In training."

"Right."

"We all have to train, Izzy."

"Of course."

Laura laughed. "You're not really upset that our machinations came to nothing, are you? Brigitte will find a very fine man."

Isabella sighed and brushed this away. "I know. So, tell me more. Where does . . . Cherry come from?"

"She lives in Tooting."

"Tooting?"

Laura heard the lack of enthusiasm in her voice. "Isabella Rudd, you are such a snob. I've heard it's got lots of great Indian restaurants."

"Darling, so has Goa. And I'd rather go there. So, how long have they been dating?"

"A week."

Isabella's eyes widened. "*A week?* And he's already madly in love with her?"

"Well, he hasn't said so exactly, but they do seem to be spending every spare minute together. This morning, they even did the commute together . . . well, until she took off in his car."

Isabella frowned. "Sorry? She's waltzing around town in his Merc?"

"Well, to her office. I'm sure she had to park it, once she got there."

Isabella looked quite worried and Laura smiled. "What?"

"Nothing. . ."

"Come on, I can tell you're dying to say . . ."

Isabella shrugged. "It's just that, you know, she's from Tooting, he's here in South Ken . . . different ends of the spectrum . . . and she does seem to have attached herself to him rather quickly."

Laura's mouth dropped. "You're not suggesting . . . No! My goodness, Izzy, that is one heck of an imagination. I could use your help on my television scripts."

Isabella laughed. "Okay, okay, sorry. Just keeping my sadly-never-to-be-son-in-law's best interests at heart."

"You know, I was thinking of inviting her to the villa, when we all go out next week."

"Saint-Tropez?" said Isabella, taken aback.

"Yes. Make her feel like part of the family."

"That's your downtime. The only two weeks of the year you actually let yourself relax."

"I know, but she won't be there the whole two weeks. I was thinking maybe she could join Daniel and me for a long weekend or something. You and Brigitte will be down the road and it'll be fun."

"Sounds great, darling. And I'll get to meet her."

"Be nice," Laura said sternly.

"Of course!" Isabella smiled. "I'm just jealous. I'd already planned the wedding."

10

"*E*XCUSE ME, NEIL, DO YOU HAVE A MINUTE?" CHERRY HAD ONLY just arrived at work and had gone directly to her boss's desk.

He raised his groomed head, saw her stricken face. "Sure. Do you want to come to the back . . . ?"

Cherry nodded and followed Neil into the back office, a small room they kept tastefully furnished for when the more private clients wished to discuss their property needs. She felt Emily's and Abigail's eyes follow her as she left, burning with curiosity. Let them look. She wouldn't be confiding in them, not since they'd rebuffed her efforts to make friends when she'd first started the job. They were tight, just the two of them, and didn't let anyone else in, especially not someone they sensed as "different."

"Take a seat." Neil indicated a brown leather armchair. She sat perched on the edge, sensed that her boss was a little anxious about whatever problem she was about to unleash onto him. He sat too, on the chair next to hers, and she got a stab of irritation at his shiny shoes, knew he paid for them to be buffed as he sat on a raised seat with a cappuccino and the *Financial Times*, completely oblivious to the man below him.

"Is everything all right?"

She looked up at him. Took a breath to hold back the tears before she started to speak. "It's my grandmother. She's ill. Really ill. I was wondering if I could have some time . . . a few days to go and see her."

"Of course!" exclaimed Neil, and she detected a sense of relief this wasn't about woman troubles. "When do you need to go?"

"This Friday." She saw him hesitate. "I know, Emily and Abigail go on holiday the same day . . . ," she trailed off helplessly.

There was a millisecond's pause while he struggled, before reassuring her. "It's okay. We can get a temp in. How many days do you think . . . ?"

"I won't stay long, just enough to see her. Only, she's abroad . . . so I might need to factor in the travel."

"Where is she?"

"France. I've already checked the flights, and if I leave Friday, I can be back Tuesday morning."

"That's fine. We'll work it out here."

Cherry exhaled with relief. "Thank you. I can't tell you what this means to me. We're very close."

Neil nodded sympathetically. "I hope she's okay. . . ."

Her eyes filled up. "Me too. It's cancer. They've just discovered it and are assessing her for chemo."

He looked as if he wished he'd never asked. "I'm so sorry."

A tear ran down Cherry's face and she wiped it away with a brave smile. "It just means the world to me to be able to go and see her, and I know she'd want to thank you too."

He brushed her thanks away modestly. "Honestly, there's no need."

"*Il est un merveilleux patron.*"

"Sorry?"

"'He is a wonderful boss.'" Cherry blew her nose. Smiled. "That's what she would say."

Neil smoothed his tie. "Well, if that's what I can do to help, then . . ." He sucked his teeth, then stood, tilted his head sympathetically. "Do you need a minute?"

Cherry nodded gratefully. He put a hand on her shoulder and then turned to leave. "*Bonne chance,*" he said, and Cherry nodded again. She waited until he left the room and then blew her nose loudly, just in case he was still within hearing distance. Paused. Listened. Nothing. She smiled. She was going to France! The *South* of France! When the invitation had come, she'd been so excited, but knew that the two little cows in the office had already booked time off, and there was no way Neil would let her go away too. It wasn't right. She'd never gotten an opportunity like this before. It wasn't fair that she should have to turn Daniel down, just because those two had the money to book a fortnight in Ibiza.

She was going to the South of France! Where her boyfriend owned his own villa! Well, it was his parents', but that was a small detail. It wouldn't always be. She hadn't even had to pay for the flight— Daniel had insisted, saying it was unfair for her to pay so much as the trip was so last-minute. She had picked her man well and she congratulated herself, hugging the information close for a moment longer, relishing it.

Then she stood, smoothed down her skirt, and affected a pose of brave serenity, before going back to her desk.

11

*L*AURA TWEAKED THE VASE OF FLOWERS IN DANIEL'S—WHAT WOULD be Cherry and Daniel's—bedroom. Provence was renowned for its early-summer blossoms, and the fields of poppies spilled out into the roads. She'd picked great bunches, along with honeysuckle-scented brilliant yellow broom. The bed was made with crisp *broderie anglaise* sheets and she looked at the final effect, pleased. There was food in the fridge and a bottle of wine chilling, ready for when they arrived in about, she looked at her watch, twenty minutes or so.

She moved around the villa, a typical Provençal-style house, checking that everything was tidy and welcoming. Finally satisfied, she went out onto the sunny terrace, from which she could see the whole of the Saint-Tropez peninsula. She gazed out at the gleaming white yachts, tiny dots in the distance, some moored, some gently drifting in the breeze. She felt different when she was here. The house in London was Howard's; this was her escape and over the years it had been a place of refuge when things had gotten on top of her at home. Since she'd gone back to work, she only got here a few weeks a year; whenever she did, it was like coming back to an old friend. It was particularly gratifying to be here now because their neighbors in London had started construction the day she left. They were embarking on their own basement extension and the excavator was deafening; vibrations were throbbing right through their house. The builders had already tripped a power cut and it had been a relief to get on the plane. It seemed the whole of Kensington was digging underground. A labyrinth of tunnels and vast chambers. Laura had visions of whole sections of London collapsing into one great big pit. A brief thought crossed her mind: How would Howard cope with the disruption? He hadn't been able to come to France due to work commitments. The answer came just as quickly. She knew he wouldn't be staying at the house; he'd be at Marianne's.

She quickly brushed this painful thought away. For two weeks at least, she could escape everything, and Daniel, no doubt, was pleased to be coming here as well. She knew he had lots of studying to do and there wasn't much chance of getting it done with the cacophony next door. Cherry would be with them until Monday night, and Laura had lots of plans for her visit. She really wanted to show her around and get to know her a bit. She was looking forward to making this trip special for her, wanted the villa to be a place she could relax too. Laura had an idea they might bond, become friendly. It would be nice.

Hearing a car on the gravel drive, she turned and went back through the house, opening the front door wide. Daniel had parked the rental car and was hauling out the luggage from the trunk. Laura opened her arms and went to hug Cherry. "Welcome! So glad you could get the time off!"

"Me too," said Cherry.

"Come in. Are you tired? Do you need a drink?"

It was early evening and gloriously warm. Cherry looked up at the house. The shutters and windows were open and gauzy white cotton curtains were caught against window frames. She was already liking what she saw. She let herself be taken inside and fussed over. She took in the large, airy reception rooms, with their big, open fireplaces, and the French country-chic kitchen, with gleaming teak worktops. She accepted a glass of chilled sauvignon.

"How was your flight?" asked Laura.

"Good, thanks."

Cherry's attention was taken by her surroundings and she didn't really engage with Laura's polite conversation. She continued to gaze around the kitchen and was struck by a painting on the wall above her, a vivid oil color of russet-roofed buildings around a sandy-colored square, with yachts on an azure sea in the background.

"What a beautiful painting!" she exclaimed.

"Isn't it?" said Laura. "A local artist."

"Is it of Saint-Tropez?"

"Yes. Of course, there are stacks of painters down in the village, all excellent, but this one, he's one of the best. We've got a few more dotted around the house."

"My absolute favorite is on the landing," said Daniel, coming in behind them and putting his arm around Cherry. "'Les Pins.'"

"'The Pines.' Sounds wonderful."

Daniel looked up at the picture. "It's fantastic, isn't it? I've always loved this artist. She's got good taste, eh, Mum? These are worth quite a bit now. He's become pretty famous. I love them. One day, I might buy a painting for myself, if there's ever one available. Most of the time, they have sold stickers on them."

"Would you like to see outside?" asked Laura.

Cherry followed her hostess through some large glass doors onto the terrace and caught her breath. Beyond the large, gleaming pool was the blue of the Mediterranean, a heart-soaring expanse that fused into the hazy sky. Lured by what she could see, Cherry walked toward the garden wall, dotted with red geraniums and leaned over to get a better look. Far below her lay the tops of the russet roofs of Saint-Tropez, which she'd just been admiring in the painting. And the yachts! There were so many of them. It was unlike anything she'd ever seen before.

"Bit of a rubbish view, eh?" said Daniel, joining her.

Cherry blinked. Speechless, she burst out laughing.

"We can go and explore later," Laura said enthusiastically. "Show you around. And we've got an invitation from Isabella for dinner."

"Mum's oldest friend," explained Daniel. "Is Brigitte here?"

"Yes," said Laura. "Brigitte is Isabella's daughter," she added for Cherry.

Cherry smiled politely.

"Hope you've got lots of stamina," said Laura. "I've got loads of ideas for your stay. Thought you might like to go and take a look at some of the vineyards, it's so beautiful up in the hills. And, of course, a little tour of the village here—it's classified as one of France's *'plus beau villages,'* and we can go to the beach, obviously, and I thought maybe you'd like to take a drive up the coast to Cannes? Anyway, there's loads to do, you can just go at your pace."

Cherry smiled along, but she inwardly prayed that she didn't have to share her entire weekend with her boyfriend's mother.

The first event was dinner at Isabella's villa down in Saint-Tropez itself. Cherry had just had enough time to shower and change and spent a stressful ten minutes wondering what she should put on. Did the moneyed dress up? Or did they just do expensive casual? Cherry didn't know and eventually settled on a fairly simple—and cheap—cotton dress. She couldn't afford much of a vacation wardrobe and the dress was something she'd bought when she was in Australia. She hoped it didn't look too faded.

Cherry noticed Isabella's eyes went to her first as she opened her wooden front door, even though she was busy helloing those she knew.

"Oh, you darling boy," said Isabella, embracing him tightly. "I don't see you for months and then you spring this"—she turned to Cherry and beamed—"lovely surprise on me." She wasn't unfriendly, but her gaze was most definitely one of assessment, of ego-laden curiosity, thought Cherry.

"Brigitte's going to be devastated, you know. . . ."

Daniel laughed. "I think she's got better taste."

"Nonsense. Still, what's done is done, and what a wonderful couple you make! And I, for one, am delighted to meet you, Cherry."

"Likewise," said Cherry, although she mistrusted the jovial

lament. She didn't really want to be meeting a load of strangers that included a girl who, it seemed, might hold a candle for Daniel. She was already feeling tired at having to fake smiles. And who was this girl, anyway? Was she some kind of ex? Cherry felt vulnerable not knowing.

"So, shall we come in, Izzy?" asked Laura, raising a stern eyebrow.

Daniel held Cherry's hand as they were led into the garden, where she was greeted by another breathtaking view. A curved infinity pool hugged the edge of the hillside, beyond which was the sea, its azure blue broken up every now and then with spray from the tufts of gentle waves. Lying by the pool were two svelte, perfectly tanned girls.

"Look who's here, Brigitte," called Isabella, and the tawny brunette squealed in delight. She jumped up from her sunbed, her small, pert breasts jiggling in their bikini top. As she came over, she threw her arms around Daniel, pressing her breasts against his shirt. Cherry stiffened, taking an instant dislike to her.

"It's so good to see you. We missed you at Courchevel this year. Where were you?"

"Studying," said Daniel briskly, "as I was the year before that, and the one before that." He took Cherry's hand. "This is Cherry."

Cherry found herself moving in closer to Daniel and clutching his arm.

"Hi," said Brigitte, noting her move. "You don't have to worry about me, we're like brother and sister."

Cherry smiled tightly, feeling awkward.

"Hello, Auntie Laura!" Brigitte called, and waved. "This is Nicole," she said, gesturing toward the long-limbed girl still on the lounger, who Cherry noticed had been watching the introductions.

Nicole slowly got up from the sunbed and made her way over at a speed that meant everyone had to watch and wait for her arrival. She kissed Cherry coolly on the cheek, but her greeting was far more friendly for Daniel. "It eez very nice to meet you," she said with a lingering smile.

Is she flirting? Cherry glanced around to see if anyone else had noticed, but Isabella was talking to a middle-aged French woman, some sort of cook it seemed, and Laura was carrying a tray of drinks from inside. Brigitte had gone back to her sunbed and was artfully arranging her body to catch the falling rays of the evening sun.

"Drink?" called Laura, and Cherry took a beer from the tray. She followed Daniel to where the empty loungers lay by the pool and sat uneasily, watching Nicole's look of satisfaction as Daniel took the lounger next to her. Laura and Isabella were at a table farther up the garden and were busily engrossed in what looked like gossipy conversation. Cherry looked down at her dress, suddenly seeing a loose thread trailing across her knee. She was too embarrassed to pull it, in case Brigitte and Nicole noticed.

"So, how've you been?" Daniel asked Brigitte. "Found a job yet?"

Brigitte raised her sunglasses off her eyes and smiled. "Cheeky." Then she immediately slid them back down again and leaned back in the chair, tilting her face to the early-evening rays. They lit her skin and tawny hair to a golden color.

"And you, Daniel?" Nicole's accent was grating on Cherry's nerves. "What eez it you do?"

"I'm a trainee doctor."

"A doctor!" She gazed at him admiringly and Cherry seethed. Did she have to be so blatant? How did she not feel self-conscious in her bikini, meeting a man she'd never seen before? Is that what money did? Give you an air of unbridled confidence? Cherry decided she didn't like either of them, but knew she should pretend she did. At least, in front of Isabella and Laura.

Daniel was still waiting for an answer from Brigitte. "Well, have you?"

"Just because some of us wanted to travel, expand our minds, and see the world before we got saddled with a grueling schedule . . ."

"You went on ski trips and summer yachts. In fact, are you sure you even left Europe?"

"Malta."

"In Europe."

Cherry wondered if Brigitte was joking, but, no, she'd lifted her sunglasses and was looking at him in puzzlement.

"Is it? Oh, well, geography never was my strong point. Lucky I'm not planning on being a global reporter or anything. I'd get totally lost."

"You'd just need to know which plane to catch."

She sat up. "Really?"

"No."

"I know you think I'm useless," she said, smiling as if "useless" was an admirable trait. "But actually . . . I am getting a job. One much closer to home."

"You are? Really joining the work force?"

"I'm waiting for Uncle Vic to find me an opening in publishing. A family friend," she explained to Cherry.

"So nothing concrete yet," said Daniel.

"You're wrong," she said triumphantly. "He's pretty certain there'll be something in September."

And she'll get it too, thought Cherry darkly. Brigitte would be hired without a thought for those who'd worked hard to gain a foothold in the industry—those who were more qualified, more passionate, and who would probably be ten times better. Those hopefuls would be pushed aside, and it wouldn't even register with her.

"What do you do, Cherry?" asked Brigitte.

"I'm a real estate agent."

"Bet you get to see some nice houses."

"I do."

Brigitte nodded appreciatively and that seemed to be all that was needed to be said. Cherry noted how she'd naturally assumed or expected the houses to be nice. Perhaps she didn't know small flats in large ugly blocks existed.

Nicole started to apply some suntan cream. She poured a small amount onto her hands, then slowly and sensually rubbed it onto her skin, inspecting her arm as she did so, seemingly pleased with it. She sat up and started to rub the tops of her shoulder blades. Stretched a little to try and get to the middle of her back. She gave a cursory glance at Brigitte, lying down with her eyes closed, and then turned to Daniel.

"*Excusez-moi,* could you pleeze . . . ?" she said, holding out the suntan lotion.

All of Cherry's hackles went up. He looked on, unsure, a little embarrassed, then held up his beer bottle. "My hands are cold, you're better off asking Brigitte," he said pleasantly.

She didn't, noticed Cherry, *the conniving little bitch.* Just smiled and lay back on her lounger.

The French woman in the apron came to the doorway and Isabella looked up. "Wonderful!" she said. "Madame Baudin says dinner is ready. Shall we eat outside?"

Brigitte got up and slipped on a flowing kaftan. Nicole stood and stretched languorously in her bikini, then went inside to freshen up, Brigitte at her heels.

"I'm sorry," mouthed Daniel, and Cherry smiled and waved a hand to indicate she wasn't going to be unsettled by a silly French girl. He waited until Nicole and Brigitte were out of earshot and then said: "Are you okay?"

"Fine," she said.

Laura came out of the villa with Madame Baudin, laden with plates and glasses, and Daniel jumped up to help. Cherry took a moment to catch her breath. All she wanted to do was go somewhere private with Daniel, a nice restaurant or something, and yet she had to endure a dinner with these people. There were pretty good odds that either Brigitte or Nicole would sit next to Daniel at the meal, neither of which she thought she could stand. The breeze lifted her skirt and she was glad she'd brought a cardigan. As she went to put it on, she saw another piece of fabric flap in the wind. It was something of Nicole's, a dress perhaps, half-spilled out of her bag. Cherry looked up. Daniel and Laura were disappearing back into the villa with Madame Baudin to get more plates. There was no sign of the girls. Isabella had her back to her and was carefully arranging glasses on the table.

It fell with a light *plip* and the pink darkened and spread in the water. The breeze gently moved it farther down the pool and it took on the shape and stillness of a drowned body. Cherry was already over by the large table.

"Can I help?" she said to Isabella.

She looked surprised and pleased that this outsider guest was not too grand to help and handed her a pile of forks. "Thanks."

Cherry began to carefully lay them out and suddenly knew how best to play this woman who would not like her to outshine her own daughter. She buried the perverse urge to do just that, it wouldn't exactly be hard; Brigitte was clearly thick as mince. No, instead she'd pretend to be polite and pleasant, meek almost.

"Hey!" exclaimed an outraged voice, and Cherry idly lifted her head.

"My dress is in zee swimming pool!" Nicole looked angrily around and stopped when she came to Cherry.

Not intimidated, Cherry met her gaze, cutlery clutched in both hands.

"What's happened?" said Brigitte.

"My dress! It is soaking!"

"It must have been the breeze," said Daniel.

Nicole was forced back inside and had to borrow something of Brigitte's while the sodden dress was hung over a lemon tree. Cherry found herself next to Nicole at dinner. Daniel was on the other side, next to Isabella.

"Poor you," Cherry said in her ear. "I hope it's not ruined."

Later that night, Cherry and Daniel lay curled up together on crisp cotton sheets. Their room was facing the back; when Cherry had closed the shutters, the sea had looked black. She was looking forward to throwing them open in the morning and seeing it clear blue on a new day. In fact, she could hardly believe her luck. The villa was incredible and the location dreamlike. The rest of the weekend was going to be spent with Daniel as much as she could possibly manufacture it.

"I'm sorry again about tonight," he murmured, nuzzling her ear sleepily.

"Don't be."

"You were magnificent."

Cherry smiled and ran her fingers across his chest.

"Did you . . ."

"What?"

"The dress?"

"Course not."

Daniel opened his eyes and she met his gaze innocently. "Like you said, it was the breeze."

He smiled and then kissed her, and she rolled on top of him and kissed him some more.

12

Saturday, June 21

CHERRY WOKE LATE THE NEXT DAY AND SAW DANIEL WAS STILL ASLEEP. She lay there quietly, enjoying the peace and privacy before Laura, whom she could hear moving about the house, hit them with whatever plans she had for the day. A thin band of light outlined the shutters, telling Cherry it was sunny outside, and she was itching to get up, but at the same time, she didn't want to leave the sanctuary of the bedroom and get roped into some sightseeing. Feeling trapped, she resented Laura's overpowering presence.

He stretched beside her. "Morning. I haven't been snoring, have I?"

She laughed and indicated the window. "No. Ready for some sunshine?"

"Do I not get a kiss first," he said, but she'd already jumped up and was opening the shutters, as she'd longed to do since last night. The sunlit sea welcomed her and it was glorious.

Daniel winced and she bounded back onto the bed. Kissed him. "Let's go to the beach!"

"Is that what you want to do today? Only . . . I think my mum might have an idea about surprising us with a fully comprehensive tour of the region's vineyards." He saw the crestfallen face that she tried, unsuccessfully, to hide. "Okay. Let's do it."

"I feel bad now," said Cherry. "If she's gone to a lot of trouble . . ."

He pulled her back down onto the bed and wrapped his arms around her. "Don't be daft. She won't mind."

After they made love, they surfaced for a late breakfast. Laura, pleased to see them, hovered around the croissants and made them fresh coffee.

"Did you sleep well? Hope the bed was all right. I was thinking that we could all explore today. Would you like to go to Château Minuty? The Matton-Farnets have been in the wine industry for almost three centuries." She smiled at them, unable to contain her exuberance.

"Mum, that's a really nice idea, but . . . I think we might go to the beach today. First day of the holidays and all that."

"Oh, right. Good idea!"

To Cherry's horror, it looked like Laura was about to invite herself along. "I was going to take my books down there, do a bit of studying," Cherry said quickly.

"You've brought work as well?" said Daniel.

"Estate agency exams coming up soon after I get back."

"I suppose I should take mine. We can test each other."

That was enough to exclude her, noted Cherry, and Laura murmured something about them all meeting up later in the day, before going off to get a book to read by the pool.

Daniel drove to Pampelonne, a three-mile stretch of golden sand that had fueled Saint-Tropez's fame since the 1950s. Even though it was still only mid-June, he'd insisted they book, as he did not want to be traipsing up and down the beach, trying to find a space.

On arrival, Cherry learned that he was referring not to a table for lunch, but to a sun lounger. Much of the beach was sectioned off to private clubs and already they were filling up. She caught sight of the total on the handheld card payer as Daniel typed in his pin and her eyes widened. *Eighty euros for two sunbeds! And you didn't even get a towel!* They'd both brought their own. Daniel knew the drill and she had already packed one out of habit from childhood visits to Brighton, sitting on the cold stones, shivering after braving the rough gray waves.

Here the sea was a clear aquamarine and the waves made a little *plip* sound as they flopped, seemingly exhausted, onto the beach. Cherry lay down on the lounger next to Daniel and the umbrella cast a welcome shade over her, for it was already hot. She looked up and saw her umbrella was made up of circular stripes of orange and white, striking against the clear blue sky. They continued across their section of the beach, a pattern of orange-and-white circles, like humbugs. Out to sea were the yachts, gleaming white and bobbing gently on the water. Some were ostentatious, some merely grand.

"Hey, there's Brigitte," said Daniel, and Cherry's heart sank. She looked up to see a group of people stepping out of a motorboat that had just beached itself on the sand. They bounded up to them, wet legs stuck with sand. Cherry saw that along with Brigitte had come Nicole and one other girl, plus two guys, all young, tanned and beautiful, and all in swimwear. They arrived and flung themselves down on the sand, sitting with arms outstretched behind them. One of the guys casually lifted his to summon a waiter for some drinks.

Introductions were made and Cherry was pleased to see that Nicole refused to meet her eye and sat a distance away from both her and Daniel. The other girl was also French, a friend of Nicole's. The two guys were boyfriends, but she couldn't quite make out who was with whom; she had to rely on who was rubbing on whose suntan lotion or playfully caressing whose hair, although none of this was a guarantee of attachment.

They spoke about trivial things: parties and each other. They consistently teased one another, throwing sand onto the girls' flat stomachs. As she listened, it transpired that they were spending the day on Nicole's father's yacht, although Cherry couldn't work out which of the luxurious floating white islands out there was his. She briefly wondered if this was what these people did most summers and almost immediately knew the answer, and also knew she was probably only glimpsing the tip of their privileged iceberg. She noticed that Daniel, although polite, seemed content just to lie back and listen idly. After a while, the drinks were finished, and Nicole stood and asked if they wanted to go onto the yacht.

Cherry stiffened. She most definitely did not. While the others were there, she felt she had to keep up some sort of required ebullience—or, at the very least, alertness—and smile and nod at the right places in the conversation when all she wanted to do was read her book. Except, if Daniel was going, then she would too. She waited for him to answer and was pleased when he politely said he'd maybe join them later.

"You okay?" Daniel asked casually after they'd left, as if knowing she'd felt a little out of her depth.

"Fine."

"Peaceful, isn't it?"

She giggled. "Yes."

"Book time?"

"You took the words right out of my mouth."

And so they both settled back on their loungers, he with some cycling book and she with an old Persephone classic. Before she opened it, she looked up at the sky. She liked its vastness, and the way, if she followed it to the horizon, she could see the curve of the earth. It made her feel like she had a place in the world, as if she could get perspective on all that was around her. She drank this in for a moment, gaining strength and peace from the steady expanse of blue; then she started to read. Before long, her eyes started to droop heavily.

She woke with the sensation of someone stroking her calf. Lifting her head, she peered down to see Daniel gently applying some sunscreen.

"I moved the umbrella," he said, pointing, "but your leg was still getting the full glare of the sun."

"What time is it?" she asked groggily.

"One."

"Already?" She'd been asleep nearly an hour and the sun had moved higher in the sky and was hotter than ever. She watched, smiling, as he continued to carefully apply lotion, his hand moving higher up her leg. He stopped at the top of her thigh, humming, pretending not to notice where his hands were. He hesitated a moment, his finger stroking the top of her leg, and then grinned teasingly.

"All done."

"Thanks."

"You're welcome. Fancy a swim before lunch?"

They went, hand in hand, down to the sea, and when they reached the water, she scrunched her toes up in anticipation of the chill, but it was deliciously warm. She waded in, Daniel diving into the wave in front of her and then he stood and splashed and she squealed. She took her revenge by scooping a cascade of water into his face and the war was on. She realized she was falling for him. Yes, she loved his life and she wanted it for herself. But she was also enjoying his company. She'd picked a man who was fun, decent too.

After lunch, they swam again and then returned to their sunbeds. Cherry was careful to back up her earlier claim and diligently pulled out some workbooks. He felt he ought to do some too, and the two of them spent a couple of hours studying, looking up at each other, and baffling one another with excerpts from their texts. When it got cooler, Cherry said she was hungry and they wandered along the harbor front, looking for somewhere to eat. Daniel texted Laura to say they'd decided to stay in Saint-Tropez for dinner and they ordered line-caught sole meunière and a bottle of Sémillon. It was from the Minuty estate, noticed Cherry, as the waiter poured her a glass. Funny to think, if things had gone differently, she would have been there today. She wondered if Laura would be annoyed that they hadn't spent the day with her.

It was late evening when they got back to the house, just as Laura was about to leave.

"Oh, you're back," she said. "I waited a while. . . . Have you had a good day?"

Daniel dumped the beach bag on the worktop. "Great, thanks, Mum. You?"

"Quiet. Relaxing," Laura quickly corrected.

"Where are you going?"

"Vincent's. I booked a table."

Daniel looked surprised. "On your own?"

"Er . . . well, I did book it for three. But it's no problem"—she smiled—"I've let him know it's just me now."

"Oh, I'm sorry." He looked contrite. "We should have come back."

"Honestly, it's fine."

Cherry thought she ought to add her apologies at this point. "Sorry, Laura. If we'd known . . ."

She thought she saw a flicker of irritation cross Laura's face before:

"Not to worry."

"It was thoughtless." Daniel moved over to the fridge. Opened it and peered inside. "Tell you what, I'll cook you something."

"No, honestly." Laura stood. "Vincent's expecting me. He wanted to catch up with the family news."

"You sure?"

"Of course."

"Sorry. Again. I don't know why I didn't think to check or anything. Cherry just said she was famished and we went and grabbed something."

She hadn't been that hungry, remembered Cherry. She'd just said she was because she preferred eating alone with Daniel to having his mother tag along. It would've been more polite, more friendly, to wait, but it was only one night, for God's sake. It wasn't like she hadn't done the whole "family and friends" thing the night before. Laura could hardly expect them not to want to be alone at *some* point. In fact, she thought, with a touch of irritation, if she'd stop trying to be there *the whole bloody time*, she might not find herself alone at dinner.

Laura looked across to Cherry and smiled. "Right, well, I'd better go. The reservation's at nine."

"We'll come with you. Have a nightcap or something," said Daniel.

Cherry really didn't want to. She was tired after a day of sun and half a bottle of wine, but she smiled as if she thought the plan was a good one.

Laura hesitated. "No, it's all right. You've been out all day. I expect you just want to relax a bit. I'll be perfectly fine on my own." She grabbed her jacket and bag and kissed Daniel's cheek.

"See you both later."

"Sorry again, Laura. We'll call next time," said Cherry.

Laura nodded and left the house. As the door shut, Cherry pulled a face. "I feel bad."

"Yes, me too," said Daniel. "Maybe we should spend a bit of time with her tomorrow?"

"I was thinking the same thing. Do you think your mum would enjoy a relaxing day by the pool? We could cook lunch, make up for tonight," said Cherry, and her burst of benevolence was rewarded with a hug.

Laura came home to a quiet house; a light was left burning for her. It wasn't quite eleven. There was a note on the table: *Waited up for a while, but fell asleep on the couch. Hope you had a great night. Fancy a day by the pool tomorrow? We're doing lunch!*

Daniel had signed it from himself and Cherry. She listened, but could hear nothing, and so went to bed alone.

13

*T*HE NEXT MORNING, LAURA EXPECTED DANIEL AND CHERRY TO RISE late again, but to her surprise, they'd already gotten up and had breakfast by the time she followed the waft of fresh coffee into the kitchen. She could hear them laughing and chatting outside. She liked listening to their youthful exuberance and enthusiasm, their limitless energy for what they wanted to do with their lives with no sense at all that the energy might run out or the beliefs might change. The mix of determination and idealism was exciting.

She especially liked not knowing how it was all going to turn out, the joyful anticipation as you reached every milestone in a child's life: Would it be a girl or a boy? What would they look like? What would their personality be like? How would they get on at school? Who would their friends be? What would they choose to study, choose to become? Having a child was the very best kind of lottery. She still thought of Rose like that every time Daniel reached a touchstone, just briefly, a curious, painful wondering that would never be answered.

She poured herself a coffee and took a fresh croissant from the paper bag. Carrying the plate and a cup and saucer, she made her way onto the terrace. She stopped almost immediately at the sight of Cherry brushing her hand across Daniel's stomach as they both lay back on side-by-side loungers, eyes closed against the sun. Cherry's hand went lower and her fingers tucked themselves into the top of Daniel's shorts, and, Lordy, Laura thought she saw a twitch. She was torn between a polite but firm cough or silently turning and slipping back inside, and the hesitation cost Laura her anonymity. Cherry had opened her eyes and, for a moment, her hand stayed where it was. She looked at Laura and then slowly removed it. She looked embarrassed. Laura decided it was kindest to ignore it.

"Good morning," she said, walking across and taking her place by the pool.

"Oh, hi, Mum," said Daniel, with a conspiratorial grin across at Cherry. "How was Vincent?"

"Very well. Wanted to know everything you'd been up to. I tried to fill him in as best I could, but you've yet to tell me much," she said lightly. "He wanted to meet you too, Cherry, and says there's a table for you tonight, before you fly home, if you'd like. No pressure, but if you do decide to go over, he'll find you some space."

"How nice," said Cherry.

Laura glanced up, but Cherry had closed her eyes.

Daniel pulled on Cherry's hand. "Come on, time for a swim. Are you coming in, Mum?"

She didn't much feel like it. She'd wait until after they got out. Do a few calm lengths. "Just going to have my breakfast first."

They got into the pool. "Is it cold?" called Laura, already knowing the answer by Cherry's squeals. It was a little pathetic, she recognized, being unable to make conversation. But no one answered. They didn't hear, they were so absorbed in each other, and Laura watched them for a while from behind her sunglasses as she bit into her croissant. There wasn't much actual swimming going on, more ducking, splashing, arms wrapped around each other. She looked away, feeling excluded and, she was ashamed to admit, rather jealous and lonely.

They climbed out about five minutes later and lay with arms hanging down, fingers surreptitiously meeting and touching.

Laura decided to go in. Swam for a bit and then floated, gazing up at the sky. She felt weightless, and with her ears underwater, the sound of her thoughts became filtered and pure. So far this trip, she'd felt distant, out of sync. When she was in the pool, her son and his girlfriend were out with eyes closed. When she wanted to go for dinner, they'd already done so and were heading for bed. When she suggested a day out in the countryside, they'd already decided on the beach. It wasn't quite how she'd envisaged Cherry's visit. She smiled inwardly; she was being silly.

Laura had hoped to get to know Cherry a bit and found herself wondering why Daniel's girlfriend didn't seem to want to talk much. She might have made a bit of an effort, seeing as she was a guest in the house. Laura stretched out in the water. Never mind, let them have their time together, Cherry was leaving the next day.

She climbed out and went back to her lounger. Cherry was talking in that low, private voice that was exclusive to lovers, and Laura pulled out her book and started to read.

She awoke to find both of them gone. Groggy, she sat up and reached for her watch to check the time. It was noon. She suddenly saw Cherry in the doorway of the house, looking at her. Had she just arrived or had she been watching a while? Laura pulled her wrap around her and sat up.

"We've made lunch," said Cherry, and she went back inside.

They ate together, and then Laura, knowing she couldn't face another afternoon playing third wheel, decided to go out for the rest of the day. As she left, she was aware she felt uncomfortable in her own home.

On Cherry's last day, Laura felt a little guilty about her churlish thoughts and resolved to make one last effort before the girl went home.

"What time's your flight today, Cherry? I was wondering if you'd like to see some of the smaller villages up the coast before you go."

"Oh . . . ," said Cherry, looking to Daniel for reinforcement. "I'm actually due quite a bit of leave. My boss has said he'd prefer it if I took it now, rather than in the middle of the summer, when everyone else wants to go away. I know it's a bit last-minute . . . a bit cheeky, and please say no if it's not possible . . . ?"

Laura tried to keep the welcoming smile on her face. "You mean, you'd like to stay a bit longer?"

"That's incredibly kind of you," said Cherry, her face lit up in the first genuine smile that Laura felt was actually directed at her.

"That's okay, isn't it, Mum?"

"Of course, it is," said Laura, recovering just in time. "How long . . . Do you have a lot of holiday to use up?"

"A fair bit."

"Mum, we were thinking of doing that trip to the vineyard you suggested. Fancy it?"

Laura was still thrown by the revelation that her houseguest didn't seem to be leaving, after all, that morning; in fact, she didn't seem to be leaving anytime soon. "No, it's okay. You go. I might go over and see Isabella today."

They left soon after and Laura made herself a cup of coffee and took it out onto the terrace. She realized she was distinctly heavyhearted about the next few days.

Isabella was more philosophical about the situation. "Darling, it's nice she wants to stay longer. Shows she's keen to get on with you."

"Does it?"

"Of course. Otherwise, she'd be leaving on the first plane out." They watched as the pool boy methodically scooped out some leaves, moving the net slowly through the water.

"There's something really calming about him, don't you think?" said Isabella. "His movements. Like some kind of tai chi."

"Is he new?"

"Madame Baudin's son." Isabella smiled naughtily. "He's come of age."

Laura lowered her sunglasses, both horrified and amused. "Isabella, you are not . . ."

"Oh, darling, relax. I just like to look." She turned back to Laura. "I quite liked Cherry actually. Despite my earlier misgivings. She seemed quite charming. Happy to pitch in. Anyway, I thought it's what you wanted. One big happy family."

"Well, yes . . . except I get the feeling she doesn't want to let me in. . . . In fact"—Laura laughed uncomfortably—"I'd go as far as to say she wishes I weren't there."

"Really? Why?"

"I don't know. Just a feeling. She doesn't talk to me much. Open up."

"Darling, give her a chance. She's only just met you. Probably terrified of you."

Laura looked astonished. "Whatever for?"

"You're the mother of her new boyfriend. And you always were very protective of him."

Laura laughed. "What on earth are you talking about?"

"Come on, you were always the territorial one at the play-groups. A real tiger mother. Do you remember the time you pinched that little boy? He was only about two."

"He bit Daniel on the leg. Drew blood. There was a row of teeth marks on him for days."

"And wasn't there some incident with a kid in Daniel's class? I seem to remember a cricket bat . . . and did the boy not end up crying or something and then . . . leave the school?"

Laura's gaze turned to the pool boy. "Do you remember being young? Late teens . . . early twenties?"

"I seem to remember a lot of parties, at least going to them, but, funnily enough, not a lot of detail."

"I wonder what Rose would've been like."

"Beautiful and talented, probably. Like her mother."

Laura smiled. "It's funny with Cherry. I was hoping . . ."

"Oh no, darling," said Isabella quickly. "Don't hope that."

"I know. Silly," said Laura. "Fanciful, really."

They sat, both enjoying the measured, slow movements of the pool boy, the regular whoosh of the water, and the drip-drip-drip as he lifted his net.

When Laura got back to the house, Cherry and Daniel were still out. She made herself a bit of lunch, but picked at it. Then suddenly impatient, she knew this was an opportunity she should be making the most of. After all, she had the place to herself and could enjoy the peace. Could swim in the pool without feeling like a third wheel.

She went to her room and changed into a bikini. On the way back, as she passed Daniel and Cherry's room, she noticed the door was ajar. She stopped and was about to close it, but then, propelled by a longing to be closer to her houseguest, peeked through the gap. She stood with her feet safely on the neutral flooring of the landing and cast her eyes about the room.

Two suitcases were stacked neatly against the wall, the clothes hung up in wardrobes. A wayward sleeve jutted through the gap between the doors. Some clothes were cast on the chair, some shorts of Daniel's and a T-shirt of Cherry's she'd seen her in the night before. The bed was roughly made, the summer duvet pulled up to reach the pillows.

On the dresser were receipts, boarding pass coupons, their passports and some books. Laura recognized one of her own favorites and, without realizing she was doing so, walked into the room and picked it up. Flicked it open to the folded-down corner and smiled, recalling the passage in the story. Was it Cherry's? She instantly warmed toward her; there was a reassurance to actually knowing something about her, even something as innocuous as the books she liked to read. See, they had things in common! And there was certainly no need for Cherry to be anxious around her.

Spurred on by this cheering information, Laura looked around. Picked up a passport and turned to the back. It was Daniel's and she laughed at his very serious sixteen-year-old face. She'd taken him to have the photo done for a school trip to Burma.

Should she? Oh, what harm could it do, it was practically an established ritual, comparing passport photos. She picked up Cherry's. Her photo was equally serious. She flicked through and there was just the one visa entry stamp in it for Australia. Conscious she'd crossed the boundaries of the passport photo game, she quickly put it back. She stood there for a second, not yet wanting to leave, aware that this was the closest she'd been to Cherry since she'd arrived three days ago, and Laura wanted to know more, to close the gap between them. At the same time, she knew she was trespassing and the insight wasn't being freely given. She gazed around the room, frustrated that she still knew so little about this girl who'd captured Daniel's heart, frustrated that Cherry hadn't let her in.

There was something sticking out of the back of the book. It must have slipped when she was looking through it. She could see it was Cherry's flight ticket and she was just tucking it back in when she frowned.

Open return. Laura pulled the ticket from the book. The flight out was for the previous Friday to Nice. Five hundred pounds. There was no return flight booked.

Why would Cherry have only booked one portion of the flight? She'd always known she was originally going home today. Laura scanned the printout looking for something to explain . . . what?

A bird flew close past the window and its abrupt movement startled her. She suddenly felt uncomfortable in the room and quickly put the ticket back. She hurried out and carefully pulled the door back to the same degree of opening as when she'd found it.

Out at the pool, she lay on the sunbed, but couldn't settle. It was a grubby thing, going through someone's belongings, and Laura was unnerved not just at how she'd done it, but how quickly and easily she'd rooted around, picking things up, snooping through Cherry's possessions, her private papers. She was embarrassed, ashamed. And yet, there was something about that ticket that she couldn't shake, something that made her uneasy.

Maybe the water would cleanse, clear her head. She waded in and set herself a task of a hundred lengths. Six, seven decent strokes and she'd reach the end of the pool. Break her focus. *Why hadn't Cherry booked a flight home again?*

When Daniel and Cherry came back later that afternoon, she was in the kitchen preparing dinner. Cherry went to change and Laura waited until she was safely upstairs and they heard the shower start to run. She started to wash the salad leaves she'd picked from the garden. Daniel was sitting at the large table, enjoying a glass of wine with her. It was the kind of moment she usu-

ally loved, just the two of them doing nothing much and she realized they hadn't done this since he'd come back from university.

"You're so meticulous," he said, amused, as she held each leaf
individually under the tap, inspecting them thoroughly as the
water trickled over.

"You'd be amazed where they hide. Look! See, I nearly missed
that one."

"Would it really be so bad if you ate a few?"

"Don't be disgusting."

He laughed and watched as she shook the leaves dry and put
them in a bowl. Then she started chopping some cherry tomatoes.

"They from the garden as well?"

"A couple of early ones." She threw one at him and he darted
his hand out but missed. He picked it up off the floor and, after a
quick inspection, chucked it in his mouth.

"Yuk!"

Daniel grinned. "Tastes just fine."

She'd have to bring up the subject soon or Cherry would be
back. "So . . . it's nice Cherry can stay a bit longer."

"Uh-huh. You got any more of those tomatoes?"

She threw him another. "Lucky her, eh. Did her boss call or
something? Just to see if she wanted to spend longer on holiday?"

"I don't know. Maybe."

"Bit weird, though, having your boss call you when you're away.
Just to see if you want to extend your trip." She smiled.

"Yeah . . . Actually, now I remember. I think she rang in to see if
they needed her to do any early-morning viewings for her first day
back and it just came up. They're quiet at the moment, apparently,
and her boss is keen for Cherry to use up some of her time."

"But originally . . . she was going home today? That was the
plan?"

"Yeah . . . why do you ask?"

"No reason."

"Come on, there must be a reason."

Laura tried to laugh it off. "I was just wondering . . . That was
what we'd agreed on."

"Yeah . . . course, it was."

She smiled casually, but her silence said something else.

It suddenly occurred to him: "Do you think Cherry had a different day in mind?"

"Did she?"

He was getting irritated now. "No! Look, we discussed the dates with you, she booked the flight, and I sent over the six hundred quid."

It took all her effort to keep a pleasant expression, to remain calm. *Six* hundred pounds?

"You paid?" she said lightly.

"Yes. A trainee estate agent doesn't earn that much."

She heard the warning in his voice and smiled genially. "I can imagine."

Anyone passing Cherry's bedroom at that moment might have been disconcerted by how still she was, so still, eyes fixed ahead with great intensity. If that person had come into the room, he would have seen she was staring at the dresser or, more accurately, the book on the dresser. That person would have wondered what about it could hold someone's penetrating stare.

Cherry repositioned it so the spine was parallel to the edge of the dresser. She knew it had been picked up, looked at, the document hidden at the back taken out. And that document's information was probably fermenting like some sort of multiplying bacteria right now in Laura's brain. Cherry was livid, but knew better than to confront her. No, there would be another way to deal with this. For now, she would keep it to herself.

14

*C*HERRY SHOWED NO SIGN OF LEAVING. THE DAYS DRIFTED BY, LAZY, plentiful, and filled with sunshine. Laura kept waiting for her to say when her time was used up, or talk about when she had to go back to work, but Cherry never mentioned it. Suggestions for day trips that they could all do together completely dried up; Laura didn't quite feel the enthusiasm she had before. They fell into a pattern: At breakfast, she would wonder what they had planned for the day. If they were going to the beach, Laura now felt a sense of relief if they did, as she wouldn't have to continue to make polite conversation. Instead she would lie by the pool, peaceful but lonely, and she found herself starting to resent Cherry's presence. This was her vacation too—and she hadn't counted on having her son's girlfriend present the entire time. She wanted some time with Daniel too, just the two of them.

She broached the subject once more with him, a few days after Cherry was meant to have gone home. To his due, he was apologetic and offered straight away to find a hotel they could stay in instead. But then Laura realized she wouldn't see him at all, so on the spur of the moment, she'd dissuaded him.

The tension was starting to get to her in other ways too. She would mislay things. Her keys would disappear from the kitchen worktop. Her toothbrush would be in the bin—fallen from the sink above. And a deep scratch appeared on her rental car, which must have happened when she'd parked in the village. It wasn't just Cherry's continued presence that was bothering her. There was also the issue of the cost of the flight. The ticket had definitely shown a fee of five hundred pounds, of that she was certain. And yet Daniel had said he'd paid her a hundred pounds more. She was well aware of the vast gulf between the two of them in wealth and she didn't like the way her mind was thinking.

Two days before Laura was to go home, it suddenly occurred to her that Cherry would likely still be at the villa when she, herself, had gone back to London. This notion irritated her so much that she was quite monosyllabic when they said they were going into Saint-Tropez for the day. She waved them off and then went outside to the pool to retrieve her bikini, which she'd left on the drying rack the day before. It wasn't there and Laura looked around. She could swear she'd hung it out the previous night. Then she saw it, blown into the dirt. She went to retrieve it and saw it was filthy, as if it had blown off when it was still wet, which was odd as it hadn't been windy at all the previous evening. Sighing, she took it inside to wash.

As she ran the tap, she considered how much, if anything, she could challenge Cherry about. She could hardly ask her how much her flight had cost, as it would sound like a direct accusation, but she decided that she would ask her again when she was planning to leave. That, she was entitled to do.

Cherry would stretch out this trip another three days. After all, funerals in France take so long to organize, and there were all her grandmother's things to go through. Neil had been appropriately sympathetic and had agreed to the extended compassionate leave when she'd phoned to tell him her grandmother, sadly, had passed away. It had been a simple decision not to tell Laura exactly how long she planned on staying; it served her right for nosing through her things. Who the fuck did she think she was, snooping through her private stuff? She was so in your face all the time, always asking questions, wanting to spend every waking minute with Daniel and her. Laura probably thought it was her God-given right to look around their bedroom. Cherry sighed.

She so wished it hadn't become like this. It would have been so nice if they'd hit it off. Cherry was of the opinion it was important to get on with your boyfriend's mother and it bothered her that she didn't.

She held Daniel's hand as they wandered around Saint-Tropez, bags slung over their shoulders, hats shielding their eyes as they walked, flip-flops kicking up sand and dust. They headed through Place des Lices, where the old guys played *boules* in the dappled shade under the plane trees; then they made their way down to the port, where the yachts looked too big for the harbor.

"What was it again?" asked Daniel, wanting to hear her say it.

"A blue short flared skirt and matching blue-and-white-striped cotton top. An exact color match," she said with a shudder.

He looked at her legs. "How short?"

She pulled his hat down over his face.

"Okay, sorry." He grinned. "So then what?"

"I was out with a couple of friends one day and saw the girl whose hand-me-down it was. And I happened to be wearing it at the time."

"So?"

"You don't understand. It was humiliating. I was so embarrassed, I ran across the road in the hope she wouldn't spot me. That was when the car hit me."

"What!" He looked at her, horrified.

She tucked her arm into his. "In the end, it was only a sprained ankle, along with a lot of bruising."

"You could have been killed."

"At the time, I was more concerned about whether or not the full story would get out at school. I was only fourteen, remember. Fortunately, the girl didn't figure out why I'd run away like that. In fact," said Cherry, suddenly realizing, "I've never told anyone before now."

Daniel took her hand and squeezed it and she smiled. Occasionally these stories that had haunted her childhood were useful; and unlike some of the things she'd said, they were actually true. Daniel was pulling her across the street.

"What?" she said, bemused, and then looked up and saw they had wandered into the narrow streets of the Old Village, where all the boutiques were, and they seemed to be heading straight for Dior. Her heart fluttered; he was intent on something, but she couldn't quite work out what. Then they were inside. She looked around at the pristine decor with its select wares, items that seemed to mock her with their superiority, and she grew nervous. It was all well and good, that hard-times story prompting him to suggest a shopping trip, but she couldn't afford anywhere near these prices.

"It's too nice to be inside shop—"

"On me," he said quietly.

She stared at him, wide-eyed.

"Anything you want. In fact, let's try on loads. I like that yellow shirt—what do you think?"

She looked at where he was pointing, then back at him again; it still hadn't sunk in.

"You'd better hurry up, because we've got the others to do yet."

"Others?" she managed to croak.

"Don't ask me what they're all called. I never remember all the names, but they do have some nice clothes." He smiled apologetically, indicating his modest attire. "So I'm told."

Cherry couldn't quite believe what she was hearing. "I can't . . . ," she started halfheartedly.

"It's my birthday present to you," he said firmly.

And that made it okay. He seemed to be as keen as she was, taking garments off racks and holding them up against her, waiting patiently outside changing rooms and giving constructive comments that proved he was actually looking at the clothing. He also paid for everything. Cherry didn't go mad; she didn't want to look greedy or take advantage of his wealth. A couple of items she turned down, saying she had too many, but she still acquired five or six pieces of designer clothing. After the last shop, with just one to go, Daniel seemed to flag, but gamely kept up his offer.

"Do you want to do the last one?" he said, nodding across the street.

Cherry sensed he'd had enough. She kissed him on the lips. "No, thank you. This has already been the perfect morning."

He looked relieved and she realized he'd made quite a sacrifice.

"You don't like shopping, do you?"

Guilt flashed across his face; then he saw her laughing.

"Can't stand it. Now you sit here"—he indicated a bench in the shade—"and I'm going across to the *boulangerie* to get us some lunch."

Cherry was happy to rest and watch him stroll up one of the streets. She looked lovingly down at her bags, still glowing with the blissfulness of it all. A stupid smile adorned her face as she ran through her head all the new clothes she had. Maybe she could wear one of the dresses tonight. The smile suddenly faltered. Laura would likely have an opinion about this lavish spending spree. Things had been decidedly distant between them the last few days—nothing that Daniel would particularly notice, but she was very aware that the liberal welcome when she'd first arrived had disappeared. Never mind that all these clothes were a gift—and one that Daniel had instigated through no conscious prompting of hers—the fact was he'd just spent nearly two thousand euros on her.

Cherry sat up uncomfortably. She didn't want to arouse any suspicion as to why she was with Daniel. It would just complicate things. As she was gazing around distractedly, she saw in a shop window across the street a painting that looked familiar; then she recognized it as being by the artist that Laura had at the villa. Gathering her bags, she walked over to the gallery and peered in. It was displayed on a small wooden easel, an oil of Saint-Tropez harbor. It cost thirty-five hundred euros and it had a *sold* sticker on it.

The bell tinkled as she walked in and she knew she didn't have long. Daniel would be back any minute. She scanned the gallery quickly and found more paintings by the same artist displayed on the back wall. *Sold, sold, sold,* she saw, and then a smaller one, an oil of Place des Lices, the dappled shade of the dozens of plane trees casting a lacelike pattern on the sandy ground. Miraculously, it seemed to be available. She would be in debt on her credit card for months, but she knew instinctively it was worth it. The gallery manager wrapped the painting, she paid, and then quickly left the shop, returning to her spot on the bench, hiding the package in one of the clothing bags. Daniel was barely a couple of minutes later and arrived slightly red-faced as if he had been running. He apologized for taking so long, but he had a baguette and a *tarte au citron* for lunch.

They sat in the square and ate, watching the *boules* players and then headed on back to the villa. Isabella's car was in the drive when they pulled up, and as they walked in, they could hear numerous voices. Brigitte was there too, along with Nicole.

"Here they are!" said Isabella, who'd obviously had a couple of glasses of wine. "Did you have a nice day?"

"Lovely, thanks," said Cherry.

"So I can see," said Isabella, smiling down at her bags.

"Do we get a fashion show?" asked Brigitte.

Cherry blushed. "No."

"Well, at least let us see what you got." She was pawing at the bags, trying to peek in, and Cherry bit back her annoyance. She pulled out a dress from one of the bags to exclamations of appreciation and envy.

"What else?" demanded Brigitte, and Cherry wished she'd shut up.

"Just a shirt and a top."

"In all these bags?" she said disbelievingly. "Come on, what's all the secrecy? Pretty, please, can we see?"

Laura had remained quiet during all this, but Cherry could sense she wanted to know what was in the bags. Isabella and Brigitte were looking at her with inquisitive, expectant eyes. She had no choice, and soon all the garments were out, being appraised and cooed over.

Cherry caught Laura looking at her in curiosity. She knew she was wondering how she'd managed to pay for all the clothes.

"You seem to have made a successful tour of the shops," Laura said pleasantly.

"Not all of them," said Daniel with relief.

"You went too?" Brigitte was amazed. "How did you manage to persuade Daniel to go shopping?"

"It was my idea," he said, smiling. He put his arm around Cherry and kissed her. "Happy birthday. Sorry it was late."

Laura's face remained impassive. Now is the time, thought Cherry. She went to the bag that held the wrapped painting and, pulling it out, handed it to Daniel. "This is for you."

He took it in surprise. "What is it?"

"Open it," she said, smiling.

He pulled off the tissue and his face lit up. "But it's . . . ," he trailed off.

Cherry nodded. "I saw it and just wanted you to have it." It had almost bankrupted her, but it had been necessary.

He loved it, she saw, but was clearly concerned. "You mustn't . . . You can't . . ."

Cherry put up a finger. "Nope. I don't want to hear it. I wanted to get you something special."

"No . . ."

She put the finger on his lips. "Shush."

He looked at the painting again, eyes lit up, and he threw an arm tightly around her neck, kissing her. "Thank you. I absolutely love it."

He was incredibly touched, she saw, and was glad she'd done it. "Yours was a present," he gently admonished.

He kissed her again. Over his shoulder, she saw Laura looking on with uncertainty. She was probably trying to work out how she'd got the euros to pay for the painting.

Let her wonder.

Laura slept badly that night. So many things were niggling her. Daniel had paid for Cherry's flights, and seemingly extra, and then all the clothes. He'd clearly spent a fortune; and to be fair, Cherry, understandably, would have struggled to pay for either. So, why the painting? How could she afford a two- to three-thousand-euro original oil when she couldn't pay for her own flights? It kept her awake until two in the morning, and she woke early too—around six. The unsettled, slightly queasy feeling in the pit of her stomach wouldn't go away, so she got up and went down to the kitchen to get a glass of water.

As she held the glass under the tap, it slipped from her fingers and smashed in the sink. Laura swore; she seemed to be so clumsy these days, dropping things, losing things. She still had to get the rental car fixed, and now it was too late, as she was leaving the following day. She carefully picked the pieces of glass from the sink and placed them on an old newspaper. Then got herself another glass and filled it, drinking slowly, the same questions from the night before still hammering away in her head like a pinball machine, but no clear answers came.

Laura stretched her aching, twitching limbs. Although it was the last day of her supposedly relaxing holiday, she felt more stressed and exhausted than before she'd arrived. Cherry had changed everything. She'd made herself at home and yet had so far proven unwilling to spend much time with her hostess. In fact, Laura got the distinct impression she was barely tolerated.

She picked up the painting Cherry had bought for Daniel. The light caught the plane trees, the sandy shadows of the square. It was truly beautiful. No wonder Daniel treasured it.

"It is an original."

Laura spun round and saw Cherry standing in the doorway.

"Just in case you were wondering."

"How long have you been there?" she burst out, irritated—guilty—although Cherry could hardly read her mind.

"Not long." Cherry smiled and walked over and took the painting from her. Met her eye. "Anything else you want to check out?"

Laura was puzzled. What did she mean? She was only looking at it, for heaven's sake! She was about to retort when a cold, dousing memory returned to her. The day she'd gone into their room. Cherry's things, her flight details. Did she know they'd been looked at, read?

Daniel appeared and put his arm around Cherry. "Still fancy the beach?"

She smiled. "Sure. I'll just get my stuff," and she went back upstairs.

"How about you, Mum? Last day of hitting the rays?"

"No, thank you."

"What's up?"

She hadn't intended to sound so curt, but she'd just about reached her limit. "Cherry had a nice holiday?"

He frowned. "Yeah. Really good. Is something wrong?"

"Oh, come on, you really don't know? She's been here quite a long time."

"I thought you said it was okay?"

Laura sighed. "I did. But let's face it, I didn't expect it to be quite so long."

"I'm sorry, I would've got us a hotel, I did offer—"

"It's fine," said Laura tightly. "I would like to know, though, why it's such a big secret, the day she's leaving."

"It's not a secret."

"But when I asked, she wouldn't say. And she hasn't volunteered any information since." Laura felt the tension of the last few days rise up in her. "How long is she intending to stay, anyway? Weeks, months, the entire summer?"

"She's leaving on Saturday."

She was brought up short. "Saturday? What, the day after tomorrow?"

"Yes, she's got to go back to work."

"Right. So, why hasn't she said?"

"She has. I've known for ages."

"But she didn't think of telling me?"

"She . . . I . . . probably forgot. Sorry, I should've thought. If I'd known we were invading your space, we would've moved out. Honestly."

Laura swallowed her dismay. *"We."* He kept saying *"we."* She had missed her son the last couple of weeks. "You know that's not what I wanted."

They fell silent. Both had more to say, but neither wanted to go on.

"We'd really like it if you came to the beach, Mum. I'd really like it. Just for a couple of hours?"

She almost did. *Almost.* "Sorry, Daniel. I've promised I'd meet up with Izzy."

It was obvious she'd made it up, and she felt bad for it, but how could she explain there was something about Cherry that didn't add up? And she was sure she wasn't imagining the awkwardness between them. It was clear from the hurt look on his face that he thought she didn't like his girlfriend.

"Okay, well, I'll see you later."

It was just a brief peck, and then he got Cherry and they were gone.

She felt guilty for fabricating the visit to Izzy, so she decided to try to make it the truth and drove down to Saint-Tropez. But unluckily for Laura, Isabella wasn't in. She stood for a moment at her friend's empty villa, wondering what to do with herself, and then thought she'd just go home again.

She packed her suitcase for the following morning, then decided to go outside and see if any of the peppers or tomatoes needed picking. She took a colander from the kitchen and managed to while away half an hour or so, even forgetting about Cherry for a bit, and then she heard voices from the kitchen. She considered staying outside for a bit longer, but she knew that would be churlish. So, with a sigh, she went in with a red and yellow pepper and four beef tomatoes.

"We're getting quite a crop this year," she started to say, and then she saw their faces. "What's the matter?"

Daniel was holding his painting. It had a tear in the canvas, about an inch long, right across the center of Place des Lices.

Laura was horrified. "How on earth . . . Your beautiful painting . . ."

"It was on the broken glass," said Daniel, "when we came in."

On the worktop was the glass she'd broken earlier and had forgotten to wrap and put in the bin.

"But . . . what was it doing there?" She looked at them both, but Cherry wouldn't meet her eye. Instead she gazed ruefully down.

It took a moment before it sank in; then she dismissed it, laughed. She stopped short, incredulous. "What?"

"Whatever happened, it was likely an accident," Cherry said graciously.

Laura was dumbfounded. "You don't really think . . . it was me?"

"No, Mum, I just don't know how it happened. We came home and found it—lying on the broken glass."

"I meant to clear it up earlier, but I forgot." Laura stopped, realizing she was sounding guilty. "Paintings don't just rip by lying on glass. They have to be torn, slashed." Upset, she stopped. "I am very sorry about your painting," she said to Daniel, "but I really have no idea how it came to be damaged." She flicked her eyes across to Cherry, who was staring at the floor, crestfallen.

Dinner was quiet; no one mentioned the painting. Laura made her excuses early and went to bed.

The following morning, Daniel loaded her bags into the back of his car. Cherry stood in the open doorway and shook her hand. "Thank you very much for a lovely stay, Laura."

That's the first time she's said it, thought Laura, and she tried to bury the irritation at being waved off from her own front step.

Daniel was quiet on the way to the airport and Laura felt a bout of sadness that they weren't on the same good terms they usually were. She wanted to try to clear the air before she flew back home. "You do know I didn't—wouldn't—dream of doing something like that to your painting, don't you?" she said, not quite believing she was having to say it.

"Yes, of course."

"You don't sound convinced."

He took his eyes off the road for a second and smiled at her. "Hey, maybe it's just one of those unexplained things."

Such as what? Laura thought. But it was clear the subject was closed. And nothing would be gained by flogging it to death. She knew she hadn't done it, and it was hardly likely Daniel had, which left either Cherry or a random accident. She couldn't make sense of the latter, but she, equally, couldn't understand why Cherry would do it. It was hard to comprehend, but there was something else distracting her, a niggling disquiet: Cherry was still in her house.

Cherry watched the car pull away and disappear around the end of the drive. So she was gone. It was a huge relief. Laura knew things, she was certain of it. Cherry knew she'd not booked a return flight, maybe even knew Daniel had paid a tiny bit more than it had actually cost. She'd been in desperate need of some new swimwear, unable to afford it, and, anyway, it was for him; it was important to her to look nice for him.

So now the suffocating mother was gone. She could let her hair down; she could be free! Free to enjoy this magnificent house.

Cherry caressed the backs of chairs as she wandered through the living room. She straightened the tea towels in the kitchen and saw the painting lying ripped on the counter. *Such a shame.* All that money on her credit card that she still had to pay off; it made her feel sick and slightly panicky. *But it had been necessary.*

Cherry needed to untangle those motherly bindings Laura still kept wrapped tight. She needed Daniel on her side, now that Laura had been snooping.

She picked up an apple from the fruit bowl and went out onto the terrace. She ate it delicately as she gazed out at the Saint-Tropez peninsula and thought of Laura here and wondered whether she fully appreciated it and how often she bothered to come. From what Daniel had said of his mother's job, she worked hard and put in long days. Cherry inwardly snorted, full of contempt for the waste of such a beautiful house. Months probably passed with no one enjoying it other than the spiders, which still managed to concoct webs every week before the cleaner got them and the birds who dipped their beaks at the edge of the pool. Cherry knew that if she owned this villa she'd be here for weeks or months at a time. She watched the famous distant harbor and felt a great sense of well-being, of belonging, as if all those yachts, the beaches, the sun-warmed streets, and the lavish lifestyle were within touching distance, there for the taking.

* * *

Lying in bed that night, Cherry picked up her book while she was waiting for Daniel to come out of the bathroom. She heard him come in and then he got on the bed and tilted the book away from her face. She looked up to see he had a small box in his hand.

"I wanted to wait until we were alone for this one," he said.

She looked at it in delight. It was turquoise blue velvet. A box like that could only mean jewelry. Tentatively she opened it up and gasped. Lying on the silk lining was a slim gold bangle set, with a single stone of soft, shimmering blue.

"It's a moonstone. For your birth month, apparently, although I have to confess that bit was a coincidence. I just liked it. Thought it would suit you."

She threw her arms around him. "Thank you. I love it!"

"Happy birthday. Again." He kissed her and then took it out of the box and she held out her slim, tanned wrist. He fastened the clasp and she watched how the stone gleamed mysteriously as she moved her arm. It was the most beautiful piece of jewelry she had ever seen. It was then that Cherry made her decision. Nicolas wasn't the only one who could get married. She was going to have Daniel Cavendish.

15

*L*AURA CAME HOME TO EXCRUCIATING NOISE. HER NEIGHBORS' basement extension was in full swing, and as irritating as it was, she had to tolerate it, for only twelve months before she'd been doing the same thing. She was supposed to be working from home that afternoon on some proposals she'd pitch to ITV at her lunch in a couple of weeks.

Soon after she got back from the airport, a writer arrived, one Laura liked and enjoyed working with, and who was favored by ITV after a respectable success with a miniseries for them the previous year. She opened the door to him and they had to shout their hellos above the noise of the excavator. They worked hard on a joint idea they had about a drama set in an exclusive private school, and despite the racket, they made good progress. The only interruption was a brief power cut from the builders, which meant that the Internet was down for an hour or so, hampering research.

By midafternoon, the writer had enough material to go ahead and write a treatment, a summary of the series. It was an investment Laura would have to bear the cost of, and at his rate, not a cheap one, but drama development was notoriously expensive. She felt it was worth it, as she sensed there was a good chance Alison and Sean would go for this project.

After he left, the builders packed up and went home too. It was late afternoon, but Laura knew the weekend would not yet have started for everyone. She toyed with the idea a bit, and then, before she lost her courage, she picked up her bag and left the house.

Laura walked the short distance to Highsmith and Brown real estate agents and browsed the window outside. Lots of beautifully photographed houses, some costing millions, some casually stating their price was on application. After she'd spent what she thought was a reasonable time looking, she stepped inside. A dapper-looking man, who was with a gentleman of retirement age, looked up. He seemed harassed, perhaps more so when a young girl approached her hesitantly.

"Hi, can I help you?"

Laura wanted to speak to the well-dressed man, not this girl, who was clearly much more junior. She knew from the website he was the manager—she reminded herself of his name: Neil.

"I'm just going to take a look at these," indicated Laura, and she moved over to a stand of house details. The girl left with a grateful nod, glad to have escaped.

Laura wondered how long she would have to pretend interest in the houses. Perhaps she could write something down, take some notes. She was about to dig in her handbag for some paper and a pen when she heard the retired man finish up. Her heart was hammering as he left, but she made herself catch Neil's eye.

He smiled at her. "Was there something I can do for you?" He was forthright, professional. She would have to be careful.

"Yes. I'm looking for something with four bedrooms. I've always fancied a mews . . ."

He indicated a chair on the opposite side of his desk. "Would you like to take a seat?"

She did.

"Perhaps I can start by taking some details?" said Neil, and Laura realized it would be better if she made up a false name and address. She panicked and could think of nothing except Isabella's, which she gave, mentally asking her forgiveness, just recovering enough to alter her mobile number and e-mail address slightly.

He started to scroll through some houses on his iPad.

"You're very busy," began Laura. *Lamely,* she thought.

"Yes. Time of the year." He looked up and nodded at a couple who were waiting impatiently; she knew she had to do this sooner rather than later.

"We have this rather lovely place," he started, showing her some photos on the screen, "in Lexham Gardens. It's not a mews, but it's four bedrooms and three bathrooms."

"Great. Can I take a hard copy?"

He delved into a file at the side of his desk and pulled out a luxurious printout. Then he began to scroll through again.

Think, think. God, I am so useless at this. "You could do with some more help."

He smiled a professional smile. "Yes, well, normally, there's four of us, but the summer season seems to have started earlier."

"Oh, so some of the staff are on holiday, are they?" *He's just said that, you fool,* thought Laura. She saw his eyes wanted to hurry things along.

"Yes. Three, in fact."

"Oh, bad planning."

As might be expected, he said nothing to this, but Laura decided to plow on. "Isn't there usually a girl in here? Dark hair, short. Young?"

"You mean Cherry? Yes, she's off too."

The sweet, ineffectual girl was hovering. "Excuse me, Neil, but is the house on Victoria Road under offer now?"

He held up his hand, a wait signal. Then he smiled at Laura. "I'm afraid we don't have anything else available at the moment, but I can certainly let you know as soon as new properties come on."

"That would be great." Laura suddenly felt silly, like she was playing a childish game, making something out of nothing. She stood and Neil shook her hand. Almost as soon as she'd vacated the seat, the couple swooped in.

Embarrassed, she walked toward the door, still trying to look like a bona fide buyer, whatever that was. Goodness knows what she'd thought she'd find out, there was nothing *to* find out. The only thing that absolutely did not add up was Cherry saying that Neil had called her and encouraged her to take more time off. He was clearly woefully understaffed.

"She's back next week," said the girl as Laura headed for the door. She looked up. "Cherry? You were asking about her. Back on Monday." There was a poorly hidden note of relief to the girl's voice.

Laura nodded. She knew. She looked for a moment at the girl and saw how out of her depth she was. Poor thing. She smiled. "Last day?"

The girl grimaced. "Tomorrow." Then regretting her unprofessionalism: "Sorry, shouldn't say that, should I?"

"I won't tell anyone."

The girl grinned. "Thanks. I was beginning to think she'd never come back."

"Delayed return?" Laura spoke with understanding and empathy; she knew perfectly well Cherry had extended her trip.

"Do you know her?"

A sigh escaped. "A little." She quickly smiled and kept the pressure valve shut up tight again. She hadn't meant to sigh; she didn't really want anyone to know about her anxiety, but the worry had been hers alone for a few days now.

"Understandable though."

Laura stopped. "Yes," she said again, not knowing what they were talking about, but something stirred, something that made her alert.

"I remember when my grandmother died. Norfolk, though, not the South of France. Bit easier to get to the funeral."

Laura was still standing there, rocked, trying to stay calm, trying to look sympathetic as if she *knew* that Cherry's grandmother had died, but every bit of energy seemed to be occupied by the unfurling realization: Cherry must have made it up. Made up her grandmother's death—did she even have a grandmother?—so she could be in the South of France at her boyfriend's villa. It *couldn't* be true; otherwise, she would have told Daniel and he would have told her.

No wonder Neil had had no choice but to let her go away when his other staff members were also off. She glanced up at him and saw him look at her strangely; perhaps he was wondering why she was still there, and it focused her enough to get out. With a brief thank-you and good-bye to the girl, who never knew just how much she'd done for Laura, she left the agency and didn't look around or slow down until she was back in her own road. Then it hit her again. She stopped in the middle of the pavement and goose bumps rose up on her arms.

Cherry had made it all up.

16

Friday, July 18

*I*T THREW HER INTO TURMOIL. WHEN SHE'D LEFT FRANCE, THERE WAS
something she didn't quite trust about Cherry, but she'd never
really expected to find anything out. Now it was real. Cherry had
lied to her boss to get time off—she'd lied to them, too, or been
economical, at least, with the truth, and Laura felt hurt. She'd
been *manipulated*. She was reminded of the scheming Cherry had
done to get her job. And then there was the money. Cherry had
seemingly cheated Daniel out of a hundred pounds, so it raised
the dark, uncomfortable question: Was Cherry a gold digger?

There had been no one to talk to. Laura had considered bringing it up with Howard, but it had been a long time since she'd
confided in him about anything. Izzy was still in France and it wasn't
the sort of thing she could discuss on the phone. So she'd left it to
brew and fester in her own mind.

Daniel was due home later that day, and as much as she'd been
looking forward to seeing him, she was now also slightly dreading
it. They'd spoken on the phone a few times and things were more
or less back to normal between them, but now she had this *thing*
and she didn't know what to do with it. His return home was only
for a few days, as he was moving out into his new flat the following
week. Laura had arranged a BBQ for close family and friends to

send him off. It would be the first time she'd see Cherry since the holiday. Cherry, who now infiltrated her mind every minute of the day, winding around like a creeper and making her uncomfortable, uneasy.

The nightmares had come back, out of the blue, dark thoughts that she'd tried to bury. They had started before Daniel was even born. She'd dream she'd had another baby, but had forgotten all about him, only remembering three days later that she'd left him in the wardrobe in a pram. Panicked, she'd pull him out, neglected, near starving, and he'd look at her, wide-eyed and confused, not knowing why he'd been abandoned. Guilty relief would swamp her, relief she'd got to him in the nick of time, but somewhere in the back of her head, she knew she'd do it again, she'd let him down again. And so she did, because the nightmare was recurring.

Later, when she really did have her baby, she'd have black thoughts, visions; and panicked "what-if's" would attack their way into her head, leaving her standing by, terrified and vulnerable, until she could gather herself enough to shake her head and force them out. She'd be walking him down the street in the pram, and as a car passed, she'd suddenly see nothing but its wheel and imagine Daniel whipped beneath it, his head crushed and mangled in the metal. She'd be in the shower and see him falling from an open window that she'd mistakenly left open, his tiny body lying inert on the paving below. A knife in the kitchen would become a gruesome blade that she would put out of sight, even though he was happily cooing in his bouncy chair. Worst, she would hear on the news about a young child snatched and she would plummet into nightmarish visions of Daniel calling for her, screaming out, confused as to why she didn't come and finally broken when he realized she wasn't ever coming for him. She would start to hyperventilate and have to get up, walk around the room to expel the images.

They had been dark hours, nights, months, but they had gradually lessened as the years progressed, although they never disappeared completely. If Daniel was late coming home from school, or later, when he was at uni, and she heard of a car crash on the M11, her imagination would start breeding ideas, one horrific thought morphing into another at rapid speed, until she forcibly stopped them, telling herself he had just got talking to some friends (which he had) or hadn't been driving to or from Cambridge on the day of the accident (which he hadn't).

Movement in front of her made her look up and she saw Alison and Sean, the drama powers from ITV, had arrived at La Galette, the restaurant they'd picked for lunch. It was in Upper Ground, not far from their HQ, but still they were nearly fifteen minutes late. Alison's PA had called to offer a girlish apology: "They're *so* sorry!" However, she had managed to make it sound anything but.

Sean came in first; with arms outstretched, he took her hands as she stood. "Laura, we're *so* sorry. Got held up with Helen at the last minute."

Helen was the comptroller of ITV, and the rumors were she was fond of summoning people to her office in a very headmistress-like way, something that won her no love amongst her staff.

"Don't worry about it," said Laura affably. She'd met Sean a couple of times before and liked him, felt he had a nose for a good script and wasn't afraid of speaking his mind.

"We only managed to get away by saying we had to see you," said Alison. Laura was sure that Helen didn't give a flying fig whether or not they had a lunch date with an independent producer, and the false bolstering of her ego made her slightly nervous—as if she shouldn't trust anything Alison said. *As well I shouldn't*, thought Laura wryly. *Nothing had changed there.*

As they took their seats, she wondered what had briefly unsettled her, and it wasn't Alison's throwaway flattery—it took more than that to put her off balance—it was this uncertainty with Cherry. She had to put it out of her mind for the next hour or so; this lunch could be pivotal to the future of her company.

Sean looked at her through his dark-rimmed square glasses.

"Thank you so much for coming, Laura, and thank you for *Pillow Fight*. I've seen two episodes now and I love them."

Laura said she was glad, while Alison sat with a magisterial smile, as though she had been the one behind it all and without her neither Laura nor the series would be what they were.

"Yes, we're really pumped," he said, beaming. Sean was younger than Alison and liked to speak on a more informal level; he worked in television because it was "fun."

"Has Helen seen it?" asked Laura.

"Not yet. It's in her schedule for next week. But we think . . . Well, it's obviously still too early to say for sure, but we've got great hopes for it."

He meant ratings, Laura knew. They wanted a big hit.

"And Sasha is *amazing*. She's going to be a big star when this comes out. Like I say, we'll have to wait on Helen and the first couple of weeks' overnights, but Alison and I would like to see a second series."

Laura smiled; this was great news indeed. "That would be fantastic."

"Alison says you might have a couple of other things to talk to us about?"

She did. The first one was the private school. She'd sent an abridged version of the writer's treatment on ahead of the lunch. As she launched into the pitch, she watched their pleasant faces remain static and knew they weren't biting.

"We like it," said Sean, ". . . like it a lot. It's just we have something very similar already in development."

It was the kiss of death. Laura left the fully developed treatment that she and the writer had worked so hard on in her bag. That was the nature of the business: Something you got excited about, and spent a lot of money and hours of time on, could be quashed in one idle sentence. It felt more of a blow than usual, but she had to move on. There was also a book adaptation for which she'd gotten the interest of a British star who was currently on an HBO series, earning ten times what she could in the UK, but who was desperate to get back to the UK, Laura knew, because she missed her family so much. They remained lukewarm over that one too, citing that their core audience probably wouldn't identify with the romantic novel as much as BBC viewers, perhaps, would.

"It feels a bit gloomy," said Sean. "What we loved about *Pillow Fight* was the suspense, the way the lead character tricked her best friend and ended up getting her man."

Alison was nodding along in agreement and then they were both looking at her expectantly. She had one last idea up her sleeve. It was a crime drama, and one or two of those on ITV were nearing their sell-by date, so there would be an appetite for a replacement. This one Laura liked, for the lead character was a formidable lady detective who had come out of retirement to avoid being saddled with her grandchildren while her daughter went (out of necessity) to work. She'd rather help pay for child care than have to do it herself. To her surprise, they liked it, and they spent the next half hour batting around some story details and who might make a good lead.

"Can you get us a treatment?" said Sean. "I think this one could really go somewhere."

Laura said she could, and lunch continued pleasurably amidst various intruding texts and calls.

She arrived home to find a rucksack in the hall and had barely got her jacket off before Daniel came through and swept her up in a hug.

"You're home!" she said, delighted.

"So are you. Just in time for a glass of Chablis and some quiche and salad. I've made dinner."

She ruffled his hair and followed the delicious smells coming from the kitchen, opened the oven door and was blasted with heat. Inside was a large mushroom quiche. "You made this?"

"Hmm."

"Fibber. It looks suspiciously like it's from Vincent."

"Okay, busted. It survived the flight well, eh?"

They compared tans and news on Izzy and Brigitte as they set the table and served up dinner. "So, how was the rest of your trip?" asked Laura. "Did you get much studying done?"

"Yep. Loads, in fact." He smiled. "I think it picked up once Cherry left. Although we did seem to spend quite a bit of time Skyping." He suddenly lit up as if he'd just realized something. "We never seem to run out of things to say to each other."

He is completely in love with her, Laura thought, trying to keep her smile in place as her heart stuttered in dismay.

"That's nice."

He looked at her quizzically and she knew the response had been inadequate.

"She's a great girl. . . ."

"But?" he prompted, eyes sharp.

"It's just . . . you've only just met."

"And?" he prompted again, and his tone had an edge of defensiveness this time.

Now was her chance. Should she say something? Dare she? How could she not?

"I've just noticed . . . she's someone who . . . You've helped her quite a bit since you've been dating." She felt herself begin to blush. *God, this is a hideous insinuation.*

"'Helped her'?"

"Financially."

His face seemed to stall in an expression of incredulity.

"Whoa, whoa, are you trying to tell me you think she's some sort of . . . *gold digger*?"

The blush flooded her face.

"Seriously?"

"I'd just noticed one or two things."

"Such as? Mum, she's not asked me for a *thing*. What was it? I paid for her flights, yes, but the clothes . . . Is that what this is about? They were a *birthday present*. If anything, she spent more on me when she bought the . . . my painting," he added.

The awkwardness intensified with the unresolved, ugly specter of the slashed painting.

Laura held up her hands. "I'm sorry, but there's something about her I just don't trust."

"Why? You don't even know her, not really."

What could she say? Confess to snooping around in their room and her amateur detective work at the office?

"I feel like I got to know her quite well . . . over the holiday," she said lamely.

He looked at her and she tried to uphold her statement with a smile.

"Mum. Do you like Cherry?"

His frankness threw her. Her hesitation gave away her answer and he knew it.

"I'm grateful for your concern, but there's no need to worry. Mum, we're dating, and I hope we will continue to do so for a long time. I'd like you to be happy for me."

"Okay." It was a small squeak of a word, meaningless really.

"Now, what about this BBQ tomorrow? You didn't have to, you know."

Should she affirm how much she liked Cherry? Reassure him? How could she, when she didn't—and now the subject was diffi-'cult between them. And she *had* liked her—she'd wanted to know her and even be close to her.

"Can I do anything to help?" he asked.

"No thanks. It's all under control."

"Right." He pointed to her empty plate. "You done?" She nodded. "I'll just fill the dishwasher, then I might pop out."

She knew where, and he knew she knew. She nodded, covering up the pang, the unfamiliar distance that was suddenly between them from his not saying Cherry's name. She couldn't bear it, her son becoming estranged from her.

She watched as he took away the plates, the tightness in her chest intolerable. Maybe she *was* wrong about Cherry. After all, Daniel was an intelligent person; he would've had a hunch if something wasn't right. She'd been stewing alone with her thoughts for two weeks, and paranoia had a nasty way of escalating things. Maybe there was some other explanation and she was on the verge of some awful, embarrassing mistake. The tension suddenly lessened. Perhaps this could all be easily solved. Cherry would be at the BBQ the next day; Laura would try to speak to her. Hopefully, there would be a chance to clarify things and she could put her mind at rest.

17

SATURDAY WAS A MUGGY, HAZY DAY AND THE DUST FROM THE BUILD-
ing work next door hung in the air. The builders were due to finish at lunchtime, thankfully, but for the moment, tiny particles
managed to lodge themselves on the skin and in the mouth, leaving a nasty, bitter taste. Laura was undaunted. She sprayed the entire garden with the hose and looked in satisfaction at the plants
and lawn, glowing as green as on a fresh spring day. Howard had
been dispatched to the butcher to pick up the meat; Daniel was
currently placing bottles of wine in the large fridge in the den.
He'd been a little cool toward her since yesterday, but she'd made
herself be bright and enthusiastic. After all, this was his leaving-
home party and she wanted them both to remember it as a happy
time.

The first guests to arrive were Isabella and Brigitte, just back
from France.

"How was the rest of your stay?" asked Daniel.

"Wonderful," sighed Isabella. "We only came back because
Richard was complaining he never saw us."

"Charming."

"And to come to your BBQ, darling boy," she said, patting his
cheek.

The back garden began to fill up: some of Daniel's friends from school, now grown up, and their parents, friends of Laura and Howard's. It wasn't a large crowd, perhaps twenty or so, and everyone knew each other well. Howard lit the BBQ, and once the smoke had gotten in everyone's eyes, it finally died down enough to start cooking the homemade burgers and marinated chicken he'd bought from the butcher's.

Just after six, Laura noticed Daniel looking at his phone, then disappearing back into the house. Ten minutes later, he reappeared with Cherry. Introductions were made and Cherry demurely made her way around the garden. Laura watched from the sidelines as Cherry met each of the invited friends. Everyone was polite and smiling and delighted to meet the girl Daniel was clearly very smitten with. She wondered when would be a good time to speak to her. She wanted to get it over and done with; hopefully, there would be some sort of reasonable explanation.

Cherry was pleased at the way Daniel introduced her. He spoke her name proudly and his fingers were entwined with hers. She was aware that she hadn't yet spoken to Laura, and she noticed that Daniel and his mother weren't quite so joined at the hip as they usually were.

"Everything okay with you and your mum?" she said.

"Sure."

She could tell it wasn't, not exactly, and Cherry was intrigued . . . and pleased. She wondered what the division could be about.

Laura went to fill Izzy's glass.

"Thanks, darling. By the way, I have a bit of a surprise for you. Your birthday. I've got you a booking at the Bazaar. For Saturday the twenty-third itself!"

"How did you manage that?"

"I told them you were Head of ITV Drama."

"You didn't!"

"Only way to get you a table."

"You'll get me fired." She hugged her. "Thanks."

It was a Michelin-starred Persian restaurant that Laura had

been dying to try, but when she'd phoned, she had been told they were fully booked up for six months. Isabella was friends with friends of the owners and said she'd try to get her in. It had to be that day, as she had a long tradition of celebrating her birthday by going out to dinner, ever since Daniel was born. Even as a baby, he'd sit in a high chair, playing with spaghetti, trying to get the slippery strands into his mouth, sometimes just the two of them if Howard was at work. She always had a cake too, knowing this would delight Daniel and each would take turns blowing out the candles. Birthdays were the one day of the year when Laura determinedly put aside whatever problems might be in her life (her marriage notably) and holed them up so they were unable to escape for the entire waking day, and she always, always made sure she went out for dinner.

"How's it feel to have him fly the nest?"

"It's not the first time."

"Ah, now I know you're being brave. This is the real one, though, isn't it?"

Laura smiled. "I'm lucky. He'll only be around the corner."

"True. In his own pad. Able to do and see what he wants. Good job you brought him up so well."

Izzy was teasing, she knew, but it suddenly occurred to Laura that Cherry might be spending quite a lot of time at Daniel's new flat, and the thoughts that had been troubling her rose up again.

"Iz . . . something weird happened on holiday."

"Oh yes?"

"I, er . . . was tidying up in Daniel and Cher—"

"Speaking of which, here he is." Izzy grabbed Daniel's arm as he and Cherry walked past. "Hey, guess what your clever auntie Izzy's managed. You and your mum are going to have this year's birthday dinner at none other than the Bazaar."

"What's that?"

"Oh, you poor, hopeless boy."

"Hello, Laura," said Cherry. "Nice to see you again."

"You too," she said politely.

"It's Persian," said Izzy. "It's set for Saturday, the twenty-third of August. I had to get on my knees and beg."

"Still a date?" Laura said to Daniel, and was relieved and pleased when he nodded.

"Can't wait."

"Oh . . . ," started Cherry softly, before withdrawing.

Daniel saw the look of disappointment on her face. "What?"

"Nothing."

"Come on, what were you going to say?"

"I . . ." She looked at him reluctantly. "I've . . . It was going to be a surprise . . . but I can always cancel it."

He smiled. "Cancel what?"

Cherry looked awkward. "I've booked a white-water-rafting trip for us—you—I wanted to take you away."

Laura's mouth dropped open.

"You did?" He kissed her. "But"—Daniel looked toward his mum—"it's Mum's birthday."

"Really?" said Laura. She couldn't quite keep the incredulity out of her voice. "That same weekend?"

Daniel laughed quickly. "I don't think Cherry meant to, Mum."

"No, I'm sure . . ." She fought down the irritation. It would be childish to insist. "It's okay. We can rearrange."

"But the reservation . . ." Daniel pointed out.

Laura shrugged. "We can go anywhere."

"Are you sure?"

"Of course. You two go away."

Daniel smiled and she knew she'd done something to make up for the day before.

"Hey, need a top-up?" he said, seeing Cherry's glass was empty. So was the bottle Laura had been carrying around. "I'll just get a fresh one from the ice bucket," said Daniel, and he headed off toward the BBQ area.

"Darling, I must just catch up with Diana. She's told me about the most wonderful yoga teacher," said Isabella, and then it was just Laura and Cherry.

* * *

They looked at each other for a moment, smiling with nothing to say. *It's now or never,* thought Laura.

"Would you mind giving me a hand getting some more wine from the cellar?"

She saw Cherry look around for Daniel and her drink, but he'd been caught up in conversation with his friend Will, and by the way they were laughing, he wasn't going to come to her rescue anytime soon.

"Course," she said, and Laura led her back into the house.

They didn't speak on the way to the elevator, and the journey down was silent too, except for the whirr of the motors. When the door opened, Cherry was invited to go first. It felt odd to be entering a twilight room after the brightness of outside and she stepped out warily. There was just a glimmer of light coming in from the window high up on the ceiling, and even though it was still light outside, the window's opaqueness and distance did nothing more than give a sensation of the fluidity of the water. The pool tiles were such a dark blue, the water had an odd impression of being deep, like the sea when you couldn't see the bottom. Then Laura switched on the lights and the sound echoed in the vast space. Cherry gasped; it was beautiful. The water was lit up now from the bottom and its inky blue radiated out from the lights like piercing sapphires caught in the sun. She saw she was standing on white marble, which continued up the walls, carved to look like Jali screens. She followed them up to the flickering reflections on the ceiling.

Laura led the way through the pool room and Cherry looked up at the opaque glass ceiling block, which muted the dazzle of the sun. Although she could see moving shadows as people stepped around it, no one actually stepped on it.

"It's always the same," said Laura with a smile, "it's as if they're afraid it might give way or something."

They headed to the wine cellar and Laura took a few bottles from the fridge. "Just a couple each of white and rosé," she said, handing some to Cherry.

As they walked back into the pool room, once again Cherry

glanced up at the ceiling, but she could hear nothing. Down in the basement, she and Laura remained in an otherworldly silence, just the sound of their footsteps.

"So, how's it been back at work?" asked Laura.

"Fine."

"They always fade so fast, don't they? Holidays."

Cherry said nothing, just smiled.

"Look . . . this is potentially a bit awkward, but . . . there's something . . . a couple of things I wanted to ask you." Laura glanced across at Cherry, but she was inscrutable. "The time you took off—was it really because you had so much leave to use up?" She deliberately kept a friendly air, wanting Cherry to confide in her.

"That's what I said."

"Only . . . I . . . Did you tell your boss your grandmother had died? And you needed to go to the funeral in France?"

Cherry stopped walking. "Who told you that?"

Laura gave an evasive smile and was thinking of a way to dodge the question, when she was suddenly distracted by a crack in the marble tiles on the wall. She looked at it, dismayed. It must be from the excavation next door and she made a mental note to talk to the builders and get them to check it out.

"What else?"

"Pardon?"

"You said there were a 'couple of things.' What was the other thing?"

Laura took her eyes from the tiling. "Oh yes. Well, it was more of an apology, really. I didn't think . . . when I invited you to come. I know the airlines put their prices up really high for last-minute tickets." She waited a moment, but Cherry said nothing. "It was thoughtless of me. Not to have considered that. And I just wanted to say, next time I'll check. . . ." She laughed. "They can be extortionate, can't they! Six hundred pounds sometimes. Just to get to France and back!" She looked concerned, as if she'd put Cherry under undue pressure. "Oh, goodness, it wasn't as much as that, was it?"

Cherry watched her. It was pathetic, the way she was fishing for information. She noticed Laura stood under a spotlight and it lit her head with a halo effect. It also highlighted her forehead and threw shadows under her cheekbones, and she was intrigued to see that she could almost see the shape of her skull.

"That was exactly how much it cost," Cherry said.

"Really?"

"Did Daniel not tell you? He paid."

"Oh. Good."

"Why are you so interested?"

Laura managed a baffled laugh. "I'm not!"

"You seem to be asking me a lot about it. As if you think there's something I'm not telling you."

"No! No—"

They were suddenly plunged into darkness; then there was a scream and the sound of glass smashing, followed by a loud splash. The strong smell of wine permeated the air and the splashing was joined by heaving gulps. Then the emergency lights switched on.

"I'm not exactly sure what happened," said Cherry cautiously, standing dripping in the garden, a towel wrapped around her. "There was a power cut and neither of us could see much. . . ." She looked at Laura strangely. "I think Laura stumbled . . . maybe because of the dark . . . and knocked against me."

Laura stopped midway with the glass of wine she was pouring for Cherry and looked up, bemused. "Sorry? I don't think I did."

Cherry shivered, snuggling into Daniel. "I don't know what to say. . . ." She looked up at Daniel apologetically, gave an awkward shrug. "You did," she said in a low voice.

"Cherry, I was nowhere near you."

"Oh, God, this is a bit embarrassing. I didn't just fall into the pool, you know," she murmured.

"You're not suggesting . . ." Laura gave a small, incredulous laugh, shaking her head. "I don't think so."

"I'm sorry I spoiled your birthday dinner."

"Oh, for heaven's sake, this has nothing to do with that," said Laura, irritated.

"I didn't know, okay, I didn't know it was your birthday. If I'd known, I would've picked a different weekend."

"It all sounds like a bit of an accident or something," said Daniel quickly.

Laura was aware of feeling like a villain at her own party. What *had* happened down there? The only explanation she could come up with was that Cherry had thrown herself into the pool deliberately, but that was so manipulative, so *extreme* . . . and then in a rush, she remembered the painting and was brought up short. *Did Cherry damage it herself? Just to cast doubts on* me*?*

She looked around and saw that people were watching, noses in glasses of wine. She saw awkward faces and embarrassed glances, people who weren't sure what to believe. When she turned to Isabella for support, she got a puzzled smile.

"Daniel, any chance I could have a word? In the house?" Laura asked.

"I'm afraid she thinks I'm a gold digger," blurted out Cherry, her voice cracking.

"No!" Laura tried to keep it light, gave a small laugh of disbelief.

Cherry turned her big brown eyes up to Daniel and tears sprang. "She thinks I'm after your money."

"Daniel, please could we go inside?" insisted Laura.

"See. You're not denying it," said Cherry, dejected.

Everyone was looking at her. Daniel had a face like thunder and Laura felt two little hot spots at the top of her cheeks.

"I think that's enough," she said quietly. "It might be time for you to go inside and sort yourself out."

"I'm taking Cherry home, Mum," said Daniel, and at her crestfallen face, he added, "She hasn't got any clothes. I'll have to."

As they turned back toward the house, Laura knew that they would go to his car and drive to Cherry's flat, and she probably wouldn't see her son for a day or so, perhaps not until Monday, when he would come to collect his things to move into the new flat.

"Anyone for a sausage?" asked Howard.

Isabella sidled up. "Darling, what was all that about? I thought you liked her."

Laura didn't answer, just watched them leave, feeling deeply unsettled.

18

*C*HERRY STARED OUT THE WINDOW OF HER OFFICE. IT HAD BEEN raining solidly for three days now, and when it rained, it was quiet—and when it was quiet, she got bored. She felt like a zoo-trapped animal, except she couldn't even expend her head-ramming restlessness by pacing up and down. Her iPad, lying on the desk, meant she could at least surf the Internet to pass some of the time, something she was sure Abigail and Emily were doing right now, as no one took such a keen interest for such an extended period of time in houses. Judging by the intense concentration on their faces, she suspected they were shopping for clothes or shoes.

She had read the *Guardian*, earmarked some TED talks she wanted to listen to, and then found herself Googling Nicolas's name, something she knew was a mistake even as she did it. There was an article in a telecoms trade journal, announcing his recent promotion to Deputy Managing Director—at age twenty-four!—a remarkable accomplishment, gushed the paper. *His dad's the owner of the company,* Cherry wanted to scream at the screen. The piece went on to list his achievements: the job and his recently getting married. There was a picture of Nicolas and his wife at some swanky charity thing, noted Cherry bitterly, and then the article had jokingly asked when he was going to provide the next heir to the company's throne. It cut her deeply.

Throat thick with hurt, she closed the page, then defiantly started to look at villas for sale in the South of France. Since returning from her trip, she'd found it an effort to get back into work mode, go back to the persona she'd created for herself and the job she had to get through as a means to an end. It was a dangerous sensation, this fidgety impatience, and she had to discipline herself. She couldn't afford to make a mistake now, not when she seemed to have actually found someone who had the potential to permanently pluck her from a life of work and drudgery. Feeling physically sick from sitting in one place, staring at her screen, trying to find something to amuse her brain, Cherry shut down her iPad, barely refraining from stabbing at it. She wanted to smash it up—she was so bored—smash it and tip the desk over. This amused her for a nanosecond and she smiled.

Cherry's mind worked well and it worked fast. It had an insatiable need for information, plans, and projects. It rebelled against enforced nonproduction, began to turn in on itself, to implode if it didn't have something to occupy it. She had too much mental energy, something she'd been aware of ever since she achieved top in her class for every subject during school. She sometimes wondered what she could have become if the option of university had been available to her—perhaps a lawyer, for she hated injustice, particularly toward the underdog, the poor man, and she thought she was good at turning a point on its side, revealing it to be something else entirely. Anyway, it didn't matter, as this was where she was now, a real estate agency in Kensington, a stepping-stone to a far greater achievement.

She stared out at the rain again, watching the steady drumming on the window and hoping it might anesthetize her into a state of tranquility. People around here didn't talk as much about the weather as those from Croydon or Tooting. They could afford to escape it and often did for weeks at a time.

She looked at the clock. At least, Daniel would be here in a few minutes to mark the halfway point of the day. Newly ensconced in his flat, he was taking her to lunch and they were going to buy some new bedding. He'd moved into his flat on Monday, but had been staying at hers ever since the party. He'd been upset with his mother, something she'd never seen before.

She'd cheered him with details of the white-water-rafting trip she'd booked (quickly, on the Sunday after the party, when he'd gone back home to pack his things). He'd deliberately timed his return to the family home, his last one as a resident, to be when his dad was at golf—Cherry was starting to get suspicious about the number of times his father played golf, and made a mental note to pursue that one—and when his mother had gone to visit a friend. He'd then effectively moved out, leaving a note for his mum, promising to call soon. Cherry was fairly certain he still hadn't made that call. She was currently trying to work out whether to encourage it; such mature, magnanimous behavior could only draw him closer to her, but letting the anger toward his mother fester some more would widen the gap between them. It was a tricky decision.

Daniel hooked his hood over against the rain and, shoulders hunched, forged his way through the few streets to Cherry's office. He was hoping to get the shopping out of the way as quickly as possible and suddenly wondered why he hadn't just let her pick something out herself. As usual, he didn't much care what the bedding was like, but he had recognized he needed some and was both grateful for her taking the hassle out of it and amused by how much enjoyment she seemed to take from buying it.

He knew he was falling deeply for Cherry and this made him happy. Everything about her, about *them*, seemed so compatible, so much fun, so easy . . . except, of course, the growing conflict with his mother. He was angry that her hints about Cherry being a gold digger had become public and caused real upset. He didn't understand why she was so set on it—everything pointed to the opposite. Cherry had bought him a ridiculously expensive painting, for God's sake! If anything, Cherry was the more generous of the two of them. Even when he had helped out, buying her airline tickets, he'd practically had to force her to take the money. Just thinking about it all made him angry again and he sighed; he hated confrontation and wished his mum would just see Cherry for who she really was and be happy for him.

It had been something of a relief to move out. It was bad enough on holiday—not wanting to fall out with his mother, but at the same time feeling uncomfortable with her growing disenchantment with Cherry. The leading questions, little comments, the general lack of warmth that seemed to increase over the days, had grated on him and he'd found it draining to keep on fending them off like a UN peacekeeper. He also didn't like his life resembling a soap opera, it embarrassed him, as did the little episode at the BBQ on Saturday.

The day after, he'd received a text, saying: **I hope you know this but just to be sure, I promise I didn't push her in, Love Mum x**. He didn't want to get into it any more and was annoyed it was still hanging over him. Consequently, he had not yet replied, although he knew that he would have to call soon, if only to stop the whole thing from escalating further. Perhaps after he'd had lunch with Cherry today, he would ring his mum and say that if they were all to get on in the future, she would need to back off a bit and stop thinking Cherry was only with him for his money. His mates had also texted, giving him a hard time the way that guys do, and Will had Photoshopped, LAURA'S SWIM SCHOOL over a picture of a daredevil diver crashing into a swimming pool, and added, **Your mum given any more lessons lately?**

In a way, his mother's recent reticence toward Cherry just strengthened his affection for his girlfriend even more. He liked uncomplicated women and she was just that; and despite her mistreatment, she had not once complained about his mother to him. He admired her for that. She just seemed to get on with it, to continue enjoying life. Thinking about her cheered him and he quickened his step. It was time to get the horror of shopping out of the way; then maybe she'd come back tonight and help him try out the new sheets.

*   *   *

The clock strained toward one and then finally it clicked over, a flag placed on the top of a mountain after a strenuous climb. Cherry had the one o'clock lunch slot this week, Abigail and Emily had to wait until two, and Neil was walking back in now. A system to cover the lunchtime "rush," although it was doubtful that flocks of people would be flooding in to rent and buy houses on a day like today. The door opened again and, as it was so quiet, all heads tilted up and Cherry was pleased to note that Daniel had such an audience. She looked up to greet him herself, but the smile died on her lips.

"Hiya, love!" called Wendy self-consciously from across the office, with a silly little wave as she took down her umbrella and rivulets of water fell to the floor.

Cherry sat there, unmoving, horror and growing panic rooting her to the chair, as she tried to fathom what the hell her mother was doing there!

Wendy was still waiting for some form of greeting and edged farther into the room, hopping toward Cherry's desk, aware that everyone was looking at her.

"Sorry, love, didn't mean to shock you or nothing, but I've not heard from you since you was away, and as I got today off work and had no plans, boss has gone and changed the shifts, I thought, well, we talked about me coming up to see you, and—"

Cherry stood abruptly, a defensive action against the tirade, a spewing of words that could reveal *anything*, and Wendy, thank God, stopped talking.

Cherry could sense everyone in the office watching her and pictured smirks, looks of pity. Her mother was wearing white Capri jeans, no doubt from the clothing section of the supermarket where she worked, and they were splattered at the back with dirt from the wet streets. As were her calves. Her gaze went farther and she saw her mum was wearing sandals—sandals on a day like today—and her toes also had mud on them. Of all the times she had felt ashamed of her mum, this was a new low.

"I'm soaked right through! It's pouring out there," said Wendy

by way of explanation. And then Cherry got a pang of guilt, knowing her mother had caught her repulsed look.

"Thought we could go for some lunch, love?"

A whole new wave of horror engulfed Cherry. Daniel would be
here at any moment. She sent a stricken look to the door. Perhaps
she could get rid of her mother somehow, make up something
about being so busy that she couldn't do it, pacify her with a promise of something else another day. But it was too late. She saw Daniel cross the road and come up to the agency. The door opened
and all heads turned again.

"Hi!" said Daniel to everyone.

Wendy turned too; Cherry froze. This was the meeting she
never wanted. Then suddenly, a blind fury overtook her: How
dare her mum make her feel like this, make her panic and stress,
put her whole future in jeopardy! Why couldn't she leave her the
fuck alone? She struggled to keep her exploding anger from lash-
ing out at her mother, and imagined shoving her back, back toward the door, kicking her out, crumpled onto the street, and
then she caught herself. The image brought her up sharply and,
horrified, she blocked it from her mind. She mustn't lose it, *not
now*. She gestured nervously toward her mother, a light flick of
the fingers without looking at her.

"This," she said tightly, "is my mum."

He came over and shook Wendy's hand, and Cherry watched
carefully for a reaction, but she saw nothing but his usual friendly
charm, albeit with a note of confusion. "Nice to meet you. Sorry,
have I got my days mixed up or something?"

Wendy turned to Cherry for an explanation, a saucy smile on
her face, as Cherry knew she'd guessed that Daniel was more
than just a friend. "Mum," she said in a low, warning voice—a
voice that implied, *Do not say anything to embarrass me*—"this is
Daniel."

"Daniel. So nice to finally meet you. Cherry has told me so
much about you."

Which was all a big lie, for Cherry had not mentioned Daniel
to her once. She was grateful for this tiny reprieve, although her
feelings toward her mother did not soften.

"Did you come to spend lunchtime with Cherry?" he asked.

She was about to wade in, play it down, suggest that she meet her mother another day, but Wendy was too quick.

"A surprise lunch," she said. "Although I think it was even more of a surprise than I intended."

"Well, I'll let you two—"

"No, no," interrupted Cherry quickly. "Mum, Daniel and I already have plans."

"We can do it some other time," he said, and then added, to fill the silence: "Or if it's okay with you two . . . why don't we all go together? It would be nice to get to know my girlfriend's mum."

It was the worst lunch Cherry had ever had to endure. Everything she'd carefully kept hidden came out: the flat in Croydon, the supermarket job, the "cute" reveals about Cherry's childhood. Cherry watched her mum blossom in a way she had never seen before. She was flushed with enjoyment and pride in her daughter. But Cherry couldn't see past her own muted, seething resentment that her mother was having such a good time at her expense. After the story of how she used to sit at the cash register at the end of her mum's shift, delighting in playing "shops" and insisting she was going to work there when she was grown up, Cherry cut her such a furious look that Wendy faltered and changed the subject.

At that moment, Cherry hated her mother with a passion. Her plate swam miserably before her and the food stuck in her throat. Daniel remained polite, of course, and even laughed a couple of times, but Cherry sensed he was dumbfounded at some of what her mother was telling him and wanted to distance himself as soon as possible.

At the point where she was unable to stand it anymore, she escaped to the ladies' room and stood with her hands deep in water in the sink, staring at herself in the mirror. She wanted to cry bitter, angry tears of despair, but couldn't as she had no choice but to go back and watch the human wrecking ball—that was her mother—reduce everything she'd built up to a pile of unrecognizable rubble. This was her life, *her* life Wendy was gate-crashing.

She clenched her fists and let out a low moan of rage at her mother's inability to see when she wasn't wanted, her inability to see how she was single-handedly destroying the only thing Cherry had ever truly cared about.

For a brief moment, she allowed herself a dark thought. Imagined her life as it would have been without her mother for the last sixteen years, if she'd been in the car when it had crashed, killing her father. Maybe there would have been some inconvenience with foster parents for a while, but it would've been over soon enough and then she could have rebuilt her life without any of the baggage she currently had to tow around. She wondered if her mother had any insurance or if the supermarket would've paid out any life premiums. Maybe she could've lived somewhere a bit nicer than Tooting. The fantasy bubble faded away and Cherry slowly became aware that she'd been in the ladies' room for quite some time, so she methodically dried her hands and went back into the restaurant. Her mother looked up as she came back to the table, but Cherry didn't meet her eye.

"Everything all right, love?"

"Fine."

The plates had been cleared while she was in the bathroom and Daniel picked up the menu. "Dessert?"

Cherry sensed that Wendy was about to accept, so she shot in with: "I have to get back to work."

Daniel paid, despite Wendy's protestations, and then they left. Both walked her back through the rain to the office and Cherry stopped them a few doors down.

"You don't have to see me in," she said tersely, and her mother glanced at her in hurt. Then she threw an arm around her neck in a tight hug, the other clutching her umbrella, which clashed with Cherry's. Cherry felt a lipstick mark land on her cheek and resisted the urge to wipe it away in disgust. She wanted no trace of her mother on her.

"It's been lovely to see you," said Wendy wistfully, and Cherry smiled tightly.

"You too."

Wendy then turned to Daniel and Cherry cringed as she gave him an affectionate hug too. In fact, she seemed more relaxed with him than she did with her own daughter, something Cherry instantly felt guilty about. She knew her behavior was abhorrent, but she couldn't help it.

"Thanks for a great lunch," said Wendy. "I can't believe Cherry's been keeping you to herself all this time."

She pulled away and, looking one last time at her daughter, took her cue to leave. Cherry watched her walk away to the tube, her sandals flicking more dirty rainwater up the back of her leg. She didn't want to look at Daniel, as she didn't want to see the new distance in his eyes, the urge to escape now that her persona had been stripped away.

"We didn't get to buy the bedding," he said.

"No."

"Doesn't matter. We'll get it some other time."

It was the first brush-off—a vague reference to a future date that would never materialize. Cherry stood miserably on the pavement, immobilized and unwilling to play her part in this breakup.

"Shouldn't you be getting back? It's after two," he prompted.

And now, he wanted to be rid of her. This was the last time she'd see him. She raised her eyes to his.

"Hey, what's the matter?"

"Nothing."

"Come on, you're not upset about the sheets, are you? I mean, I know you wanted to get them, but I thought it was more important we spend time with your mum. Especially as she came all this way here to see you."

Cherry stared at him, checking for signs of genuineness.

"I did the right thing, didn't I? I got the feeling you weren't so sure. Is everything okay between you two?"

"Fine," she said slowly.

"Good. Because she seems really nice. Funny." He smiled. "Only I'd have a word with her about all that childhood stuff, if I were you."

Cherry wasn't sure she'd describe her mother as funny. "Cringe-worthy" was more like it. But more to the point, she couldn't believe what she was hearing. Daniel didn't care. Her mother was a Croydonite who wore a fake tan and thought that a cruet was a sliced raw vegetable to eat dip with, and he didn't seem to care one bit. She'd gotten away with it and the immense flood of relief was intoxicating. But Daniel and her mother wouldn't meet again—not for ages, she quickly vowed. It had been far too close for her liking. Cherry had always known deep down that they would have to meet at some point if she was going to get engaged to Daniel, but she would have planned and prepped it to within an inch of its life. Two or three hours max, somewhere public where they could easily escape, and she would have visited her mother beforehand, perhaps taken her something new to wear as a gift and warned her on what not to say. At least now, it was out of the way. Cherry would never forgive her for turning up like that, but all in all, it had worked out quite well. She thought back to his last question and gave him a celebratory kiss. "Yes, you did the right thing." Then she gazed up at him, happiness flooding through her. This man was amazing. She had to have him.

19

*L*AURA FOLLOWED DANIEL AROUND HIS FLAT, POLITELY ADMIRING IT. He would point out the obvious ("This is the bathroom") and she would answer with something equally mundane ("Nice tiles"). All the fun of seeing her son's first "grown-up" pad was lost. It saddened her and she could sense he disliked their new distance too. He'd been in his new place a month now, but it was the first time she'd been to visit.

"It'll be hard the next few weeks," he'd said, "now I'm at the hospital."

She knew it was true. His new job as a junior doctor was all encompassing, but it just highlighted another thing about him that she knew hardly anything about. They had spoken on the phone a few times since the fateful night of the BBQ, short conversations that had mostly revolved around small talk, but the party was still an obstacle to any in-depth or relaxed chat. It was impossible to say what she had to say over the phone, and so Laura had waited for a chance to speak to him, face-to-face, and here it was. The nerves were made worse by the fact she missed him terribly and all she wanted to do was throw her arms around him and have them make up, but she couldn't. Not even Izzy had fully understood. They'd met up for coffee shortly after the BBQ and Laura had tried to explain what she'd found out: Cherry's seemingly fictitious deceased grandmother and the disparity over the cost of the flights to France. Since the BBQ and Cherry's evasiveness, she was convinced again that something was up. Izzy was sympathetic, but pointed out there could have been any number of explanations. Worse, she'd said she should be careful not to interfere too much. Paranoia had a way of alienating people.

Laura looked for signs of Cherry as they went around: clothes, shoes, bottles of products in the bathroom. There was some conditioner and a toothbrush—nothing else that she could see—and so with some relief, she supposed that meant frequent stays, but not yet the semipermanent status that preceded moving in. She also looked for the reassurance of condoms or a packet of birth-control pills, but couldn't find any.

Daniel made ham baguette sandwiches for lunch. He pushed a plate toward her as she sat down at the breakfast bar. "Ta-da."

She smiled. It looked huge. But delicious. "Thank you. It's a lovely flat." She inspected him next; he looked tired, no doubt from all those hours that junior doctors had to put in. She reached into her bag. "This is for you. I wasn't sure what you might need . . . ," she trailed off, not wanting to highlight the fact she hadn't seen his new home before now, and ruminated, not for the first time, that a few months ago she would probably have helped him move in.

He opened it up. Inside the stylish wrap was a top-of-the-line alarm clock that woke you with a gradually brightening sunrise that could also be accompanied by a dawn chorus, waves, or a rooster wake-up call.

"You can choose how long you want your sunrise to last for," said Laura. "I thought it might be useful, now you've started on the foundation training, all those shifts and night work. It's meant to help regulate your sleep/wake cycle."

"I love it," said Daniel. "Thanks. 'A sunrise every day, no rain.'" He read the side of the box. "Seems it can also boost your mood and productivity levels. I'll have no excuse not to write up good notes now."

"Is it going okay?" asked Laura.

He lit up. "Hard, but I'm loving it. I've even got a bit more re-laxed about writing prescriptions. You should have seen me the first time—I checked and double-checked the British National Formulary and re-read the patient's notes about three times. It took me twenty minutes to do a five-minute job. And the rounds! My supervising physician rattles out instructions like a machine gun. I've learned to write very fast."

She watched him glow as he spoke and saw the five-year-old boy who'd bandaged his action men with toilet paper and told her he was going to be a doctor when he was "growned up, when I'm ten." And now look at him! She felt so proud, but something else was pricking away at her, childhood memories making her emo-tional. She quickly shook them away.

"And how about you? How did *Pillow Fight* go down with the great British public?"

"Not bad. It's all about tonight, episode two. If we get good rat-ings, we should be okay for a second series."

In fact, the first episode had opened to decent viewing figures, but had dropped off a little halfway through. Nothing to worry about, Alison had told her. The press reviews had been good. The other piece of news was that Alison had also called to say how much she and Sean had liked the treatment for the new crime drama idea—"It's *superbly zeitgeisty*, and what a *sensational* charac-ter"—and wanted to commission a script, to be completed as soon as possible. The rumor was that one of their mainstays was going to be axed and a replacement was needed. Laura had no hesitation getting the writer on board and sent her away to come up with sixty pages of brilliance. With any luck, Cavendish Pic-tures was going to be very busy over the next few months.

"Fingers crossed, eh."

"Did you see it?"

"Cherry and I watched it together. We both thought it was bril-liant."

Mentioning Cherry reignited Laura's nerves. She played with her sandwich, wondering how to start.

Daniel stopped midchew, then swallowed. "What?" he said challengingly.

She had to tell him about what she knew. The reasons why she thought Cherry wasn't all she made herself out to be. She had to get him to listen to her.

"Look, I know we haven't seen eye to eye over Cherry lately, and I understand your frustrations at some of the things I've said, but I deliberately left a few things out. Things that I've done and I'm sorry."

"Go on."

"I was also very embarrassed, and that's why I didn't tell you. At first." That got his attention. She took a deep breath. "You see, when we were all in France, I went into your bedroom when you were both out one day."

His eyebrows rose in indignation.

"I didn't plan to. I just happened to pass by and the door was open and . . . well, I went inside. I found Cherry's flight details and there were two things I noticed about them. First of all, she hadn't booked a return flight, which I thought was odd when we'd agreed on when she was going home, and second, it turns out she'd only paid five hundred pounds for it. You gave her six hundred," she prompted.

He didn't say anything, just looked at her, and Laura thought it best to plow on.

"That's not the only thing. When I came back to London, I went to Highsmith and Brown. Someone there told me Cherry had gone to France to go to her grandmother's funeral."

"What?"

"I'm pretty sure she said it to get the time off. I think she needed something big in order to be allowed the leave at a time when they were very short staffed."

"They probably got her mixed up with someone else. Mum, I'm not being obtuse, but is this really all you have to go on? To think she's some sort of gold digger? They could both easily be mistakes—maybe Cherry forgot how much she paid and this person you spoke to at the agency . . . Who was it, her boss?"

"No."

"Who then?"

"A temp, I think."

"There you go!" he said triumphantly. "They probably haven't even got the right person. And if Cherry was going to fleece me for money, I think she'd go for more than a hundred pounds."

"No, you don't understand—" she said desperately.

"Please, Mum," he snapped. Then he took a deep breath. "It's your birthday tomorrow. Let's not fall out about this now. Can we save it for after I come back from this weekend?"

Laura bit her lip. The more she heard about Cherry, the more convinced she was that the girl was bad news. Daniel had told her that Cherry had tried to change the booking that had clashed with her birthday dinner, but the company had no other availability that summer that worked around his hospital shifts. She didn't believe a word of it. In fact, she was beginning to think it wasn't just about the money. This trip, Laura suspected, was designed to show her who had the biggest place in Daniel's life. Cherry was intent on taking her son away from her.

A sudden thought came to Laura. What if Cherry managed one day to extract a proposal from him? An avalanche of misery suddenly descended. Cherry would machinate a lifetime of distance, and all the things she'd been looking forward to would suddenly be out of bounds: watching his career grow, myriad family events, Christmases, birthdays, holidays. She'd have to wait for rarely granted permission to see her own grandchildren. . . .

"Look, while we're away, I'll ask her about it, and you and I can talk next week. Deal?"

She was brought back into focus. She looked at him and knew that, unless she wanted to alienate him further, she'd have to accept. She nodded.

"Would you like something else?" he said, looking at her barely touched baguette.

"No, no, this is just great." Her appetite had waned, but she took a bite with gusto. "Are you looking forward to tomorrow?" If nothing else, she would keep asking him about his time with Cherry to see if she could glean anything more.

"Can't wait. There's been so much rain the water's up to grade four. The thrills start at eight in the morning."

Cold water and speed, it sounded like hell to Laura.

"You are . . . being careful, aren't you?" she said.

He frowned, not sure what she meant. "It's all a legit company. . . ."

"No, I don't mean that."

"What, then?"

She raised her eyebrows in a way that said, *Do I have to spell it out?*

His mouth dropped open. "Mum! I'm a doctor. I don't think I need a lecture on contraception."

He started to laugh and then couldn't stop until tears were rolling down his face. "Oh, Mum," he managed to gasp out, "you are funny sometimes."

She smiled wanly, but her stomach was still churning, as she knew it would continue to do until her questions about Cherry were answered.

20

Friday, August 22

"**A**RE YOU SURE YOU DON'T WANT ME TO DO SOME DRIVING?" ASKED Cherry as they sped down the highway somewhere near Birmingham. She'd offered, cajoled, begged him to let her do the whole journey, but he said no, she'd been working and he'd had the day off. So she had to be content with setting the GPS and picking the music, not an unpleasant side of the bargain. She hadn't told him exactly where the post code would eventually take them, it was to be a surprise, but its double *L* prefix gave visions of Welsh villages in the mountains, with snug country pubs. It was important that she didn't tell him, the surprise element adding to the memorability of the trip. It had been timed carefully, not just to eclipse Laura's birthday, but they had been dating nearly three months now and Cherry knew they needed a marker. Something memorable. They got on well, but she wasn't about to let things carry on, drifting pleasurably. She was of the firm belief that events cemented relationships, took them to a new level. The more you did together, the more memories you created. The longer it felt you'd been together, the relationship would then move up a notch. You couldn't go on at level one forever; you had to progress. This weekend was progress.

The night before, they'd sat on the living-room floor wrapping

Laura's birthday present. Daniel had been working crazy hours, so she'd offered to get something and he gratefully accepted. They agreed on a silk shirt and she'd been let loose on the King's Road with his credit card and PIN, a nice, dangerous feeling. A taste of the future. It had given her a sense of self-possessed contentment, of superiority over the shop assistants. There was nothing so pleasurable as spending other people's money. He liked her choice and was relieved she'd also thought to get paper and ribbon, along with a card. She wrapped the shirt while he penned the card, and, of course, with them sitting side by side and her involvement so far, he asked if she'd like to sign it. She hesitated, as if she were considering the probable rejection and then decided to be generous-hearted and offered the olive branch of her signature. As she marked her name indelibly with a flourish, she knew it would cause real anxiety. Daniel and Cherry's first joint card.

It started to rain. Soon the windscreen wipers were going at full pelt against the spray and the downpour.

"Think it's raining in Wales?" said Daniel, an underlying excitement in his voice.

Cherry checked her phone. "It is," she said, smiling. "We don't want it too much, though, or they won't let us go down the river."

"True." He let out a noise of exhilaration. "I can't wait for this. Do you know, not one of my ex-girlfriends ever did something like this for me!"

Cherry pretended to be surprised, as if it were the most natural thing in the world to selflessly pick a weekend away that your boyfriend would love. "Honestly?"

"No. It was really always about them. I mean, they might have come up with the idea, but there's no way they'd be sitting in the car next to me ready to give it a go. They'd be too worried about their hair or the cold or something." He leaned over and squeezed her knee. "You are amazing."

"I just thought, you know, it would be a good way to let off some steam, after all the pressure of starting at the hospital." She could see her thoughtfulness really touched him.

"Thank you."

"My pleasure, Dr. Cavendish."

He smiled and she knew conversations like this helped to make the trip even more memorable, highlighting her selflessness and reaffirming his feelings for her. The rain continued all the way to Snowdonia, and the GPS eventually led them to a small, white-washed, picturesque pub, at around half past nine. Both peered through the rivulets on the windows as they parked, unable to see it properly in the dark and the rain. Daniel switched off the engine.

"Shall we?"

She nodded. "Go!" she yelled, and they jumped out of the car, while he grabbed their bags and they ran laughing into the pub.

It had been all of ten yards, but they'd managed to get thoroughly wet.

"You must be the Laines," said the short, stout fellow behind the bar with a thick Welsh accent. "I'm Ted. We was wondering when you might get here. 'Specially in all this weather."

Cherry blinked at him through the droplets on her lashes and smiled. She'd made the booking in her name and didn't bother correcting his assumption they were married. In fact, she was delighted he'd said it, and something about the way the trip had started so perfectly made her think it was going to be a very successful weekend.

"Do you want to see your room and then come down and have a pint, something to eat?"

"Sounds great," said Daniel, and Ted lifted the bar hatch and took them through the lounge area, which was populated with a mix of elderly locals, mostly men in worn green quilted jackets, and a few other young faces—people who'd also come to experience the white water on the River Tryweryn. At the back of the room was a door that led to some narrow steps. They followed him up and came to a long landing, off which were the bedrooms.

"How was your journey?" said Ted. "Came from London, didn't you?"

He said "London" like it was a foreign country.

"That's right," said Daniel as Ted opened the door of room number 3.

"This is your place for the night. Everything's self-explanatory, but if you need help turning on the taps, you know where to find me." He nodded at them; then he disappeared back to the bar.

Cherry immediately started to look around. It was a small room filled with a double bed, an old wooden wardrobe, a low table with some local leaflets, and two bedside cabinets. The bed itself looked laughably small, as doubles did when you had a king or, in Daniel's case, a super-king-sized at home. It was covered with a thick duvet and a green-flecked throw was folded across the foot end. Another door led to the bathroom, where to her relief, the towels looked clean, as did the shower. And the suite, thank God, was white, not some awful aged pink or avocado green. It had been the only place available that was close to the river and it was cheap—something she'd been relieved about, given she was already in so much debt.

She came back into the bedroom to see him bounce onto the bed like a kid. "Come on," he said, holding out his hand.

She smiled and joined him. They tested out the springs, definitely some wear and tear, but not noisy, thankfully. Then they lay, side by side, for a moment, and Cherry felt herself roll toward the middle. She raised an eyebrow.

"It'll be more cozy," he said.

She laughed and jumped up, going to peer out the window. Outside she could just make out what looked like a stable and a lot of open fields.

"You hungry?" said Daniel from the bed.

"Starving."

Ted had lit a fire; it was that nippy. The mornings had started having that autumn chill to the air, the seasons on the turn.

They found an empty table, with cutlery wrapped in a dark green paper napkin and place mats with black-and-white etchings of the pub on the front.

"It's only lamb pie tonight," said Ted, bringing over two steaming plates. "My wife got a touch of the sniffles, so didn't get around to doing the chicken."

"Lamb's perfect," said Daniel as Cherry glanced up at the blackboard menu. It seemed the pub only served pie. Lamb pie, and on a good day, chicken pie. The chalk also declared there was beef pie, and she wondered what had happened to that.

"Beef's all gone," said Ted, catching her look, and went off to get their drinks.

She looked at Daniel, but he seemed to be charmed by the place and Ted's no-nonsense attitude. The background Welsh lilt of the locals added to the ambiance, and the pie was delicious, and the pub toasty with that lovely intimate feeling created by the warmth of a real fire, and the rain beating against the window-pane. Out of London, Cherry felt more relaxed. She was easily more sophisticated than these surroundings and there was no need to be on constant guard or check she was maintaining Kensington standards. Daniel raised his glass and she clinked it.

"To a wonderful weekend," he said, then paused and looked at her with something deeper than fondness, something more meaningful than affection. "To us. I'm very happy to have met you, Cherry."

She met his eyes and smiled. That was exactly the sort of look she had hoped this trip would produce. "Likewise," she said softly.

The rain stopped sometime in the night. Cherry had been aware of it as she'd woken, uncomfortable and irritated by the mattress that sank in the middle. It was pitch black, and utterly quiet outside, and the silence seemed to seep in and lie thick in the room, watching her. She got a sudden longing for home, for bright streetlights and the sound of sirens. She felt like she didn't belong there. She had no idea of the time or how long until the alarm would wake them at seven. She lay there for what seemed like ages, staring into the darkness, listening to Daniel's soft breathing beside her. She felt very alone in that dark room for a moment and almost nudged him awake so she could snuggle in close, feel his arms around her. But just thinking about it made her loneliness seem silly, childish; she didn't quite know what she'd say if she woke him. She closed her eyes and willed herself back to sleep. At some point, it must have happened because the next thing she knew, an increasingly loud beeping was coming from Daniel's phone.

Breakfast was toast, eggs, and marmalade, the pub this time only populated by the half-dozen or so of the younger clientele from the night before. Then they drove the short distance to the rafting company's HQ, where a purpose-built stone building housed the equipment, changing rooms, and a small cafe. As they walked through the muddy parking lot, awash with puddles from the rain, to register and find their guide, they saw a large sign outside the HQ building: TODAY'S WATER: GRADE 4.

"That's pretty fast," said Daniel, and Cherry felt a stab of nerves. She, unlike Daniel, who'd taken on rapids in Colorado, had never been white-water rafting before.

A young man, with sun-bleached hair and a clipboard, stood outside the building, welcoming people. He was dressed in a wet suit, one that looked like it was expensive and professional; together with his outdoorsy hair, speaking of months on the river, it emphasized her own ineptitude. She didn't like the feeling of the unknown, of something she had no control over, and had been unable to research or test first. They were checked off and then went into separate changing rooms to get fitted for wet suits, buoyancy aids, and helmets. Cherry didn't talk to the other giggling girls who were in there, squeezing their bodies into neoprene. She got dressed and locked her things away and then went outside, carrying her helmet. Daniel was already there, with another couple and the outdoors hair guy, who'd ditched the clipboard. Once she arrived, their group was complete.

"Hi," said their guide, "now we're all together, we'll do some introductions and then I'll go through the safety briefing. I'm Gareth. . . ." He smiled through his beard and indicated that Cherry should go next.

"Cherry," she said, waving, and then it was Daniel, and next the couple were Jane and Paul from Bristol. *She looks like an accounts clerk,* thought Cherry, *safe and slightly dowdy, and he, like someone who works for the local council.*

"Right," said Gareth, "here's what you need to know. I will be at the back of the raft and will control it, but you will be required to paddle as well, or at some point we will fall in. At no point do you stand up on the boat or you will fall in. When you do paddle, listen for my instructions on which side of the raft needs to do the work, or"—he paused for impact—"yes, you got it, you will fall in."

Idiot, thought Cherry, *does he think he's funny?* She caught Daniel's eye and bit the inside of her cheeks as she saw him trying not to smile.

"If you do fall in, you *will* have your buoyancy aid on *and* your helmet, which is the type with holes in it so the water can drain out quickly. The best thing to do if you go into the water and you can't get back in the raft is swim for the bank. I will radio for someone to come and get you, and depending on how far you are down the river, you'll either be minibussed or walk back up to the start. When we get to the bottom of the run, there is a quieter patch, which we will need to paddle out of quickly so we don't get caught in the rapids farther downstream as these lead to a series of small waterfalls that are too fast-flowing for today's trip. Once we're out, we get the boat on the trailer and then everyone gets in the minibus and you get a ride back up to the top. Then we do it all again! Any questions?"

Everyone looked at each other, but no one had any.

"Great. Can everybody swim?"

Wry titters from the group and then they followed Gareth to the riverbank. He apportioned the places: Jane and Paul at the front; Cherry and Daniel at the back. Each took a handle of the inflatable raft and, under Gareth's instruction, pushed it into the water. They followed and Cherry felt the icy cold against her neoprene boots. They climbed in, the girls nervous, the boys full of bravado and excitement. Gareth got on the back and instructed everyone to start paddling. At first, it was calm, the water a semiopaque algae green, the bank serene and tree-lined. A pleasant meander down the river, but then all of a sudden, the water dropped down as it ran over a series of boulders on the riverbed. It created a rush of pummeling white water that flooded the raft, soaking them, but they had no time to take in what had happened as the boat surged forward on another rapid, then crashed into some rocks. She held her breath as they spun around a full three-sixty degrees, then hurtled faster downstream, where more waves engulfed them, these at shoulder height. Cherry spluttered from the cold that slapped her face, then screamed with laughter.

"Paddle left!" yelled Gareth, and she realized, being on the left side, this was meant for her and Paul and they were supposed to be helping propel the raft over the next set of rapids. She wildly plunged the paddle in the water, feeling completely ineffectual, particularly as she lurched sideways in the boat as it plunged over another boulder. Then another swift gradient change and more frothing water that came up over the side of the raft. And so it went on, an exhilarating twenty minutes, all four of them thrown about laughing, clutching their paddles in the air, trying to listen to instruction and use them when required. Suddenly the commands became more urgent: "Paddle to the right bank! Paddle!" shouted Gareth, and this must be the part, thought Cherry, where you had to get to the side to avoid the waterfalls. Even though the water had calmed considerably, it was harder than she thought, and she struggled to fight against the current as they all paddled to Gareth's increasingly insistent shouts, eventually bringing the boat close enough to the bank that it was no longer dragged downstream.

"Everybody out," said Gareth, and they climbed out of the raft, and dragged it up onto the bank, where a team of two guys helped them pull it onto the back of a trailer. Cherry was grateful for the help; her arms and legs felt rubbery and she took Daniel's hand as he hauled her out of the water.

"That was brilliant," he said, giving her a wet, river-tasting kiss. She grinned back at him.

Once they were all in the minibus, its seats and floor wet with river water, it set off back up the hill. Gareth, who was in the front, turned around to face the four dripping passengers. "Everyone want to do it again?"

"Yes!" they yelled in unison, polite barriers well and truly knocked down.

The second time was just as fun, as was the third, with Cherry and Daniel changing places and sitting up front, which was even wetter and more thrilling as you faced the rapids head-on. They even got to grin at the professional photographer who was on hand, halfway down the run, to take snapshots that you could buy afterward. They'd been promised one more run if there was time, and Gareth seemed to think they could squeeze it in.

Each couple reverted to their original seats, and started with the now-familiar, gentle paddle down to the first rapid. Cherry, having been bounced and tossed down the river three times now, was starting to feel tired. It took more effort to paddle when Gareth shouted his instructions, but the run started as intoxicatingly as those before. The water was as relentless in its determination to hurl them downstream, get them off its back.

"Paddle left!" yelled Gareth, and Cherry felt a mild irritation at having to do so; her arms were aching and she was tired of hearing his self-important bellows. In the hesitation, the raft was caught in a sudden rapid; as she raised her paddle, she was lifted up into the air and her arm swung outward and whacked Daniel on the front of his head. She opened her mouth in alarm, but in the blur of movement that followed, she hardly saw him propelled upward, more heard the thud as he landed on a rock that jutted from the riverbank.

She strained to see over her shoulder, flicking her head from side to side as the raft belted down the river, expecting him to be waving at her, amused that he'd been thrown from the boat. But he wasn't moving. Gareth was trying to look backward too, both of them fighting the power of the water so they could see what had happened.

"Paddle right!" screamed Gareth suddenly, and Jane and Paul, the laughter dying on their lips when they saw one of their party no longer in the boat, plunged their paddles in the water. Cherry was losing sight of Daniel, but then she caught a glimpse and he was still lying motionless on the rock. She tried to stand to get a better look.

"Sit down!" roared Gareth, and she flinched, then sat back down and followed his urgent moves to paddle them to the bank.

Gareth was already on his radio, calling in help, as he ran up to the rocks. Cherry climbed out of the river, slipping on the bank and back into the water twice; then Paul yanked her hand to help her. She ran upstream to where Daniel lay, confused as to why he wasn't getting up. It was only when she saw him close up that fear flitted through her body. He was draped over a rocky outcrop, lying on his side with his head lower than his body and his feet still dangling in the water. His face was pointing downstream, but his eyes were closed. His helmet had been knocked backward and she saw a red welt on his forehead, which she suddenly realized, in horror, was what she'd inflicted when she'd accidentally hit him with her paddle. Gareth was leaning over, taking Daniel's pulse.

"Oh, my God! Oh, my God," she said, clambering over the wet rocks to get to him. She knelt down and touched his hand, which felt cold from the river. "Is he okay? Daniel, Daniel, talk to me." His face remained white and still; the only movement came from his legs, which were jerking up and down in the flow of the water.

The minibus pulled up in a screech of mud and two staffers jumped out, carrying a first aid kit. Behind them, on the bank, stood Paul and Jane, arms folded, helpless looks on their faces.

"He's breathing, isn't he?" she insisted angrily, not believing the alternative but saying it, just to eliminate it.

Gareth nodded. "We need an ambulance." One of the staff was already on the phone.

"Daniel, Daniel," Cherry implored, stroking his cheek with her thumb. She squeezed his hands tightly as if that might wake him up. When it didn't, she squeezed his arm.

"Don't move him," shot out Gareth, and she stared at him incredulous, none of it making any sense. The sound of sirens grew louder and then an ambulance flew up to the riverbank, stopping abruptly, its light still spinning, and two paramedics came running, carrying a stretcher. They took over. As they rolled Daniel carefully onto the stretcher, bluntly telling her to get out of the way, they painstakingly took off his helmet and Cherry saw another mark, a red circular lesion on his temple. The paramedics expertly packaged him away, simultaneously asking questions about what had happened, had anyone moved him, how long had he been there, who was his next of kin. As they deposited him into the ambulance, a red helicopter whirred into view above them, then landed somewhere beyond the trees. Just before they closed the doors, one of the paramedics spoke to her:

"You're his girlfriend?" She nodded, too stunned to speak.

"The air ambulance will take him to Wrexham Maelor."

"Is that a hospital?" she asked, but they didn't answer, too preoccupied, or they just didn't hear. The sirens started up again as they took him up the hill and toward the helicopter.

She still hadn't moved when she saw it rise up into the air, and she didn't know if it was because she had stood there a long time or the ambulance had been extremely quick. But the sight of him being taken away, of the noise of the blades fading into the sky, emphasized the shocked silence on the ground. She shivered, suddenly freezing cold.

"Where is it?" she said, meaning the hospital.

"We'll give you a lift, or you can follow us in your car," said Gareth.

She suddenly realized she still had to change and the idea of being delayed a minute more panicked her into action. She started to run back up the hill.

21

Saturday, August 23

*L*ATER, LAURA WOULD NOT REMEMBER IT AS BEING HER BIRTHDAY—
although she'd never have another one without brushing up
against that wild terror, a sensation of stopped breathing, of panicked, unasked questions and an overwhelming, animalistic need
to be with her son—but she would remember it by the smell of
roses. It had been a scent that she loved, but that would soon have
the power to plummet her into a dark place. Stooped in the garden, near the fence, she'd been pruning the dead heads away
from the new blooms when the phone rang. She distractedly
picked it up, still snipping away with the secateurs.

"Hello, can I speak with Mrs. Cavendish, please?"

She remembered being mildly irritated, half-expecting some
marketing company who'd gotten hold of her number or the
dentist calling to remind her of an annual checkup date.

"Mrs. Cavendish speaking."

The voice paused a millisecond, and in that moment, it got her
attention.

"Mrs. Cavendish, I am a nurse, Nurse Hadley, from Wrexham
Maelor Hospital in Wales. I'm afraid I have some bad news about
your son."

22

*T*HE JOURNEY TO WALES WAS AGONIZING. EVERY TRAFFIC LIGHT, EVERY car hogging the fast lane, not getting out of their way, every time the autocratic highway speed signs flashed at them to slow to sixty, then forty miles an hour, she would move restlessly, angrily in her seat. The physical pull to be next to Daniel was so strong, if they weren't going as fast as possible, her body started to move itself, as if to make up for it. All the while, Howard sat beside her, driving, a pained expression on his face.

She'd had to call him on the golf course, and to his credit, he answered immediately—she never rang, preferring to leave him to it, knowing she was all but excluded from that side of his life— so perhaps he'd known something was wrong. While he was driving back to her, she threw a few essentials (toothpaste, change of clothes for them both) into a bag, then sat in the hall chair when she wasn't pacing in frustration. She rushed out as soon as she heard the car pull up outside and he didn't even have time to switch off the engine before they were back on the road.

The first few minutes of the journey were spent repeating over and over what the nurse had told her, which was very little. "Your son is unconscious after falling from a raft in a white-water-rafting accident." He was currently "in surgery," but she couldn't or, more likely, wouldn't give any details on why or what, but instead asked them to get there "as soon as they safely could." When Laura had pressed for details, anything to try to make sense of it

all, Nurse Hadley always answered with the same thing: "It's better that you speak to a doctor when you get here." Although
Laura understood why, she felt a deep hatred for her at one
point, so desperate was she for clarity and reassurance.

"He's obviously hit his head," said Howard.

"You think so?" said Laura, although deep down she also believed the same thing, she just didn't want to admit it.

He nodded.

"And the surgery?" Laura's voice trembled.

Howard didn't say anything at first, as they both knew that
whichever way you looked at it, this was bad. "We don't know yet,"
he said gently.

Laura saw him glance at the GPS again and shared his anxiety
at the time. Two hours to go, with an estimated arrival of 5:07 p.m.
She looked at her watch, where two hours on registered 5:05; she
could be with Daniel a whole two minutes earlier, she thought,
before realizing what a ridiculous notion that was. Two hours was
two hours, her watch was just a bit slow. They said the accident
had happened at 10:15 a.m., and so Daniel would have been almost the entire day without his family by the time they arrived.
Thinking this made her almost shake with a sense of neglect.
What if he was waiting for her, for someone to hold his hand?
What if the presence of her or Howard at the hospital would
make a difference to his surgery? Howard, in a rare moment of
tenderness, rested a hand on hers.

"He's in the best place and they'll be looking after him. And
they'll call. They'll call," he emphasized, meaning with good or
bad news. Anything significant.

It was at this point that Laura realized he wasn't dressed in his
golf clothes, meaning that he'd either changed after she'd called,
which seemed highly unlikely considering the urgency, or he hadn't
been at golf at all. She didn't answer, just squeezed his thumb, an
acknowledgment she'd heard.

They were led into a small room, a consultation room that
Laura sensed had been used to tell a lot of people bad news, to
ask them to make difficult decisions, maybe occasionally to im-

part something joyful. It felt like a room that had a burden to it. She and Howard stared at the walls, the safety posters, the help lines, and the vase of surprisingly real, fresh flowers on the table. They were waiting in silence for the doctor to come and speak to them, having exhausted what little they could squeeze out of what they already knew.

There had been no sign of Cherry.

The door opened and Laura started. In walked two doctors. Laura urgently scanned the face of the one who led—a kindly, bright Asian woman—trying to read it for news.

"Mr. and Mrs. Cavendish," the doctor said, indicating the chairs, "thank you for coming so quickly."

Neither sat. "Where is he? Can we see him?" asked Laura.

"Very soon, of course. And I know you're anxious to." She indicated the chairs again and they lowered themselves into them, as did the doctors.

"I'm Dr. Raina, the neurosurgeon, and this is Dr. Kennedy, the anesthetist." She indicated the man on her right, a gangly redhead who smiled at her. "We've been looking after your son since he came into hospital this morning. Daniel suffered a head injury when he was white-water rafting this morning. After investigation, we found it had led to a subdural hematoma, which is a bleed on his brain. We took him into surgery immediately and successfully removed the buildup of fluid."

Laura was trying very hard to concentrate, but her mind kept lurching at the mention of certain words: "bleed," "immediately," "successfully." She was grasping for meaning, an understanding of the seriousness of what they were telling her, so she could arrive at a point where she could stop thinking the worst.

"He's now recovering in intensive care—"

"So he's okay?" blurted out Laura.

Dr. Raina smiled kindly. "The operation was a success. He's stable and now we give him time to recover. In order to help him do this, we are keeping him anesthetized, so that his brain can have a better chance of healing."

"*Healing?* So it's . . . damaged?"

"I was referring to the fact it's taken a knock and he's been in surgery. In terms of brain damage, the scans do not indicate that this is the case."

She almost cried with relief. "Can I see him?"

"Yes, of course. We'll take you and your husband there now. Remember, he won't be awake and he's going to look a bit different from the last time you saw him. We've had to shave off some of his hair so we could complete the surgical procedure, and he's going to be attached to a lot of machines that are helping monitor him while he recovers. He's also on a ventilator."

"So he's not breathing?"

"Not independently. We'll keep him like this for a couple of days and then work to get him off ventilation."

Suddenly to Laura, what had seemed horrific, but manageable, was a whole lot worse. The gangly redhead shifted forward in his seat. "He can't breathe independently because he's sedated to a level that the brain is resting."

"Did you have any questions before we take you up to the unit?"

Laura looked bleak and Howard took her hand. "Not at the moment. We'd just like to see our son."

Dr. Raina smiled. "I'll take you to him now."

They followed her to a unit with busy nurses full of low-key banter and practicality, too upbeat, too normal, for the seriousness of the situation. Then they were introduced to Daniel's nurse, a woman who received them with a quiet, unfazed confidence as if she dealt with loved ones' serious head injuries every day, which, of course, she did.

Laura braced herself just before the nurse pulled back the white divider curtain that separated Daniel from the other beds on the unit. She could hear the beeps that foretold of her son's presence and knew it was going to be bad, but the sight of him still hit her like a concrete brick against her chest. Machines held on to him, the wires and tubes entering his body like a plague of alien parasites. It was difficult to see where he ended and they began; they were one mass of flesh and plastic. One side of his head had been shaved completely, the exposed skin deathly white.

His face was pale, almost grayish in color, and swollen as if he'd been in a fight, but without the bruising. The ventilator was fixed into his mouth, making his tongue protrude grotesquely; the plastic and bands that held the ventilator in place cut lines across his cheeks. Across his forehead was a red welt. He lay still, his eyes shut; and after a moment's shocked hesitation, she ran to him and tentatively took his limp hand, touching him the way she would a fragile newborn. She tried to speak, to say his name and let him know she was there, to reassure him, but her voice cracked and she had to stop, not wanting him to know she was losing it. She just let silent tears roll down her face.

"Can he hear us?" Howard asked the nurse.

"We've got no reason to believe he can't," said the nurse. "In fact, we encourage you to talk to him, offer him comfort, even though he can't communicate back."

"I'm okay now, I'm okay," said Laura, through deep breaths, as she pulled up a chair without letting go of Daniel's hand. She sat, without taking her eyes off him.

Howard took a chair on the other side of the bed.

"I'll leave you alone for a while," said the nurse, and she drew the metal rings around the rail until they were enclosed, the three of them in a white, beeping bubble.

After a few seconds, Laura heard a stifled choking sound; she looked up to see Howard crying, his hand in a fist and pressed against his mouth, trying to suppress the noise. He shook his head and squeezed his eyes between finger and thumb as he wiped away the tears.

The last time she'd seen him cry was the night Daniel had been born. He'd finally come into the world at six in the morning after twenty-four hours of excruciating labor, complicated when Daniel's heart rate had dramatically dropped, which had resulted in an emergency caesarean. She'd lain exhausted, dazed, and Howard, sitting in the chair by her bed, held tiny Daniel while tears suddenly streamed down his face.

"I'm sorry," he'd said, embarrassed, as he hurriedly tried to wipe them away, but they kept on coming. "I thought . . . I thought you were going to die, or he . . ."

Laura had known what he'd meant. It couldn't happen again.

"Hush, we're fine now," she'd said, and it had been a moment of closeness, of the three of them, Howard at his most raw. It was a Howard that she knew *only she* would see, and that no one could take away from her.

"I'm just so happy," he'd managed to spill through his tears and she'd smiled, full of love for him.

"Are you okay?" she said softly over the bed.

He nodded. "Sorry."

She wished she could once again tell him it was all going to be fine.

The nurse came back in and started to check Daniel's IV fluids and Laura watched silently. They'd been told the nurse stayed with him all the time, and she was grateful. After a moment, she turned to Daniel and started telling him about her day. Awkwardly, at first, for she was unused to his bleeps, his silent responses. When she faltered, Howard came in. After a while, they got up a good rhythm, each supporting the other. After a couple of hours of keeping up a cheerful run of nonsense, the exhaustion started to set in. It was then that another nurse subtly drew back the curtains and spoke the words Laura had been waiting to hear:

"Someone's outside who would like to see Daniel. Cherry?"

Laura stiffened. "No," she blurted out. "I don't want her here."

Howard glanced at her, but she refused to budge. "I'll go and see her," he said.

"Tell her we want his things."

Howard nodded and left the cubicle. Laura held her son's hand tighter and silently vowed to stay at his side all night and all the next day if it kept Cherry away from him. Something that she knew was unfeasible, but what she could do, as next of kin, was stop Cherry from visiting. She burned with a deep emotional rage when she thought about her, about her stupid little plan of one-upmanship, and how in order to score a point, she'd ended up putting Daniel in the hospital. She wanted to know what had happened, but she couldn't stand to see her. Whenever she pictured Cherry's face, Laura felt such a blind anger, she lost all rationality. Laura knew that if she was in the same room, she'd not trust herself. Howard would find out.

23

*T*IME HAD A FUNNY WAY OF MAGNIFYING ANXIETY. CHERRY SAT IN THE
coffee shop, nursing her third cup, and would occasionally look
up at the clock and get a flutter of apprehension when a largish
chunk, more than a five-minute block, had passed. She'd escaped
down here, at about the time she thought Laura and Howard
would be arriving, to think about what she was going to say to
them before she went back up. The day had been long and nightmarish. She'd come out of the changing rooms to find the police
waiting outside, apparently a routine procedure when an ambulance had been called to an accident. Gareth had already spoken
to them and she felt a chill of fear. It was an accident, hitting
Daniel on the head with her paddle. But it wasn't that which had
propelled him out of the boat, it was the waves; the river was
clearly too swollen, too dangerous to ride, and she felt a stab of
anger toward the cocky Gareth with his patronizing jokes.

She'd driven Daniel's car to the hospital, followed by the police. When they arrived, the nursing staff told her that he'd had
to go straight into surgery, but they wouldn't say why or give her
any details, something that worried her even more. So she had no
further reason to delay talking to the police. She gave her version
of the events, tearful as she relived the accident. Then it was over.
They asked if they could call anyone for her, get a friend to come
and sit with her, but she'd refused. After she'd assured them she
was okay, they left, saying they would be in touch again.

Cherry was now free to go over her thoughts. She allowed the ripple of guilt to come to the surface, to examine it, and see if it had any credibility. She knew she should have paddled when Gareth had shouted his instruction at her, but for a split second she couldn't be bothered. This had possibly had a bearing on where the raft had gone to next, to a section where the rapids were particularly violent; that might have been what caused her to throw her paddle up in the air and hit Daniel. Perhaps this had unbalanced him so he'd not been able to stay in the raft when the wave hit and threw him out of the boat. Perhaps, in striking him, she'd knocked his helmet so that his head was unprotected at a crucial point when it hit the rock. Perhaps. But it was all conjecture, she reasoned with herself. No one knew if her apathy had started the chain of events, if one thing had *actually* caused the next. None of it could be proven. And she'd said none of it to the police.

They had asked her about the blow to his forehead, and genuinely tearful and remorseful, she'd told them her paddle had flipped upward, out of her control. They themselves said that his helmet had been dislodged, but it could have been the fall onto the rock that had done it, not her. Secretly, she was relieved the blame could not be laid at her feet. She thought about poor Daniel lying unconscious on the rock and wished with all her heart that she'd done as she was told, paddled when asked. Then perhaps they'd be at home now, back in his flat in London, making dinner together.

She'd gone to check at the desk, to see if there was any news on his progress. She was relieved to hear the operation had gone well and he was now recovering. A doctor would come and speak to her, and then she would be able to go and see him. In the meantime, Laura and Howard had been called and were on their way. Cherry timed her afternoon; she'd have forty-five minutes with Daniel and then she'd come back to the coffee shop, give his parents some time alone with him.

When she first saw him, she'd been rocked at how he looked, how suddenly vulnerable and dependent. It upset her more than she expected and it reinforced how much she'd fallen for him.

Cherry finished her coffee. She'd been sitting so long she'd gotten to "know" some of the other people waiting. There was a young couple, the woman heavily pregnant and looking exhausted. He had a permanent excitement about him, and would every now and then knead her lower back with his thumbs. Then there was the late-middle-aged woman, dressed well in a cream coat and amber silk scarf. She was alone, but somehow this didn't suit her; she looked like the sort of woman to always be with a husband. Cherry had spotted a ring and wondered if she was here to see him. Both had been here as long as she had and they felt like comrades, each with her own vigil, but united by an essential need to be in the hospital. They'd caught each other's eyes, the pregnant woman when her devoted husband had gone to get a refill. She'd sighed and sat back, her hands around her enormous belly; the middle-aged woman with her hands around her warm cup; both had smiled. Cherry stood nervously. It was time to go back to the unit.

The nurse looked up as she approached and said that Daniel's parents were with him and she'd let them know Cherry was here. When she disappeared, Cherry tried to imagine the conversation that was going on. She was not surprised, but, nonetheless, still perturbed to see that Howard came back alone.

"Hello, Cherry."

"Can I see him?"

He put a hand on her shoulder and led her away. "Not right now. Why don't we go and get a coffee."

They went back to the place she'd vacated all of five minutes ago, but somehow, in the time she'd been away, her allies had left. This threw Cherry—she felt deserted and it made her even more nervous. She sipped at her fourth cup of the day, and feeling like a child awaiting a reprimand from the head teacher, she waited for Howard to speak.

"How are you doing?"

It was a good sign, his asking after her. Made her think they were on the same side. "Fine. Okay. I'm still a bit shaken up, but it's Daniel I'm worried about."

"We all are," he said brusquely.

She nodded, her earlier optimism evaporating.

"What happened out there this morning?"

Cherry told Howard the same story she'd told the police. Once again, she cried when she mentioned the paddle that hit his head. She hated saying this bit, as she felt it incriminated her. She made it clear, conversationally, that it wasn't the blow that caused the injury. At the end, she was expecting questions, but Howard just stirred his coffee, and it unnerved her. Did he believe her? She could hardly ask him, for doing so would suggest that she might have been lying.

He looked at her. "Do you have his bag, his things?"

Cherry had forgotten about them; she'd hurriedly grabbed them from the locker at the rafting center and stashed them safely in the holdall they'd shared. She had felt a sense of responsibility and care for looking after them. She'd assumed she would be the one to do so, and it felt odd to give them up. She hesitated, but he continued to look at her, so she retrieved the holdall, which she'd been carrying around all day, from under the table.

"There's both of our things in here. . . ."

"You keep the bag."

She pulled out Daniel's personal possessions and handed them to Howard over the table. He took them and placed them on the chair next to him.

"I need to find somewhere to stay. The nurses said he's going to be here for a few days at least."

"I don't think Laura's going to let you see him. Not for a while."

Stunned, she stared at him. "She can't stop me."

"I'm afraid she, we, can. As his next of kin."

The hurt deepened. "You too?"

"My wife is already extremely upset over this. Minimizing her stress can only help Daniel to get better."

"What about me?"

"It's just for a while. Until he's got through the worst."

Cherry blazed with anger. "She doesn't seem to understand that I love him."

He watched her for a moment. "Did you book this weekend to deliberately upset my wife?"

Her eyes flashed to the floor.

"Because if you did . . . then you don't love him that much, do you?"

She sat numbly as he got up.

"Are you going to take Daniel's car back to London?"

She shrugged: *I suppose.*

"Drive carefully," he said kindly.

She watched as he walked away, Daniel's things under his arm: clothes, wallet, phone, flat keys. She had effectively been dismissed.

24

"*F*ROM HIS SCAN, WE BELIEVE HE SHOULD BE REGAINING CONSCIOUS-
ness," said Dr. Raina. She waited while this news sank in.

They were back in the consulting room. It was early morning
and the sun was streaming through the window, making the dust
spin in the light. Dr. Raina was compassionate, but professional,
passing on facts without embellishment; Laura and Howard were
exhausted and frightened. Laura had spent three days at Daniel's
bedside and then last night the doctors had stopped the sedation.
At some point over the following twelve hours, he should have
come round.

Laura's voice sounded small, shriveled. "So, why hasn't he?"

"We don't know yet. We'll start investigating this morning. He'll
have another scan and we'll also perform brain EEGs and other
test activities."

"How long will it all take . . . ?"

"We'll have some results in later today, but I must warn you that
they may not give us the answers we need," Dr. Raina said gently.
"The brain is very complex and sometimes it takes a while until
we find out exactly what's stopping someone from coming out of
a coma. Sometimes they recover before we do find out."

"Can you tell . . . Can you tell how long he's likely to stay like
that?" Laura felt Howard put his hand gently on hers.

"I'm afraid not. We just don't know. The good news is that he is breathing unassisted, so he's off the ventilator."

Laura nodded, but she couldn't help feeling these were scraps of good news. Small things to cling to when the bigger problem loomed large and dark.

Dr. Raina's beeper went off and she looked down at it. It was clear she was required elsewhere. They could have kept her, but there didn't seem to be anything else to say.

"Will you keep us updated, Doctor?" said Howard.

"Of course, I will. As soon as we have any news, I'll be in touch. Can I suggest that you take a rest for a couple of hours? Have a change of scene?"

He nodded just to close off the conversation, but neither Howard nor Laura knew where they might go. Their only reason for being there was Daniel.

"Daniel, it's time to wake up now," said Laura as she leaned over his bed, holding his hand and scanning his face for signs of life. "Open your eyes."

He lay there, unmoving, the beeps still sounding in some torturous rhythm.

"Can you wiggle your fingers? Your toes?"

She stared, but still nothing.

"Just a flicker."

"Come on, Daniel," she said, growing increasingly desperate. She determinedly pulled up a chair, squeezed his fingers hard, too hard probably, but she just wanted to get through to him. Any movement, any sound, just something to tell her he was there, he was trying.

"Please?" she begged, her voice cracking; silent, frantic tears rolling down her face.

By the next day, nothing had changed. The tests had not thrown any more light on why Daniel wasn't regaining consciousness and he lay there silently, eyes closed, palms down on the sheets. It was the same the next day and the next. Laura had already been making inquiries, calling friends of friends, researching on the Internet, and had found out that one of the best specialists in the country worked at the Chelsea and Westminster Hospital in London. After speaking to Dr. Raina, it became clear that they could request for Daniel to be transferred, something that was arranged quite swiftly.

Laura hoped that the move might produce some change in him, but was disappointed. The new specialist said the same; it was impossible to predict when he might come out of his coma, and it began to sink in that it could continue for many weeks or even months, and this sent her spinning into a whirlpool of terror and anguish that threatened to get out of control. She had to stay positive, she reminded herself, a word that was becoming rapidly overused, but it was all she had to cling on to. Her son's life had been reduced to a series of clichés: *"Take each day as it comes." "Just be there for him." "Stay positive."*

After ten days, life came knocking. Howard had to get back to the office for some urgent meetings. Her PA had tentatively left a message saying she had a few things to pass on whenever Laura was ready. They had to be important or she wouldn't have bothered her.

They fell into a routine. She would go to the office in the morning and work from home in the afternoons, visiting Daniel for at least two hours every day. Howard would go in the evenings, on the way back from work. Laura had decided to let Cherry see Daniel as well. She was prepared to do anything that might help bring her son out of his coma. If Cherry spoke to him, maybe her voice could trigger something inside his brain, something that would bring him back to her. She was allowed to visit early evenings twice a week, on Tuesdays and Thursdays. Laura gave strict instructions that this was the only time Cherry could visit and she had to be out by the time Howard arrived at eight. Wondering if the nursing staff was sticking to the rules, she spoke to Howard once about it and he said he hadn't seen her.

Laura had come back to some bad news. The decision makers at ITV were unwilling to commission a second series of her drama as the ratings had continued to fall, and, so regrettably, it wasn't something they could continue with. But they had "high hopes" for the new crime drama script and were looking forward to seeing it. In the meantime, she was still able to pay staff salaries for now. She'd been on the verge of calling Howard about the decision, wanting someone to talk to about it, but had stopped with the phone in her hand. After a momentary closeness, brought on by their son's accident, they had drifted apart again. Each returned from the hospital with little to report, as neither really thought to talk about what they had said to Daniel. They had been apart for so long, they had separate lives. If Howard tried to discuss his life with Laura, he would have to start from the beginning, and it was the same with her.

Laura could never get used to the idea of Daniel lying there in the bed, and her heart tightened every time she saw him. She talked brightly, incessantly, after researching comas in books, the Internet, cornering friends of friends who worked in neurology. Reports were to be found where recovering patients could relay full sentences of what had been said to them when they were in their dark place. It was just a matter of time. Or so she obstinately believed.

The year drew on, and Isabella had her usual Christmas party, carols around the piano and a lot of champagne and mulled wine. She'd been such a good friend since the accident and had been there every single time Laura had wanted to talk, providing words of encouragement and tissues. She knew Christmas would be a difficult time and told Laura she understood if she didn't want to come, but Laura felt it was important to keep life as normal as possible, even though she started every day with a heavy pain in her chest.

Once she was there, though, she felt like an outsider. She wasn't interested in drinking, and the festive atmosphere never caught on for her. She also felt that people were awkward around her, didn't know how to talk about Daniel, and so most didn't mention him, except maybe to say, "Give him our love," which they would do with a pained, fatalistic expression. This was something that she read to be so desolately pessimistic, it angered her. *He is still alive!* She wanted to scream it out. *He is still there, a part of me. He hasn't bloody gone yet,* she whimpered to herself. After a couple of drawn-out hours, she slipped away home.

Then Christmas itself came. She and Howard spent it with Daniel, in the long-term care provision, a special nursing home he'd been moved to. It gave her comfort to be with him, to make sure he wasn't alone.

As the new year turned, it seemed joyless and bleak. Every day, fear would attack her when she was doing the most ordinary things, putting on her tights, locking the front door. *When? When?* She sometimes shouted it out loud when no one was listening, a word that evaporated like vapor as it left her mouth, leaving no trace and no answer. *When would he recover?* The waiting was torturous. She stared into the black chasm of an unknown distance, but remained agonizingly defiant. She would never give up.

25

Thursday, February 12

IT HAD BEEN MORE THAN FIVE MONTHS SINCE THE ACCIDENT. TINY signs of spring were appearing. Snowdrops had sprung up in Hyde Park, snuggled around the base of trees. Because London had its own microclimate, all those buildings and people, there were even a few crocuses, splashes of yellow and purple. Laura sat in the back of her cab on the way home from her afternoon meeting. The sun had made a late appearance and it was above 50 degrees for the first time since October. She felt an urge to get outside, feel the air on her face, and she tapped on the dividing partition between herself and the driver.

As she stepped out of the cab, she knew it had been a good idea. The sun was so sweet and she saw something she hadn't seen in weeks: shadows on the pavement. It had been so long, they seemed slightly strange to the eye, a novelty. It lifted her spirits, which had been frozen in gloom for several months. The ITV meeting had been good; Alison and Sean had read the script of the crime drama and liked it. In fact, they were as committed to the project as ever and were keen to see the next draft as soon as possible. Assuming the writer went away and satisfactorily wrote in all the notes that had been discussed today, Laura felt she might get a green light.

The sun and fresh air were helping, but Laura's headache still hung around, threatening to erupt into a migraine. She'd never had one before Daniel's accident, but could now claim at least one a month. She dug into her bag for the tablets she always carried around, but found the packet empty. Knowing the migraine, if it came, would be debilitating, she stopped at a pharmacy and went in to buy some. She waited in line at the counter, concentrating on the shelves behind the assistant until she found what she was looking for. Then it was her turn. The girl in front of her turned around. It was Cherry.

Laura hadn't seen her for months, so it was a shock, even more so because of how she looked. She'd lost weight, but she was also pale, with purple shadows under her eyes. The glow that Laura had noticed the first time she'd seen her, that day she'd peered in the real estate window, that glow had gone.

Cherry recovered first. "Hello, Laura."

"Hello, Cherry."

They both stood there, bound together by one man, yet unsure of their own relationship.

"I think it's time we had a chat, don't you?" said Laura.

They went to a high-street coffee shop, something busy and impersonal. As soon as they found their place in the queue, Laura regretted asking Cherry along. What did she have to say to her? She thoroughly disliked her, and, yet, she wanted to know what it was like when she visited Daniel. She'd just talk to her enough to satisfy her suspicions—that he was as unresponsive with Cherry as he was with her and Howard—and then she'd make her excuses and leave.

They found a table that was covered in sugar grains and Laura wiped them away with a paper napkin. They sat and Cherry was clearly not in the mood to strike up conversation as she gazed out the window at the people walking past. Laura contemplated her for a moment.

"Shouldn't you be at work?" It came out harsher than she'd intended, accusatory.

Cherry gave her a hard stare and then took a sip of her tea, in no hurry. "It's my day off. I work Saturdays."

Chastened, Laura realized something else. "But you see Daniel today, Thursdays."

"Yes."

"So you come into town especially."

This irritated Cherry on two fronts: Tooting *was* town, albeit farther out, and of course she did. "Yes, Laura. He's my boyfriend."

They fell into silence for a moment and Cherry went back to staring out the window.

"How have you found . . . the visits?" asked Laura.

Cherry shrugged. "I worry I'm boring him with talk of houses."

"Do you think he's listening?"

"I don't know. Sometimes."

Laura was quick: "Why, what's he done?"

"Nothing, I mean I don't want to get your hopes up or any-thing—it's more of a feeling. He's too special, too interested in things, in people, not to listen." Her eyes glazed with tears and she quickly rubbed them away. "They don't know when he's going to wake up, do they?"

"No."

"I miss him." Her voice was so small, so lost, that Laura's heart cracked, for just a moment.

Cherry pulled herself together. "Sorry, I know you do too." She lowered her head, fiddled with her teaspoon, and then looked up again. "And I'm sorry for taking him away, and on your weekend too. If I could only turn back the clock . . ." Suddenly she was sob-bing loudly, conspicuously, and Laura stared, horrified. Then as other customers glanced over, she grabbed a paper napkin and thrust it at Cherry.

"Here. Dry your eyes."

"I'm sorry, I'm really sorry. . . ." But she managed to stem the tears. Laura noticed that she looked even more of a mess than be-fore. "Sometimes," continued Cherry, "sometimes I feel like I'm going to fall apart, bit by bit, find parts of me dropped onto the floor." She attempted a smile.

Laura watched her. She wasn't sure about this new repentant, grieving Cherry. She didn't trust her. This was the girl who'd lied and manipulated her way into their lives, thrown herself into a swimming pool and insinuated that Laura had pushed her. She had deliberately ruined Laura's birthday weekend, and then had taken her son on a trip that had put him in the hospital for five months. But then, she did seem rather upset. Perhaps, after all, she had a conscience.

"Maybe you should go home."

"I can't. I'm waiting until six."

She meant the time Laura had allowed her to see Daniel. "Look, I'm sure he won't mind your not going tonight. Howard will be there later anyway."

"I can't, I—"

"I'll be honest with you, Cherry, you look a state. Go home, have a bath, and get some rest. In fact, why don't you take some time out. When's the last time you had a proper break?"

"What do you mean?"

"A week away. A change of scene. Some time when you don't think about Daniel."

"I always think about him."

Laura began to get irritated and could feel her compassion wearing thin.

"For heaven's sake, get yourself some sun. Take a holiday or something. Daniel will no doubt be in the same state when you get back."

"Do you think?"

Laura reluctantly nodded.

Cherry gave her a watery smile. "I think you might be right. I could do with getting away."

Laura nodded again, then stood. "Good-bye, Cherry."

"Good-bye, Laura."

Cherry watched her leave, and when Laura had disappeared down the road, Cherry decided to get a chocolate brownie from the counter. After all, she had something to celebrate. The truth was, she was exhausted. Exhausted from visiting, from waiting, from wondering. She wasn't sleeping well, and the doctor had prescribed some Zopiclone, which had helped at first, but the pills left her listless. At first, just after the accident, she'd missed Daniel terribly. He'd become such a big part of her life and they'd spent so much time together, but then, after a while, the sadness spread beyond him. She was also feeling a terrible loss for her new life, for their—her—future.

Things had changed rapidly since the accident. There were no more dinners at nice restaurants, no staying in his swanky flat. She winced every time she thought of that beautiful, expensive place going to waste, empty with no one to enjoy it. She'd even had to give the car back the day Howard returned from Wales. He'd phoned her at the office and asked her to park it outside his house and drop the keys through the letterbox. Christmas had been utterly miserable. Wendy had invited her back to Croydon and it had been just the two of them around the fold-up table with a turkey crown and paper hats, which she had removed at the earliest opportunity.

Every time she saw Daniel, she urged him to hurry up and get out of his coma so they could be together again, continue with the life she'd planned for them. But more than five long months had passed, and so far, nothing had changed. Cherry had religiously visited him twice a week, every week, when she could quite easily have made excuses not to—but she hadn't—and the vigil was beginning to take its toll. She started to wonder how long she would be expected to stay girlfriend to a man who couldn't respond to her in any shape or form. She was young; she had plans; and the longer she sat by that bedside, the more she wondered what other opportunities were drifting away. She'd planned on getting engaged in about four months' time, a year since she'd met Daniel, and if that didn't happen, which it didn't look like it would, then she'd have to start all over again. When she thought like this, she fell into an agitated despair, mourning what could have been.

It was made worse by the fact that work wasn't going too well lately. She was too clever for it, and it bored her. She had to work extra hard to keep up her agent's persona, but she felt trapped. She couldn't leave, because if she didn't have a job, she'd lose her flat and Croydon loomed. She could look for another position, but she'd only been there a year and it wouldn't look good on her résumé. What she was desperate for was a break, a chance to rest, take stock, get a new perspective on things. She'd saved a bit and could book something cheap, a last-minute trip. But she hadn't wanted to disappear on a two-week holiday to Mexico and come back all tanned and relaxed, because she didn't want Laura thinking she was callous. Now, however, she had permission. She smiled. The tears had come at the right time.

26

Tuesday, February 24

*T*WO WEEKS LATER, LAURA GOT A PHONE CALL FROM THE NURSING home. Her heart was hammering, but the doctor's message was not the one she'd been hoping for.

"Mrs. Cavendish, I'm afraid I have some bad news."

"What's happened?"

"I'm afraid Daniel's no longer able to breathe unaided. He's been readmitted to the hospital and they've had to put him on the ventilator."

Her world crashed yet again.

She was first to the hospital. The specialist, Dr. Murray, came to speak to her immediately and explained that at 9:20 a.m. Daniel had stopped breathing; as a consequence, he suffered a cardiac arrest. The team had successfully resuscitated him, but he was now back on a ventilator. Howard arrived in the middle of it all and she listened to the report again, the words digging like knives in her heart. It was as if Daniel, after all this time, was slipping away, but she couldn't understand why.

"What caused it?" she asked Dr. Murray. Laura was desperate to make sense of the change.

"He's contracted pneumonia. I'm afraid that patients who are in his condition are highly susceptible to it."

Laura lashed out from distress and frustration. "He can't be perfectly fine one day and the next get pneumonia and have a heart attack. It doesn't make sense!"

Dr. Murray remained patient. "Mrs. Cavendish, he's not perfectly fine. He's in a coma. It's often difficult, or impossible, to predict the outcome of such an injury."

It didn't satisfy her. She felt as if she'd taken her eye off the ball, just routinely visiting and waiting, hoping. She should have been *doing* something.

"We have to wait and see if he can regain the full use of his lungs," he continued. "We'll try taking him off the ventilator again later today, and if that doesn't work, we'll adjust it to encourage him to make more effort to breathe, but the machine will still support him."

"What if he has another arrest?"

Dr. Murray paused. "He's been in a coma for a long time. We have to think about what's in his best interests."

A growing horror took hold of Laura. "You mean, you might not . . . You might just let him die?" she said incredulously.

"Not necessarily. If it's still your wish, we'll do our best to resuscitate him."

"Yes, it is my wish!" said Laura, tears springing.

When they were left alone, Howard and Laura sat in silence for a moment.

"They're doing their best," said Howard.

"Are they?"

He was slightly shocked. "Yes, of course."

"Oh, Howard, I don't mean to say they're negligent or anything, and I know there are some amazing doctors here—Murray's one of the best, after all—but I just feel we've been blindly letting this go on when we should have been keeping an eye on things." She went to sit beside him and held her hands together in her lap. "We've been here before, remember. What if we'd . . .

if I'd taken Rose to a hospital the minute she didn't take her first feeding?"

"Now hold on—"

"I know what you're going to say, what everyone has always told me, that I did what I could, I wasn't to blame. But those 'what-if' questions don't just go away. And I promised, Howard, I *promised* that I'd always look after him, I'd watch out for him, I'd ask the questions that he wasn't able to. I'd step up. He was my second chance."

He rested a hand on hers. "So, what do you suggest?"

"There's another guy . . . He's American. I didn't do anything because I thought we were in safe hands, we *are* in safe hands, but I want to increase our options. He's a new appointment at a private hospital in town, one that specializes in neurological conditions. Oh, I can't bear it, Howard—what if we're missing something? What if we've allowed ourselves to become complacent? I just think we should see him, get him to see Daniel."

"Won't that mean moving him?"

"Yes, but there's everything in that hospital that there is here, and this specialist too. Dr. Bell, his name is. I can make a call and I bet it's just a question of authorizing Chelsea and Westminster to move him and they'll take care of the rest."

"Is it safe to move him? When he's so ill?"

"We can ask."

Howard considered what his wife was saying and Laura mistook his silence for reluctance. Her voice cracked.

"If he . . . doesn't make it, Howard, I don't think I'll be able to live with myself knowing I didn't try everything, to do the absolute best for him. This Dr. Bell might say the same thing, but let's, at least, get another opinion."

Howard looked at her. They were two people lost, looking for any sort of rescue. As much of a long shot as it was, it was better than staying marooned on the island. "Let's go and speak to Dr. Murray."

They could tell he didn't think it would make much difference, but he didn't prevent it, and Daniel was moved to the Wellington Hospital by ambulance two days later.

Laura was on her way to see Daniel, when she remembered that Cherry was due to visit later that evening, as it was Thursday. She would be wondering what was going on, as it had been a couple of days now since Daniel had left the nursing home. She made a call and spoke to one of the nurses she knew well, but was surprised to hear that Cherry hadn't been in touch for a while.

"She's gone away," said the nurse. "Cancun for two weeks. Did she not say?"

Laura remembered their conversation. "Oh yes, yes, of course. When did she leave?"

"Last Monday, I think."

Laura was hopeful at her first appointment with Dr. Bell, but his assessment, unfortunately, was much the same. Daniel wasn't responding to being weaned off the ventilator. Three days after being admitted, he had another cardiac arrest. Laura and Howard were called to the hospital and Dr. Bell gently warned that the situation did not look good.

"I'm afraid it's extremely possible that he may have another arrest very soon, and when they continue like this, it's very difficult to keep the patient alive."

"How long?" asked Laura.

"It's hard to say for sure, but it could be as soon as twenty-four or forty-eight hours."

Laura returned to Daniel's spacious, sunny private room and sat quietly by his bed. She'd tried, she'd really done all she could, but it seemed it wasn't enough. She took his hand and her heart broke. Brittle for so long, it shattered into a thousand tiny pieces that splintered and tore at her insides.

That was it. That was all she had left of him. After twenty-four years, she had perhaps one or two days of him, just lying there, pale, unresponsive, helpless. She suddenly had an overwhelming sense that she didn't want to share him. It was the same when he was first born, she couldn't stand people holding him for too long.

It felt unnatural being parted from him, even though he was just across the room. She wasn't able to sit still, she would flex her arms agitatedly, fight the impulse to just pluck him back from Howard's cooing mother, who always left Daniel reeking of her perfume so that she had to bathe him. She wanted him back in her arms. She wanted to cherish every second of these last days, eke them out, even though she knew the sand would be running through the hourglass.

But Cherry was back tomorrow, and when she heard the news, she would want to see him. Laura couldn't stand the idea of her being near her beloved son. She didn't even want to hear her ask to visit him, or have her come to the hospital and beg the staff. Cherry had taken so much of Daniel away from her, the thought of her encroaching on these last few hours filled her with a desperate raging fury. But she knew Cherry would. Deep down, Laura knew that even if she asked Cherry to stay away, even if she explained how she felt about needing to be alone with him, Cherry would still want to come. The finality of it suddenly hit Laura; clutching his hand, she wept on his bed like she'd never wept before.

It was late when she got back home and Moses, unaware of all that was going on in her wretched life, rubbed himself around her legs. He was hungry. Laura had come back to feed him, but also to pack a few essentials. The cab was waiting outside for her, ready to take her back to the hospital. Howard was there now, but he would take a break when she arrived, and she planned on spending the night by her son's bedside.

She opened a tin of cat food and had barely put it on the floor when Moses was wolfing it down, purring as he did so. Next she went upstairs to grab what she'd need for the night. She packed some pajamas, a toothbrush, and wash things. Also a change of clothes.

It came to her in a breathtaking moment. She stood bolt upright in front of the wardrobe, clutching a fresh shirt as a cold shiver raced through her body. This was it. It was bleak, hideous, but it was a way out. The only way out. She paced up and down, shaking, wondering if she could do it. But now, the thought was in her mind, her feet had been uprooted, and she was carried along in a current she couldn't fight.

She would do it tomorrow.

27

I LOVE MY SON. THAT WAS ALL THAT COUNTED. IT DIDN'T MATTER THAT she was about to do something heinous. An opportunity had been granted to her, a beacon of light through the devastating last few months, and Laura knew she had to take that opportunity. She'd agonized over it for hours; but now that the decision was final, she felt a wave of terror at what she had to say. The words that were going to break her into pieces. This was the first time. She briefly considered rehearsing it, but the words—the word—wouldn't form properly in her head. Her instinct was to bat it away violently.

Crossing to the sink in the en suite bathroom, just off the private room at the hospital, she looked at herself in the mirror hanging above. A brief check that her soul was still intact through her worn blue eyes reassured her further. No flashing green irises, no demon-like pinhole pupils. She looked more tired though, and she was shocked to see how much she'd aged. There were more lines around her eyes and mouth. There was also a sadness, a haunting despair that she had desperately tried to keep at bay with this new expensive hospital, the best doctors she could find, and brittle hope. For a moment, she forgot what she was about to do and thought only about what was soon to happen.

The heartbreak was a physical force that made her double over, clutching the sink. After a few seconds, she stood. Nothing had changed.

Cherry was back today. Laura had checked and the flights from Mexico usually arrived at Heathrow early in the morning. She looked at her watch. Maybe she'd be back in her flat in Tooting by now.

A lump formed in her throat as she held her phone, but she swallowed hard. She had to get this right. *Any mother would do the same,* she reminded herself again and again, a mantra to get her through it.

She dialed the number carefully. She went cold, then clammy, in alternative waves, buffeted around by her agony. Her life was soon to end. The life that had meaning. Holding the phone with two hands, trying to stop their shaking, she waited for the rings in her ear to be terminated. At last, they stopped and the voice that answered sounded curious, unknowing. No wonder, as Laura had never rung her before and her number wouldn't be recognized.

"Hello?"

"Is that Cherry?"

"Speaking."

"Cherry, it's Laura Cavendish."

There was a brief silence while Laura knew that Cherry was running through her brain, trying to work out why she was calling.

"Cherry, I'm afraid I'm ringing with some bad news. . . . Daniel died a few days ago." *Oh, God, it hurt, it hurt.* She squeezed her eyes tightly, but it didn't stop the flow of tears.

There was a stunned silence from the other end of the phone; then: "What?"

"He had a heart attack—one of several, actually—and he was admitted back to the Chelsea and Westminster. They were unable to save him."

More silence.

"I know it's a lot to take in. . . ."

"Why didn't you call me?"

"I know you wanted to get away for some rest . . . and it didn't seem fair, you'd only just gone away. I'm sorry, it was a difficult decision, but I thought it best."

"I see." It was the statement of someone who didn't know what to say, who still hadn't fully processed what she was being told.

Laura caught a glimpse of her reflection in the mirror. The anguish it showed on her face was real. Her heart was hammering; she just wanted it to be over.

"When's the funeral?"

Laura felt her chest tighten in apprehension. "We've already had it. It was family only."

If she could've seen Cherry's face at that moment, she might have given herself away with guilt. The ultimate banishment from Daniel's life had hurt Cherry badly.

When she put the phone down, she felt empty. No relief, no gleeful triumph at having got Cherry off her back. But she also felt a kind of peace. Now she could go and say good-bye to Daniel. The doctors didn't know when his last moment might be, and she didn't want it to take them by surprise, before she'd said all she wanted to say to him.

She took a moment to compose herself and splashed some cold water on her face. Then she opened the bathroom door and went back into his room, where he lay on the bed in the same position he'd been in the last few months. She was alone with him for a couple of hours, as Howard had gone home to get some fresh clothes.

She pulled up a chair and, looking out the window, saw that it was one of those early-spring days that was a kindness from nature, an unexpected gift. She suddenly wanted Daniel to have it too and she opened the window. The air that came in was fresh, but not cold, full of life, and she could hear birds singing. She sat back down again and held his hand.

"It's a lovely day." She couldn't manage any more and stroked his hair to give herself a moment, thinking she had to do better than this or she'd ruin it. Now was not the time to fall apart. She tried again. "Just in case I don't get the chance to say this to you later, in case—" She stopped abruptly. She'd been about to say, *"in case you have to leave suddenly,"* but something had stopped her, some maternal protective mechanism. She'd thought long and hard over the last few months about whether Daniel could hear what was being said to him and she thought—hoped—he did. She'd been about to tell him about all their memories, everything that she loved about him, but knew now that she couldn't. What if he didn't know he was dying, but could hear everything she said? Laura shuddered in horror. He'd be stuck, listening to the end of his life being pronounced, but not able to communicate, to ask for comfort. It would be like being buried alive.

She climbed awkwardly onto his bed and gently laid her cheek next to his, being careful not to dislodge any of the plastic tubes taped to various parts of him. Then she took his hand. In her head, she relived two memories. One was of a baby girl, a perfect little person with blue eyes and fair hair who'd died in her arms, just a few days after she'd been born. The other was of an equally perfect little boy, who when he was small would wake and climb into her bed with his toy monkey, snuggling up to her and sharing one of the monkey's ears, the softest, most treasured part of the toy with her. They would lie there, warm and close, whispering secrets to one another.

"Daniel, I hope you're not scared, not of anything, because you don't need to be. I'm here, I always will be, no matter what. And I'm staying now until . . . until . . . I'm staying."

28

*C*HERRY HUNG UP AND LET THE PHONE REST ON THE SOFA NEXT TO her. Daniel was dead. She couldn't take it in: He'd *died;* he had vanished; he was no more. While she was on holiday! She suddenly realized she hadn't even asked Laura the exact day. What had she been doing on that day? Lying lazily on a sunbed on the beach? Wandering around Chichen Itza? Or maybe even having dinner with Elliot. It had been a fleeting thing, that much she'd made clear, but she'd needed the relief spending time with him had given her. He'd approached her in their hotel bar and found that they were both traveling alone and their holidays overlapped by four days. They ended up spending pretty much all of those four days—and nights—together. Cherry didn't feel guilty, she saw it more as a necessary healing balm for the last few months. Then he left and she got on with the rest of her trip.

It disturbed her that she didn't know when Daniel had died, that she couldn't match an event of such magnitude to a moment in her own life. She almost called Laura back, there and then, but as soon as she had the phone in her hand, she dropped it. She didn't feel up to asking questions yet; it was all still so unreal. A movement at the window caught her eye, people walking past, going about their lives oblivious to what was going on inside her flat. She jumped up suddenly, went to make a cup of tea. As she was holding the kettle under the tap, it hit her. She burst into tears, great wracking sobs, and dumped the kettle in the sink;

then suddenly she remembered that the next-door neighbors could see in if their back door was open and the flat above them could see in if they looked down at a certain angle. She recoiled, hating her flat, Tooting, *poor man's London,* and the way people all lived on top of each other. Instead she went into the bedroom, which was a little more private, and lay down, fully clothed, on the bed.

Daniel was dead. She thought she'd felt lonely, cast adrift when he was ill, but she realized that was nothing compared to now. She'd always believed he'd recover; she had read numerous accounts, reports on the Internet, studied it in books and journals, until she felt she could pass as a doctor herself. But instead he'd left her. And her new life, the one she'd planned, had disintegrated. She couldn't even say good-bye. She shrank inside remembering Laura's words, *"Family only."* She wasn't included. Was she not good enough? Not worthy? Not rich enough? Yet again, she'd been slighted. It was like Nicolas, all over again. Neither Laura nor Howard recognized her as a proper girlfriend, as someone who had meant anything to Daniel. Where was he buried? Or had he been cremated? Where were his ashes? She didn't know the answers to any of these questions and was left in a vacuum of ignorance.

She felt a sudden, violent anger toward Laura for keeping everything to herself. Laura had cut her from his life. And she, Cherry, was stuck in a dead-end job that she was growing to hate, with no escape on the horizon. She couldn't go through it all again. She realized that Daniel had made the job palatable, not just because he would eventually lead her out of it, but because he was what she looked forward to at the end of the day. Talking to him, exchanging stories about the people they'd each had to deal with, he as a trainee doctor at the hospital and she as a real estate agent. The way he'd held her and kissed her had made her feel good, feel as if she had value. Now that was all gone. She was a nobody again. The people she'd aspired to be like had unceremoniously kicked the door in her face. In the end, Laura had won.

29

*L*AURA DIDN'T LEAVE THE HOSPITAL, FEARING THAT IF SHE DID, Daniel would die when she wasn't there. She called Mrs. Moore to put aside some clean clothes and sent a cab to pick them up. At night, she slept on a temporary bed next to his that the nurses had put up for her. Howard came as much as he could, but his work meant that he had to spend at least a couple of hours in the office every day. The nurses said that often they could tell when a patient "didn't have very long" and would tell Laura so she could call her husband if that time came. Four days in, she noticed that some of the flowers were dying. It depressed her that they should mirror what was going on in the bed and she plucked them out with distaste. She didn't even want them in the bin in the room and took them outside to dispose of elsewhere. As she closed the door behind her and started to walk down the corridor, she heard something, a deviation from the rhythm of the beeps that had become as familiar to her as her own heartbeat.

A nurse rushed past her. *Jesus,* thought Laura, *he's died! He's died as soon as I left the room.* She let out an anguished wail and ran back in, rushing up to the bed, desperate to hold him, for it not to be too late. Dr. Bell had come in a split second after her. "Mrs. Cavendish, if you could just give us some room," he said, and the nurse firmly took her by the elbow and moved her aside as he ran his eyes over Daniel and the monitors.

"He's trying to breathe."

Laura stared incredulously. "He's what?"

"Breathe. On his own." Dr. Bell smiled and looked at the read-outs. "Three breaths in the last minute. Well, well, well."

She shook her head. "I don't understand."

"He's breathing independently. Some of the time. It's good news," he said cautiously. "I think we'll trial him with the ventilator, change it so it reduces the amount of work it has to do. Let's see if he can take on more."

"Oh, my God."

"He'll be carefully monitored over the next twenty-four hours as we see how much his lungs want to take on."

"Then what?"

"Let's just deal with the next few hours first," said Dr. Bell kindly.

Laura was ecstatic—for a few minutes—and then she'd swing back to despair again. It was just a cruel trick, medicine playing with her emotions, offering a strange grasp at life before Daniel left her for good. She stayed glued to his bedside, watching him, staring at his chest, her eyes willing on every breath that he seemed to take. She asked the nurse exactly what each of the numbers on the machine meant, which were related to his lungs, and got obsessed with willing it to register another breath. She barely slept that night, lying close to him on her makeshift bed, getting up every hour or so just to check the monitors.

Early the next morning, she and Howard waited impatiently for Dr. Bell's prognosis.

"He's doing extremely well. In fact, I think we should take him off the ventilator."

Laura turned to Howard and they exchanged radiant, tense smiles, hardly daring to believe what was happening.

"I'm just going to remove the ET tube." As he disconnected the ventilator, then gently took out the endotracheal tube that fed down into Daniel's lungs, Daniel suddenly coughed and his eyes opened.

"Oh, my God," said Laura, her hands to her face.

"Daniel, can you hear me?" said Dr. Bell, placing an oxygen mask on him. "You're perfectly safe, you're in the hospital. My name is Dr. Bell and I'm here to look after you."

Daniel stared around wildly, uncomprehendingly.

"Don't panic, everything's fine. I'm going to hold your hand and I want you to blink if you can hear me."

For a few seconds, nothing happened. Then he blinked and Laura was filled with a joy that weakened her even as it exploded through her body and tears poured uncontrollably down her face.

"You're in the hospital and your mum and dad are here."

"I'm here, I'm here," said Laura, wiping away her tears as she went to him and took his other hand. He looked at her, but she wasn't sure if he could see.

"You've had an accident, but you're getting better," said Dr. Bell.

Daniel's eyes closed again and Laura panicked. "What's happened?"

"It's perfectly normal. He'll come round gradually, regain his orientation over time."

"So he's okay?"

"We'll know more later, maybe over the next few days and weeks, but this is very good."

Daniel's recovery started slowly, and Laura, at first, was constantly reminded of how much he couldn't do, how it took him two weeks just to sit up in bed, how he still needed to be fed, how the sores on his body and lips took so long to heal, but gradually she noticed little parts of him coming back to her. A smile, a hoarse word, a moment of lucidity—and after each of these, she was amazed at the progress he'd made.

"It's because he's young and he wants to get better," said Dr. Bell, and Laura felt an immense pride that Daniel was so determined.

She would stare at him in wonder, amazed by the transformation. The doctors repeatedly reminded her that there was a long way to go: He could still have some damage to the brain; his memory could be affected. Laura, though, was filled with euphoria and brushed these warnings aside. So caught up was she in his recuperation that at first she forgot about Cherry. Then, in the kitchen one evening, preparing a meal for herself and Howard, it came back to her like a steam train, fast, thundering, flattening everything in its path. *I told Cherry he was dead.*

It was a huge problem, but something she didn't want to deal with at that moment. All her thoughts were taken up with Daniel's recovery and the work involved, the physiotherapy, the speech therapy, the time spent just talking to him, encouraging him. She didn't want that interrupted or complicated in any way, and Cherry was most definitely a complication. Laura had a vision of Cherry sucking the new life out of him, telling lies, emotionally manipulating him with her eye on the prize, and she felt a wave of fear. Although recovering well, he was nowhere near his optimum strength, and Laura pushed aside the guilt and told herself it was the best thing for him that Cherry was kept away for now.

She went down to the den to get some wine for their meal and saw Howard thrashing out laps in the pool. She realized she'd have to think of something to tell him, something to explain Cherry's absence. Thank God he hadn't asked about her; presumably, he'd also been so involved in Daniel, he hadn't thought to. What on earth could she say? She felt panicked as she remembered what she'd done, the lie she'd told, and quickly moved through the pool room to the cellar and grabbed a chilled bottle of Chablis from the fridge. As she made her way back upstairs, she saw something wet on the floor, a patch of glistening tiles, and she bent down to investigate. It seemed to be water, but it hadn't come from the pool. A languid drip fell onto her hair, and, startled, she looked up. She was right underneath the opaque window. She frowned. Had it come from there? It was too far to see, but that would mean there was a leak.

"What's the matter?" called Howard.

"I think we've got a leak."

He swam over and stared up at the ceiling. "What? We've only just got the tiles repaired. Bloody next-door builders."

"I'll get in touch with them."

Later, as she and Howard sat down at the table, she tentatively broached the subject.

"By the way, I spoke to Cherry a few weeks ago."

"Yes? What day's she been visiting?"

Laura hid her trembling hands under the table. "She's moved on."

He put down his glass of wine. "What?"

"Yes, I'm afraid she came to the decision just after she returned from holiday."

"That was ages ago. You didn't mention it."

"I didn't think it important—too caught up in Daniel, you know, the bad news we thought we had."

"So she doesn't know he's come round?"

"No, she does. That's why I called her." It was another lie, her fourth now. One was breeding another.

"Does he know?"

"I haven't brought it up, and he hasn't mentioned her. But I think he may have guessed." She paused. "I think we need to protect him. If he does say something, I think it might be easier to take if he thinks she walked away some months ago."

Howard was silent for a moment, angry at what his son still had to go through, then nodded.

For a moment, Laura couldn't quite believe how easy it was. Then she breathed a silent sigh of relief and pushed the whole thing to the back of her mind.

Two months after regaining consciousness, Daniel finished his physio session, and after getting back into his chair, he sat back exhausted. It hurt him, she could see that in his eyes, and she was about to tell him how well he was doing when he spoke first.

"Where's Cherry?"

A thick layer of dread stuck in her throat. This was her chance, the moment she could put things right. She could just say something about Cherry giving him space to recover, that she was dying to see him. She could tell Cherry—What? That she'd been delirious? Deranged with grief that her son had been given only a day or two to live?

Life had taken on a new joy, a new purpose, since Daniel had come back to her. It was as if someone or something had decided at the very last second not to take away her remaining child, despite her failing to keep her promise. Because she *had* failed. She'd said she would protect him, never let anything happen to him, and in return he would be kept safe. No carelessness like with Rose, no misjudged calls. *That had been the deal.* And she'd failed to keep her side of it.

She'd invited Cherry into the family. Yes, Daniel was dating her, but Laura had encouraged it without even a thought to who the girlfriend was. She'd asked her to come to France. God, at one point, she'd even looked upon her as some sort of surrogate daughter. Laura shuddered. She'd failed so abysmally and yet had been given another chance. What kind of mother was she if she just let Cherry waltz back in again? She suddenly sat up straight. Was she mad? How many warnings did she need to get?

"She's not been to see you for a while," she said regretfully, pained. It wasn't a lie, but it wasn't the whole truth either. The look on his face told her everything; he'd deducted that she'd left him when he was in a coma.

He stared out the window for a bit and Laura looked away, feeling awful. She had a sudden urgent impulse to tell him it wasn't true. But the seconds ticked on and she said nothing.

Daniel continued to improve and didn't mention Cherry again. But Laura still worried. What if he tried to get hold of her? Once, when they were in the hospital gardens, taking a slow walk because his leg muscles were still so wasted, she tentatively brought it up. They'd been talking about his old school friends visiting that weekend and it seemed like the right time.

"Are you going to get in touch with Cherry?"

"No."

And the subject was closed. Although she was relieved that he seemed to have moved on, part of her knew it would only take a simple call to unravel everything.

His phone was in a box upstairs, in her dressing room. She went home that night and was going to delete Cherry's number, just to make sure she left their lives forever, but then realized that it would look a bit odd if it was the only one gone. So she took the phone outside on the patio and smashed it, taking the SIM out and destroying that too. She stared at the pieces and then hurriedly gathered them up and tied them in a plastic bag. She buried them under some rubbish in the trash can, glad the garbage men were coming the next day.

The whole thing made her distinctly uncomfortable. The only reassurance was that she knew she was getting to the end of the fallout of her lie. The loose ends were being tied up. No one knew anyone's number by heart anymore. Everyone relied on their mobiles so much; they told their owners where to walk, whether they were going to get rained on, and they stored their contacts so that most people didn't even know the number of their own mother. Daniel was no doubt the same and would have inputted Cherry's number into his phone once only—not even that if she'd called him from hers and then he saved it, and he would never have dialed it again. The phone would have done the work for him. She got him a new phone, telling him the old one had gone missing somewhere from hospital to hospital. It had a new number, just in case Cherry should accidentally call him.

But there was still one thing. Something that made her stomach churn with worry.

Cherry still worked a mere ten-minute walk from the house. If Daniel were to pass by her office . . . well, it didn't bear thinking about. It tormented her, kept her awake at night, and she didn't know what to do. It was the doctors who gave her the idea. It was only temporary, but it would give her some time to think. They said that Daniel was ready to go home soon, but he still had weeks of physio to do: swimming, walking, and lots of recuperation. She knew exactly what to do; they would go to France, where it was warm. Daniel agreed without a murmur and Laura was deeply relieved. She booked their flights for the day he was discharged.

30

DANIEL REACHED FOR THE EDGE OF THE POOL AND MISSED. HIS FACE went underwater for a second before he lunged again, this time making contact. Ignoring the pain, he turned to do another lap. His clothes still didn't fit him properly and there was no way he was going to buy a whole load of new ones; for one thing, the idea of having to shop for them drained him of energy, and energy was one thing he was short on right now. No, he had to put on bulk and muscle and then he could stop hitching his jeans up over his backside—and that was with the belt on.

By the time he completed his target, he was so tired he just rested his head on his arms at the side of the pool. As ever, when he wasn't distracting himself with exercise, his mind was full. He was still coming to terms with how much his life had changed. He'd woken from the coma not recognizing his surroundings, or indeed his physical self. His last memory had been the moment before the accident, of being in the raft and hurtling down-stream. His job and his girlfriend, both of which he loved, had vanished. Day-to-day life had slowed to a pensioner's pace, but even if he wanted to pick it up, he physically wasn't able to handle it. It frustrated him that he was trapped inside his own body.

He sighed and climbed out of the pool, throwing a towel over his shoulders. The sun was shining and June in the Côte d'Azur was glorious; he soon chucked it off again to bask in the warmth. He sat for a moment at the teak table and looked down at Saint-Tropez in the distance, its russet roofs aglow in the sunshine. The whole village seemed to face the sea, something that he found both charming and reassuring. He hadn't yet gone down there, though, and they'd already been in Gassin a week.

He wasn't particularly sentimental, but he was finding this trip hard. There were reminders of last summer—and Cherry. He was in the same room where they'd slept together. There would be even more reminders in Saint-Tropez. Part of the problem, he knew, was that he was having trouble accepting he'd been dumped when he didn't know how it happened. And hadn't even been mentally present. His last memories of Cherry were exceedingly happy ones, and it was as if a great chunk of his life was missing—which it was. He was torn with wanting to ring her, acting like it was all a big mistake, but then he'd remind himself that she'd given up on him. And he hadn't thought she was like that. Their relationship, however short, had felt solid. It had felt like it had longevity, that they had a future.

He often wondered what he would have done if it had been the other way around, if Cherry had had the accident, and he liked to think he would have stayed with her a lot longer. So, what had made her leave? Yes, he was in a coma, but his mum had said she'd disappeared before Christmas, early November, in fact, so he'd only been "under" for a couple of months. He wondered how she'd come to the decision—was it easy? Did she want to be let off the hook? And then there was the thing she didn't know. That he'd come out of it. But he couldn't call her to tell her that—if she came back, he'd never know if it was because she really wanted to or was doing it out of some sort of duty. He couldn't call her period as his phone had gone missing somewhere in transit from the locker at the rafting center to the various hospitals and he didn't know her number.

His stomach rumbled and he stood and went in search of some lunch. It fascinated him how much he ate, must be nature's way of replenishing the wasted body. He could wolf down whole baguettes, loaded with butter and cheese. As he headed into the kitchen, he saw his mother at the table, reading something on her laptop. She looked worried, her brow creased. When she saw him, she plastered on a smile and pulled the screen down.

"Mum, do you need to go back to work?"

She hesitated, so when she spoke, Daniel knew she was lying. "Don't be silly. I can work here."

He sat down opposite her. "You've taken off too much time to look after me." She started to protest, but he laid a hand on her arm. "Don't think I don't appreciate it. I wouldn't have gotten here if it hadn't been for you, but . . . all those months in the hospital, coming out here . . . it's time you put yourself first for a bit."

Relief swamped her and she was unable to hide it. To her delight, her crime drama had been green-lit and they were due to start filming at the end of the year. That meant it was suddenly all systems go: Further episodes needed reading and editing; casting needed to be done; directors interviewed; key crew hired; locations scouted for. Not to mention, she was supposed to be chasing down the builders who were supposed to be repairing the garden window, and she just couldn't do all this from the South of France. It wasn't only work that was a distraction. The ever-present shadow of Cherry, working just down the road from their house, kept her awake and she knew she was running out of time.

"Are you absolutely sure?"

"Never been surer."

She put her hands on either side of his head and kissed it. "I'll come back for weekends."

"You don't need—"

"Shush. That's the deal."

She flew home that night. It was an emotional farewell and both blinked back the tears. "Thanks for everything," said Daniel as they hugged tightly. "I couldn't have done it without you."

"I'll call you," she said. "Every day, just to make sure you're doing your exercises."

Once he was alone, Daniel missed her more than he thought

he would. He lay in bed and, as usual, his mind turned to Cherry. He just wanted to know why she'd decided to break it off. And then an idea formed. He would call her office, speak to her there. And if it was hard, too public, then he could get her mobile number again, call her when she finished work.

He felt a certain fatalistic peace once he'd decided what to do, although he wasn't looking forward to the conversation. He was certain he would be rejected a second time—and twice from the same girl was hard for any man to stomach.

The following morning broke warm and cloudless. He got up early and walked to the *boulangerie* to get a fresh baguette, then ate breakfast outside. He'd slept okay; but now that he was up and the moment to call Cherry was creeping nearer, he felt nervous. He turned on his phone and Googled the real estate agency, Highsmith and Brown. Seeing the photo of the shop exterior on the website made him more nervous still. He couldn't call yet; it was only seven in the morning in London and she wouldn't be at work. To pass the time and stop himself from overly rehearsing what to say, he decided to take the put-off trip into Saint-Tropez.

It was easy enough to drive, as it was too early in the morning for the tourist crowd and the traffic was refreshingly manageable. It was market day and he found himself wandering around the busy stalls in Place des Lices, full of early-summer vegetables, bundles of broad beans, towers of artichokes, and sweet-smelling peas in their pods. He bought a few and some early nectarines and then, still finding physical exertion draining, sat down on a bench, a couple of streets from the market. He rested in the sunshine, then checked his watch. It was a quarter to ten. In fifteen minutes, Cherry would be at her office. His heart tightened and he looked around to take his mind off the impending call. It was then that he realized where he was. Across the street was the designer clothes shop that Cherry had said she didn't need to go into on their shopping expedition. He was sitting on the very bench where he'd left her when he'd gone running off to get lunch and her gold bangle. He sat up abruptly, the warm wood suddenly uncomfortable. Unsure of what to do for a moment, he gazed around distractedly and then his eyes fell on the gallery. He saw a painting in the window that was unmistakably by his favorite artist and realized that this was where she must have bought his gift. It struck him suddenly that it was odd that the gallery was right opposite the bench, as if the painting were an impulse buy, but then, he reasoned, so what if it was?

He had an urge to move, to get away from the bench, and decided to go inside the gallery. The bell rang behind him and he made his way over to the artist's collection. He stared at the paintings: the beach, the square, pine trees in the landscape. He hadn't seen his own painting for months and assumed it was still hanging in his now-vacant flat, its tear repaired, but still visible. When she'd given it to him, he'd felt a rush of love for her. It had been such an incredibly thoughtful, generous thing to do. So, why had she changed? Because she most certainly had. She'd left him only ten weeks after he'd fallen into a coma. *Ten weeks.* But then, they'd been dating barely more than that before the accident.

The paintings glowed around him, their vibrant colors and Mediterranean light prodding away at some forgotten joy that he'd felt when he first saw them. It gave him an unexpected strength and he thought about the call he was about to make. He wondered how surprised she'd be, whether she had prepared herself for such an eventuality. She probably had. There was some stock answer as to why she'd decided to leave him, how hard a decision it had been, but she'd felt like she had no choice. He shook his head at his own stupidity. What else had he expected her to say? That she had no interest in dating a coma victim? Maybe she'd met someone else. Whatever had happened, she'd been gone more than seven months. *Seven months.* She'd probably forgotten all about him.

He laughed, a dry realization becoming clear. For her, the breakup was a long time ago, time enough to heal and move on. As it would be for him. He suddenly knew he didn't need an explanation. No good would come out of this call, and he flinched at the idea of her hesitatingly, reluctantly, suggesting that they meet, or—he suddenly had an awful thought—she should come out to France to see him, talk things over. He'd had enough of feeling weak, of having people feel sorry for him. The paintings seemed to be spurring him on, their colors seeping into his veins. They gave him far more joy than pain, and it was then he knew he'd started to let go of Cherry. It was an uplifting moment. He left the shop with a new lightness.

31

Tuesday, June 16

WHAT WAS SHE GOING TO DO? HE WAS GETTING STRONGER BY THE day. Soon he would follow her home and then it would be a matter of days before he bumped into Cherry and everything she'd said would blow apart. Laura squirmed as she walked, her stomach so knotted she had to stop for a moment. How had she thought she'd get away with it? She must have been *insane.* Worry affected everything she did—she couldn't work, eat, sleep, without being consumed with a growing panic. Stopping outside Daniel's building, she took a deep breath, then again and again, puffing out her cheeks, trying to get rid of the sick sensation in her stomach. She held herself still for a moment, waiting for some respite, then let herself in.

Daniel wanted to move back to the family home when he came back from France, at least to begin with, which suited Laura just fine. She liked having him around and had offered to go to his flat to get him some clothes. He'd also asked if she could get his laptop. She said hello to Ian, the porter, then checked Daniel's mail locker—just a bit of junk. Most of his mail had dried up some months before.

She went upstairs and opened the front door to a musty, stale smell, the summer sun having cooked the air inside many times over.

Going into the bedroom first, she knew vaguely from his instructions what he kept where: T-shirts, shorts, underwear, a jacket he particularly liked. The room had a strange *Marie Celeste* feel to it, a glass of water left on the bedside table from the previous summer, a layer of dust on its surface, a pair of dirty socks on the floor. They'd had a cleaner come in a couple of weeks after the accident, but Laura had only instructed her to empty the garbage and the fridge. Everything else she had wanted left untouched, hopeful it was only a matter of days before Daniel came round.

She filled his clothes into a large bag he had stuffed at the top of the wardrobe. He also wanted some of his study books, as he'd been accepted back into the hospital training program, a year deferred, but he said he'd get those himself when he got back in two weeks. *Only two weeks.* What was she going to do? The cold sweat broke out again and Laura hurried on, this time to the kitchen. Medical books and papers were left on the breakfast bar, some open. A newspaper from the previous August, yellowed in the sun. Daniel's laptop was also there, plugged in, and Laura was about to pick it up when she noticed its standby light winking. He mustn't have closed it down fully the weekend they left for Wales, instead just sandwiched the screen down. It was probably best she did it, before carting the laptop over to the house.

Laura lifted the screen and it sprang back to life. A visual reminder of Daniel's life all those months ago, just before the accident. One by one, she closed them down: the *Guardian* newspaper, a site selling fancy mountain bikes, the weather in Wales. It felt odd, looking at a snapshot frozen in time, still lit up and yet forgotten about—and a lifetime ago. A medical site and then something else. A Twitter account. *That's odd,* she thought; Daniel wasn't on Twitter. And then she saw. It was Cherry's. The acidic bubbles erupted in her again. Cherry was going to bump into him, Laura knew it. She'd get back with him and there'd be no stopping her this time. She'd take everything. Anxiety filled her, magnified by not knowing anything about Cherry the last few months. Where was she? What had she been doing? Laura couldn't help being drawn to her adversary, needing to know something, a battle-weary defendant's need to position the enemy before the final defeat.

She looked at it again and something sank in that she hadn't noticed before. The password box was filled with x's. All she had to do was click on the "login" button.

She could find out anything she wanted, just by scrolling through. Her finger hovered over the key. It was *wrong*, an invasion of privacy, probably illegal.

And then she had an idea. She gasped and the adrenaline made her sit bolt upright. It was brutal, disgusting, but it might get rid of her problem. She sat for a moment, taking quick shallow breaths, not quite believing it. *Clicked*. But she didn't waste time reading the entries, after all. Instead she began to type.

32

Tuesday, June 16

CHERRY SAT AT HER DESK AND SILENTLY SURVEYED THE OFFICE. ABIgail and Emily stood, side by side, gazing intently at a screen, checking the photographs of a new house they'd just taken on. She wondered why she'd never really bonded with them; was it because they recognized a kindred spirit in each other's background? She didn't know, and was past the point of caring. They cooed over the glass staircase and roof terrace overlooking Hyde Park and she despised them for it. It was pathetic, really, facilitating the buying and selling of some of the most expensive properties in London while getting paid a pittance to do so. Insulting, really, and all the time thinking that being in close contact with the houses themselves was a "perk." You got to walk on handwoven rugs and polished maple flooring; but nine times out of ten, there was a clause in the contract saying it was imperative shoes were removed on entering. That was something Cherry would have done, anyway, but being told to do so—like some serf who didn't know how to respect something of value—got her back up. The owners were all laughing at them, these people with their millions of pounds in the bank. "Look, but don't touch" would be their motto, and others were to kowtow and gush and remain deferential or risk losing their business. It stank.

It was also excruciatingly boring. Cherry had been there a year and a half now. She felt trapped; it was as if her life was seeping away, valuable time and her youth leaking into the ground and disappearing. This scared her and fueled the boredom further until she went round in demented circles trying to work out what to do. This wasn't how it was meant to be. Daniel had been her escape route and it had all been going so well. She still missed him, was still hurting from his death, and the pain was made worse by the fact she felt partly responsible. The life change, the plummet to the start of the Chutes and Ladders board, well, she had to take some responsibility for that. She'd done it to herself. If only she'd concentrated on that raft, if she hadn't hit him, he'd most likely be here now. They'd be living together, perhaps even engaged. She'd be well on her way to a life of freedom. *Freedom!* From drudgery and work and fear. For a moment, she imagined what it would be like to always have money before the bitter taste of reality came back.

Cherry recognized she was in a bad place. She'd been impatient, curt even with a couple of clients lately, and Neil had overheard and taken her aside for a stern talking-to. She boiled inside while he was speaking, but knew she had no choice but to toe the line. The ever-present cloud of Croydon loomed, its tendrils reaching closer to snatch her back to obscurity and a humdrum life with no prospects. She'd tried scouting for other men, a new boyfriend, but every single, or potentially single, man who walked through the door irritated her. They were all so self-important, barely looked at her, spoke to their friends as if she wasn't there, while she seethed and fretted and wished again that she'd never booked a white-water-rafting trip.

Then there was Laura. She hadn't heard from her since March, when she'd called to tell her Daniel had died. No one had rung to make sure she was okay, that she was coping with her grief. No one had asked if she wanted to see the gravestone or whatever there was. Her insides corkscrewed with the hurt and humiliation of it all.

Two women were heading her way. She'd heard the door open,

but hadn't bothered to look up, but now she realized that she was the only one who didn't look busy. She cast a resentful look over to Abigail and Emily, but they were oblivious. The women arrived at her desk. One was about twenty or thirty years younger than the other, and the older one still looked impeccable. She guessed they were mother and daughter.

Cherry took their details and listened to what they had to say about the apartment they wanted. The daughter needed a "little pad" for when she started university. They were looking now, as she wanted to "try it out" over the summer. She wanted a garden or, preferably, a roof terrace. There had to be a porter and a gym. It needed to be light and near to the King's Road, for she wanted to be close to the "fun."

There weren't that many that fit all her criteria. Cherry showed her one, then another, detesting this difficult-to-please, honey-haired, golden-limbed girl, who was only a couple of years younger than herself. Judging by her skin color, Cherry suspected she'd probably already had two or three holidays this year and was now being offered every opportunity Cherry had craved, but had never had: university, independence, a mother she was close to, so much so they went shopping for apartments together.

Jealousy stuck in her throat and she wanted to snarl at her for being so spoiled, so self-involved, that she couldn't see how lucky she was to have a flat in Kensington—and who gave a fuck if it had black, not white, cupboards in the kitchen! Surely, her darling mother could fork out for a whole new interior if she whined about it enough. Instead she smiled, albeit coolly, and said in a bored tone that she only had one other to show her. She got it up on her screen and this time the gushes poured out.

"Oh, I love it. Look, Mummy, it's got a cute little oven. I could learn to cook!"

Cherry flinched; she hated hearing grown women calling their parents "Mummy" and "Daddy." And the cute little oven was a top-of-the-line La Cornue. Mummy smiled indulgently, amused, and Cherry knew the girl was one of these types who thought it was amusing to claim she burned eggs, and any attempt at cooking anything would have more focus on how she was adorably in-competent than actually putting any effort in.

"Can I have it? Can I, please?"

"If you ask me and Daddy round to dinner first."

The girl squealed in delight.

Cherry felt sick. She looked unabashedly at the clock. Thank God she could go home in ten minutes.

"Can we look at it now?"

The mother had spoken and caught her unaware. "I'm afraid that's not possible." The lie didn't sound convincing and the mother frowned.

"Why not?"

"Because I want to go home, and the thought of spending one minute of my own time taking you and your overprivileged daughter to a place I'll never dream of having in my entire life makes me want to turn this desk over" was what she wanted to say. Instead she settled with:

"We need to give the owners twenty-four hours' notice."

"But I thought you said the place was empty."

Cherry turned to the girl. So she had been listening. "Never-theless, we do still need to let them know."

The look of displeasure on the girl's face gave her a surge of satisfaction, of power. She felt a need to damage that self-appointed, God-given right and take something away, let her know what it felt like *not* to get what you wanted.

"Can't you just ring them now?"

Cherry stiffened. She didn't like the way she was being spoken to. *You need this job,* she told herself quickly, plastering on a smile. She didn't see Neil making his way over from the back office, Emily just behind him.

He addressed the clients first, all smooth charm. "Excuse me for interrupting, but Emily here can take care of your viewing. Cherry, would you mind just sorting something out in the office for me, please?"

She stared, bewildered, but his arm was out, indicating the way, and she had no choice but to stand. The honey-haired girl gave her a mocking look as Emily slipped into her warm seat.

Cherry felt the atmosphere change to one of obsequious wish making as she followed Neil to the back.

"Take a seat," said Neil.

"What's this about?" she asked, trying to regain some dignity, but still she sat down.

"I'm going to make this quick," he said, "as I think it might be better all round."

Her stomach flipped over. Was she in some sort of trouble?

"Your latest comments, on the clients we have here. It's just not acceptable."

"That girl out there, she was a bit strident," defended Cherry, "rude, actually, with me. Demanding. But I didn't say anything to her."

"Not her. Not anyone specific. Or perhaps everyone." He leaned over to the desk, where a computer was lit up. "'Once again, my day is filled with arrogant, rich wanker foreigners who seem to persist in wanting to buy the whole of London. I've had enough of them, throwing around their millions and taking all our houses.'" He stopped reading and looked at her. "You've even mentioned this agency by name in another message."

Cherry stared at him in horror, leapt up to see the screen, and realized he was reading from two tweets—*her* tweets. "But that wasn't me. I didn't write those!" she said hotly.

He considered her a moment. "It's your account—"

"Someone's hacked in. It happens all the time, you read it in the papers—"

"This is incredibly damaging."

"No shit! God, to think you think I wrote that!"

"I meant to the agency. We've already lost a sale. A Chinese businessman has pulled out of a house that was due to close at the end of the week. Found somewhere else. With someone else. It's worth over thirty-five grand to us in fees. And I've just spent half an hour on the phone with a client, trying to persuade her to keep her two apartments on with us. She declined."

Fear gripped her; she had to get through to him. "But, Neil, please, this wasn't me. You can't blame me for something I didn't do."

"I'm sorry, Cherry, but I just don't think it's working out—"

"No—"

"It's not just this. I sense a general attitude change. . . ."

"My boyfriend's just died! And now you're firing me. I'll sue you."

"Or you can go quietly and we'll pay you two months' salary."

It was paltry. Insulting. She burned with rage. "Six. And a reference."

"Three. And that's my final offer. Clients need to know they're welcome here, and they can work with us. And I'm sorry, but I think a reference is out of the question, given the circumstances. I think it would be best for us all if you could take your things home now."

Minutes later, Cherry barged defiantly down the street, not caring if she knocked into people. She got more than a few disapproving looks, but couldn't give a damn. Who had done this to her? Was it some joke? Could it have been Emily or Abigail? Then the tears came. She quickly swallowed to push them back. A hard pain formed in her chest. With no reference, she had very little chance of finding another job. No job meant no money to pay for her flat. She was going back to Croydon.

33

Monday, July 27

AS USUAL, SHE WOKE AT SIX A.M. NO ALARMS, JUST A USELESS HABIT, as now she had nothing to get up for. She would lie in bed wondering. Who'd done it? Nothing else had been posted. She'd closed her account, but the damage had been done. She would stay in bed, silently, until just past seven so she missed her mother. She listened to Wendy turn on the shower, the dull drone of the hairdryer through the thin bedroom walls, the clink of the teaspoon in the mug, then finally the soft thud of the front door.

Even then, Cherry didn't get up, not at first. She wanted to make sure her mum didn't come back for something forgotten, had enough time to get on the bus that took her to the vast supermarket three miles away. At about seven-twenty, Cherry got out of bed. It was a single, wedged against the wall of the small second bedroom. The covers were the same as she'd had when she'd lived there as a schoolgirl, pink and floral. The entire room was the same: the beige Ikea wardrobe with the shadow white doors, which sold in the thousands, castoffs of it on eBay not even fetching ninety-nine pence; a mass-reproduced picture of New York on the wall, probably also from Ikea; some tissues in a "designed" box. She felt the same stifling despair as when she'd lived there before.

Cherry had had to serve notice on her flat after she'd been fired from her job. She'd packed up her belongings and they were now rammed under the bed and at the bottom of the wardrobe in the tiny room, her last vestige of privacy. Most of her gear she hadn't bothered taking out of the boxes. There didn't seem to be any point.

When Cherry had called her mother to ask, haltingly, if she could stay temporarily, Wendy had known better than to ask too many questions.

"There's always room for you here, love," she said kindly; but to Cherry, the open words just sounded like a trap she could never escape. She'd mentioned something vague to her mum about redundancies, and Wendy had tutted, saying, "Bad luck." She had been extra sympathetic about Cherry losing her boyfriend and then her job in a matter of months. It was a real hard blow.

Cherry had been living there four weeks now and showed very little sign of getting a new job and getting out. The truth was, she didn't know what to do. She would spend her days walking, down past Reeves Corner, where the ground was still flattened by the fire damage started in the riots, past the nail bars, the betting shops, and the ninety-nine-pence stores, with their tartan plastic holdalls dangling overhead as you walked in. In the heat, the pavements themselves seemed to sweat, giving off a sour, sticky aroma.

She walked incessantly, waiting to be inspired: an idea, a plan, something to tell her what to do. She wanted to feel driven again, to regain the focus and ambition she'd had eighteen months ago when she'd started out at the agency. She walked until her mind went round in circles, past boards outside recruitment offices taunting her with offerings such as administrator at eight pounds per hour. Dull, dead-end, menial jobs.

Even Central Library couldn't motivate her. It seemed to be full of the unemployed and loafing students with big ideas, but no willpower. She shouldn't be here with these freaks, these failures; she should be in a flat in Kensington, planning an engagement party. She burned with the unfairness of it all, the waste, the lost opportunity.

She left the library and stood hopelessly outside, watching the buses accelerate past her. It depressed her, being aimless. She considered going farther, across George Street and down toward East Croydon station, but then what? She couldn't afford to go anywhere, and where would she go, anyway? She was trying to escape from herself. She turned back and started a slow walk back to the flat.

Cherry tried to be home before her mother returned from work. Not to welcome her, but because she felt she should earn her keep as she wasn't paying anything and she needed the free board and lodging. She'd scour the fridge full of her mother's markdowns from the supermarket and make something for tea. Wendy always complimented her efforts too much, something that annoyed Cherry, for she knew it was an attempt to buoy her up.

"Ooh, what have you made today?" she'd say, opening the oven door and sniffing dramatically. "You do spoil me. You've no idea how nice it is to have something cooked when you've been on your feet all day."

They sat down and Cherry made sure the conversation was geared around her mother's day at work: how many staff had turned up sick, what Holly's daughter was recording on YouTube, (a ballad on guitar apparently), and whether the saucepan promotion had brought in more customers. Usually, after this, Cherry washed the dishes while her mum watched *EastEnders*. Cherry hated to be in the room while it was on. It was another thing to drag her down to the lowest-common denominator and she preferred to be alone.

Tonight, however, Wendy came into the kitchen.

Cherry looked up in surprise. She could hear the theme tune coming from the living room.

"Aren't you going to watch your program?"

"In a minute, love." Wendy looked awkward and alarm bells

rang loud in Cherry's ears. Was her mum going to ask her to leave?

"I was thinking . . . you spending all day here, alone. Can't be good for you. Especially with, you know, Daniel so recently gone."

Cherry stiffened and her mother hurried on.

"I hope you don't mind, I took the liberty of speaking to my manager, told him a bit about you, how clever you was and all that, and, well, there's an opening coming up at work. In the Technology and Gaming Department." She said this last bit as though it was a real coup.

Cherry recoiled. *Work in a supermarket?* Was that all her mother thought of her?

Wendy spotted her face. "I know it's a bit different from what you was doing before, but you don't have to stay there for long. It could be a stopgap."

She was supposed to be engaged to a doctor with a trust fund and heir to a multimillion-pound fortune and a villa in the South of France.

Wendy took her silence as encouragement. "Or you could work your way up, you know. They recognize talent and promote people pretty quickly."

She'd rather die than work in that supermarket. Her confidence knocked to an all-time low, she dried her hands. She had to remain calm and civil, or living here would become intolerable.

"Cup of tea, Mum?"

"Lovely. So . . . what do you think?"

Cherry pretended to think it over. "Maybe. But I want to try some other avenues first."

Wendy smiled. "Course. But if you want to talk to him, I can set you up a meeting"—she snapped her fingers—"like that."

"Thanks, Mum. Why don't I bring your tea in, you're missing your program."

Wendy did as she was bid, and as soon as her mum left the room, a tear rolled down Cherry's cheek. She quickly brushed it away—red eyes would only prompt questions. Taking the tea in, she feigned a headache and said she was going to lie down in her room.

She lay on her bed and realized she'd reached rock bottom. Maybe you had to get this low to get your fighting spirit back, because she knew now she had to get out of there. The first stage was to forget about what might have been: stop looking back and thinking about where she'd be now, if Daniel hadn't died. A vision of his flat came into her mind again, but angrily she pushed it out. She was done with it. It was time to forget about Daniel, once and for all. He was gone. What she needed was closure.

34

*T*HE MORE TIME THAT PASSED, THE SAFER LAURA FELT. SHE WAS EVEN starting to forget—a day or two would go by and she'd realize she hadn't even thought about what she'd done. Sometimes, on a particularly good day, she could convince herself it didn't happen. Distant, like a dream.

And time was continually moving on. Why, if this came out in ten, twenty years, their lives would have all changed so much—new jobs, new girlfriends—she and Daniel would laugh about it. *Maybe.* But it would certainly have lost its razor-sharp edge, which was getting dulled with every passing day, even if it wasn't quite quick enough for Laura.

She'd gone onto the agency website two days after she'd posted the message and seen that Cherry's profile had been taken down. So she'd risked a call. Asked to speak to her and had been told she no longer worked there. The relief was intoxicating. Even Isabella had noticed a difference in her.

"You look, I don't know, lighter, happier," she said at lunch, and took her hand. "You've had a hell of a year, can't imagine what you've been through, and now look. He's back at home, healthy, recovered—no wonder you look so good."

Laura smiled and allowed Izzy to attribute her new well-being solely to Daniel's recovery.

"So, can I tempt you to a bit of shopping now to celebrate?"

"Iz, I have a job."

"Darling, I know." She waved a regretful hand in the air. "I just think of all those afternoons wasted. Now you're in a better place. . . ." She paused, and Laura looked at her suspiciously. "He's early fifties, divorced, all his own hair and his own business. Does triathlons for fun." She shuddered. "I feel like sponsoring the poor lamb just to make it seem worthwhile."

Laura tapped her on the hand with her teaspoon. "I've told you before, Howard and I are fine rattling along, albeit in our own dysfunctional way."

Isabella snorted. "*He's* all right. Sorry, I'm just protective of you."

"I sort of need him. I don't know why, maybe it's habit." All this elicited was a sympathetic squeeze of the hand. Knowing she'd pushed it far enough, Isabella changed the subject. "So, what else is new with you?"

"Well, other than the new series with ITV . . ."

"I don't think I've congratulated you on that properly yet. You *and* Daniel."

"He's back at the hospital next week."

Izzy clapped her hands. "You're both very busily employed!"

"The good news keeps on coming. Next door's building work has finished, at last, thank God, so they can finally start the patch-up job on our pool window."

"This is all brilliant. And here's a bit of news for you. You know, what's her name . . . Cherry."

Laura's chest tightened.

"Well, you know my friend Angela, the one who still wears the size-six bikini, she's selling her house. They're using Highsmith and Brown. Apparently, Cherry's been fired. So she's gone for good! I still can't believe how badly she treated Daniel. I got her very wrong, didn't I? Sorry, Laura."

Laura smiled politely. She was just thankful it was all over.

And it was, it *was*, she reminded herself later. Not just Cherry, but what had happened to herself. The person she'd become, whom, looking back, she didn't recognize. It was as if someone else had done that thing, and it scared her, the lengths she'd gone to. Maybe now, knowing that Daniel was going to recover, she wouldn't have done it. But hindsight was a wonderful thing, and at the time, all the medical evidence indicated that his days were numbered. She had genuinely thought she was spending her last few hours with him and she'd been bewildered, heart-broken, and desperate. She more than likely wasn't thinking straight. Something must have flipped in her brain. It was best she forget and get on, but now that she had her sanity back, she knew something like this *must never happen again.*

35

"THIS IS PRECISELY THE REASON I'VE NOT YET MOVED BACK TO MY flat," said Daniel as Laura produced a flaky chocolate croissant, warmed in the oven. Truth was, he didn't see a reason to move. In fact, he was beginning to wonder why he'd even bothered with it in the first place. Living at home was working out just fine, not because he got treated with breakfast every now and then, but he enjoyed the company. Both he and his parents worked long hours and irregular shifts, so it was a bit of a lottery whom he saw when, but that meant they appreciated their time together more. Always close to Laura, Daniel found he was getting to know his dad better too. He and Howard had ended up in the den a few nights ago, with a couple of beers and a movie.

"It's cold out," said Laura. "You need an extra layer." And it was. Autumn had started with a vengeance and the wind was hammering against the window, the trees nearly already stripped, even though it was still only the middle of September.

"I think that could just as well be a sweater," said Daniel, wolfing down the croissant. "This is also bad for the arteries. You know I'm on the cardio ward, don't you, Mum? Hardly a great example for the patients."

"You're the picture of health." Laura beamed, squeezing his

cheek. She just had time to flick through the paper before leaving for the office.

"So, what do you reckon?" said Daniel.

"About what?"

"Should we rent out the flat? I'll just stay here?"

Laura put the paper down. "You know you're always welcome, and I love seeing you the rare times you're not at the hospital. But it's up to you. I understand if you need your own space."

"Will you get me chocolate croissants every day?"

"Nope."

"Hmm . . . could be a deal breaker."

Laura stood. "Hard luck. It's time I left."

Daniel leaned in confidentially. "What's happening in this new series, then?"

"Can't tell you."

"*Can't* or *won't?*"

"Bit of both. I'm planning the finale this morning with the writer. And if I don't leave now, I'll be late."

The wind blew her sideways as she crossed the road to her office and Laura laughed, a spirited, delighted laugh that was all the more noteworthy as laughter had been so scarce for so many long months. It was a joy reacquainting herself with happiness, simple pleasures, and she never tired of reminding herself of the most beautiful, exhilarating fact that *Daniel was okay*. She'd wake in the morning, or be picking some apples in the supermarket, or be supposedly concentrating in a preproduction meeting, and say it to herself and an explosion of fireworks would go off somewhere inside her.

He'd returned from France looking more or less his old self. More important, he sounded like his old self, happy-go-lucky—and his ambition had returned. If anything, it was stronger than before. While he'd been away, he'd arranged his place back at the hospital for his Foundation year one. He said he felt as if he'd been given a second chance. Something had happened when she'd left him to come back to London; he'd struck up a friendship with a local woman who ran her parents' business. Laura had met her briefly one weekend when she was out there; Vivienne had stopped by and she and Daniel had gone out for a drink. She was at least a decade older than he was, had the confidence that came with it and no time for self-pity. He wasn't one for wallowing, but her no-nonsense spirit had accelerated his recovery. He'd come back tanned, relaxed, and somehow a bit tougher.

Laura buzzed herself into her building and walked up the stairs to where Willow sat outside her office. She was her new PA and eager to please.

"Your visitor is here," she said. "I showed her into the meeting room."

The writer was a little early, but that was fine. Laura was looking forward to the session; it was one of the most fun stages of developing a drama, making up the stories, and the writer was smart and imaginative. Laura went over to the meeting room and opened the door.

Cherry was sitting at the round glass table, flicking through a magazine.

"Hello, Laura."

In a state of utter shock, Laura said nothing.

"I suspected it might be a bit of a surprise to see me, but not an unpleasant one."

Panic overtook her and Laura quickly turned away and closed the door. *Why is she here?* She took a moment to try to compose herself before turning back around. Made her voice as calm as possible, even though her heart was racing. "Hello, Cherry. I'm afraid you've caught me at a bit of a bad time. I've got a meeting starting any minute now."

"Oh. Well, I'll take that minute, if it's all the same to you." She didn't wait for permission. "It just became very important to see you. Since we last spoke, when you called me just after Mexico with the news . . . Well, all these months have gone by, but I've had a hard time accepting it."

Laura didn't say anything. She still couldn't work it all out. *Think, think.* It had been, what, six, seven months? Cherry's hair was longer, which made her even more attractive, more sensual. Laura knew she had to keep calm and then when her writer arrived—damn Willow for not knowing the difference—she'd just have to politely, but firmly, ask Cherry to leave.

"Despite what you may have thought, Daniel meant the world to me." Cherry's tone suddenly became harsh. "Why didn't you ever call to make sure I was coping okay?"

"I . . . I'm sorry. I was just so caught up in my own . . . grief."

"Yes, and I suppose you had the funeral to arrange as well. No, hold on, you did that when I was on holiday. Couldn't wait. What day did he die, by the way? I'd really like to know where he's buried, just so I can go and say good-bye."

Laura was unnerved by the questions, coming without even a pause to hear answers. Cherry was watching her and Laura was grateful she'd already thought some of this through.

"I'm afraid it was a cremation. And we took the ashes to France, which he always loved."

Cherry stared at her and Laura looked away. "I'm sorry, Cherry, but I really do have a meeting starting—"

"Just one more thing."

Laura was beginning to feel impatient. *Okay, so Cherry is probably grieving, but it's taken her all this time to get upset about it?*

"What is it?"

"If Daniel hadn't died, would you have been happy for us to be together?"

Laura stalled, tried an affectionate, exasperated smile. "What kind of a question—"

"Oh, good. Because I always thought you'd do something to stop us. It's nice to know I was kind of a part of the family. Even if you didn't invite me to the funeral." Cherry stood. "Thank you, Laura. This has helped a great deal. I just needed some sort of closure. It all happened so suddenly and there was nothing concrete for me to see or visit. It just didn't seem real, you know?"

Feeling slightly sick, Laura nodded.

"I can see you're busy, so I'll be off." Cherry stuck out her hand, and after a moment's hesitation, Laura shook it. Then Cherry turned and left the room. Feeling shaky, Laura clasped the side of the table, loosened her scarf. She waited a minute or two to give Cherry time to leave the building; then she went back to Willow's desk. There was no sign of her writer yet.

"If my ten o'clock arrives, please take her to the meeting room. I'll be two minutes."

Willow nodded, startled by her boss's face, and decided it wasn't the time to tell her that the previous guest had gone into her office first, before being told that wasn't the meeting room. Willow had caught her rifling through some papers on Laura's desk. "Oh, silly me," Cherry had said, and then followed Willow to the large room next door.

Laura hurried back down the stairs. She'd pulled it off, but was still feeling shaken. She needed a coffee fix, a strong one, and there was an Italian cafe right across the road whose double espressos she'd turned to in the dark days of Daniel's illness to get her through the exhaustion. She pressed the door release to get back out on the street and stepped onto the pavement. Then she yelped with fright. Cherry was standing outside, leaning against the wall.

She smiled. "Well, you've saved me some time. I thought I was going to have to wait until you finished your day and I was just wondering what to do with myself."

Laura stared at her, uncomprehending, her mind was already confused by Cherry's sudden appearance, by her coming to the office.

Cherry leaned forward. "I know he's alive," she whispered.

Laura stammered, "What are you talking about?"

"What kind of mother are you, who would lie about her own child's death?"

She felt the blood drain from her face. The self-loathing was creeping back in.

Cherry's voice turned hard. "You tried to take everything away from me. I am going to do the same to you."

Laura gaped. Cherry held her gaze for a moment; her eyes

cold, unforgiving. Then, when she was sure the message had been understood, she turned and walked away.

Trembling, Laura watched her go. She tried to pass it off as a juvenile, silly threat. But there was something in Cherry's tone that had frightened her deeply. She instinctively knew that no matter how hard she might try, she wouldn't be able to dismiss it. Laura would be waiting. Waiting and wondering what was going to happen.

36

CHERRY KNEW THAT IF LAURA HAD BEEN JUST THAT LITTLE BIT more generous with her information, had told her all those months ago about Daniel's ashes going to France, phoned again to check she was okay and allow her to ask which day he'd died, she'd never have called the hospital. Not the new hospital, of course; she hadn't even known about that one. No, the Chelsea and Westminster, where he was supposed to have had the fatal heart attack. Wary of calling Laura for the missing links, the information she needed to move on with her life, she'd called the ward. However, as she suspected, they refused to tell her anything as she "wasn't next of kin." Next came the wracking tears, then the claim that she didn't know when he'd died, because she'd been so traumatized by all the visits, by seeing him in a coma for so long, that she'd become ill herself and so had only found out through gossip that it might be the case.

"Is he really dead?" she wailed dramatically, and then had asked for access to the hospital bereavement services, which she knew they weren't allowed to refuse. She also knew that once she was put through, she would get the information she needed. How could they counsel the bereaved without knowing the where and when? Instead she'd been astounded to hear that Daniel hadn't died (so the bereavement services were not available to her), but they wouldn't tell her anything else. At first, she'd been so utterly gobsmacked, it hadn't sunk in. She was convinced they'd made a

mistake, some silly yet appalling hospital error. For a brief moment, she wondered if she could sue them and what the sums
might be for psychological damage. Then she started to think about
the possibility it was true. It was too big to ignore, so she'd gone to
the hospital and waited outside the ward for one of the cleaners
to come out, one she recognized from her vigil during all those
early weeks and whom she'd regularly struck up conversation
with on her lonely afternoons. The woman had initially refused to
be drawn out, but Cherry's five crisp ten-pound notes had helped.
She told her that Daniel had been transferred to a private hospital, the Wellington, in northwest London sometime in late February. She wouldn't say anything else, but Cherry had enough. On
calling the Wellington, she'd been told they couldn't give out any
information, but he'd been discharged on May 26. If you were
dead, you weren't discharged.

A cold realization had started to form. She remembered the
sudden funeral, the fact it was family only. It was all very conve-
nient to tidy him away before she got back. At first, the idea pop-
ping into her head was so incredibly callous, so *unbelievable*, that
she thought she must have made a mistake. No one hated her
that much, she thought tentatively, but couldn't quite bury the
wounded feeling that maybe, just maybe, they did. Amidst the
hurt, she forced herself to face up to the possible fictitious scenario that had duped her. The only way to find out for certain was
to confront Laura, so she'd gone to her office. The final confir-
mation came from watching Laura's face that morning.

Just think, if she'd been a little kinder, a little more human,
she'd have gotten away with it.

She'd taken away everything that Cherry had worked hard for,
cherished, aspired to, her whole *raison d'être*. In one cruel, mega-
lomaniacal swipe. Had Laura been laughing at her all this time?
Talking about the poor little Croydon girl who'd got ideas above
her station? To think she'd tried so hard to be friends! *How dare
she,* Cherry thought. *How dare she think that because she has money,
she's better, that she could control the lives of other people.*

Cherry would not be humiliated again. It had taken all her

strength when she'd seen Laura that morning not to fly at her, but that would've been a waste. Cherry wanted her to feel exactly as she felt, that sense of injustice and helplessness when someone just comes up and snatches away what you care about and grinds you into the dust with their heel while they're at it. No, Laura needed to be taught a lesson.

Cherry also wanted Daniel back. She'd been given another chance, and this time she wasn't going to mess it up. No stupid white-water-rafting trips. She had to tread carefully; after all, he'd probably been told she'd given up on him, dumped him when he was in a coma. Her heart suddenly stopped. What if he'd met someone else? *Oh, please, don't let that be true,* she thought, and knew she had to get a move on. So between her two goals and the pressing urgency, she had a lot of thinking to do, a lot of planning to sort out. Her mind switched on and it was a joyous feeling. Energy flooded through her for the first time in months. Her mum, home midafternoon after an early shift, was the first to notice the change.

"Have you got a job, love?"

"Yes, Mum, I have. A very important one."

She was pulled into a bear hug. "Congratulations! What is it?"

"Putting right a wrong."

Wendy looked puzzled. "Are you working for a charity?"

Cherry considered; her mother might as well think this as anything. "That's right."

"Good for you, love. It's about time more people out there did something for someone else. I'm thinking of doing the midnight walk, you know, for breast cancer. Do you fancy coming with me?"

"Think I might be a bit busy with the new job, Mum."

Cherry felt alive. This was the project, the focus she'd been looking for. She escaped to her bedroom and started by writing a list of everything Daniel had ever said about Laura, his parents, anything that might be of some value. She had an excellent memory, something she was particularly pleased with herself about, and had used to full advantage throughout her life. Once, she'd been off from school for a few days with the flu and the dreaded French verb test was the day of her return. All she'd had to do was scan the workbook while they were lining up to go in, and she knew the conjugations of *"souhaiter"—to wish*—perfectly.

When she was done with her list, there was quite a lot on it, some of it really useful. She was going to have a lot of fun. But the first thing she was going to do was see Daniel. Laura wouldn't tell him about her coming to the office, not immediately, because then she'd have to explain why. And that she couldn't do without admitting she'd lied about his death. No, she'd likely build herself up to it. But Cherry knew she wouldn't leave it too long, wouldn't dare to. She'd be too afraid Cherry would get to him first. So Cherry decided to make sure she did just that. She threw on her jacket and told her mum she was going out for some air.

She walked the ten minutes to Wandle Park and found a quiet bench. The park was quite busy with dog walkers, mums pushing prams, and some of the kids out of school, but it was still big enough for people to have their own space; no one came near her. Making sure she dialed a prefix that would hide her own number, Cherry phoned Laura's office.

"Hello, can I speak to Willow, please?"

A click and she was put through.

"Hello, Cavendish Pictures."

"Oh, hi, Willow, this is Rachel Thornton, PA to Alison Forest at ITV drama." Such a good idea of hers to chat with Willow earlier when she'd gone to the office. She'd found out she'd only been there a few days and it was her first TV job. It was unlikely that she'd be familiar with people's voices and she was usefully green. "I'm calling about *The New Life of Heather Brown*."

"Oh, I so love this project."

"Me too. It's one of my favorites on our slate."

"Really?" Willow was delighted.

"Absolutely. Such a good script."

"I can't wait to see it made," gushed Willow.

"You should ask Laura if you could come and visit the set."

"Oh, my God, I'd love that."

Cherry smiled. Willow was so trusting. "Listen, Alison's asked if Laura can come in for a meeting tomorrow morning. She's got some issues on the casting and is keen to lock it down ASAP." ITV was so helpful in putting all their executives' names on their website as they detailed their upcoming dramas. It had all been incredibly simple and hadn't stretched Cherry at all.

"She's got an hour between ten and eleven?"

Willow sounded worried for the future of the drama. She was so unsuspecting, Cherry almost felt sorry for her. "That's great. We'll see her then. Alison's out of the office and off-line this afternoon, but any questions she'll answer fully tomorrow."

And that was it. Cherry just had one more thing to prepare for. She started to make her way back home to her mum's flat. It was time to open the boxes.

37

Wednesday, September 16

*T*HE NEXT MORNING, DRESSED CAREFULLY IN THE ELECTRIC-BLUE dress that Daniel had bought her in France, the one that showed off her raven hair, Cherry made her way along Cadogan Square. As she turned into the front path of number 38, she felt herself grow heavyhearted. She rang the bell. After a few moments, she heard footsteps coming to the door. It opened and Cherry looked up and screamed. Then she fainted, falling halfway across the threshold.

When she came round, Daniel had pulled her into the hallway and shut the door. She tried to sit up, but her head hurt. She'd hit it when she fell, something that she'd been prepared for. She stared at him in shock, still terrified.

"Are you all right?" he said matter-of-factly.

She was silent.

"What's wrong?"

"You're . . ."

Daniel frowned at her. "What?"

"Alive."

"Yes. Last time I looked."

"I don't understand. . . ."

"Do you need some water?" He sounded impatient, like he wanted to get on and for her to leave.

She continued to stare at him, a hurt expression on her face. Tears welled up. "You could've just told me it was over."

She struggled to get up and open the front door, but he put out a hand to stop her.

"What did you just say?"

"If you didn't want to see me anymore. I could have handled it, you know. Being dumped. No need to let your mum do your dirty work. Was it her idea or yours?"

He looked baffled. "What are you talking about?"

"So, what? You're just going to deny it now? Sorry, but I deserve better." She gulped back some tears and tried again to wrench open the door.

"Cherry, will you please tell me what's going on?"

She stopped and looked at him. "Your mum. Telling me you were dead."

The hallway fell silent.

"Say that again."

Cherry frowned. "She phoned me. Back in March. She told me you'd died when I was away."

Daniel stared. "She did *what?*"

Cherry felt it wasn't really necessary to repeat it. His face was fixed in utter astonishment.

"Cherry, do you have time for a coffee?"

She did. He started toward the kitchen.

"Not here, though," she said quickly. "If it's okay with you, I'd rather not be . . ." She looked around uncomfortably and he understood.

"Let me just get my things, put my work away."

"May I use the bathroom?"

"Course."

Daniel disappeared into the hub of the house, and after a couple of seconds, when she could no longer hear him, she slipped upstairs and into Laura's bedroom. Closing the door softly, she glanced at the desk and saw the notepaper she'd spotted on her tour, when she'd come for dinner all those months ago. Embossed with Laura's name and address. Silently she moved across the

room, noting how the thick carpet muffled any squeaks or footsteps. She took a few sheets and slipped them into her bag; then
seeing a handwritten note, something about a woman having a
strenuous time looking after her grandchildren, she took that
too. It must've been no more than two or three minutes before
she was back downstairs.

"Ready?" said Daniel, appearing from the kitchen with his
jacket.

She nodded.

They went to a coffee bar a few streets away. It was better that
way. Laura would soon find out she wasn't required at ITV Towers
and Cherry didn't really want her barging in on them.

He sat and listened while she told him what had happened—
awkwardly, of course, as it would be difficult to hear, and she didn't
want to hurt his feelings any more than she had to. She tried to
keep it brief. She tried to be careful; there was still a long way to go.

He didn't say anything for a while; then he rubbed his face in
his hands. When he looked up, he was just as bewildered. "Why
didn't you ask to go to the funeral or something?"

The insinuation was that she could've worked harder to flush
out the lie. "I did. She said it had taken place when I was away.
And there was no gravestone, as your ashes had gone to France."

He stiffened and she knew it must be hard hearing how your
mother had discussed your own funeral. He picked up his teaspoon and slowly stirred his coffee without looking up at her.

"I'm sorry you had to go through that."

She nodded. "It took me a long time . . . Well, I never really got
over it. That's why I went to your mum's office yesterday. I was just
desperate to talk to her, hear about what had happened after
you'd . . . you know . . ."

"You went to her office?"

"She didn't mention it?" Cherry countered. "Well, no, I guess
she wouldn't." Silence lapsed for a moment. "Are you okay?"

"Why did you come to the house?"

She noticed that he wasn't opening up to her yet. "I came to

bring her these." She opened up her bag and pulled out an envelope. Inside were some photographs.

"It's our trip. The white-water rafting. I just thought she might
like to see the last photos of you. . . ."

He took them in his hand. There they were, the two of them
laughing and screaming as they hurtled down the river. Cherry had
dug out the pictures the night before from the boxes stashed in the
wardrobe. They'd been taken by the professional photographer
and she'd got them from the center a month or so after the accident for her own memento.

She had a sudden surge of conscience. "I hope they're not too
upsetting," she said quickly. "Because of the accident—"

"No." He looked at her. "It was a nice thing to do."

She gave a small smile. "So . . . when did you wake up?"

"March. A few days after she called you. When I was fit enough,
we went to France. Better recuperation. Warmer."

"You look really well."

He nodded, accepting the compliment.

"Can I ask . . . what she said about me? About why I'd stopped
coming to the hospital?"

"She didn't go into much detail. Just made it sound like you'd
left a long time before."

Cherry's face crumpled. "I know we didn't always get on . . .
but I didn't think it was that bad."

His face was set in a stony expression.

She sat awkwardly for a moment and he saw and seemed to
snap out of his mood. He sat up a little straighter, focused a small
smile on her.

"Are you still studying?" she asked.

"I'm back at the hospital. They've given me another place."

"That's great."

"Yeah. You? I noticed you'd left the agency . . ."

"It didn't really work out."

He looked surprised. "No?"

"No, things got a bit . . . My mind wasn't really on it." She
shook her head, not wanting to go into it further.

"Hang on, was this because . . . of me? Of what you'd been told?"

That is sort of true, thought Cherry. Here was another thing she could hold Laura accountable for. She gave him an awkward smile.

He exhaled in irritation and she could tell he was biting his tongue when it came to his mother. "I think I owe you quite a bit."

She grinned. "I'm just glad you're still here."

"Must have been quite a surprise when I opened the door."

"Yep."

They both remembered her faint and laughed.

"So, what else have you been up to?" he asked.

"Not much. I'm staying with my mum at the moment."

"Send her my best. Explain I'm alive first."

"I will. How about you?"

"Just got my head down, doing the hours."

They looked at each other a moment.

Heart in mouth, she spoke first. "Did you meet anyone else?"

"No." He paused. "Did you?"

She'd heard the hope in his voice. She smiled and shook her head.

38

Wednesday, September 16

*I*T HAD STARTED OUT AS A MORNING OF STUDYING. DANIEL STILL thanked his lucky stars that his memory hadn't been affected and he had mercifully retained five years of medical school. There had been a note for him when he'd gone downstairs: *Need to speak to you. Will be home this afternoon, can you be around? Mum x* He'd gotten to his books over his toast and the time had melted away, unnoticed, until the doorbell had rung. He remembered he'd been annoyed at the interruption and had gotten up thinking it was hopefully just the postman.

When he'd first seen Cherry standing at the door in the striking blue dress, which he remembered from their trip to France, she made something leap up in his chest. But he quickly reminded himself she'd left him. Then she screamed and fainted, something that he found both baffling and annoying, although this could've been due to its arousing a sense of chivalry in him that he oughtn't to feel.

The news, when he heard it, didn't make sense at first. He couldn't understand it. He tried to think of every reasonable explanation, but the thing he kept coming back to was that his mother had lied. She'd made up a story about him dying. Gradually this notion tunneled its way into his brain and sat there, refusing to leave. To make things worse, he realized that she'd not only made up this terrible thing, but she'd perpetuated the lie, long after he'd recovered. She'd sat by his hospital bed until he'd gradually gotten the strength to leave it, pushed him around the gardens, then spent days encouraging him during physio. There had been plenty of time to bring up the subject. And all the time he was struggling to cope with everything that had been thrown at him—not only his injuries, but the sharp pain of a breakup as well. He'd gotten through, of course, but once or twice he'd gone to bed feeling so incredibly miserable, it had been an effort not to break down.

How could she have done this to him? Why? He knew she didn't like Cherry, but this was . . . sickening. He tried to breathe away the pain that had lodged itself in his chest. Part of him wanted an explanation, but he didn't trust himself to speak to his mother yet. He didn't want to hear what she had to say; her floundering or her thin justification would just repulse him. For the same reason, he didn't call his dad either. He didn't want to incriminate his mother, for he knew that with their relationship being as it was, his father would think her despicable. He couldn't deal with any of that yet.

It didn't take long to pack his few possessions. He looked round his room and knew this would be the last time he'd leave. Then he went downstairs. When he'd read the note from his mother that morning, it hadn't made any great impact. He was around and happy to see how he could help. Now, however, he could see the restrained urgency between the lines—she wanted to get to him before Cherry, and no wonder.

If Cherry hadn't had the random, compassionate thought to bring over the photos, his mother probably would have reached him first. He wondered if he would have reacted differently if it had been she who'd told him. He tried to imagine the words coming out of her mouth: *"I pretended you were dead. I made up a funeral."* They sounded farcical, yet at the same time breathtakingly callous. It reminded him of the sort of thing reported in sensationalist newspapers: mothers who pretended their children had cancer in order to elicit substantial donations.

He turned the note over, wrote something on the back; then he put it back on the worktop. He hitched his bag onto his shoulder and left the house, pulling the front door shut behind him. As he walked down the road, he thought there was one good thing to come out of this revelation: he'd seen Cherry again.

39

Wednesday, September 16

*T*HE RECEPTIONIST AT ITV TOWERS RANG THROUGH FOR ALISON WHILE Laura filled in the visitor slip.

"Mrs. Cavendish?"

Laura looked up.

"I've got her PA on the phone. She says there's nothing in the diary."

"What?"

"Alison's out of the office."

"When's she back?"

"Not until this afternoon."

It was ten in the morning. "But I have a meeting—"

The receptionist held up a finger and listened to something through her headpiece. "Her PA's coming down."

Laura moved aside for the throng behind her and checked her diary. She had the right time, so Alison must have forgotten. And it was supposed to be urgent. She watched the screens broadcasting a mix of the news and the morning's property program and wondered, irritated, when she'd be able to fit Alison in. This afternoon was already full and she wanted to get back home early to talk to Daniel.

Rachel, the PA, came through the revolving doors. "Laura,

there seems to be some mistake. We don't have an appointment for you this morning."

"But you rang Willow. Yesterday afternoon."

She frowned. "No, I didn't."

"She spoke to you. Something about casting?"

"I promise you, I didn't."

Something clicked in Laura's brain, and with it, a growing sense of foreboding. She knew who was behind this. "My apologies, I'll talk to Willow. She must have been mistaken," she said, and quickly left the building.

Once outside, she tried to still her racing heart. Someone had a camera set on a tripod outside, pointing at the main entrance, right where she stood. It unnerved her, as if Cherry could somehow be watching on a screen somewhere, the all-seeing eye. *How had she found out?* Laura quickly moved away from the lens of the camera.

That question had gone round and round in her head last night, but she couldn't work it out. There was one thing she was sure of, though—Cherry was behind this stunt. But why would she do something so silly, so juvenile, as to send her on a wild-goose chase, a meeting that didn't exist? It was harmless in itself, unless she'd been deliberately placed out of the way.

Jesus. Daniel.

Laura walked into her ominously quiet house and knew almost instantly that Cherry had been there before her. There was a lingering sense of dread as she made her way through the empty rooms. The note was left on the kitchen worktop and said simply: *Seen Cherry. Decided to move back to the flat, after all. Think it just makes things easier all round. Time I stood on my own two feet and got a little independence anyway. Dan.*

The last sentence had been an add-on, she could tell. Something to soften the blow. She laid the note down and sat heavily. What had Cherry told him? How had she painted it? Whatever way served her best, she knew.

She pulled out her phone and was about to call Daniel, then

had an image of Cherry there, listening at his ear. No, this was a conversation that had to be between just the two of them. She sent him a text instead: **Daniel, I know you're probably and justifiably upset and furious at me, but, please, will you let me explain? Can we meet later?**

The response was swift: **Tomorrow. Five at the flat. But I only have an hour.**

It wasn't quite what she'd wanted to hear, and her heart sank. At least, Howard was away on a work trip, so she wouldn't have to explain why their son had suddenly left home.

Moses came in from the garden, delighted to see her at such an unusually early hour. He leapt up onto the worktop and rubbed his face against her knuckles, her hands propping her head up in despair. She scratched him behind the ears. "Oh, Moses, I've done something really . . . awful." She had. She'd started this by telling that monstrous lie.

40

*C*HERRY SAT ON THE SEAT ON THE PLATFORM AT NOTTING HILL TUBE station and waited for her watch to reach seven minutes past four. Then she stood. It was time to start heading up to the street. Daniel, she knew, was prompt, so it was just late enough to make him hope she was still coming. She bounded up the steps, so as to get just a little out of breath, and then ran out of the entrance. There he was, standing outside an upmarket sandwich establishment, trying not to look as if he might have been stood up.

"Sorry I'm a bit late," she said, "tube was held up at South Ken," and he smiled, all doubts melting away.

"No problem." They stood self-consciously, both smiling awkwardly at each other, feeling like they were on a first date. Strangely, it seemed a bit premature for kisses—even though just over a year ago, they were sleeping together. This afternoon was a movie date, a mutual appreciation for Steven Soderbergh. Once they'd both admitted they were still single, the next most natural thing was to arrange to go out. Cherry had had to think of something low-key to ease them in, something that wouldn't feel too strange, something innocuous that wouldn't make him question whether he was doing the right thing. The film was about to leave the theaters and she'd said how it would be a shame to miss it; he agreed, and she said she was thinking of going that afternoon, so if he needed a break from his studies? He didn't think about it long and they made a plan to meet later. Cherry went home to shower and change. She wanted to look her absolute best, as she had big intentions for the afternoon. They walked along the street toward the Gate cinema; at the curb, he put his hand out protectively as a car came flying around a left turn. Cherry felt a rush of warmth, a fuzzy sense of attachment.

They crossed the road safely and headed toward the front of the building. Outside, the poster brought bad news.

"It looks like it's already gone," cried Cherry, even though she'd known this when he suggested the venue. Sitting silently in a cinema would persuade him to come out, but it was not going to resurrect their relationship.

He stepped closer. "What? It can't have."

But it had. Something new about aliens had taken its place.

"What about the Electric cinema just down the road?"

"Good idea," said Cherry.

They walked the couple of blocks to the Electric, but that was just as bereft of Steven Soderbergh's genius, something else that Cherry had already known. Daniel looked sheepish and thumped his fist on his forehead. "I'm so sorry. I've dragged you all the way up here for nothing."

"Outrageous! How are you going to make it up to me?"

He smiled. "We could find another cinema?"

"Or the zoo?" she jumped in quickly. "I've always wanted to go."

"Really?"

She noted his hesitation. "You're not keen."

"If you'd like to . . ."

But neither of them moved. Cherry could feel the afternoon slipping from her control. Whatever they did, she had to decide now.

"Tell you what, why don't we just walk toward the park? It's such a lovely day." She turned, not giving him a chance to refuse, and they set off toward Kensington. It wasn't the most promising of starts, and in quiet desperation, she knew she was going to have to work harder. She suddenly thought a walk wasn't such a good idea, after all—they were awkward around each other and needed something to distract them, something to talk about. She turned excitedly to him.

"Jazz."

"What?"

"They do a bit of R and B too. And great fish and chips."

"Shouldn't that be shrimp Creole?"

"We could make a request."

She held her breath and sent a silent thank-you to her memory. The aloof and elite Abigail and Emily to thank. She'd never penetrated their joint wall of friendship, but listening carefully to every conversation they'd had at the agency had been useful, after all. More than once, they'd raved about a bar with "the best" live music, but never thought to ask her along. She'd wistfully checked it online one night when they'd gone along after work and she was further put out by the fact it *did* look good, not too up itself or pretentious. She knew it opened at four; in fact, they'd probably even get a table this early on.

She looked at him excitedly. "Fancy it?"

Her enthusiasm was infectious. "Where is it?"

"Ten minutes."

"Walk?"

"Cab."

He hailed one and they climbed in. Cherry gave directions and a few minutes later they were driving down a little back alley. Nestled between a wine shop and a jewelers was the bar.

Once they were inside, Cherry knew immediately it had been a good idea. They had a table to themselves and there were just enough people already there to make it feel like a gathering of friends, people who through luck or skill had managed to skive off work early.

Daniel was looking at the menu. "Is it too early for cocktails?"

Cherry grinned and shook her head.

"This place is great, how did you find it?"

"It's one of my favorites," said Cherry casually, as if she spent numerous nights hanging out there and was now sharing it with him. They were drawn in by the singers, a young white guy with a prominent Adam's apple and a statuesque black woman in a purple sequined dress. She was in her late fifties, but her voice was strong and defiant. The young guy would occasionally flirt with her on stage and she'd treat him with dignified disdain. This amused him and between them they had an electrifying presence together.

Cherry glanced at Daniel and looked for signs that his mother had been in touch since she'd seen him that morning. Laura would've found out about the nonexistent ITV meeting hours ago, and no doubt she'd be extremely suspicious of who'd actually sent her there, and had probably worked it out. She'd likely panicked, wanting to talk to Daniel, but so far he'd not mentioned anything. He was still behaving as if he hadn't spoken to his mother, which meant he didn't know about how she'd threatened Laura the day before. In fact, Cherry wasn't all that worried: If Laura did bring it up, she would just deny it. It was all rather melodramatic and far-fetched and Laura was the one with the record of grotesque lies. In fact, instead of being a worry, Cherry felt sure she could make it look as if Laura was behaving worse than ever and this would push Daniel to her even quicker. She'd wasted enough time and was sick of being down and out. Thankfully, Daniel had paid the cab and put his card behind the bar for the drinks.

The band changed songs and the woman started up something feisty and proud and her voice filled the belly. Murmurs of appreciation went around the room and Daniel impulsively stood. He held out his hand and led Cherry to the other couples in the small dance area. She smiled. The ice was well and truly broken. There was no going back.

As he held her hand and spun her around the floor, Daniel thought again how lucky he was that Cherry had decided to make an unplanned visit to his parents' house that morning. And how lucky his shifts had worked out so he'd been in at the time. He'd been given something back from all that had been taken away from him after the accident. He got a stab of hurt when he thought about his mum and how quickly he'd moved out, but he quickly quashed it.

The flat had smelled musty. He immediately opened all the windows and ran all the taps, which gurgled with air locks. His old electronic travel card was lying on the coffee table, put there after he'd returned from work the day he and Cherry took the trip to Wales. It had been lined up neatly with his work ID and all his old mail. He checked through the postmarks. They stopped sometime around early November, probably when his mother had managed to get hold of most people to tell them he was in a coma. He quickly looked through, but they were all junk mail, bills, and so on. He chucked them all in the trash. Then he opened the fridge. It was empty. He had a sudden urge to fill it and make the place feel more like home, so he left his rucksack lying in the hall and headed out. When he came back, he turned up the music and made himself some lunch. The place felt better already, but what he couldn't get rid of was the ache in his chest. And for the first time he felt angry. He'd been cheated out of something he cared about. All those months when he could have been with Cherry, the girl he loved. Why? Why had his mother gone to such lengths?

The vibrant music and powerful singing released something in him and made him feel free. The singer finished on a heartfelt note and a small outbreak of applause rippled around the room. Daniel led Cherry back to their table.

"Quite a mover."

She blushed. "No . . ."

"Did we ever go dancing?"

Her face clouded over. "Don't think we had time."

"What else didn't we do?"

"Swim with dolphins."

"Which couples swim with dolphins?"

"It's an option. Have our portrait painted."

He smiled. "Buy matching T-shirts."

"Throw a dinner party."

"Have 'our' song."

"Argue."

He considered. "No, we didn't, did we?" In fact, he realized, they'd never had more than a healthy debate. It was a nice thought.

"I've moved back to the flat."

She stared at him. "What do you mean?"

"It was left empty. Ever since the accident."

"What did Laura say?"

"I haven't spoken to her yet. I left her a note back at the house. It just seemed like it was never going to be an easy conversation and I needed some time to think."

Cherry nodded. "Was that today? After we met up?"

"Yes."

She could tell he was still hurting. She put a hand on his, then raised her glass. "Happy new home," she said warmly, and clinked.

By the end of the night, he knew what he wanted to do. They left the bar, and before it became too big a thing, he asked her, "Do you want to come back?"

She stared at him a moment and he wondered if he'd gone too far.

"It's okay if you don't—"

"No, I'd like to."

They were silent in the cab on the way back, each content with the other's company and his or her own thoughts. Daniel opened his front door and she stepped inside. As it closed behind them, they moved together into a kiss. Cherry pulled urgently at his shirt and they were naked before they reached the bedroom.

Afterward, as they lay in bed, both were happier than they'd been for a long time. The missing months had melted away and they felt as attached to each other as they had a year ago, only more so because of what they'd been through. Cherry's leg was looped over his and Daniel looked at her beautiful, lightly tanned skin, luminous in the semidark.

"Cherry?"

She snuggled into his side. "Yes?"

"Move in."

Her heart beat rapidly against his arm. She propped herself up on her elbow and looked at him, wide-eyed.

"Here?"

"Of course, here. I don't want to waste any more time. My accident taught me that. And I don't know about you, but this"—he indicated the two of them—"feels as good as it was, better even. I just want to be with you."

"I want to be with you too."

"So, will you?"

She paused. "What about your mum?"

"She's not coming."

"No, I mean—"

"I know what you mean. She'll just have to get used to it. It's my life and I want you in it. If you'd like to be."

She kissed him. "I would."

41

Thursday, September 17

*L*AURA BUZZED DANIEL'S FLAT FROM THE STREET. SHE PULLED HER handbag in tightly over her shoulder; then realizing her palms were damp, she quickly dabbed them on her jacket. It was a new sensation, being nervous about visiting your own son. She gave a small wave through the glass door to Ian, whom she could see was at his desk, then finally an answer. She smiled up at the camera and heard the door click open. On the first floor, he'd left his front door open. She knocked and peered inside for him. "Hello? It's me." It felt odd not to be greeted, as though she was trespassing. He came through from the kitchen and stopped still in the hall. Laura was instinctively about to go and embrace him, but his folded arms and flat expression kept her at bay.

"Tea?"

"Yes, please."

He turned and went back into the kitchen and she was left alone for a moment.

"Mint?" he called, and she followed and took a seat at the breakfast bar and watched as he made the tea. Neither of them said anything. He pushed a mug toward her, and then, holding his, leaned his back against the counter and looked at her expectantly.

"I'm sorry," said Laura. "Truly, deeply sorry. They'd just told me you were likely to"—she paused, remembering the awful meeting—"not make it. In fact, you didn't have a lot of time. I was devastated and, knowing I was about to lose you, I wanted . . . I wanted you to myself. To give you all of myself. I wanted the last few hours to be like they were when you were little. Just us."

"And then?"

"What do you mean?"

"Well, I woke up. At no point did you tell Cherry I'd recovered. And you told me she'd left me months before."

"I know, I—"

"Did you not think I missed her? That I could've done with her when I was recovering?" His voice ached with hurt and she felt an urge to put her arms around him, but he wasn't a child she could comfort anymore. And, anyway, she was the source of the hurt.

"Daniel, it wasn't an easy decision. I agonized over it, even after you'd come round."

"That makes it even worse. You held my future in your hands, tossing it this way and that."

"No, you misunderstand—"

"At least, if you'd known for a fact she was bad news, it would make it easier to stomach."

Laura took a deep breath. "Look, I know it's been hard, and I should've been the one to tell you, but . . . well, this isn't going to be easy to hear. . . ."

He stiffened. "What?"

"Cherry manipulated me out of the way yesterday. She faked a call to my PA, pretending to be ITV, and told me I had to be at a meeting yesterday morning. Meanwhile, she went to the house to drop the bombshell."

Daniel put his cup down in exasperation. "Mum, she didn't know I was alive."

"No, you see, she *did*. She'd come to my office the day before."

"Yes, she told me."

Laura was surprised. "She did?"

"Said she'd gone for some closure. You hadn't told her anything about my funeral, or where she could visit my nonexistent grave."

She tried to ignore his sarcasm. "Is that all she said?"

"What else was there?"

"She threatened me. Told me she knew you were alive, and in revenge for what I'd done, she was going to take everything from me."

He made a small exhaling noise, incredulous. *"What?"*

"I'm sorry, Daniel," she said. "I know you like her, but she *is* bad news."

"'Revenge'? 'Take everything'? How's she going to do that?"

"I don't know."

He was staring at her in a way that made her feel uncomfortable. Hurt was etched across his face, along with something else he was trying to fight. *Dislike.*

"She came to the house yesterday morning to bring you some memorabilia," he said. "Photos of our trip to Wales. She thought you might like them."

Her heart missed a beat. "She's clever, don't you see? She's playing you."

The buzzer went. Daniel picked up the phone, listened, and held down the door release.

"Expecting someone?" she said apprehensively. She thought she knew who.

His look confirmed it and Laura sat up straight. "What are you going to say to her?" she asked.

There was a rap at the door and Daniel left. Laura could hear quiet murmurings in the hallway. A few seconds later, he came back, followed by Cherry.

"Laura," she said demurely. "I hope I'm not intruding."

Laura looked at her. She was as cool as you like, and not a trace of their previous conversation could be read in her face.

"He knows everything."

Cherry looked puzzled. "About what you said to me? The lie?"

"No . . . ," she began heatedly before pulling herself together. "About you. Coming to my office and threatening me."

Cherry looked at Daniel, wide-eyed. "I don't know what she means."

"Oh, come on. . . ."

"I'm sorry, Daniel," said Cherry softly, "I know she doesn't like me, doesn't want us seeing each other, but I'm finding this very hard to deal with. Maybe we should rethink our plans."

"What plans?" said Laura, anxiously looking at Daniel.

He was silent for a moment.

"Cherry's moving in. *Moved* in."

"She's *what?*"

"I'm not. I can't cope with this." Upset, Cherry turned to go. "Look, I'll just get a cab, take my things home again."

Daniel grabbed her arm. "No—"

"She's moving in *now?* You don't waste any time, do you—"

"Mum!"

"Whose idea was it?" Laura demanded.

"What?"

"For her to move in?"

Daniel was losing patience. "Mine, of course."

"Are you sure? Think back. Are you sure she didn't plant the idea?"

"No."

Cherry was in the hallway, dragging her bag to the door.

"Cherry, wait!" Daniel ran over and put his hand on the door to stop her from opening it.

Laura took a deep breath. She spoke awkwardly, under her breath. "Daniel, this is what I've been saying . . . about the money. There was the ticket too, remember? Telling you the flight to France was six hundred when it was only five. *I saw the ticket.*"

She saw him hesitate.

"Daniel, please believe me. Everything I'm telling you is true."

He looked at Cherry, who, she saw, was doing her best to look perplexed. "Are you talking about when I came to your villa?" she said. "I don't understand. . . ." She blinked, hurt, then started rummaging in her suitcase. "You think I tried to scam money out of you? I didn't. . . . Look . . . I'm sure I have it here somewhere. . . .

I kept it, a keepsake . . . it was our first trip together . . . here!" She produced a piece of crumpled paper with a flourish. "My ticket!"

Daniel took it. "That's all I ever asked you for, right?" continued Cherry.

Laura frowned at the piece of paper in Daniel's hand. It *looked* the same, but the amount was six hundred. . . . "That's not right. That's not the ticket I saw. . . ."

"I need to go," said Cherry, tears welling in her eyes.

"Not yet." Daniel turned to Laura. "Mum, I think you'd better leave."

"But can't you see? She must have made that up, printed another one or something. She's lying!"

He spoke quietly. "Mum, it's not Cherry who's the liar."

Laura broke her gaze from him when she could feel the tears prick; holding her head as high as she could, she left the flat.

As she made her way out onto the street, Laura could feel Cherry watching her from the window. She daren't look up; she didn't want to see her gloating, triumphant face.

The dark was creeping in, casting the room in a reverential gloom, but Laura lay on the sofa, couldn't muster the energy to get up and switch on the light. In fact, she quite liked it, lying there, Moses on her stomach, purring rhythmically, both of them watching the shadows take hold. It suited her mood. She knew she'd lost her cool earlier, but Cherry's performance had gotten to her. Now, lying here and looking back on it, she felt frightened at how much Cherry had controlled the entire incident. She was probably enjoying it, reveling in the way Daniel was turning against his own mother. She'd tried calling him when she got back to the house, but it had gone to his voice mail. She'd left a message, asking him to call her back, but he hadn't so far; she didn't expect a response tonight. In fact, she honestly didn't know when she'd hear from him again.

The lift door opened in the hallway and Moses pricked his ears. Howard must have come up from the garage.

He came into the room and flicked on the light. Laura winced and covered her eyes.

He was surprised to see her. "What are you doing here in the dark?"

"Nothing. Relaxing."

Howard stroked Moses, who was weaving in and out of his ankles. "Hello, boy." He looked up. "Where's Daniel?"

A knot formed in Laura's chest. She'd have to tell him. "He's moved back to his flat."

Howard stood. "When?"

"Yesterday."

"Was he not going to say good-bye?"

"It's not as simple as that."

He looked at her, waiting for more. Under pressure, she got up and moved into the kitchen. Poured herself a glass of wine from the fridge.

Howard followed. "What's going on?"

"Daniel and Cherry are back together."

He looked surprised. "What . . . After the way she dumped him?"

"She didn't dump him. I told her . . ." There was a long pause. "Yes . . . ?"

"When we thought he wasn't going to make it . . . I told her he'd already died."

Howard stared and then started to laugh, a wild, incredulous bark. The laugh dried up. "You're not joking, are you?"

"She didn't love him, I'm pretty sure. . . . I *know* she wants him for his money."

He rubbed his hand across his hair, making it stick up. "Oh, my God."

Laura topped up her wine. "Do you want some?" she said, indicating the bottle.

Still reeling, he shook his head. "What about when he woke up? Did you not think to tell him the truth?"

"Oh, Howard, how could I?" she said, frustrated at his lack of understanding. "And now he's found out, through Cherry, who's manipulated herself back into his life."

"*Cherry's* manipulated?"

"She's a very clever, very determined young woman."

Howard reached for the bottle and a glass. "Maybe I will have that drink."

He looked at her and she wished he'd wipe the judgmental expression off his face.

"So when he found out, he felt the need to move back to his flat, and judging from your mood when I came in, he's not best pleased with you," Howard observed.

"He doesn't see her for who she really is."

"I think it's you who's not seeing."

"But she's—"

"Not her, you. Look at yourself. At what you've done." He shook his head. "How on earth did you think you'd get away with this?"

"You're forgetting. At the time, we didn't think . . . The doctors told us he was dying. I just needed those last couple of days. As a mother, under the circumstances, I don't think that's too hard to justify, is it?"

"'As a mother . . .' He's a grown man, Laura. You don't have to think what's best for him anymore. How do you think he felt when he woke up and you—Christ, me too—told him she'd left him. Me, consoling with a load of bullshit about how she wasn't worth it if she wasn't going to stick around." He was angry now and slammed his glass down. "Does he think I was in on this?"

"I don't know."

"Well, you'd better bloody tell him I wasn't. No, don't, I'll tell him." He sighed heavily. "Cherry's okay. What exactly have you got against her?"

Laura flashed a look of exasperation. "I've told you. She's after his money, his future, thinking she can just hang on to his coattails and get herself another life."

"And you know this how?"

"Little things. She's lied about stuff. Money. Fabricated excuses to get time off to go to France. But it's more than that, it's . . . I don't know . . . a feeling."

"What, mother's instinct?"

"Don't dismiss it," she snapped, hurt.

"You're deluded. Just let go, let go of him." He looked at her with a new distance, as if he didn't know her. "Stop making excuses for your obsessive behavior. You've driven him away—you—and you've only got yourself to blame." He shook his head as he looked at her, as if hit by a great sadness, then left the room.

She heard him go upstairs, and after a while, the footsteps faded out. She sat down and, pouring some more wine, found her hand was shaking. She hadn't said anything about Cherry's threats, but she had a feeling Howard would've just thought she was being sensational, or what was it he'd called her? *Deluded.*

42

*T*WO WEEKS LATER, SHE STILL HADN'T HEARD FROM DANIEL. OUT-
wardly she put on a show of being levelheaded and rational, acting as if it would all blow over. Inside she was a writhing mess of
anxiety. There was no one she could talk to about it. She and
Howard were more estranged than ever and didn't even seem to
achieve their occasional meals together now. He'd send her a text
telling her he had a late meeting at work and she'd end up having
a solitary dinner in the kitchen. Eating alone soon lost any appeal
and she'd gotten into the habit of not cooking, sometimes not
really bothering to eat at all. She had lost a few pounds. As she inspected her face in the mirror above her dressing table, she noticed her cheeks were a little more hollow. But it wasn't really the
sunken look that was different; it was the dullness of her eyes. She
quickly glanced away. Tonight might take her mind off things.

She was going to a dinner party at Isabella's. A handful of friends
had been invited, Isabella said, then had followed by asking if
Howard would be working, rather than asking if he was free to
come. Laura hadn't pressed for an invitation for him. He wouldn't
go anyway—not with the way things were between them. She wasn't
really in the mood for lots of jolly conversation, but it was better
than staying at home.

She hoped Isabella was going to be too busy to ask much about Daniel. She hadn't told her friend he'd moved out, and she didn't want to get in an awkward corner making up something to avoid explaining about the lie. No, the plan was: to get out of the house, have a change of scene, mingle with some old friends, and then come home early. She was also going to avoid drinking too much, didn't want to start feeling desperate or maudlin and end up blurting something. She preferred not to even think about it; it was like a shameful secret, a big dirty black goblin that sat on her shoulder, poking her in the back of the neck every now and then, just to remind her it was there.

She slid the lipstick expertly over the edge of her cupid's bow, just as she heard the elevator door open. Howard was home. It instantly made her nervous. She snapped the lipstick shut and put it down. Then she left her bedroom. It was good he was home early, she told herself, as there was something she wanted to ask him, had been wanting to ask him for a while now.

She headed into the living room, where Howard, still in his work suit, was pouring himself a whisky.

"Good day?" she asked with forced brightness.

He turned, saw with some surprise that she was dressed up, but didn't comment. "Fine. Yourself?"

Laura wasn't going to tell him she'd tried calling Daniel for the third time since he'd thrown her out, and had, for the third time, gotten his voice mail. She'd not left a message, didn't see how she could really expand on the previous two. But the lack of communication was killing her, and somehow she had to get onto the subject. "Yes, great, thanks. You up to much tonight?"

"No, not really. Been a long week."

"Meant to be a nice weekend. You catching up with anyone? Seeing Daniel?"

It was about as subtle as a brick, but she kept her fixed smile in place.

"Not got any plans to," he said slowly.

She braced herself and any pretense left her. The question had been burning away for days and she had to know. "Has he been in touch? You know, since he moved out?"

Howard took a sip of his drink. "Yes."

It cut her down, even though it was the answer she'd secretly expected.

"Is he okay?"

"I take it you've not spoken to him."

She didn't feel the need to reply.

He was awkward. "He's fine. Busy at work. Doesn't have a lot of spare time. You know how it is, these trainee doctors."

Knowing he'd lied to spare her pain made it all the worse. If Daniel had time to speak to his dad, then he had time to speak to her.

"Is Cherry still living there?" Her voice sounded tight, strangled.

He looked at her. "You want me to answer that?"

Laura took a deep breath and glanced around the room without really looking at it.

"Leave it, Laura."

Hurt, she looked at him. She didn't want to get into another argument. "Right, well, I'd better be off."

"Going somewhere nice?"

"Just to Isabella's."

"Well, enjoy."

She was about to say, why didn't he come too, seeing as he was back earlier than expected, but he'd already turned away, was fixing himself another drink. She nodded at his back and went into the hall, put her shoes on and left.

She was the last to arrive. Isabella had hired caterers, whose staff was also acting as a sort of butler, and a young woman with sleek dark hair, who reminded her of Cherry, took her coat. She was led into the front room, abuzz with chatter and good humor, and she recognized most of the people there: Diane and her husband, Phillip, who'd come to the BBQ last year, as had Sally and Edward. A couple of others she'd seen at Christmas, but no one since, as socializing had taken such a knock over the last few months. No one noticed her. She stood just inside the doorway, on the periphery, unable to join the flow of the party.

Laura felt as if she didn't belong, as if, should she go over and try to join the conversation, they'd turn with cool glances. She'd lied that her son was dead. Laura was under no illusion what these people would think if they knew. They'd reel in shock and a collective muted horror. Even if they knew the truth about Cherry, it wouldn't be enough to justify what she'd done. She'd said the unsayable and allowed it to permeate deep into other people's lives. They'd put themselves above such sordidness. They'd judge, gossip, some maybe even getting a kick out of the eyebrow raising, the subtle amusement at her expense.

She was starting to regret coming, and wondered about just backing out and going home, when Isabella spotted her. She waved delightedly and headed over.

"Darling, you're almost late, I hope it's not because you've been working yourself too hard." She didn't wait for an answer, but kissed her on the cheek and signaled for the waitress to bring over some champagne, holding her own glass out at the same time for a refill. "Come and meet my new friend, Andrew. You look great, by the way. What a beautiful dress. Silver gray does wonders for your eyes."

Laura was pulled in the direction of Isabella's husband, Richard, who was talking to an energetic, wiry man with gray hair and a tanned, weathered face.

"Andrew, allow me to introduce you to my great friend Laura."

"Hello, Laura." He held out his hand warmly and she took it as Isabella looked on.

"Laura is a television producer, and Andrew runs an exporting business. Oh, we're ready," she said as a gong went off in the dining room, and Laura found she'd been seated next to Andrew.

As she looked around the table, she realized they were the only two people in the room who had arrived alone. A flash of suspicion crossed her mind and then it became clear during the first course.

"So, what do you do for fun?" asked Andrew.

Laura smiled. "It's questions like these that always remind me I need to take more time off."

"I know what you mean. Running a business, it's a monster that chews up all your waking hours."

"So, not much time for anything else?"

"I do try and keep fit."

"What's your thing?"

"Triathlons, mainly. Set myself a target twice a year."

Laura kept smiling, but inside she was deeply uncomfortable. She'd expressly told Isabella not to set her up. It felt like another weight on her shoulders, an evening she had to spend being polite to a man that she had no interest in, at least not romantically. What had he been told? Christ, it was so embarrassing. She was suddenly angry, which made her feel exhausted, which in turn angered her more. She got through the meal as best she could. More than once, she wondered what Daniel was doing. When was she ever going to hear from him? The questions whirled around her head, tormenting her while she fended off polite questions about the difference between a director and a producer. She announced her departure as soon as was reasonable. Andrew said a perfunctory good-bye and she felt a flash of guilt—he knew she hadn't been keen on her dinner companion. *Damn Isabella for being so interfering.* She came over then, said she'd escort Laura to the door.

"I wish you weren't leaving so soon." Isabella peered at her, noticed her tense mood. "You are okay, aren't you? Not coming down with anything?"

"No, Isabella, I'm not."

"What's wrong, then?"

"You either think I'm some sort of floozy or consider my marriage dead, neither of which is a particularly great sentiment from a so-called friend."

It was harsh, too harsh, but it was said. Laura immediately felt guilty when she saw Isabella's look of surprised hurt. But somehow she didn't know how to, or didn't want to, make amends.

* * *

Laura left and got into the waiting cab that had been called for her. Her mood didn't improve on the way home. When she got in, she found Howard not there. She went up to the second floor; seeing no light under his door, she tentatively knocked, then quietly opened it. His room and his bed were empty. He wasn't in the den, either, and with a sinking feeling, she realized he must have gone to Marianne's. She felt a flash of anger; she should have chatted up Andrew, after all. Not that he'd be interested now. Why was she able to burn bridges so easily these days?

Alone, she went into the kitchen and fixed herself a glass of wine. This wasn't how she'd foreseen her life: her marriage a sham, despite her heated protestations to Isabella, and her only child estranged from her. She was suddenly hit with such a severe slice of loneliness, she was winded. What would happen if she lost them, both of them? The sadness that captured her stripped her raw and she got up from the kitchen table.

Leaving her wine behind, she hurried up the stairs, tripping on a step halfway, then ran into her room. She sat at the desk. She had to do something. She couldn't just let Daniel go on, not knowing how she felt, letting that girl twist everything. A photo was hung above the desk, a black-and-white shot of her and Daniel when he was a baby. She looked up at it now and saw his delighted, adoring gaze as she held him above her head. Something caught in her throat. She'd poured so much into him, so much of herself. He was her joy, a person she had in part created in every sense of the word, her investment, her baby. She'd taught him how to write his name, to catch a ball, to ride a bike. Encouraged him to debate, to have an opinion, to stretch his mind. Shown him how to cook and how to treat women. If he wouldn't let her in the flat and wouldn't answer her calls, she'd have to try something else. An e-mail was risky; Cherry used Daniel's computer, this much she knew. And she couldn't post a letter—there was a good chance it would be intercepted. The only option was to give it to Ian, the porter, with strict instructions it was only to be handed to Daniel. She picked up her pen and started to write.

43

Friday, October 2

*I*T WAS HIS FIRST DAY OFF FROM THE HOSPITAL OR STUDY IN WHAT
seemed like weeks. Daniel felt an urge to escape and they got up
early and went to Cambridge. Cherry had never been and said
she wanted to see where he'd lived and studied all those years.
They strolled along King's Parade and Trinity Street, the formal
university buildings watching over them like a collection of stern
but fond headmasters. He pointed out which window had been
his bedroom and where he'd gone for bacon sandwiches on a
Sunday morning after a heavy night out.

She listened to him exclaim and laugh as the memories came
back, but it wasn't wistful nostalgia, which she was pleased about.
She didn't like not knowing about a great chunk of his life and
didn't want him to yearn for it and the girls that might have been
a part of it. After she'd seen the sights of his university days, they
decided to join the tourists.

It seemed a shame not to take a boat on the river, and Daniel
watched as Cherry lay back, her eyes closed against the unexpected warm sun, summer's last gasp before autumn fully took
hold.

As usual, his stomach flipped over when he looked at her. She
was so incredibly beautiful. Her long, dark lashes underscored
her eyes like naughty smiles, and the hollow of her collarbone was

bathed in sunshine in such an inviting way that he wanted to dip his fingers in its warmth. It wasn't just that he was deeply attracted to her. Daniel could spend hours with her without getting bored. She was clever and sometimes he wondered why she'd settled for a job that had seemed to him to be beneath her ability, but he'd respected her choice, and, anyway, she wasn't doing it anymore.

The recent, uneasy thought popped into his head again: Cherry didn't seem to be doing—or looking to be doing—anything. His face clouded over. He wouldn't have thought like that if his mother hadn't been so adamant about Cherry's motivation for being with him. She was wrong, Cherry was genuine, but still, Daniel couldn't shake a nagging sensation. Why was his mum so convinced?

He hadn't returned her messages yet, as he didn't know what to say to her. He was tired of trying to remain tactful under countless accusations of what his girlfriend was really like. He was tired of having to defend her. If he was honest, he was sick and tired of the entire subject and just wanted to get on with his life. He couldn't ignore Laura forever, but he knew that as soon as he called, she'd bring it up again. And then there was that nagging thought, the thing he couldn't quite tune out. He was becoming increasingly aware that since Cherry had moved in, she hadn't said anything about getting a job.

"What are you thinking about?" Cherry had one eye open and was watching him.

He smiled. "Nothing. Just hoping it doesn't rain."

Cherry gazed skyward. Wisps of white gauze over cornflower blue. "Don't think so." She reached up and let her hand brush against the draping tendrils of a weeping willow as they glided downstream.

"Nice to get out of London."

"Are you back in the hospital tomorrow?"

"Yes." He batted away a couple of midges, coming in too close to his face. "You?"

"Saturday . . . thought I'd have a lazy one. Watch a movie."

"And after that? I mean, the rest of the week?" He'd tried to sound casual, but he saw her stiffen.

"What do you mean?"

He pushed against the riverbed with his pole. "I just think it must be boring for you. Being in the flat all day."

"I'm not in it all day, I go out."

"Yes, but you were—are—always so ambitious. When you were at the agency. . ." He smiled at her.

She was silent for a moment. "Do you think I'm sponging?"

"No—"

"It's just I can't really pay you any rent at the moment, you know that."

"I don't want you to—"

"Bills are hard too."

"I know, it's okay—"

"But I do help out with groceries." She looked at him, her eyes defensive, hurt.

Daniel was squirming. He didn't really want this dissection of their domestic life, and was beginning to regret bringing up the subject.

"I'll change that. Starting next month."

She sounded determined, but the look on her face was one of resignation. He had no idea what she was talking about.

"I've been offered a job," she explained.

He stopped punting and looked at her in delight. "Wow! You have? What is it? Why didn't you say?"

"Because it's not great. Only assistant, not full agent, and the money's not much. I was going to keep looking, but—"

"Don't take it."

She looked at him in quiet exasperation. "I think, in light of what we've just discussed, I should."

"No, please. There's no rush. It was just that I was thinking . . . you're smart, you obviously want to do something with your life, and it must be so *frustrating* hanging around . . . when you're not out, that is." He was aware he was now ignoring the notion that she was taking advantage of living in his flat.

Cherry sat up and took his hands. "I really think I should. At least as a stopgap. I've got another idea. . . . I wasn't going to tell you yet, not until I have it all worked out, but I've been thinking of setting up a company. But until then, if I take this job, I could afford to pay you a thousand a month. I know it's not much—"

He put a finger to her lips, embarrassed for putting her on the spot. Ashamed too, because, strictly speaking, he didn't pay for his apartment either; it had been bought by his father. And here she was offering up what would be half—probably more than half—of her salary from a job she was too bright for and didn't want.

"I don't want to hear another word about it. More to the point, what's this company?"

She paused. "You sure?"

"Yes. Now come on, spill."

"Well, it's still early days, but with my knowledge of property . . . I think there's still money to be made in renovation."

"I'll invest in you."

"Really?"

"Of course."

She smiled politely. Daniel started punting again. A silence fell between them.

He felt he should make amends. "What are you thinking?"

"What if it . . . you know, the whole money thing, comes between us?"

"Why should it? Okay, okay, I know it just did, a bit, but now we know we can deal with it." He looked at her and guessed what she was thinking.

"It's not just us though, is it? Your mum thinks that's why I'm with you."

"That's got nothing to do with us."

"It has, though. I'm never going to be as rich as you, you know that. We'll always be different. You'll always end up paying more than me as long as we live your lifestyle. Sometimes it's a struggle to keep up, to not mind. I do have pride, you know." Upset, Cherry looked toward the bank.

Daniel stopped punting and sat down in the boat. "It's okay. . . ."

"I wish I could buy this, buy that, but I can't. That's just the way it is. If it bothers you, you must say so."

"I'm sorry, Cherry."

She turned to him then and gave a small smile. Allowed him to take her hands. "Of course, we could always move to Croydon."

He laughed. "Wouldn't bother me."

She grimaced. "Would me." And he laughed again.

"I'm afraid of what she'll do," she said quietly, "afraid I'll lose you."

She sounded so fragile, on the verge of defeat, and he felt a sudden fierce urge to fight for her. And a fear. He realized he'd let something toxic in, into what was theirs, their space, their love, and he was angry at himself for allowing his mother's words to influence him so much. He'd never been so happy, and if he wasn't careful, he'd drive Cherry away. And then he knew he couldn't go on for months with his mum's constant disapproval, her dissuasive arguments. It was like pulling a tooth—the more you thought about it, the worse it seemed. Better for his mother for it to be over. One short, sharp tug.

"Marry me."

Her look of shock made him laugh. Then he realized in a flash of panic, she might say no. He went onto one knee, the boat rocking precariously, and took her hand as she giggled and yelped.

"You'll tip us in!"

"Will you?"

She laughed again and a joy radiated over her face. "Yes!"

44

*B*ACKWARD AND FORWARD, SHE SLOWLY TILTED HER HAND, ENTRANCED by the leaping colors that flashed at her before vanishing and being replaced by other, seemingly brighter colors. It utterly captivated her and she knew she'd never get bored of it. They'd gone shopping immediately, Daniel saying he wanted to make it official, propose to her properly, and he apologized for not being better prepared.

At first, Cherry had been so stunned she didn't quite believe it. She allowed herself to be pulled along to a small, exclusive jewelers just five minutes from the boathouse, where she was presented as "my fiancée." The assistants had cooed over how "romantic" the proposal was, and she and he were asked if they had a preference for a particular type of stone. This made Cherry sit up and take notice; she had to exert some influence here if she was going to get what she wanted.

In fact, Cherry knew just what she wanted—a diamond, of course, a distinctive one—but there was an opportunity here to fantasize with a rainbow of jewels, some of which would appear later in her life in a different form. A gift for her birthday, their first child perhaps, an eternity ring. She tried on a sapphire first, surrounded by smaller diamonds, then an aquamarine, which was the color of the Caribbean Sea, then a bloodred ruby, before she sensed a note of restlessness in Daniel, and the assistant was clearly beginning to lose interest too. So she chose the one she'd spotted a full ten minutes before. It was a two-carat, square-cut diamond in a platinum band.

She left the shop wearing it. As she walked along, her right hand in Daniel's, with the other she rubbed her thumb against the underside of the ring, smiling and feeling its cold hardness in some sort of private acknowledgment that they were going to be friends for life.

After Daniel had left for work the next day, Cherry had tried her ring in each room, seeing how it looked in certain lights and against particular fabrics and then with numerous outfits too. She experimented in how it looked when she poured some water from the kettle, when she was on the phone, hand held aloft, when she typed on a keyboard. She became more delighted with every scenario. She draped the ivory curtains in the living room around her waist and twirled, her heart soaring with happiness. *She'd done it!* She was going to marry someone who would keep her from her old life forever. She would never have to worry about struggling, about money, or the pure drudgery of a dead-end, monotonous job, like her mum had had to endure. She was better than that and she could hold her head high.

Stuff Nicolas and his bigoted views. Maybe they'd buy a house on the Webb Estate. Imagine if it was next door. If Nicolas and his stupid wife just came out one day and there she was. She delighted herself for a good while with this notion and the imagined looks on their faces; then she began to grow restless and looked out the window. She wanted to go out and tell someone her good news. Take her ring on a trip to someone. She found herself driving toward Croydon and thought she'd surprise her mum. She'd go and see her and wait to see how long it took her to notice.

Wendy, so unused to impromptu visits, was convinced there was something wrong. In the end, Cherry had to show her the ring, just to shut her up, which spoiled her plan of waiting to see when she caught sight of the ten thousand pounds of rock on her finger.

"Oh, my good God," exclaimed Wendy, clutching her hand, "is that real?"

"Of course, it is."

"Are you . . . ?" Wendy's face lit up, and Cherry grinned and swerved to avoid the ensuing kiss.

"Congratulations!" Wendy clasped a hand over her mouth and her eyes shone with threatened tears of happiness. "To think, my girl, marrying . . . oh, Cherry . . . to *Daniel*. He's so *lovely*. . . . Honest, I liked him so much. Oh, it's like a fairy tale. Like that Catherine and William. I'll have to go somewhere proper for me dress, Designers at Debenhams or something. . . ."

As Cherry drove back home, she passed various old haunts that used to bring shame or dread. The restaurant where she'd worked, the school. They were nothing to her anymore. She was a different person, a better person, and they would never be able to threaten her again. As she escaped their stranglehold, she felt a new freedom and it was exhilarating.

She got back just before two, still in a state of bliss. As she walked past the porter, he called out to her, "You on your own, love?"

"Yes. Daniel's at work."

Ian stood up from the desk and disappeared into the room behind, calling back over his shoulder. "That'll explain this, then."

Cherry wondered idly what it was he'd gone to get, when her eye was suddenly drawn to an envelope tucked into a small cubbyhole, which she knew he reserved for registered mail that he signed for on the residents' behalf. It was a handwritten letter and it was addressed to Daniel. She was about to ask if he wanted her to take it for him, when she recognized the handwriting. Laura's. Without thinking, she snatched it up and slipped it into her handbag just as Ian came back through with a large bunch of flowers.

"Unless you have another admirer."

"They're beautiful!" She read the card tucked into the foliage. "'To my fiancée, on the first day of our engagement.'"

"Yep, ring's still blinding me," joked Ian, shielding his eyes from Cherry's finger.

Back in the flat, Cherry sat down on the lemon sofa and took out the letter. She fingered it for a moment, thinking. It was probably a plea, full of pathetic begging—but then again, it might have more poison about herself and she couldn't afford anything to upset this engagement. She'd already mentioned she wanted a winter wedding and was planning something for January—the sooner, the better, as far as she was concerned. There was still the hurdle of Laura, and despite all Daniel's protestations that he decided what went on in his life, Cherry was a little worried. Laura would have to keep her interfering nose out—and that included letters to Daniel blackening her name.

She opened it and read quickly:

> *Daniel,*
>
> *I'm sorry you don't feel you can return my calls and I know that's in part because you don't want to hear what I keep saying. But I can't stand back and watch when there's something very wrong. I also know you love Cherry and it's hard to hear negative things about the person you love, but all I ask is that you consider what I've said. Investigate it. Believe me when I say that I would not exaggerate just to destroy a relationship simply because I didn't approve. This is a situation much more serious than that. Maybe you could do some simple unobtrusive inquiries. Remember the story about her grandmother who died—the one Cherry told her boss? That's exactly what they said and yet she didn't mention anything to us at all. Why not? Was it not true? Or perhaps there's something else, something about her past that you could find out. Has she ever told you about any of her ex-boyfriends? Who they were? Why it ended?*
>
> *If you find that there's nothing in my fear, then you can tell me so and I'll back off, but please just try. I don't care what she does to me, as long as you try, and in a way I wish she would do something, just so you could see. It goes without saying that I miss you hugely and I want more than anything for us to be on speaking terms again.*
>
> *With love,*
> *Mum*

Cherry placed the letter on her lap and knew immediately that Daniel mustn't see it. It would have to get lost, mislaid by Ian.

There was a chance he'd mention it to Daniel, might even say it was from Laura; but as Daniel was not talking to her, he'd probably not bother to find out what it had contained. She stood suddenly. Laura didn't yet know of the engagement, but Cherry knew Daniel would have to tell her. His mum needed to back right off and do what any prospective mother-in-law did when her son got married: recognize her new, diminished place in his life and *keep her mouth shut*. Laura needed to know whom she was dealing with and what was best for her. Cherry screwed up the letter and stuffed it in her pocket.

She waited until Monday, as there was a better chance that Howard would not be at the golf course. Daniel had mentioned which one he was a member of, and as she drove through the gates of the Royal Surrey Golf Club, she saw it was as exclusive as it had looked online. With the car wheels crunching on the gravel, she slowly passed the clubhouse, with its ivy-clad brick, and headed for the car park.

Cherry stopped the car in a quiet corner, where no one else was around, but where she could still see the clubhouse. She got out and started to walk toward the entrance. Pushing open the large double doors, she stepped inside. It smelled of beeswax and money, and the carpet was thick and plush. As she walked along, she noticed wooden boards hung on the walls listing winners of tournaments. She stopped and read their gold lettering, rows of names going back to 1875. Then she saw his name. *Mr. Howard Cavendish, 2015 winner of the Winter league.* It was paired with a *Mrs. Marianne Parker.* They also won in 2014, 2012, and 2011. *Wow, quite a couple.* They disappeared for a while, but then she saw them listed again in 1995. It was a long gap and Cherry wondered what had happened; maybe they'd been off form. The most recent winners also had their photograph displayed, and Cherry's eyes were drawn to one of Howard with Marianne. She studied it, looking for something of interest. He had his arm around her rather broad shoulders and both were smiling at the camera.

"Can I help you?"

A middle-aged man, dressed in a blazer and pale chinos, had stopped beside her.

He was the kind of man who knew everything about his golf club, a man who would have very strong ideas about who should be a member and the etiquette involved. She was glad she'd worn one of the suits from her days at the agency and she gave him a disarming smile. "Are you the club secretary?"

"Yes," he said expectantly, clearly waiting for her to tell him who she was.

"I was just wondering if you could give me some membership information, a brochure or something?"

His suspicion receded slightly and she was handed a glossy brochure, then had to listen to a sales spiel. After a few smiles and complimentary comments about the course, she managed to escape. She made her way back to the car and sat inside, wondering what to do. Howard spent a lot of time here, she knew, and she wanted to find out why. She opened the brochure and dialed the number printed on the inside cover, disguising her voice.

"Oh, hello, I'm meant to be meeting a friend of mine, Marianne Parker, today, only I've forgotten what time we said, and I can't get hold of her. Could you possibly tell me our tee time? Two o'clock? Oh, my, I've missed it, haven't I? I'll have to catch up with her later. I'm so sorry to have bothered you." She hung up before he asked her any more.

So Marianne was here. It might be worth waiting a while. Chucking the brochure on the seat, Cherry settled back. After about an hour, she saw a woman, who looked like the woman in the photo, exit the clubhouse. Cherry narrowed her eyes, feeling certain from her build, her brown hair, that she was Marianne. She watched Marianne talk to a female friend she'd come out with; after a couple of minutes, they embraced and went to their separate cars. Marianne got into a BMW, a new convertible in silver. Cherry waited until she drove off and then carefully, cautiously, followed.

Marianne headed back into town, along the A3, and Cherry made sure she stayed at least two cars behind all the way. They crossed the river at Battersea Bridge and then headed north toward Kensington; the roads got busier and the drivers more erratic, the farther into town they went. Cherry almost lost her a couple of times. When they reached Swiss Cottage, Marianne turned off toward Hampstead into what were residential streets. Audis and Range Rovers jammed up against one another in quiet exclusivity. Then the BMW slowed and pulled into a space outside a three-story, redbrick Victorian terrace home. Cherry stayed back and watched as Marianne locked the car and made her way up the path to the storm porch and into the house. Cherry waited a moment, wondering what to do next, but there was nothing more to see.

She was just starting to pull away when another car came toward her from the opposite direction. Alarmed, she quickly reversed and parked back against the curb. The other driver slid into a space just a little farther up the street, undid the belt, and climbed out. Keeping her head down, Cherry watched as Howard went up the path to Marianne's house. *Howard!* She waited for him to ring the bell, but her eyes widened as she saw him take out his own key and let himself in. Cherry stared at the shut door in excitement and let out a little laugh. *So that's what he was up to!* And for some time, judging by the years of photos of them together. Cherry thought about the woman she'd just seen. She was a brunette to Laura's blond complexion, and more sturdy, more ruddy-cheeked. Cherry wondered what it was like knowing your husband's mistress was not as pretty as you. Must be even more of a punch in the gut. She slipped the car into gear and drove away.

45

*I*T WAS TIME FOR AN APOLOGY. TIME TO EAT HUMBLE PIE AND ADMIT she was wrong. She'd been too harsh, too quick to judge. This, Laura admitted, heavyhearted, about her abominable behavior. She waited in some trepidation at the front door, and as she glanced around, she noticed how the nights were drawing in. It was cloudy and the still grayness seemed to blanket everything. A few seconds later, her buzz was answered.

"I'm sorry," she said anxiously, quickly, as she was feeling brittle and wasn't sure if she'd be able to hold it together if Isabella was still angry with her. "I completely overreacted and I shouldn't have spoken to you like that."

Isabella deliberated a moment; then she opened the door wider and indicated for Laura to come in.

The relief was so great she thought she might burst into tears, but that would be absurd, so she bit the inside of her cheeks to stop herself. She seemed on the verge of tears too often now.

"Drink?" asked Isabella as she led her into the drawing room, where Laura had come for the party just a few days before.

"Yes, please," and she watched silently as Isabella mixed two gin and tonics. "It was a lovely party," she started feebly.

"I think we both know that's not true," said Izzy, handing her a glass, "at least not for you."

Laura was chastened. "Sorry. But I did expressly ask you *not* to set me up with him."

"I didn't set you up—he just happened to be at the same dinner party. He and Richard have been doing some work together, and Richard wanted to extend the alliance socially. He was there as Richard's guest. . . ."

"Oh, God, now I feel even worse. . . ."

"But I admit I did place you next to each other at dinner. Not to set you up," she said quickly, "but I just thought you might enjoy the company. No, not like that, I don't mean that you're . . . lonely or anything, it's just everyone knows each other inside out. I thought it might be fun for you, someone new."

Laura ruefully remembered her polite, aloof responses over dinner. "I don't think it was much fun for him."

She was half-expecting an admonishment of some kind, but Isabella took a long swallow of her drink, then said: "He'll get over it."

There it was again, the dam bursting and relief swamping her, and she started to well up. *For God's sake! This is ridiculous.* She blinked quickly, knowing this overreaction to a kindness, a much-needed reconciliation, was all because of Daniel and, to some extent, Howard. She hadn't had a reply to her letter and was beginning to wonder if she ever would. What if they didn't speak before Christmas, or Christmas passed them by altogether? What if it went on even longer, for a year, two? Perhaps they'd just bump into each other on the street one day. Nod an acknowledgment to each other. Perhaps so much time would pass, they'd get used to being without each other—but this thought was so unbearably sad, it almost made her stagger, collapse weakly onto the sofa.

"Laura, is everything okay?"

She'd barely heard the question and adjusted her gaze so she was refocusing on her friend.

"You seem a bit . . ."

"What?" Her voice caught.

"Preoccupied. Has something happened?"

Laura tried to smile. "Like what?"

"I don't know."

"Honestly, things couldn't be better."

Izzy didn't believe her, she could tell.

"You can talk to me, you know. I'm your friend. Forget this silly little spat." Izzy squeezed her arm warmly, softened her voice. "You and I, we've been through everything."

She almost confessed then. She longed to, in her head. But how did she start? The lie had made her too ashamed—she couldn't bear for anyone else to know what she'd done, and she was afraid of what Izzy would think of her. She looked at Izzy's face, open and kind, and forced a smile. "Really, there's nothing."

Izzy studied her carefully, then acknowledged she was being pushed away. She looked hurt. "Fine," she said quietly, and in that word, Laura felt a door close between them. It was awkward then, and she heard herself making excuses.

"Suppose I should be getting back. Haven't fed Moses yet." She knew Izzy was aware she was just making stuff up. It was feeble and depressing, and she suddenly had to get out of there. Usually, when they said good-bye, they had something in the future to look forward to: *"See you tomorrow." "Meet you for lunch, Tuesday." "I'll give you a call about yoga."* This time, there was nothing.

"See you soon," Laura eventually went for as she briefly kissed Isabella's cheek and then walked down the path and looked for a cab. She hesitated before looking back, as she was unsure of what Izzy's expression would be. Then, when she did, meaning to smile and reassure them both, she just caught sight of the front door as it was closed shut.

The house was cold when she got in, and dark. She switched on the heating and went to make herself some tea, but when she got the milk from the fridge, she saw a half bottle of wine and poured a glass of that instead. She knew drinking wasn't going to help with her melancholy mood, but what the hell. She debated over whether to make anything to eat and then decided she would, for Howard too, as it was his first day back after a work conference. He hadn't texted her to say he'd be late.

Having something to do made her feel a little better and she switched the radio on and started a Bolognese sauce. By the time she heard the elevator come up from the den, dinner was ready. She decided that instead of the dining room, they could eat in the kitchen tonight. It would make a change and would be good for them to sit somewhere different, somewhere old habits would not take hold. She was just setting the table as Howard walked in. He stopped when he saw what she was doing.

"Hi. Hungry?" she asked brightly, her hands full of spoons and forks.

He looked across at the stove.

"It's spaghetti Bolognese."

Howard nodded and went to wash his hands at the sink.

"Can I get you a drink?"

Howard tensed. "Will you stop?"

"Stop what?"

"This stupid pretense."

Laura smiled, genuinely confused, which seemed to irritate him more. Then she noticed how cold he was, how angry.

"I never had you down as being so . . ."

"What?"

He hesitated. "Spiteful."

She was startled to find how much he could still hurt her. He put his hand in his pocket and pulled out a letter, then put it on the breakfast bar. She looked at the envelope. It was addressed to Marianne Parker. She instinctively recoiled. *His girlfriend's letters? Why is he bringing them home?* Then she looked closer, frowning. The handwriting . . . *It's mine.* She slowly drew the envelope toward her.

"Open it. Although, of course, you already know what's inside."

She pulled out the notepaper—*her* notepaper from her writing desk—and unfolded the letter.

Dear Marianne,

I've been wanting to write this for a while, but it's never quite seemed the right moment. And then I realized there never was going to be a right moment. What was I waiting for? You to do the decent

thing and get your bloodsucking proboscis out of my husband? I'm
sick of being ignored, taken advantage of. You are a vile human
being. You just take what you want without any thought to the effect
it might have on others. And you do this with seemingly no con-
science. I hope you're punished for this, that the worst things happen
to you and your family. I hope you suffer some horrible accident. It
would be karma if it were disfiguring.

It would be justice.

There, I feel better now. Some things just have to be said.

Laura Cavendish.

She dropped the letter like it was corroding the skin on her fingertips. "I didn't write this."

Howard pulled a face.

"I promise, I didn't." But it looked like her handwriting. Then in a rush, she knew. Her mind grew stricken as she tried to work it out. How had Cherry done it? How did she know what her handwriting was like? How had she managed to forge it so well, and when had she gotten the notepaper? She saw Howard watching her.

"Howard, Cherry's forged this note, made it look like it was from me." She pushed the letter toward him. "It *looks* like my handwriting, but it's not quite the same." Suddenly she noticed something. "Look at the *P*'s, I don't quite join the loop, and she does, *look*."

He sat silently for a moment and she could tell he was trying to hold his temper. "*Cherry?* Really, Laura? In a minute, you're going to tell me she's also responsible for the crisis in the Middle East and global warming."

"No, no. You have to listen. Howard, about a month ago, she came to my office. Told me she knew that I'd lied about Daniel. And she said she was going to take everything away from me. She's *threatening* me. Somehow she got this paper. She's been in the house. . . ." The thought chilled her.

"Why didn't you say anything about this before?"

"I didn't think you'd believe me." She could tell he didn't now, and it made her frustrated. She looked at the letter again. "How did you get this, anyway?"

"It arrived this morning."

"And you just happened to drop by and be there to comfort Marianne? I thought you were supposed to be at a work conference?"

"Laura, I want a divorce."

Something clamped around her heart and stopped it. *"What?"*

"Marianne's leaving her husband."

"How nice for you."

"Don't be like that."

"Like what? You want me to congratulate the two of you? I've had to stand by and turn a blind eye for *years* while the two of you . . . !" Laura exploded.

"I'm sorry."

"No, you're not. You're thinking of yourself."

"Okay, yes, mostly I am. I'm unhappy, aren't you?"

Laura didn't dare answer; she didn't want to admit it.

"It's been *years,* Laura. How long are we supposed to go on? Do you want to spend the rest of your life living like this? The two of us barely functioning together? Don't you think you'll look back and think it was time—valuable, *precious* time—wasted? How much longer do the two of us even have? In a few years, I'll be sixty. *Sixty!* If I can't do something about it now, when do I change things? When I'm seventy? Eighty? But, also, I think you're unhappy too. If I go, it leaves you free to change things. Maybe find someone else."

Anger burned in her. "I don't need your relationship counseling, thanks. I planned for the first marriage to work."

He looked at her sadly. "So did I." Then he stood. "I think it's better if I don't stay. For what it's worth, I was at a conference. Marianne came to see me this morning at the office."

Of course, it would be that the one time she confronted him on his infidelity, he was innocent. Laura hated the whole sorry situation. She wanted to kick and scream at the unfairness of it all.

He picked up his jacket. "Has Daniel been in touch?" he asked quietly.

"No."

There seemed nothing else to say. Howard went into the hall-

way. Laura waited, then, urged by a need to see him leave, maybe
to hope he wouldn't, followed.

"Are you all right?"

"Fantastic, considering my husband's just left me."

"You can divorce me. You have the grounds. But, actually, I
meant, are you all right about Daniel?"

Tears burned in Laura's eyes. She wanted to say no, wanted
him to come and comfort her, for them to have a relationship where
this could happen. But they didn't, and loneliness swamped her and
made her bitter.

"Seems he takes after his father in choosing the wrong woman."

She'd meant Marianne, but too late realized it could have been
her. Humiliated, she turned and went back into the kitchen. She
waited until she heard the elevator descend to the basement and
knew Howard would be getting into his car. Sure enough, she
heard the vehicle elevator rise. Somewhere out there, he drove
off to the woman he loved. She picked up her wine and her hand
shook. Was this all part of her punishment? Had she started herself along this long, awful, destructive path? The wine stuck in her
throat.

I am a liar.

The house seemed very big and very empty when Laura got up
the next morning. For the first time since she'd moved in, she
didn't feel entirely comfortable in it. She suddenly "saw" it, was
conscious of doors, walls, and furniture. Things that she'd been so
used to that they were comfortingly invisible suddenly appeared
odd, as if she didn't quite recognize them. A chair in the corner of
the living room. Mirrors reflecting her face back at her. She was
keen to leave it and get to work as quickly as possible.

She got a cab, which took her as far as Drury Lane. There was
some disruption up ahead, the traffic was solid; and even as they
waited, an ambulance wailed behind them, desperate to reach its
injured charge, but unable to move. Cars inched up onto pavements. Laura decided to walk the rest of the way. In the time
she'd paid the driver and left the cab, the ambulance had edged

forward only another few meters and she felt for the person who was waiting for it. *Never be in an emergency in London,* she thought ruefully. *You could lie bleeding to death and no one could get to you because of the congestion.* She headed in the direction of whatever crisis was taking place, planning to turn down a side street.

Just before she veered away, she looked up toward the incident. Two or three cars had obviously made contact—she could make out some crushed doors and a ruptured hood. Then, awfully, a man, a cyclist lying in the road. His bike was a short distance from his feet, the back wheel mangled. She was about to go and see if she could help, but there was an ambulance car already there, with two paramedics obviously waiting for their backup. The police were holding people back. She shuddered and hoped he was okay. He looked young; he had a backpack on. She thought about his mother when the ambulance finally went past her, lights flashing frantically, a desolate wail every now and then to remind people to get out of the way.

She turned off down a narrow street, then another, and headed toward the office. She walked quickly; the accident had unsettled her even more and she wanted to get to work. The show was gearing up for filming and the heads of departments—art, costume, makeup, camera, and the director—would start prepping in a couple of weeks. When she thought about that, she got the familiar surge of excitement, mixed with an anxiety-infused thrill at what they were about to begin, the juggernaut of production, all for a few minutes a day caught on camera. She had to go and visit some locations today and later meet with the casting director to view tapes of auditions for some of the secondary characters.

Laura's right shoe was sticking to the pavement, so, in disgust, she stopped and lifted her foot behind her. *Chewing gum! Yuck!* As she was trying to scrape it off, there was a noise, a cough. Someone behind her had stopped as well. She lowered her foot and stood there for a minute, fear seeping in as an acknowledgment of her stupidity crept up on her. She was in a sort of quiet backstreet, enclosed by buildings on both sides, a link between two thoroughfares. She sensed the tension of someone holding their breath. Her heart started hammering and she saw there were only a few yards to the end of the street. People crossed in front of her. People who wouldn't know if she was attacked in this narrow alley. She suddenly ran forward, her foot feeling tacky, holding her back, as she grasped for the exit, certain someone was following her. She burst into the road and ran wildly away from the alley, only stopping when she was a good distance away. There were plenty of people around her now. Only then could she look back.

There was no one there. No one except for busy commuters and meandering tourists, who were all intent on their own agendas and took no notice of her. She stared at the opening to the alley, but nobody came out. She waited for what seemed an age, made herself stay a bit longer, then wondered if she should go back and see if anyone was loitering in there, but she shrank at the idea. No, she wanted the sanctuary of her office and to immerse herself in her work. It was the only thing that could take her mind off her worries. She turned and hurried away.

46

Friday, October 23

*I*T WAS AMAZING HOW QUICKLY A PERSON COULD FEEL AT HOME, thought Cherry as she broke the eggs into the butter and sugar mixture and pressed the button on her—correction, *their*—brand-new candy-apple-red KitchenAid. The blades beat obligingly, and after a few seconds, she switched it off. It had been over a month since Daniel had thrown his mother out, and three weeks since their engagement, and she was baking a cake. Just a little something for him, a surprise while he was out with his friends before he went back to the grueling schedule at the hospital, but it could just as easily be a celebration. An anniversary.

Sometimes she couldn't believe her luck. She was living in the most amazing apartment, which would be her—*their*—home for the foreseeable future, and this was just the beginning of the most wonderful life with the most wonderful man. He'd given her the biggest closet, the most drawer space, and his credit card to buy a few things to "make it feel like home." He'd laughingly begged to be let off any shopping trips, and both of them knew she'd rather go alone anyway. She'd even finally bought his—*their*—new sheets. She added the flour, then spooned the finished cake mix into the two tins and put them in the oven. Satisfied, she set the timer.

While the cake was cooking, she would think about her business idea. Do a bit of research. It was important to keep up the appearance of looking for a vocation, even if she made it part-time once they were married. She sat with Daniel's laptop on the perfect lemon sofa, framed by the cream-and-gold-papered walls, imagining what she looked like. She'd achieved a level of living that she reveled in proudly, and all she had to do was exist in it to feel quietly euphoric.

To think, Laura had done her utmost to stop this from happening, to stop her from sitting on this sofa, living in this flat. Laura would've gladly ruined her whole life without a second thought. She would still stop it if she could. Cherry could not allow her to think she was a pushover, that she could be bullied. When she'd said she was going to show Laura what it was like to have someone trample all over everything you cared about, she'd meant it. It was the only way the woman would understand what it felt like. Would maybe think twice before doing it again. Because a part of Cherry was scared that all this could still be taken away from her. She'd never wanted to fall out with Laura, but Laura had made their relationship impossible with what she'd tried to do.

She lay back and let her eyes rest on the oil she'd bought for Daniel in Saint-Tropez. Although repaired, it would never be as good as it was before she'd slashed it, but it had been the best investment she'd ever made. Soon she would go back to her mother's and collect the rest of her things. She hadn't wanted to go before now, as she was enjoying herself too much. Most of it, she just wanted to be rid of, the old Cherry having been annihilated long ago, but there were the books. Boxes and boxes of them. The books were innocent. They were gateways to a different future, a new life, and she wanted to keep them with her. She was expecting Wendy to suggest she bring Daniel round for tea, something that she would stall indefinitely. The old feelings of guilt crept back in; and she thought, not for the first time, that if her mum wasn't so *wrong*, she wouldn't have to feel this way.

She wondered idly how long she and Daniel could go on in this blissful bubble—without either mother getting in the way. As far as she knew, Laura still hadn't spoken to him, and Cherry had made sure he hadn't gotten her letter. He'd spoken to his father though. It had been last week and she'd had to hide her delight when Daniel had told her that Howard had left Laura. *Good.* Apparently, he'd been screwing that Marianne for years, which was just as she'd suspected. He'd rung Daniel and told him the minimum, just that they were getting divorced, and Daniel wasn't to worry. She'd held Daniel's hand supportively as he repeated the conversation and hoped it had been her letter that had triggered the decision. It had taken her quite a lot of practice to get the handwriting just right. How smooth was the writing? Did Laura keep her pen on the paper? Were there any areas where the pressure on the pen was lighter or firmer? Then she made a master alphabet and practiced and practiced before composing her note. She'd gambled on only two things: Howard not turning up at the golf club while she'd done her investigating, and Marianne not recognizing Daniel's car—something she was fairly confident about, since Marianne wasn't likely to have spent any time at the Cavendishes' house. And it had been a stroke of luck Howard hadn't seen her. Then it had just been a matter of posting the letter, from a place away from Chelsea and Croydon. She'd settled on the center of town and popped into John Lewis and ordered her bakeware at the same time. It was amazing how you could just go around the shop picking things and then someone would arrange to have them delivered, like you were the lady of the manor. You didn't have to go online and do it yourself or anything.

The timer went off. Cherry went back into the kitchen and pulled the cakes out of the oven. She sniffed approvingly, then left them to cool. She slipped on her jacket and grabbed her keys. *Her* keys! *Her own* set! Life was good. And now she was going to get another little surprise, something that would be just hers and Daniel's.

Cherry tried to keep her anger buttoned down, but it was hard when she saw puppies and kittens desperate to get out, their soft paws clambering over one another, trying to get a grip on the glass sides of their boxes as she walked past, eager for her attention. They'd probably been bought from puppy mills, poor things, been taken straight from their mothers and dumped in this pet shop. She knelt down by one of the cages. Smiled at the soft balls of fur that wanted to get to her, would probably purr deafeningly from human contact if she picked one up. These were the unlucky ones; their lives were destined by the fortunes of their birth. No nurturing start in life from a reputable breeder and, likely, a questionable home when—if—they were ever bought by someone. What kind of future did they have? It was always the same in life; it was all about where you were born, and to whom.

She gazed at the kittens, all five of them, but it was too many to deal with, and, anyway, Daniel preferred dogs. There were fewer puppies, just two left of a litter of three cocker spaniels. *Same as Laura had when she was young,* Cherry remembered. With light brown, almost golden fur, the male had a white patch on his tummy. She indicated the puppies to the man who ran the place, who was feeding some fish.

"They ever get walked?"

"Every day," he said brightly, automatically.

She thought about challenging him—it was obvious he was lying—but it probably wouldn't change things. "I'll take the boy," she said, and he placed the puppy carefully in a pet carry box, with holes punched in the side. He produced a birth certificate and medical documents, which she took with the same apathy as he gave them.

"You want a leash?"

She glanced up at a rack behind the cash register. "Yes, please."

As she walked out of the shop, she looked back at the remaining puppy. She was standing still, watching silently, and Cherry suddenly got a pang of guilt. The poor thing never saw daylight, and had no space to run around. She probably didn't have any care or comfort at all beyond what was necessary to keep her as a commodity, something to make money from. And Cherry had just taken her brother. She hesitated. Maybe there was a way to end her misery in this place.

"I'll take the other one as well," said Cherry.

The puppy wagged her tail as she was also lifted out of the pen. Cherry got out her purse.

"Another leash?" asked the man.

"No . . . it's okay," said Cherry. "But I will have one of those large boxes of hamster food."

She drove to Richmond Park, the box of puppies on the front seat. Once parked, she picked it up, along with the plastic bag with the leash and the hamster food. The two little wriggling soft bundles tried to lick at her hands through the holes in the cardboard box. She pulled her coat tight and walked through the park, one of the few places in London where you could actually get away from people. Ahead she saw a copse of conifers; she made her way toward them. As she ducked under, the sounds of the open spaces shrank away. She was hidden and alone.

Kneeling on the soft earth, she opened the box and the two puppies were delighted to see her. She scratched each one under the chin. The sound of brakes rasping to a stop made her look up and she stiffened as a kid came close by on his bike. She watched through the trees as he spun his pedals, looking at the chain for something, then after a few seconds, rode off. She waited until it was quiet, the puppies licking her hand; then she took the girl out of the box. *It would've been cruel to leave it,* she told herself; and she could, at least, make it quick. Putting both her hands around its neck, she twisted sharply. It went limp. She took the box of hamster food and discarded the contents onto the ground, then placed the unmoving puppy inside the empty box. Then she got out her phone and dialed.

"Hello, I'm calling to report a cruelty . . . some kittens. It's a pet shop that I've just been in. They seemed really distressed, thin. And I saw the guy who worked there—he . . . God, it was awful. He just threw one back into the glass cage. From a distance, as if it was a ball. Lobbed it. He thought I was on the other side of the shop, looking around. No, I didn't buy any. Yes, it's Pet's Kingdom in Worcester Park. My name? It's Polly Hammond." She gave a false number and continued, even more desperately now. "You will go there, won't you? That's what the RSPCA does? I'm sure they're from puppy mills. Can't you close places like this down?"

She checked her watch. Daniel would be home in two hours. Just enough time to go to the post office, then get back to ice the cake. She clipped the leash onto the other puppy, and he was delighted that he was getting a walk outdoors, probably the first since he'd been born. She watched as his paws bounded through the grass—real grass!—and her heart warmed at his obvious euphoria. Then a sudden sharp intake of breath. She hadn't bought one of those ball-throwing things! *How utterly thoughtless.* Dismayed, Cherry apologized to . . . Rufus. She would call him Rufus and vowed to make it up to him as soon as she got to some shops.

"This is *delicious,*" said Daniel, again, as he took a large bite out of his second slice of cake. Cherry leaned over the back of his chair, kissed him on the cheek. "You're sure it's not the beer making it taste good?"

"No way. Will and Jonny say hello, by the way."

"Hello back."

"He's—Will's—waiting to hear on an interview. Big promotion if he gets it."

"So, it seems, you guys had a good time?"

"Great." Daniel was suddenly conscious it was one of his rare days off. "You didn't mind me going off with the guys, did you?"

"Course not. I've been very busy. . . ."

"Oh yes?" He grabbed her, pulled her onto his lap, and planted a chocolate-tasting kiss on her lips. "Doing what? Other than acquiring our new friend here." He reached down to pick up the puppy, and the dog immediately tried to lick his face.

"Rufus! Naughty!" Cherry took him away. "You don't mind, do you?"

"No, I told you, he's great. You do know that with me at the hospital, you're the one most likely to be cleaning up the accidents on the floor?"

"I'm going to have him expertly trained in no time." She put her arms around his neck. "And in answer to your question, I've been planning a very special day."

"Aha . . . and do I get a say on this very special day?"

"Of course. As long as you think it should be in January." She held her breath a moment as she watched him mull it over.

"Bit cold?"

"Honeymoon in the Caribbean?"

He nodded, good point.

"Very soon? It's only, what, three months away?"

"Do you really want me talking weddings any longer? I could make it stretch a year, if you prefer."

He laughed. "No thanks."

She was pleased to have gotten her way. "I've also found a venue. If you like it, we can start sending out invitations."

"Yes." He sounded wistful.

"What's up?"

"Oh, you know, parents getting divorced. The whole thing with Mum . . . I haven't even told her we're engaged yet."

"Maybe we should just run away," she said lightly, "get married on a beach somewhere."

"It would save a lot of hassle. Quick, easy, just us two."

She caught her breath. She hadn't thought for a moment he'd take it seriously, but it was a brilliant idea, actually. "You know, I think you can organize them in as little as a couple of weeks."

"Really? It sounds great."

"Could you get the time off work?"

He laughed. "You're serious."

Her face crumpled. "You're not?"

"Well, I don't know. . . . I mean, we want our family and friends there, don't we?" Cherry got off his lap. "Oh, God, sorry, I didn't realize . . . I thought we were just messing about." He followed her to the kitchen and took the plate from her hands and put it in the dishwasher. Then he laced his fingers into hers. "Is this because you think my mum's going to ruin it?"

"She's not going to be thrilled. No doubt she'll try and stop it."

"How's she going to do that?"

It irritated her, the way he wasn't taking her concerns seriously, and she pulled away.

"Cherry, stop. Sorry. It's just . . . you know I love you. We're

what's important now. This thing that's going on with my mum . . .
well, I'm sure it'll get sorted out. We've got three months."

"She'll try and put you off me."

"Let her try."

"She'll make up some story again. Tell you about things I've
supposedly done."

"I don't think she will, you know"—Cherry frowned as Daniel
spoke—"but if she does, I'll put her right."

She mulled over his words, waiting to be mollified. "You know,
I've also been working on my business plan today. It's coming
along well. Just in case you were thinking—"

He drew her to him. "Shush. I do not think you are with me because of my money, despite what my mother may say."

She gazed at him, checking for genuineness, then wrapped her
arms around his neck and gently kissed him on the lips.

47

Monday, October 26

SHE SOMETIMES THOUGHT SHE WAS GOING MAD. SHE *WAS* MAD. HOW
had she gotten caught up in this? Laura couldn't see a way out.
Fear followed her everywhere. She would sit in the evenings, trying to watch television, but unable to concentrate fully as a mix of
anxiety and loneliness settled on the sofa next to her. She hated
being able to see through to the hallway, dark and silent from
where she perched on the sofa, so Laura started to leave all the
downstairs lights blazing. This way, there was something to welcome her when she got up to get another drink or just wandered
into the kitchen, wondering whether she could be bothered to
make something to eat.

At night, she was more conscious than she ever thought possible of Howard's absence and her lone presence in the house.
She'd started bolting the front door, top and bottom, at first just
when she went to bed, then as soon as she got in from work. She
rarely walked anywhere, preferring the safe capsule of the cab.
She was afraid of being followed. She was afraid of not knowing
for certain if she *had* been followed.

She walked up the stairs to her office now, the drizzly Monday
morning clawing at the windows outside. Willow went to make

her a filter coffee from the machine in the kitchen. Laura went into her office, switched on her laptop, and looked to see if the end-of-series latest draft was in. Her writer had promised it for today, but writers often promised things, then didn't always stick to deadlines. In a few weeks, they would start shooting and she was grateful for the distraction that would bring. Her mobile rang and she looked at the name on the screen, then picked up.

"Alison."

"Hello, Laura."

"How are you?"

"Not great."

Alert, Laura sat up straight.

"I've had our lead on the phone."

Laura was instantly wary. Why would Julie call the channel and not her?

"I'm afraid I've got some pretty bad news. She's been sent a package, from you, the note said. It arrived this morning."

Cold fingers of dread walked down Laura's spine. "What was it?"

Alison sighed. "I don't quite know how to say this. It was a dead puppy."

"What?" she whispered.

"In some sort of box. The note also said something about her solving her first crime."

"Christ!"

"She was hysterical. Still could be, all things considered."

"I'll call her."

"No."

"But I need to—"

"Laura, Julie doesn't want to talk to you. To anyone, in fact. She's walked."

"*What?*"

"We need to stand everyone down."

Willow appeared at the door with the coffee, but Laura furiously waved her away and she cowered out.

"Now, just a minute . . . she can't just walk off the production!"

"We can sue her if we want, but I think she'll have a pretty good case when she's been receiving threatening parcels in the post."

"We'll recast."

"*Who?* You know funding was subject to casting. The Americans won't go for it."

"So you're *canceling* the show."

"Laura, we don't have a lead actress. We don't have a show."

She started to panic. "You have to let me talk to her. I'm going to call her now."

"She won't answer. She's switched off her phone. Thinks there's a possibility someone's got the number . . . ," Alison trailed off, leaving a heavy silence in the air.

"Alison, you know this has nothing to do with me, don't you?"

"Of course, but that's not the point. Someone's got it in for her. Do you know who?"

She thought about lying, but considering the magnitude of the disaster, realized she had to give a worthy-enough explanation.

"They haven't got it in for Julie. I think it might . . . It's me. There's a girl, a stupid girl, who's on some fantasized vendetta."

"I see. Are you calling the police?"

Laura paused. "Are you?"

"Julie wants it hushed up. Nothing to the press, either, obviously. I don't think we'll need the police in order to get our insurance payment." She paused. "Laura, how did this girl get Julie's address?"

Laura went cold, glanced guiltily around her office. "I have no idea." She held her breath, waited for Alison to say something more; for a moment, she thought she was going to, but then: "Right. I'm sorry, Laura, it seems like a sad end. The lawyers will be in touch. We'll have to catch up again, when all this has blown over."

When would that be? Months, years, probably never. And ITV wouldn't be the only door slammed in her face. The abrupt end of such a high-profile show would be around town in a matter of days. Through the office window, she saw Willow rise from her desk, and, then seeing her, she sat down again.

Laura sat in silence as the true scale of her loss started to sink in. The production fee, the repeats, the second, third, fourth series. The international sales, the DVDs. The hoped-for accolades.

Her reputation. Her company. Her career. All gone. She felt a sudden surge of rage. *How dare she!* Laura grabbed her bag and, tight-lipped, strode out of the office.

Laura's anger didn't subside in the cab, rather it smoldered into red-hot embers that would reignite the minute they were aggravated. She felt herself tense as they got nearer Daniel's flat . . . and then she saw her. Walking along, as happy as you like, in her skinny pants, designer jacket and heels, expensive bag held over her shoulder with stylish, glove-clad hands. She was casting benevolent smiles around as she might, seeing as she'd wormed her way into the biggest scam she could. Laura thrust some cash at the driver, then got out and marched up behind her. When she was within touching distance, she clamped a hand on her shoulder and Cherry reeled around. Pushed her glasses onto the top of her head.

"Laura! You scared me."

"What the *fuck* do you think you're playing at?"

"I beg your pardon?"

"Oh, cut the act. You know exactly what I'm talking about."

Cherry cast an eye sideways at the curious glances they were getting from passing shoppers. "Has something happened?"

"You get a kick out of posting dead animals to random strangers? Do you know what this has cost me?"

"I really don't know what you mean, Laura, but I don't like your tone."

"The show is canceled and *you* . . ." She was shaking with anger and jabbed her finger at Cherry's face—

Suddenly she stopped. She was going to shout at her more, threaten her, but Cherry didn't look scared, not even unnerved. Her eyes were cold. A ripple of unease went through Laura. She took a deep breath. "Whatever it is you're doing, whatever vendetta you're on, I'd like it to stop. This has gone too far. What you've done . . . it's completely unreasonable. You're angry with me, and I understand that, but this is . . . well, completely disproportionate."

Cherry was quietly watching her. *Maybe*, thought Laura, *maybe I'm getting through.* The silence went on for longer. And longer.

"Boo!" Cherry was right up in her face.

Laura gasped out a strangled scream, staggered back.

"You know I had a bit of bad luck recently. Someone hacked into my account, sent a tweet that my boss thought was from me. Got me fired."

Laura's eyes flickered with guilt and she quickly looked away.

"What does it feel like to lose your job, Laura?"

"You're insane," she whispered.

"Sounds like you're having a run of bad luck too. The divorce, the show . . . You know, they say it comes in threes. I really hope that's not true."

Laura stared at her, outraged, but at the same time, a primeval fear swept over her. "Are you threatening me?"

"You really do have a habit of reading the most fanciful things into what I say."

"I know it was you."

"You know nothing. And you should think very carefully before saying that again. Remember, Laura, threes. Or fours. Or . . . well, let's not get too ahead of ourselves."

Cherry turned and walked away, and Laura could do nothing but watch, rapidly being overtaken by a terrifying sense of disempowerment.

Laura sat in her living room opposite two officers from the Metropolitan Police Department. She'd put off calling. It signaled a seriousness to the situation that she'd been avoiding. And there was Cherry's reaction . . . for it would mean she'd find out. But she had no one else to turn to.

The first time they'd come to the house, a few days after her run in with Cherry, she'd told them everything, like some great dam bursting, and the relief of sharing the burden had been so sweet. Then, as per police procedure, they'd gone away and done their investigations. Laura had been more jittery than ever before, waiting, praying they'd get back to her soon so she could stop looking over her shoulder.

Now they were back and Laura knew systems and processes would be put in place. Soon this would all come to an end. They'd recapped the facts with reassuring clarity and the tea had been drunk, the biscuits eaten. One lone Florentine was left on the china plate and the male officer would longingly look at it every so often. The policewoman looked down at her notebook.

"So, just to be absolutely clear, you're not receiving any nuisance or malicious calls?"

"No."

"Any electronic communications?"

"No."

"And you're not being followed?"

"No. Well, I don't think so." Laura caught a whiff of boredom, disengagement, emanating from the policewoman as she shut her notebook and alarm bells started to ring.

"I've told you, she's not harassing *me*, not directly anyway."

"Laura, we've contacted both Marianne Parker and Julie Sawyer and neither wishes to pursue anything about the alleged communications. In fact, Mrs. Parker says that she believes the letter came from you, and Ms. Sawyer denies receiving a puppy or any kind of animal in the post."

"She's a well-known actress. She doesn't want the publicity, that's all. But it happened!"

"Do you have proof?"

"Well, of course not, but . . . what about Cherry? Have you spoken to her?"

"There's nothing to speak to her about, as there's no complaint."

Laura leaned forward in her seat. "No, you can't do this. . . . You can't ignore everything I've told you. She *threatened* me. . . ."

"I'm afraid there's nothing we can do."

"Christ, what do I have to do to make you take me seriously?" she exploded.

Neither of them answered at first. Laura swallowed the hard lump in her throat.

The policewoman spoke: "Laura, we are taking you seriously. We just have to follow the proper channels."

She mustn't get hysterical, but this—these people, she was *relying* on them. "Please. I don't know what else to do."

The policewoman showed a note of sympathy. "If you do start to receive any unwelcome communication, then this might be useful." She put a leaflet for the National Stalking Helpline on the coffee table. Two minutes later, they left.

Weary, Laura cleared away the cups and saw the Florentine had gone. He must have swiped it on the way out. She sat down heavily on the sofa. Abandoned. Alone. The creeping fear that now permeated every time she was left with her thoughts started up again. She knew Cherry had picked the cocker spaniel deliberately because of the dog Laura had owned as a child. The puppy was as much for her as for her actress. What else had she said, revealed many months ago in front of this girl? She'd never remember, never know, unless Cherry decided to remind her.

Laura's life suddenly felt very unstable; it could be picked apart, interrupted. She'd gone into the office earlier that day and looked around for missing papers, cast contact lists, locking some documents away and shredding some others. Then she'd deleted some e-mails, things she wouldn't like other people reading. She'd wondered if Cherry could break into her e-mail account, her company server. These things were probably in the realm of a computer-savvy kid—look at that young boy who hacked into the pentagon computer system. She'd quickly contacted her IT company and they'd tried to reassure her, but she'd insisted on a higher level of security. The sense she was being followed had intensified. When she'd left her office to hail a cab, she'd stopped at a shop window, pretending to look in, then turned her head sharply to see if anyone was watching her.

Laura quickly got up from the sofa, double-checked she'd bolted the front door on her way to the kitchen. Her mind was still full of the puppy. Who in her right mind would send a dead animal to someone? It was then she realized Cherry must have killed it herself or packaged it alive. In horror, she stopped still, a chill running down her spine. Cherry had no fear of anything, of being caught. There seemed no limit to what she was prepared to do. She was ruthless and her revenge was palpable. Nothing tempered her; nothing could stop her. She seemed to have no moral boundaries and her brain was lightning quick, devious, and imaginative. She'd made sure that none of it could be traced back to her.

Laura was suddenly afraid for what was left. What else did she care about that Cherry was planning to take from her? Her mind went off in all directions, spasming from one horror to the next. She reached for the phone. She couldn't call Daniel or Howard. It had to be Isabella.

48

*L*AURA FOLLOWED ISABELLA INTO HER KITCHEN AND STOOD THERE nervously, knowing she didn't have long as Isabella had to leave for the Cotswolds later that afternoon. When she'd phoned, it had been a bit awkward between them. They hadn't spoken since she'd gone over to apologize. And then Isabella had said she was going away—for what seemed to Laura to be a very long week. The thought of another seven days of being imprisoned in her house, fearful of every knock on the door and every lonely night, her mind turning somersaults as it tried to work out the unknown, was too much to bear. She'd begged to come over.

"Cup of tea? Or something stronger? I can't as I'm driving."

"How is your mother?"

"Complaining that the doctors are trying to kill her, but at least she's taking her medication. George has had enough and it's my turn to babysit. Then my darling brother can take over again, especially seeing as he only lives next door, albeit a Range Rover ride away, and I don't believe for one second his trip to Strasbourg is 'crucial to his election success.' So, Builders? Mint? Chamomile?"

"Yes, please."

Isabella was going to ask which, but Laura had turned away and

was looking out the huge glass bifold doors that led out onto a
sunken, white, minimalist garden.

"You ever feel exposed? As if someone could get in?"

"Darling, it might be large and worth six mil, but it's still a terrace. I'm enclosed on all sides."

Laura turned back to accept the cup of chamomile, and noticed her hands were jittery.

"Want to tell me about it?" said Isabella.

"I don't know where to start."

"Sit down."

She did, grateful that someone else was taking control of the
situation. She twisted her cup in her fingers, trying to phrase what
it was she knew she had to say.

"I don't want to rush you, but if I don't get up to Mother's before evening, she'll be calling the randy colonel at the end of the
lane and asking him to send out his helicopter."

"A few days ago I heard from ITV that my, our, project has been
canceled."

"*What?*"

"Izzy, this is going to sound bonkers . . . horrendous. . . . Oh,
God, I'm not losing the plot, but you might think so when you
hear what I'm about to tell you."

"Go on."

"I've been afraid to say . . ."

"You can tell me anything," said Isabella softly.

"Promise not to judge."

"Course."

Laura looked at her; it had been a throwaway promise to continue the conversation. Now that she had Isabella's attention, she
didn't know where to start. She fiddled with her cup and then
suddenly, unexpectedly, started to cry. Almost as soon as the first
tear made a run for it, she pulled herself together, quickly retriev-
ing a clean handkerchief from her bag. Izzy put out a comforting
hand.

"What is it? Laura?"

"Cherry's back."

Izzy sat up. " 'Back,' in what sense?"

"She's living with Daniel. I said something to her months ago that wasn't true. It made her go away, but then she found out I'd lied and she wanted him back. He's invited her to move in with him. Meanwhile, to punish me for what I said, she's told me she's going to take everything away from me. Daniel's not answering my calls, Howard wants a divorce. A few days ago, I found that she'd sent a dead puppy to the lead actress on my new project. My salvation project."

Isabella's mouth was ever so slightly open as she took all this in with growing incredulous outrage on her friend's behalf.

"'A dead puppy'? What in heaven's name did you say to her?"

"I told her Daniel had died. While she was away in Mexico. She came back and I didn't want her to see him. I phoned her up when she'd come off the plane and told her he was dead. And she couldn't see him as we'd cremated him and scattered the ashes."

Isabella was still trying to smile some encouragement, but the corners of her mouth twitched and fell. Laura saw confusion in her friend's eyes, along with disbelief.

"You said you wouldn't judge."

"No! I'm not," said Isabella quickly.

"At the time . . . I thought he was dying. I thought he only had a few days left."

"And then . . . ?"

"I'd found out a few things . . . stuff she said, and it was pretty clear to me she'd attached herself to him because of his money. So . . . I kept quiet."

Laura waited for Isabella to speak. "Say something. . . ."

"I don't know what to say. I can't believe . . . I mean, I can understand you wanting some time with Daniel . . . but, *Laura* . . ."

Laura's head fell into her hands. "Oh, God, don't, don't . . . I've made such a mess of things."

"Okay, okay. It's fine. We can fix this."

"Can we? How?"

"What you did . . . was appalling. But I remember how terrible it was for you, how desperate the situation was. What does Daniel think about this?" asked Isabella carefully.

It took a moment for Laura to answer. "I haven't spoken to him in nearly two months."

Isabella reached across the kitchen table and gave her hand a squeeze, something for which Laura would be forever grateful.

"My God. *A dead puppy.* I mean, this girl, is she mad?"

"Mad . . . clever . . . extremely focused. I don't know. Probably all three. But she's got it in for me and I don't know what to do. I'm scared to go home."

"I take it Howard's not there? Have you told him about all this?"

"Some of it. It wouldn't make any difference." Laura spoke over her friend's look of exasperation. "Anyway, I don't want him there."

"Have you told the police?"

"Yes. They can't do anything. The actress doesn't want any publicity and is denying it. She's left for a sojourn in Ibiza. And the letter Marianne got that was supposedly written by me—well, she still claims it was written by me."

Isabella's eyes widened. "Cherry *forged* a letter? What did it say?"

"Oh, just nasty, venting stuff. The kind of thing someone who'd been cheated on for years might want to say. It made Howard realize that time was a-wasting. He's decided to seize the moment. He wants a divorce."

"The bastard," muttered Isabella.

"And . . . I confronted her."

"Who? *Cherry?* What did she say?"

"She told me to back off. Or more bad luck would be coming my way."

"Jesus! She's insane. Who does she think she is? She's just some *kid,* for Christ's sake. Same age as ours. My God, if Brigitte ever tried anything like this . . ." Isabella took a deep breath. Gave Laura a look of condolence, of pity, a look that made her feel quite alone. "Oh, Laura . . ."

"I know," she said quickly. "I know I did something awful . . . ," she trailed off, wanting to ask Isabella if she'd have done the same, but was afraid of the answer. "I don't know what to do," she said helplessly.

"Can you try to speak to Daniel again?"

"He won't. Believe me, I've tried. And written. I think she intercepted the letter."

Isabella's phone rang on the table. She glanced at the screen. "Mother."

"You have to go."

She nodded awkwardly and sent the call to voice mail. "I'll call her back in a minute."

Laura stood and blew her nose as she took her cup to the sink. "Don't rush."

"It's okay. You need to get on."

"We haven't sorted anything out."

"I'll be okay."

"Come to Mother's?"

Laura gave a small smile. "You just want an ally."

"You're right." Isabella pulled her into an embrace. "I'll be as quick as I can, and you have to promise to call me if anything happens. In fact, I'm going to call you. Every day."

"Thanks."

"I'm sorry we fell out."

"We didn't . . . not really," said Laura. "I'm glad you're getting out of here, actually."

Izzy laughed. "What, you think that little jumped-up so-and-so is going to go for me?"

"She might." Laura remained sober. "You're all I have left. And she's capable. She'll stop at nothing."

Laura checked the house when she got home, put on every security lock, but she couldn't help feeling creeped out every time she went into the kitchen to fill her glass of wine. The fridge made a loud *thur-wup* as she opened the door; the wineglass seemed to echo on the granite worktop. She stopped and listened to the empty house: silence. Maybe it would help if she played some music. She turned on the radio, but the classical program was melancholy and all the other music stations jarred on her mood too; they seemed meaninglessly noisy and oblivious to her need to soothe her nerves. So she switched it back off again, but now the house seemed quieter than ever. God, she wished Isabella were there.

Laura took a deep breath. She had to pull herself together. Cherry was not lying in wait somewhere in the house. Aware that she'd had nothing to eat since breakfast, and it was now nearly six, she opened the fridge again and pulled out a tub of *tzatziki* and a red pepper, which she roughly chopped. She sat at the worktop, eating her rudimentary supper, her mind wandering. What was Cherry going to do next? Laura was certain that there would be something else. How far would she go? She ran through her mind all the things she cared about: the house, her friends . . . *Christ, there was Moses.* She jumped up and ran to the bifold doors, opening them and calling him urgently, banging his food dish to make him come running. When he did, and after thorough checking, she found him unharmed, she slumped with relief. But she shut the doors after that, much to his disgruntlement. "Sorry, Moses, but I need you in tonight. There's a crazy girl out there wanting to get me. And that means maybe you too."

She sat back down at the breakfast bar. Couldn't settle. Then despite knowing he didn't want to speak to her, she grabbed her phone and called Howard. He didn't answer. Deflated, she left no message. She went to ring Daniel, but unable to stomach another silent rejection, she put down the phone.

Trapped in her house, she stared out the window at the darkened garden, wondering where Cherry was, what she was thinking, what she was planning.

49

A DRIVER BLASTED HIS HORN AS LAURA NAVIGATED WHAT HAD TO BE one of the worst roundabouts in London. She was south of Croydon in Purley, a traffic-choked one-way system of a town, suffocated on one side by this monster roundabout, which was now spitting her out into the entrance road of an extremely large supermarket. She jolted over the speed bumps and headed for the car park, passing megadeals shouting at her from the posters along the route: three boxes of doughy pizzas, with fake smiling Italians, for three pounds. She parked and took a moment to think.

She'd lain awake last night for several hours, listening. In her mind, she'd wandered through the house, each room shadowy, capable of hiding someone. She'd pictured movement behind the curtains, heard the sound of breathing behind the door. In amongst the fear, she got flashes of anger, of being afraid in her own home, of losing contact with Daniel.

Cherry was just a *kid;* as Isabella had said, if Brigitte ever tried anything like that . . . she'd what? Certainly wade in, perhaps put a stop to it. It was then she had the idea. She got up and switched on her laptop. She had to find Cherry's mother. It wasn't a certain thing by any stretch; in fact, there was a very good chance it would be the worst move she could make. Cherry knew how to cover her tracks and gave off an air of the innocent victim, and a mother thought her child more perfect than anyone . . . but mothers also knew their children better than anyone else did— and maybe, just maybe, she knew something about Cherry.

Laura peered through the windscreen. This place was where Cherry's mother might work. She'd remembered Daniel had once said she worked in a supermarket, and, hoping she might have the same surname as Cherry, Laura had searched staff and managers under "Laine." She'd gone through about three chains until at Tesco she'd found a woman called Wendy Laine. The store's location was about right—still commutable from Croydon, but Laine was a common-enough name, so it was entirely possible she had no connection.

If Cherry's mother did work there, Laura wasn't sure how best to approach her. Her story was outlandish and shocking—no mother wanted to hear that her child had done something awful. What if she was defensive, angry? What if she punched Laura or something? What if Cherry had already told her about the lie, and the woman hated her on sight? Anxiety and fear pushed Laura out of her car.

A woman in tracksuit bottoms, a size too small, walked past, dragging a girl no more than three, with pierced ears and a brash Disney T-shirt. She was lagging behind, more intent on eating whatever sweet was wrapped in the long, lurid, yellow-and-green paper than following her mother, whose cart was loaded up with bags, at the top of which were cartons of the frozen fake-Italian pizzas.

Laura locked the car, then made her way to the supermarket entrance. Wendy Laine was a checkout manager, the website had said, but she would obviously work shifts. There was no way of knowing if she was working today—except, as she walked in, she saw a board by the entrance with all the managers on duty. Wendy's name was there, and next to it was her photo. Laura stared and was disheartened. This woman's hair was a rather bright shade of reddish brown and she looked nothing like Cherry. A security man was watching her.

"Everything all right?" he said, a note of suspicion in his voice.

"I need to see Wendy Laine, please." *Is there any point?*

"What's it about?"

"A personal matter."

He looked as if he was about to argue, but then moved away, down one of the aisles, presumably to get her.

Two minutes later, a petite woman appeared at Laura's shoulder. "Can I help you?"

Laura scrutinized her for a resemblance to Cherry, but still saw nothing.

"Hello, I'm Laura Cavendish."

The woman frowned a moment, then broke into a delighted, albeit perplexed, smile.

"Daniel's mum?"

Her heart jumped. "That's right."

"Cherry never said . . . Are we meant to be meeting?"

"It's more of an impromptu thing. I didn't tell Cherry I was coming."

"It's almost time for me break. Hold on—" She fiddled with her radio. "Holly, can you cover now? I'm going for a cuppa."

Laura heard a fuzzy agreement and then followed Wendy to the cafe, a bland, natural-light-starved cubicle at the side of the shop. "They do a lovely latte," said Wendy, insisting on paying as she got the staff discount.

Laura ordered a peppermint tea, Wendy a latte, and the two sat down at a small round table with brown edging.

Wendy looked at her curiously. "It's nice to meet you finally. I've been asking Cherry to introduce us for ages, but she's always had some excuse, mostly that you don't have much free time. Course, we're both working mums," she said, smiling.

Laura returned the smile. She thought that Cherry had said nothing about their falling-out; Wendy was too amiable, delighted even to be in her company. In fact, she was so pleased to meet her, so openly warm, that Laura had an unexpected stab of guilt for what she was about to do. She took a deep breath and clasped her hands on her lap.

"Wendy, a few months ago, I did something rather awful to Cherry."

Her face was blank. "Did you? She never said."

"Cherry and I haven't always seen eye to eye, and when Daniel was not expected to live . . . you know he was injured?"

"Yes, terrible news, I felt so sorry for you—"

"Yes, well, when the doctors said he was unlikely to live, I told Cherry he'd died, just so I could spend those last few days with him alone. Just his father and I."

It didn't sink in at first. "You what?"

She didn't say it again.

"Oh, my God."

"And when he *did* live, I didn't tell Cherry. I did a terrible thing, and I'm sorry for the hurt I caused them. . . . But since Cherry found out, she's . . . well, to put it bluntly, threatened me with destroying my life."

"Come again?"

Laura was wary. She'd caught the indignation on Wendy's face, the flash of anger. "I know it's probably very hard to hear. I would find it hard—"

"Now, just a minute. How do you get off coming here and telling me my daughter's some sort of monster?"

"I didn't say that exactly—"

"What have you got against her?" said Wendy, voice raised.

Laura laid her hands on the table. "Wendy. Please. Please hear me out."

"Go on," Wendy said begrudgingly.

Laura explained about the letter to Marianne, the puppy, and all the while, Wendy's face tried to deny the shock.

"This is pretty far-fetched."

"You think I made it up?" cried Laura. "I didn't want to come and tell you this, and I certainly didn't want to upset you or offend you, but I don't know what she's going to do next, and that makes me . . . extremely nervous." She paused. "And I don't know how to stop her." Laura looked at Wendy, hoping she'd have some word of comfort, some solution to make the nightmare go away, but she just looked like a woman whose pleasant morning cup of tea with another mother had soured beyond anything she could have imagined.

"Who do you think you are . . . coming in here, insulting me and my daughter . . . ?"

She went to stand, but then Laura did too, begging.

"Don't go. *Please*. I don't know what to do. My own son won't talk to me. You've no idea what that's like."

Did she imagine it, or did Wendy flinch? After a moment, she sat down again, much to Laura's relief.

"She's moved in with him, your Daniel, hasn't she?"

Laura nodded. "He thinks I'm so against Cherry, it's clouded my judgment." She looked awkward. "Recently I've not been too keen on the relationship."

"Why?"

Should she tell her? It might push the insults too far. Might make Wendy fly at her. "I had a notion that Cherry might like my son primarily because of his money."

Wendy shook her head angrily, vindicated now. "No way. She had that job—over thirty grand a year it was."

Laura was embarrassed. "She doesn't work there anymore."

"No, but she's looking."

Laura spoke softly. "I don't think so."

"But Daniel, no *offense*, Laura, but he's still training, isn't he? Not exactly loaded yet, and I can't see him forking out for both of them. And he lives in a posh bit of London, doesn't he? Must be one helluva mortgage."

"He has a trust fund. And the flat . . . it's paid for. His father bought it."

Her eyes opened wider.

"Daniel has five thousand put into his bank account every month. Even though he has a career, which we hope will blossom, he doesn't actually need to work." She stopped, seeing her words finally had sunk in. Wendy had colored and, for the first time, seemed out of her depth.

"Bloody hell." Silence fell between them. She'd closed off. Embarrassed about not understanding the scale of riches. Laura had a fear she was about to lose her and took her hand and held it tightly. "Please, Wendy. I don't know what else to do."

The other woman didn't seem too comfortable with having her hand held and Laura awkwardly pulled away.

"And now she's getting married," said Wendy to herself.

Laura reeled beneath a million tiny shards of pain, her ears ringing.

"You didn't know."

"Married? Daniel and Cherry are getting married? When?" she said, panic rising.

"January."

Her hands started shaking. "No, please, God . . . I can't . . . Please, Wendy, I know she's your daughter, but please don't let her do this."

"You don't understand what you're asking me."

"It's gone beyond the money. It's turned into something where she wants him, wants all of him, and me not to have him. I'll never see him again. She'll cut me off completely. You know your daughter better than anyone—please, anything you can do."

Wendy sipped her drink, then slowly put the cup down. It clattered noisily in the saucer, the china thick, designed to withstand the handling of the masses.

"No."

A tightness gripped Laura's chest.

Wendy stood. "You must understand, Laura. She's my daughter."

Laura watched as Wendy, trembling, walked away.

50

CHERRY LET HERSELF INTO HER MOTHER'S FLAT AND DIRECTED THE moving man she'd hired down the hallway to her bedroom, where the boxes were neatly stacked. It had been the right thing to do, move the last of her things when her mum was at work, as it made it a lot easier not having to dodge questions about when Wendy could come and see her new home. She didn't want her mother coming over and "oohing and aahing" about everything, making embarrassing comments about how expensive or fancy everything was or, worse still, bringing a housewarming gift from the supermarket. As usual, Cherry felt guilty about these thoughts and decided she'd take her mum out to dinner somewhere nice, maybe in a few weeks, once she was properly settled in. In fact, she'd leave her a note promising this. *Yes, that's the thing to do,* she thought, pleased, and she went into the living room to find a piece of paper.

"Mum!"

Wendy was sitting on the sofa. "Have you come to say good-bye?"

"I—I didn't know you were here." She frowned. "Aren't you supposed to be at work?"

"I swapped my shifts."

"Oh, right."

"You don't sound too pleased."

"Oh no—doesn't bother me. Why would it?"

Wendy stood. "You didn't seem too keen on the idea when I originally offered. I thought it would be nice. You know, to see each other."

"Of course, it's nice. It's just I didn't want to put you out."

Cherry was uncomfortable under her mother's gaze. What was all this about? She wanted to get her stuff and go, and certainly didn't plan on hanging around for an impromptu bonding session.

"I don't think that's true, Cherry. I think the truth is, you don't like spending time with me."

Cherry's stomach twisted, but she laughed. "What?"

"I'm not rich. Comfortable, I like to think, and I work hard."

"Of course, you do," Cherry said quickly, reassuringly.

"Don't patronize me!" snapped Wendy, and Cherry flinched. "I think, Cherry, that I am an embarrassment to you. Unworthy of you."

Cherry's heart was hammering in her chest. "What are you going on about?"

"I work in a supermarket, I don't wear fancy clothes, I don't speak as well as some people. You always wanted to better yourself, had high expectations, expensive taste. That's why you was so upset about that Nicolas. I knew you was too good for round here, never thought you was too good for me." Wendy's voice cracked, but she pulled herself up. "A woman came to see me in the shop yesterday."

"Who?" Cherry asked anxiously, but deep down, she knew.

"Laura Cavendish. I wasn't going to say anything, but what she told me . . . It was keeping me awake all night. She was begging me to help her. To stop you." She paused. "Is it all true?"

"Oh, don't be so melodramatic."

Wendy stopped still. "Oh, my God," she whispered.

"Did she tell you what she did? She lied to me! Told me her own son was dead so I wouldn't be able to see him anymore."

Cherry waited for her words to have the right impact, for her mum to back down, like she always did. For her to be afraid of upsetting her daughter, for her to say what Cherry wanted to hear, so as not to estrange her even more. But Wendy was looking at her differently—in a way that Cherry had never seen before and it scared her.

"I can't believe you did that," said Wendy. "All that stuff. You killed a puppy . . . ? What's wrong with you?"

"Oh, Christ, will you stop going on about it. I saved it from a miserable existence. You should have seen it, poor thing, all cooped up with nowhere to run, no light, no air. It had a shit life. It had no future because of where it was *born*," she spat.

Wendy's voice caught in her throat: "You mean *you*, don't you?" She took a step toward her. "After your dad died, I worked hard all those years. Nearly killed me sometimes, but you never went without. I didn't see you as much as I wanted to, but I hoped you'd see something good in what I was doing, look up to me. I may not have had much. But I *worked* for everything I ever got. Never sucked it out of someone else like a leech!"

Shaking, Cherry slapped her across the face. Wendy gasped and put her hand to her cheek.

"Excuse me?" The man with a van was hovering awkwardly in the doorway.

Cherry reeled around. *"What?"*

He held up his hands. "It's all in. I'll be off." He couldn't leave quick enough.

Cherry apprehensively turned back to her mum.

"I know you're ashamed of me," said Wendy quietly, "but I'm also ashamed of you." And she turned away.

Cherry's eyes blazed. Suddenly she felt like the nobody Croydon girl again—the one whose future was limited, who couldn't keep a boyfriend who came from a better background. She was overwhelmed with emotion and needed to get out. She rushed out of the flat and clattered down the stone steps and into the air. The man with the van had gone and was now making his way to

Kensington. Cherry marched, trembling, down the street to Daniel's Mercedes, arms folded, eyes stinging.

How dare she! How dare that fucking woman stick her nose in . . . Hate poured from her, contaminating the very air she breathed. *What the fuck was Laura doing, coming to see my mother. As if I was a child! She is stifling, suffocating—the way she behaves about Daniel. So fucking possessive! It isn't fair to control other people's lives like that, smother other people's dreams. . . .*

Cherry fiercely wiped away her tears with the heel of her hand and clamped her throat shut so no more would come. As she got in the car, her anger settled like a hard stone in her chest. So Laura was intent on breaking her up with Daniel, she hadn't listened. The more she tried, the more Cherry raged. Why couldn't Laura just fuck off? Disappear? If only some bus would come and knock her over. Some accident or something. That was the thing about accidents, you never saw them coming, but one little slip, one badly timed moment, and you were history. Wiped out. The problem no longer existed and no one was to blame. That would be fantastic. Cherry wallowed in the idea for a moment, steeped in resentment and self-pity.

But then reality hit. Accidents didn't just happen when you wanted them to. Still angry, she drove away sharply, slamming the car into gear. Hands tight on the wheel, she stared hard ahead, cursing at anyone who didn't move fast enough off a green light, anyone who hesitated at a roundabout. She drove toward the Webb Estate, not quite aware of doing so, then stopped the car and looked through the mechanical gates, shut fast. Blinding lights came up close behind her and she watched as another car went past, the gates gliding open for it. Without thinking, she put the car into gear and followed in its slipstream. The other vehicle turned off down one of the residential streets and Cherry took the route she remembered, to Nicolas's.

She arrived in Silver Lane, flanked on either side by four rows of silver birch trees, and stopped halfway along. There it was, the large, detached, eight-bedroom mansion. She moved the car another few feet, so she could peer through the trees up to Nicolas's bedroom. She wondered anxiously, hopefully, if she would see him. His arms around his wife, silhouetted in the window. Maybe he'd spot her. Come down. She'd make sure he saw her ring, then casually drop Daniel into the conversation.

Suddenly she felt like a complete fool. He'd gone. He and his wife. They'd have their own place now; they were living their own lives. They'd moved on. With a crushing sense of humiliation, Cherry drove out as quickly as she could.

51

*I*T WAS SIX A.M. DANIEL, FULLY DRESSED, LOOKED AT CHERRY SLEEPING in their bed, her shiny dark hair falling across her slightly flushed face. Her arms were outside the duvet, the skin smooth and inviting. He wondered whether to give her a kiss good-bye. They'd had their first fight the night before and hadn't yet made up, not properly. And he still didn't really know what it was all about.

The evening had started pleasantly enough. While Cherry was at her mum's flat, Daniel had had a call from his friend Will, delighted to find him not on a shift. Will was looking for someone to celebrate with, as he'd just learned he'd gotten the promotion. He invited himself round and they were waiting for Cherry to come back, so they could all go out together. Daniel was aware none of his friends had seen Cherry since just before the accident; and now that they were back together, it would be good if they got to know each other a little better. The guys grabbed a couple of beers from the fridge while they were waiting.

"Got to say, Dan, you're pretty forgiving. Especially after the way she gave you the elbow," said Will as he popped the top of his bottle.

Daniel remained noncommittal. He didn't want to incriminate his mother by divulging the whole story, so he settled on a vague: "It wasn't as bad as you think."

As was the way with men, Will didn't dwell on the subject long. He clinked his friend's bottle with his own. "Good luck to you," he said without malice. "What do you fancy doing tonight? We could try out that new Japanese—you know, the one Theo's friend owns. Cherry like Japanese?"

Daniel didn't know. The front buzzer sounded, and answering, he saw on the screen the man with the van already unloading the boxes onto the street, ready to carry them upstairs. "She'll be back in a minute," he said, "we'll ask her." The man carried the boxes up the stairs and into the apartment. He barely said hello and wasn't interested in a cup of tea. Daniel asked him where Cherry was and if she'd followed him back; the mover raised his eyebrows.

"Hope not, mate. She slap you about like she does her old lady?"

Daniel's mouth dropped, and realizing he'd said too much, the man was in a hurry to leave.

"Got to get going, if that's all right, mate. You got the cash?"

"Hold on, what did you mean, 'slap about'?"

"Now I ain't getting into no domestic. If you don't mind, I'll get paid and be on me way." He stuck out his hand stubbornly and Daniel could see he wasn't going to be drawn further. He paid him his two hundred quid and the man was gone. The remark left Daniel with a sense of unease, although he thought that the man must be mistaken somehow. He rejoined Will in the living room.

"Everything all right?"

Daniel was quick to smile. "All good. So, are you getting your own office now?"

As he listened to Will talk about his job, he kept an ear out for Cherry's return. About twenty minutes later, he heard the key in the lock. The living-room door swung open. She looked tense, strained, and not pleased to see Will. Daniel jumped up to give her a kiss, which she accepted on her cheek. He turned to indicate their guest.

"Will's got the new job."

"Oh, right."

"You know, Risk Engineering Manager."

"You said." She took a breath, knew she had to try harder. "Congratulations!"

Will raised his bottle. "Cheers!"

Daniel put his arm around her. "He came round to see if we wanted to go and celebrate with him. Fancy coming out for some dinner?"

"Um . . . I've got a terrible headache, but you two go and celebrate."

Embarrassed, Will took a swig of his drink. He obviously felt he'd stumbled into some sort of lovers' tiff.

Cherry stood there for a moment, aware of what she'd done, but unable or unwilling to make amends. She felt like she was suffocating and needed to get out of the room. "I'm just going to get changed."

After a split second, Daniel scrambled after her and followed her to the bedroom.

"Is everything okay?"

Cherry tugged off her tights and threw them on the floor. She lay down on the bed. "Fine."

"Your mum okay?"

"Yes, she's good."

She was obviously blocking him. He didn't know how to bring up what the moving man had said, and instinctively knew it wouldn't go down well. "It doesn't look like everything's okay," he said gently.

"Honestly, everything's fine. It's just this headache."

"I'll tell Will I can't go out. Make something up—"

"Just go," she snapped.

There was a silence.

Cherry rolled onto her side, forced a smile. "I'm sorry, it's just been a long day, that's all. But you go out," she added hurriedly, "I think I might just try and get an early night."

Daniel went to the restaurant alone with Will, telling him something about Cherry having a migraine. It had been a bit of a halfhearted affair and he got the feeling Will was regretting asking him to come out. Daniel had brushed off his query of whether "everything was all right back there," and considered calling Cherry, but he thought she might be asleep. When he got back around ten-thirty, she was.

Just like now. He looked at her beautiful face once again, the eyelashes dark against her cheek, and decided a kiss might wake her. He grabbed Rufus, who'd snuck in behind him, and had a tendency to jump on the bed and lick your face. Then he crept out of the room and went to work.

Cherry woke at eighty-thirty with a nagging thought, like a fly that buzzed around the room before going quiet; then just when you'd forgotten about it, it started up again. Then it came back to her. She'd behaved stupidly the night before and she cringed as she thought of how she'd made up that lame excuse for Daniel's friend. What was his name? *Will.* She'd met him a couple of times before, many months ago. He was okay, but a bit pleased with himself, a trait that irritated her. Just the same, she should have been charming; she should have gone out to dinner with them both. It had gotten awkward with Daniel and she'd tried to make amends, but all she could think about at the time was her mother, what had happened.

She suddenly curled up in a tight ball of pain and guilt. *I hit my mum.* It made her feel sick with guilt; but, she thought fiercely, Wendy was wrong about why she was with Daniel. She loved him. It was just good luck that he was wealthy. Good luck that she'd had a hand in, yes, but wasn't there a famous saying that you make your own luck? Cherry cringed as she went over the events in her mind again. The thing she'd tried to hide for so long—the horrible, shameful fact that she was ashamed of her own mother— had come out, and all because Laura had been going round saying stuff, hurtful stuff, to Wendy. The anger rose up again: *God, how I hate her.*

There was one point last night when she'd almost broken. She'd wanted to tell Daniel everything: how she'd manipulated him by pretending she didn't know he was alive, what she'd said and done to Laura to teach her a lesson, and how Laura *wouldn't just leave her alone,* but she knew that she couldn't. *Not ever.* She'd sent him off to some restaurant and had lain in bed, wondering if he'd call before she fell asleep. At some point, he'd come back and had gotten into bed without waking her, and had done the same in reverse this morning.

Restless, she jumped out of bed. Those old married couples in the news who always said never to go to sleep without resolving an argument were right. She shouldn't have left it to fester while they slept. She had to make amends and decided to surprise him when he came home with a nice meal. A cliché, she knew, but it would work. She wandered into the kitchen and pulled down some of the cookbooks she'd bought from the local bookshop for their kitchen, flicking through the pages. Rufus barked at her and she picked him up and let him help choose. They settled on a *tagine.* Exotic enough to show she'd made an effort, but actually pretty easy, judging by the instructions.

That decided, she started making coffee, and the fly buzzed inside her head again. The Laura fly. It made her skittish and she hated the feeling. If only she could swat it, crush it, wipe its entrails into a piece of paper towel, and then chuck it away. Maybe someone had done it for her. Partially amused with the idea, she turned on the TV, looking at the breakfast news for signs of an accident: a woman who'd put a foot in the road a second too soon and was pancaked, or who'd been knocked off the platform on the underground. It wasn't likely. Laura generally didn't take the tube. Something had to happen to her. It was so effortless, really, just a tiny thing could upset the equilibrium. Intrigued by the simplicity, she decided to Google it: *How to cause an accidental death.*

She opened up the laptop and started to type in the search engine, when her fingers froze over the keyboard. Jeez, that was close. Cherry knew that it was impossible to completely eradicate a browsing history. Thank God she'd only gotten to "cause." It wasn't like she was actually planning on doing anything. But just in case, she closed down the computer and decided to have a little fun with her imagination instead.

Lightning . . . bit difficult to control. Being stung by a bee . . . maybe Laura was the type to suffer from an anaphylactic reaction. Could you train bees somehow? Maybe you could put something on the skin that would attract them.

There was still a fairly high failure rate in this scheme, though. It would depend on the person being irritated enough to bat the insect away, and the bee actually releasing a sting.

Hmm . . . what about drowning? It would require a strong current— and no observers. Poisoning . . . ? Oh, why couldn't Laura have been different? Why is she so possessive, so insistent that I'm not good enough for her beloved son?

By lunchtime, she was feeling a lot better. Of course, she wasn't intending to go round to Laura's house and put bleach in her tea, but it had been good therapy to speculate.

After lunch, Cherry went shopping for the ingredients for her makeup dinner and then started cooking. The *tagine* filled the flat with the scent of cinnamon, bay, and cumin, and the meringue roulade stood regally on the worktop. At half past six, she set the table; twenty minutes later, Daniel came home. She waited for him to come into the kitchen. Straightaway she saw that she'd done the right thing. The sight of the table, with its carefully laid-out wineglasses and cutlery, raised a smile and diffused the coolness between them.

"What's this?" he said.

"My way of saying sorry. For being a miserable old bag yesterday."

"You were a bit."

"Hey!"

He put down his keys and wallet. "I was worried. Still am. Is everything okay?"

She smiled. "Of course, it is. Like I said, I was just having a bad day. Honestly. Have you seen the pudding?"

Daniel came over to investigate the long, white, sugary, twirled dessert oozing with cream and strawberry compote. He stuck his finger in and made a face of appreciation. "That is *good.*"

Relieved to be off the subject of the night before, Cherry smiled. "You have a good day?"

"Saw an angioplasty."

"Is that where they open up a blocked artery?"

"The patient visibly improved right there, in front of my eyes. Blood started flowing better around his body and his skin tone changed immediately."

"Must be amazing to see."

"It is." He paused. "Mum rang me today. Left a message. First time in weeks."

It was like a knife in her back, but she forced herself to stay casual. Took the couscous out of the packet and tipped it in a bowl.

"I feel bad. Don't like falling out. She sounded upset."

"What did she say?"

"Same as the others. That she was sorry. Wanted to make amends."

Cherry nodded matter-of-factly.

"It's difficult for me—you do see that?"

"I know."

"I don't like you two not getting on," he said with a sigh. "My fiancée and my mum. You should be on shouting terms, at least."

Cherry smiled at his lame joke.

"Can't we try and work something out? And you know, we still haven't told her about the engagement."

"Of course! Nothing would make me happier."

"Really?"

"Yes." She kissed him. "It makes me sad when we don't get on and you're caught in the middle." She turned to open the oven and check the *tagine,* well aware she'd left Daniel taken aback at how easy it had been to persuade her. Men liked a nonconfrontational life, but she knew what she'd said was too easy, and nothing had actually been resolved. Neither would it be, but by the time he realized that, and brought it up again, Laura would have disappeared—hopefully.

"That smells delicious," he said, looking at the *tagine.* He put his arms around her and kissed her on the back of the neck. "Thank

you, Cherry. You're amazing. I know she hasn't made things easy
for you and I appreciate your not holding it against her."

"Careful, hot!"

"I feel I should go and see her."

Cherry turned. "What? Tonight?"

"Only for half an hour or so. After dinner. Is that a problem?
She's been having a rough time. You know, with the divorce and
everything."

A wave of panic crashed over her. The last thing she wanted was
Daniel getting the full story of how Laura had been to see Wendy.
"I'm . . . just not feeling that good, that's all."

"What's up?"

"It's not much, just that headache. From last night." She rubbed
her forehead, trying to think quickly. "Can't seem to get rid of it."

He waited a moment and then said: "You need to sit down. Go
on, I'll just take a shower, then finish the couscous.' " She allowed
herself to be led into the living room and onto the lemon sofa. As
soon as he left the room and she heard the shower run, she sat
up. The tense, nervy feeling escalated. It was like the devil on her
back and no matter how she sat, she was restless, wanted to escape
from it. She put some music on to try and blast it away. Then she
lay back down on the sofa and closed her eyes, trying not to think
about the fly buzzing around her head.

"I thought you had a headache?" Daniel had walked in, wearing a clean T-shirt and jeans, hair tousled and wet from the
shower. Rufus had followed him and was jumping around, trying
to lick his ankles.

She started. "I do. I mean, I took a tablet."

"They don't work that fast," he said, turning down the volume.

Damn him for being a doctor, she thought, knowing he was right
and she couldn't argue. Instead she threw the full radiance of her
smile at him. "You've cheered me up. I think the stress of the
move has been getting to me."

"You're not happy to be here?"

She looked at him in surprise. "I'm extremely happy." She

wanted to ask, *"Aren't you?"* but something stopped her. "Are you hungry?"

"Starving."

"Shall we eat?"

He followed her into the kitchen. "Glass of wine?"

Her face fell. "Oh no!"

"What?"

"I forgot the wine!"

"Don't worry about it."

"No, I mean I wanted everything to be perfect." She grabbed her purse. "I'll just go downstairs to Henry's, get a bottle of Shiraz or something. It's time for Rufus's walk anyway," she said, holding his exuberant body still as she clipped on his leash.

"You don't have to."

She was already out the door. "Why don't you hold off on the couscous till I get back. You know what he's like, doesn't always perform when you want him to."

The door slammed behind her and she tried to still her rapid breathing. She didn't wait for the elevator, hurrying down the stairs instead, with Rufus all eager pedaling legs behind her. The fresh air helped to calm her and she walked the short distance to the wine shop, then tied Rufus up outside. There were usually a handful of customers discussing wine with the importance of a peace treaty, but she was the only one in the shop and was served quickly. Clutching her bottle in a thick plastic bag, she stood outside. She wasn't ready to go back to the flat, not enough time had passed for the atmosphere to dissipate, and so she untied Rufus from the post and took him for the walk she'd claimed he needed.

Laura sat and flicked through the channels, irritated by the lack of quality television. She did not want to watch another life-style show flimsily dressed up as a serious cooking program. Un-settled, as usual, on her own, she had spent the day mooching around the house feeling agitated. After her disastrous visit to Wendy, she was at a loss as to what to do next. There was nothing she could do, and this frightened her, made her feel like a sitting duck.

Laura considered checking her phone again, but she already knew that Daniel hadn't replied to the message she'd left. The hollow ache in her chest flared up and she stood quickly, looking for a distraction. She would try to read some of her book.

She went upstairs to her bedroom, but the book wasn't on the bedside table as she'd thought. In a knee-jerk panic, she wondered if anyone had been in the house. Only Mrs. Moore, she remembered, with a tinge of embarrassment. Perhaps she'd moved the book elsewhere when she'd cleaned. Laura looked across at the windowsill; then pulling the curtains back a touch, she found the book and was about to let the curtain drop again, when a movement outside caught her eye.

Cherry was standing on the opposite pavement, under the streetlight, staring up at the house. Laura instantly recoiled, dropping the curtain. It fell partially closed, leaving a small sliver of a gap, a dazzling slice of light into which Laura knew Cherry could see perfectly. If she wanted to leave the room, Laura would have to cross this opening. She stood there, scrunched up into herself, backed into the wall. . . . *God, I am cowering.* She stared at the back of the curtain, an angry whimper escaping, before she pulled her breath in sharply. *I mustn't let her do this.* But Laura was paralyzed.

She stood there for what seemed like ages, unable to decide whether to look again, to see if Cherry was still there, when she heard a dog barking. A small dog, as it was a light, happy sound . . . or perhaps a puppy. *A puppy.* Laura pulled the curtains back and there, being coerced by Cherry out of the opposite neighbor's garden, was a brown cocker spaniel puppy. It bounded around her, tangling itself in its leash and licking her hand as she bent down to stroke it.

Laura stared. *The same as the one sent to her actress.* The one Cherry had killed. *What the hell is she doing coming around to the house. . . . My God, she's* taunting *me.*

Then suddenly Cherry looked up and Laura was filled with a frenzied rage at her casual arrogance. Without thinking, she dropped the curtain and ran downstairs so fast she almost tripped.

She flung open the front door and launched herself onto the pavement.

The street was empty. She drew a sharp breath and looked up and down, but Cherry had gone. The night was still and dark, with just small pools of light spreading a short distance from the foot of each streetlamp. Then something else appeared from behind the wall of her opposite neighbor. A fox. It saw her and stared brazenly for a moment before turning and trotting up the street. The fear returned and Laura realized the door was open behind her. Heart hammering, she quickly retreated and, slamming it shut, bolted it.

Daniel stared in bewilderment at the slammed door. Cherry hadn't wanted him to go and see his mum—that much was obvious. Part of him didn't blame her; she had, after all, been treated abominably but . . . Oh, who knew? He suddenly felt exhausted and sat listlessly at the table. The wineglasses, cutlery, napkins, even flowers, for God's sake, suddenly seemed like a full-on attack, and then he instantly felt guilty. She'd gone to a lot of trouble to make amends tonight. Perhaps he was being inconsiderate, suggesting he go and visit Laura. His phone beeped and he picked it up, expecting a photo of a wine label, Cherry's suggestion for the evening, but it was a Facebook e-mail telling him of a message request. He didn't immediately recognize the sender, and when he opened it, he read it, confused: **Hi, Daniel, I hope you don't mind me getting in touch, but there's something I want to talk to you about. Could you give me a call when you can? Thanks, Wendy**

At the end of the message was a London phone number.

It took a second for him to realize the e-mail was from Cherry's mother. He was curious as to why she could be messaging him, and something made him call back, there and then.

"Hello?"

"Wendy, it's Daniel."

"Blimey, you was quick."

"I got your message."

"Oh, good."

She was unforthcoming with much else and he felt he had to prompt. "You asked me to call."

"I know, I know. Is Cherry with you?"

"No, she's gone to the wine merchant."

She fell silent and he realized he sounded a bit of a snob: *wine merchant*. But it wasn't just that, it was as if she was plucking up the courage to say something.

"I found you on Facebook."

"Okay."

"This is extremely hard for me to say . . . but I feel I need to." She paused. "Your mum came to see me the other day. She said some stuff that I didn't like hearing. . . ."

Daniel could feel himself getting riled and must've exhaled or something, as Wendy continued with: "I know what you're thinking. She's got it in for Cherry. And she has in a way but . . . oh, God . . ." Wendy took a deep breath. "This is about the worst thing I ever done, but . . . there's a good chance your mum's right."

"Oh, Wendy, no, no . . . you can't let Mum get to you. She's got a real problem with Cherry, and I'm really sorry about it, but—"

"Just shush and listen." Wendy paused. "Like I said, I think she's right."

He had no choice but to ask. "Right about what?"

"Oh, my God, do I have to spell it out? It's bad enough having to say this about me own daughter . . ." She paused. "Cherry's not as sweet and simple as she makes out. She wants to win. She gets an idea in her head, and she wants it. If that idea's a life where she doesn't have to work in some crappy job, like . . . a supermarket, then she'll do anything to get it. And she's not gonna give up easily, which is why she's made your mum's life hell, and I can't say for sure where she'll stop."

Daniel was playing with the fork on the table, pushing the tip of the handle so it sprang up in the air. Suddenly it clattered onto the floor.

"Are you still there?" said Wendy.

"Yes. I am."

"I'm sorry to be saying this, and I wasn't going to, but you was so nice to me. That day we all went to lunch. Even though I gate-crashed your own time with Cherry, you was so friendly, made me feel really welcome, I'll never forget it. Anyway, I couldn't just let you go on being in the dark or nothing. And I know about the awful thing your mum done, but still . . ." Wendy's voice was wavering and Daniel could tell she was on the verge of tears.

"Listen up. When Cherry was a kid, about fourteen, she cut up a girl's school shirt while she was out doing PE. Two holes in the front, just 'cause she nicked her idea in a school competition. Prize was fifty quid. The girl didn't even win, Cherry did, but I think she was making a point."

It was a small thing—a stupid, small thing that a teenager would do—why, then, did it make his blood run cold?

"Anyway, I think I've said enough, so I'm going. I'm sorry, Daniel. I feel like this is partly my fault. Like I didn't bring her up right or something . . . I'll be seeing yer, okay?" She hung up.

Daniel put the phone down on the table and stared uncomprehendingly around the room. All of a sudden, the hole his mum had stubbornly, unwelcomely, been trying to pry open in his relationship had widened. He didn't know what to do with what Wendy had told him; he needed time to think. He heard the sound of the key in the lock and jumped up as Cherry came in.

"'Australian, savory and powerful, with intense spicy . . .' What's up?" She looked up from the label.

"Nothing," he quickly reassured her.

"Something's happened."

He smiled and held out his hand. "Shall I open it?" She watched him as she handed it over, and he could tell she was deliberating on whether to press him; he was thankful this was a makeup dinner and she backed off. Browbeating him was not on the menu. At the same time, he was disturbed by the strong, almost survivalist, feeling he had to keep his phone call with Wendy a secret. He poured them both a glass as Cherry served up dinner. It was delicious, but the conversation didn't ever get into full gear. They were both wary, unable to fully relax, and Cherry claimed a return of her headache. The meal was eaten quickly and then they ended up in front of the TV. At half past ten, neither saw much point in staying up longer, and they went into the bathroom separately and then got into bed.

"Do you fancy your book?" said Daniel, and Cherry knew by this that he did. He wanted to escape into something other than their evening.

"Actually, I might just crash," she said, and switched out her light. "But you read."

He did for about ten minutes before turning out his own light. As they lay in bed, Daniel sensed she was still awake. He called her name once, softly, but she didn't reply.

Once she heard him drop off, she allowed her mind to tick. She knew cracks were appearing. Something had happened tonight, something he was keeping from her. Something that had made him suspicious. Cracks had a way of widening, deepening, faster and faster, as they took hold. She had to resolve this soon or he'd slip away.

52

Saturday, November 7

*L*AURA HEARD THE MAIL FALL ONTO THE DOORMAT. AS USUAL, SHE approached it with some trepidation, but it all looked fairly ordinary. A collection of statements buffered with some junk brochures selling cashmere sweaters and overseas investments. She flicked through it and stopped at an expensive cream envelope, thick with the paper it held inside. The doorbell rang before she had a chance to open it and she found herself peering through the hall window, aware she was behaving like a timid old lady. It was the builders, come to repair the leaking window. She made them a cup of tea while they assured her they would have the glass out by the end of the day, and hopefully back in the next. Once they were out in the garden, she took her post to the quiet of the living room. She opened the thick envelope first.

> *Dear Mrs. Cavendish,*
> *I am writing on behalf of my client, Howard Cavendish. He feels that a notable amount of time has passed since he first discussed the issue of divorce with you, but so far has not received any correspondence detailing your request to start proceedings. He is still very acceptable to you instigating proceedings rather than him, but you must make this known within fourteen days or I will be bound to file*

a petition to the courts. In order to facilitate the process, I recom-
mend that, if you haven't already, you get independent legal advice.
  I look forward to hearing from you in due course.
  Yours,
  Alastair Lloyd-Edwards

Laura dropped the letter on the coffee table. Did it matter? Who cared who divorced whom? The relationship was over, and no one seemed to notice or think that this might be the important thing. Or maybe it wasn't, not for Howard because of Marianne. Maybe their marriage hadn't mattered to him for years. She was suddenly exhausted and knew she wouldn't bother to reply.

She hadn't been to work much either, vaguely aware this was feeding into Cherry's ambitions for her. However, since the cancelation of her drama, she'd lost all energy. She wasn't sleeping well at night; her skin was pale and there were shadows under her eyes. She was afraid to go out. Food was delivered by the supermarket. When the post crashed on the mat, it startled her and she approached it like a wary animal, afraid of what it might be.

And then there was Cherry's nocturnal visit. Laura wondered how long she'd stood there, what she'd been looking for, what she was planning. When Izzy had called first thing to check in, she'd been so angry about it she'd threatened to call the police, there and then, but Laura knew she'd receive a similar response to the one she'd already had. They couldn't do anything until Cherry made her first move. She realized she was waiting. Waiting for something to happen, and it was slowly strangling her.

She had to do something. She had to see Daniel. Laura grabbed her bag and jacket and headed out.

She approached the double doors with the large elevated sign: CARDIOLOGY. A young black nurse was sitting behind the desk as she walked in, apprehensive now that she'd actually made it.

"Can I help you?" asked the nurse.

"I'm here to see Dr. Cavendish."

"He's in surgery."

"Oh, right. When . . . when might it be over?"

The nurse glanced at the clock. "Hard to say. Another two hours, at least."

Her face fell.

"Anything I can do?"

"No, it's fine. I'll come back then."

Laura made a swift exit before the woman asked any more questions. She had a dread of hospitals since Daniel's accident, but she resigned herself to the wait. The minutes ticked by excruciatingly slowly, and she stretched out a coffee for forty-five minutes, then suddenly thought: *What if Cherry meets him after his shifts? What if she comes here?* Her stomach constricted and she jumped up and nervously wandered around the charity shop full of knitted garments by well-meaning patrons, then the gift shop full of cuddly toys and metallic balloons on sticks, and then finally the minimarket. At about half past three, she went back up to the ward.

"Is Dr. Cavendish free yet?" she asked the same nurse, who looked up and nodded down the corridor.

He was deep in conversation with someone and didn't see her at first, so she got a chance to look at him unchecked. It was the first time she'd seen him in his uniform and her heart swelled with pride. Then he looked up.

She didn't know if he was pleased to see her or not. At first, she thought she caught a glimpse of relief, gladness, but it turned into a frown before she could be sure. He walked over.

"Mum, what are you doing here?"

"I came to see you."

"I'm at work."

"Yes, I know, but I can't come to the flat, can I?" Laura tried to stem her anxiety. "I . . . I left you a message yesterday. I've left lots."

She saw a flash of guilt. He pulled her away from the nurses' station, conscious of gossip and alert eyes. "I'm sorry. It's just . . . there's been a lot going on." He paused. "Wendy got in touch."

Laura looked at him, shocked. "What did she say?"

A nurse called his name. Daniel turned. "Coming... I can't talk here."

"I can wait until your break."

"That's five hours away and I don't always get one."

Seeing her crestfallen face, he relented. "I'll come to the house."

"When?"

"I don't know. . . ."

"After your shift?"

"It's going to be late."

"I don't care. But phone first," she said quickly, knowing it would be dark when he came knocking on the door.

"Okay, I'll try."

"Promise?"

He took her by the arm and led her toward the double swing doors. She stopped and turned to him, pleading. "Please?"

He was surprised by the emotion in her voice. "Okay. Now go home and get some rest. You look exhausted."

Laura left, and on her way home, she found herself shaking. She was so thankful, so grateful, that she was on speaking terms with her son again; it brought home to her how much she'd missed him. And Wendy had been in touch. She was apprehensive about what she'd said, but Daniel didn't seem angry with her anymore, so perhaps some good had come out of her disastrous visit. The problem of Cherry was still very much present, but she blocked that out for now and concentrated on small mercies. Daniel was willing to meet up. Maybe he'd start to believe her.

53

"*H*EY, MUM, I'M JUST GOING HOME TO CHANGE. IF YOU STILL WANT to talk, I'll come over. If you're asleep, though, don't worry, as I'm pretty tired too. We can always do it tomorrow. I'll give it half an hour or so, and if you haven't called me back, I'll assume you've gone to bed."

"To hear the message again, press two, to save, press—"

She'd missed his call. Furious with herself, Laura checked when the message had arrived. Only twenty minutes ago, thank God. She rang him back straightaway, cursing herself for falling asleep and not hearing the phone.

She'd come back from the hospital and tried to keep busy; then as the day wore on, she found herself getting more anxious. What if he changed his mind? What if Cherry called him about something and he had to go straight home? As the evening drew in, she'd tried to distract herself by reading, but eventually the toll of the weeks of sleepless nights had overtaken her and she'd fallen into a deep, dreamless slumber.

She got up from the sofa and paced the room, listening. With every ring, her heart sank further, and then she got the dreaded voice mail.

"Daniel, I missed your call. I still want to meet. You said you'd still be up? Please, can you come over? Maybe you're in the shower or something . . . let me know. I'll wait up, so don't worry about it being late."

She hung up and was suddenly swamped with a sense of isolation. She looked at the clock: 10:43. There was still time. She tried to settle down in front of the TV. After ten minutes, she got up and made a cup of tea, putting her phone in her trouser pocket; she did not want to miss another call. It was while she was waiting for the kettle to boil that she realized Moses still wasn't in. She opened the bifold doors and, standing safely in the light, still inside the kitchen, banged his food dish on the patio. He didn't come running. Instead she heard a faint, pitiful meowing from somewhere at the bottom of the garden.

"Moses?" she called, and he answered with a mewl. Something was wrong.

She'd have to go out to get him. She looked out at the dark garden and cursed her cat. Switching on the outdoor lights, she could see the path through the middle of the lawn, the builders' plastic barriers, the stainless-steel water feature, but nothing in the shadows at the far end. The end where Moses's cries came from.

Laura decided to do it as quickly as possible. She stepped outside and the coolness of the night enveloped her. Forging up the garden, with more courage than she was feeling, she kept her mind focused on the job at hand, calling Moses until she could locate his mews. It wasn't until she got right to the back, where the trees covered the fence, that she saw him, or rather his paw. It was batting through a piece of broken fence, trying to move it so he could get through.

Laura bent lower so she could see better. Somehow a piece had been dislodged, but it was swinging back over the hole every time Moses tried to move it. *The foxes must have done it,* thought Laura, as it was only a few inches wide and she'd seen them coming into the garden from the back.

"Don't worry, I'll get you out," she said, and pushed the fence section to one side, but for some reason he wouldn't come through.

"Come on, hurry up." Laura could feel the shadows start to encircle her, and she wanted to get back inside, but Moses still wouldn't move.

"What's the matter?" she asked, the hairs prickling on the back of her neck. She turned to look back to the house and it seemed a long distance away, all of a sudden, across a great expanse of garden that she had to cross. To the sides, beyond the reach of the lights, it was still dark and she could see nothing. She reached through the fence and tried to grab Moses by the scruff of his neck, but he was reluctant to be caught; then she finally got him. She put him on her shoulder, where he started purring uncontrollably.

Laura looked back toward the open door of the house, with the light flooding from the kitchen. The breeze picked up and the trees rustled behind her. She shivered. As soon as she ran, she felt as if someone was chasing her. She clutched Moses and heard herself whimper, didn't dare look round. Fear pricked at her skin, escalating as she fled across the garden, until finally she leapt inside and slammed the door shut behind her. She frantically tried to turn the key, but her hands slipped. She dropped Moses; then with two hands, she wrenched the key across and heard it lock. Gasping, she peered through the window. There was no one there.

Her phone beeped in her pocket, startling her. It was from Daniel, a text: **Sorry, was in the shower. Coming over now.**

Oh, thank God. She almost cried with relief. "Daniel's coming, Moses."

Laura hated being in the house alone. It was getting late, and would be even later by the time he arrived—maybe she could even persuade him to stay the night. She sent a quick reply, then went back into the living room and sat on the edge of the sofa, waiting for him to arrive. *Daniel is coming.* She was suddenly swamped with a feeling that was almost euphoric. Her phone was still in her hand. Was it too late to call Izzy? She decided to give it a try.

"What's happened?" her friend asked quickly.

"Oh, nothing, nothing. Sorry, I know it's late, but nothing bad's happened. In fact, the opposite. Daniel's coming over to chat. I saw him at the hospital today and he said he'd come over after his shift."

"Oh, darling, that's brilliant. About time."

"I think—I think he's getting a little bit suspicious, or something. Realizes all's not what it seems with Cherry."

"*Really*. How do you know this?"

"Just something he hinted at in the hospital."

Izzy took a deep breath. "Hallelujah."

"I know," said Laura softly. "I know."

After they'd said good night, she flicked through the channels to try to pass the few minutes until he arrived. The 911 shows and dated films from the 1990s did nothing to help her sense of alienation, as if all those with normal lives, normal families, had long since abandoned the TV to the outcasts and the solitary.

At 11:28 p.m., Laura heard the doorbell. She jumped up and quickly went to let Daniel in. *Never before have I wanted company so much*, she thought as she opened the door. Almost as soon as she had, she let out a startled wail, but Cherry was already inside and had shut it behind her. Laura backed away, knocking into the hall table.

"What are you doing here?" she managed.

"I know it wasn't me you were expecting," said Cherry, putting her bag on the table as if she lived there. Laura watched, her heart beating rapidly, as she tried to work out what Cherry was doing and saw she seemed relaxed, pragmatic, as if she paid a call on her late at night on a regular basis.

"Where's Daniel?"

Cherry didn't answer, just looked at her strangely, and Laura suddenly got a ripple of fear. "What have you done with him?"

Cherry shook her head, amused by Laura's vigorous imagination. "Nothing! But that attitude is something we really need to talk about." She held up a hand and felt herself getting snappy. "I'll say this bluntly—you're way, way too suspicious. I'm sick of it.

If you'd ever given me half a chance, you would have discovered I'm not so bad."

Cherry thought that Laura looked agitated, scared even, and for a moment she got a flush of satisfaction before checking herself. She was here to try to sort this out. Laura didn't deserve it, but she was willing to bury the hatchet. She'd done a lot of thinking the last couple of days and, in all honesty, life would be a lot easier if she didn't have to carry on with this vendetta. She'd done enough, she thought, to make her point; and if Laura would back down, she was prepared to forget all about it. At first, pursuing Laura had been satisfying, but it was a time-consuming ordeal and felt rather like trying to break a horse. How much did the woman want to take, for God's sake?

Her benevolence gave her a warm feeling, a sense of righteousness. She'd come to her conclusion after a day of waiting, of brick walls and inaction, and she'd been bored—and irritated that for a time she'd lost control of the situation.

Daniel had been on a later shift today and this had given them the chance to have breakfast together. The atmosphere had been one of forced amiability, and neither of them had mentioned the night before, even though Cherry was intent on finding out what had shifted his implicit trust, what had made him behave disingenuously around her. Instinctively, she knew if she asked him outright, he'd pretend not to know what she was talking about. She discounted the idea he'd found something incriminating of hers; she was careful, so careful, that nothing existed except her hopes and dreams, her plans in her mind. Anyway, she was an honest and genuine person. She could love him, support his career, look after their house and children.

No, what she needed was to check his phone. That would hold the most likely source as he'd been fine until she'd come back from getting the wine. He must've spoken to someone or heard from someone while she was out. Fully expecting to snoop when he was in the shower, she was annoyed to see he took it into the bathroom with him so he could play music from his iTunes. The phone didn't leave him for longer than a minute, two perhaps after that, and before long he was kissing her good-bye and leaving the apartment, taking her source of intelligence with him.

She sat heavily on the lemon sofa. For once, she was stumped and realized she'd just have to wait until he came home and then engineer a situation where he was away from his phone and she could check it without being caught. She kicked herself for not thinking of this first thing—and now she was wasting a whole day. In order to get his mind on his return, she sent him a text, something suggestive, lighthearted, and teasing, which sent the message that she was oblivious to his suspicion and dying to shag him. Hopefully, one or the other would distract him and/or bring him home as soon as possible so she could get another look at his phone.

Cherry idled the day away, waiting, thinking, planning how to get to his phone and practicing how to deal with the outcome. There was a good chance it was Laura who had called and she held imaginary conversations with Daniel while pacing the room, distressed yet calm: *"Daniel, I don't know what to say. We know she's intent on driving me away. Do you not think she's a little—I don't know how to say this—obsessive?"*

She also rehearsed her hurt reaction to the accusations so many times, she was beginning to believe her own denials. It was a good sign. In the breaks, she treated herself to some wedding websites, starting to plan where it would be, what she would wear. It wasn't as much fun as it should have been, because she couldn't fully relax until things with Daniel were back on an even keel.

When he came home, Cherry went to the front door to greet him, solicitously taking his bag and massaging his shoulders.

"That's nice," he said appreciatively, rolling his neck, but he didn't stand there long and made his way into the kitchen to get a drink. "I said I'd go and see Mum tonight—if it's not too late for her," he said as he poured water into a glass.

It was one of the scenarios she'd predicted. "It's well past ten," said Cherry, acting surprised, but without bitterness, careful not to alienate him. For the first time since he'd come in, he looked her in the eye and she kept up the appearance of nonchalance.

"I know. She might be asleep. I left her a message telling her to call if she's still up for it." He kissed her briefly. "I'll just get a shower," and he went into the bathroom, but this time, he left his phone on the worktop. Excitement flared inside her, but she waited until she could hear the water running and was about to pick up the phone when it started to ring. Startled, she snatched her hand away. *Mum* was illuminated on the screen. Cherry waited for the rings to finish and then came the *blip* to say there was a message. She picked up the phone and dialed into Daniel's mailbox.

"Daniel, I missed your call. I still want to meet. You said you'd still be up? Please, can you come over? Maybe you're in the shower or something . . . let me know. I'll wait up, so don't worry about it being late."

Cherry didn't want him to go over. She needed more time, didn't need anything to accelerate the already-fast-burning touchpaper. She pressed 3 to delete and then got rid of the text announcing the voice mail as well. Next she looked at the call history. Laura's call was listed at the top and, in a couple of swipes, she deleted it. She scrolled down through the remaining calls from what she supposed were work colleagues, Will, his dad, and then she saw it.

It wasn't listed as a name, but as the number in full. The only one she knew by heart, as she'd lived there. Her mother's house. Her mum and Daniel had had a conversation at eight thirty-seven the night before. Quickly she thought back. It was exactly the time she'd gone out to get the wine. Her heart was pounding. So he knew everything, or at least enough. That's why he could hardly look her in the eye when she'd come back, and why he'd been distracted and distant since. It was also why he was going to see Laura tonight.

Except he wasn't, she reminded herself quickly. She'd removed the message. Cherry often found that her brain was at its optimum under pressure, she got a physical buzz from solving problems against a ticking clock, and tonight was no different. In fact, tonight was inspired, genius, and most of all felt like *exactly the right thing to do.*

She would go and see Laura.

Cherry felt an odd sense of fatalism, as if by recognizing what to do, she'd started a sequence of events. She didn't know what they were yet, but somehow knew they would hold her answer.

Cherry had to prepare herself and quickly. The shower had gone off and he'd be dressed in a minute. She scrabbled around the kitchen and grabbed two slices of bread, slathered them with mayo, and put in some sliced beef and arugula. Poured a fresh glass of water and put them both on the worktop, just as he came in.

"Expect you're hungry. Thought this would be quick, especially if you end up going to see your mum."

He looked touched by her thoughtfulness. "Thanks. Has my phone rung?"

She shook her head. Daniel checked the kitchen clock and she followed his gaze. It was ten to eleven.

"I said I'd give her half an hour. I'll eat this, and then if she hasn't called, she's probably crashed."

Cherry watched attentively as he wolfed down the sandwich. After he finished, hands clasped, he stretched his arms up in the air, expelling the tiredness of the day. Then he picked up his phone again and Cherry held her breath, wondering if he was going to call Laura. But he put it back down.

"Might crash, myself," he said. "I'm on a six a.m. shift tomorrow."

"Don't blame you," said Cherry, putting his plate in the dishwasher.

"Sorry, I haven't been much company tonight, have I?" He yawned, a massive tidal wave of exhaustion that took him by surprise.

"Go to bed," Cherry said sternly. "I'll join you in a minute, just going to put this on," and she started to fill the dishwasher with powder. She deliberately took her time, and when she went to the bedroom, he was, to her satisfaction, fast asleep. Cherry congratulated herself on her sandwich. She'd added half a Zopiclone,

left over from the days just after Daniel had "died," when she
thought she'd lost everything and had had trouble sleeping. A
half would be effective enough to put him into a deep slumber,
but not so powerful he'd have any telltale signs in the morning.
She'd crushed it into powder and the peppery garlic mayonnaise
had helped disguise the faint taste. There was only one thing left
to do. She took Daniel's phone, which he'd left charging on the
worktop, sent a text, and then deleted the record: **Sorry, was in
the shower. Coming over now.**

"I thought it was time we resolved this . . . difference of opinion," started Cherry tactfully. Laura was just staring at her, looking a little moronic, if Cherry was honest. It made Cherry feel
good, honorable even, that she was prepared to offer an olive
branch. "Instead of you continually trying to push me out and
me . . . retaliating"—she saw Laura stiffen at this subtle acknowledgment of her schemes—"why don't we just quit before it gets
out of hand?"

What was wrong with Laura? Why was she still staring as if she'd
had a lobotomy or something? She clearly had to spell it out. She
moved forward and saw Laura flinch.

"Stop being so jumpy. I just fancy a sit-down, that's all." She led
Laura into her own living room and relaxed onto the sofa. Laura
was still standing, framing the doorway.

"I suppose it's too much to ask for a drink . . . ? Oh, never
mind. Let me just say what I came here to say. I've tried really
hard, Laura, to fit in, to be a good person, ideal girlfriend for
Daniel. . . ." Remembering something, she looked around the
room and laughed ruefully. "I was so nervous that day I came for
supper, the first time we met, and all you did was make me feel
like an outsider. It was you and Daniel, no room for anyone else.
But I'm not on the outside, not anymore, and you just can't seem
to get that. But I'm prepared to forget about everything. We
should be friends. I *want* us to be friends."

Eventually Laura spoke. "Are you mad?"

Cherry looked around, as if Laura was addressing someone

else. "No. I really don't know what I've done to make you dislike me so much."

Incredulous, Laura opened her mouth to speak, but Cherry knew what she was going to say and it irritated her. "Oh, I know, the puppy, the letter to Marianne, although Howard decided to divorce you himself," she added spitefully, "but those things were *after* you'd been such a bitch to me. That lie . . . it was . . . unforgivable."

Laura flinched.

"Can't argue with it, can you? I was just giving you a little taste of your own medicine." Cherry got up and pushed past Laura into the kitchen. The room was shadowy, lit only by the under-cupboard lights.

"Do I have to make myself a drink?" She sighed, getting a bottle of juice out of the fridge.

Laura eyed her warily, but didn't speak. She saw her phone, where she'd left it, and wondered if she could get to it and dial for help without being noticed. But then, surely, Cherry would hear it being answered and she was very unsure about the girl's state of mind. Laura knew she should probably be trying to talk to her, reason with her or something, but she was nervous, didn't know what she was dealing with.

Laura slowly opened up a cupboard, took out a glass, and slid it across the worktop. Cherry looked at it in pleasant surprise.

"Thanks. See, it's not so hard. Being nice." She poured some juice. "You're making Daniel miserable too, you know." She saw Laura's eyes light up at the mention of her son and sighed impatiently. "He doesn't know I'm here, and he's not currently in any physical condition to come over. He's *asleep*." Then Cherry added, to Laura's look of alarm, "And he probably won't wake for some time."

"What have you done to him?" Laura asked angrily.

Cherry stopped mid-drink. "You know, you should listen to yourself sometime. He's a grown man. He doesn't need his mummy interfering in his life." She looked at her. "We make a good couple, he and I. I'm a good person. I've done nothing wrong. I worked *hard* for this."

"So you admit it?" Laura said quietly.

"What?"

"That you set out to get Daniel. You picked him because of what he's got."

Cherry banged her glass on the table in anger. This woman was so narrow-minded, wasn't prepared to see things from another's point of view. Laura didn't like the fact that she wanted to get on, to better herself.

Christ, poor people were allowed *to think about money because they didn't have any.* "Oh, for God's sake." She walked over to the back doors and looked out. It was dark, but the garden lights had been left on.

Upset, Laura watched her, and unable to hold back any longer, she unleashed all her pent-up fear and worry. Her voice wavered. "You say you're a *'good person.'* I've never heard anything so outrageous in my life. You're a conniving, manipulating liar. You're only interested in one thing, and that's what you can get for yourself."

Cherry tensed her shoulders. "No—"

"You're nothing but a self-serving parasite—"

"No, I'm not—"

". . . and my unfortunate son just happened to be in the wrong place at the wrong time when he walked into that real estate agency—"

"Stop it—" Cherry put her hands over her ears.

". . . and you are systematically ruining his life, and even your mother is embarrassed to call you her daught—"

"SHUT UP!"

Cherry's scream hung in the air; for a moment, neither said anything. Cherry tried to calm her breathing, control the impulse to fly at Laura, rip the self-satisfied and judgmental expression off the face of this privileged woman. She concentrated on the garden, taking measured breaths and forcing back the fury that threatened to engulf her. Shaking, she tensed her arms, bunching her hands into fists.

All of a sudden, Cherry was engulfed by sadness, a sense of defeat, which threatened to destabilize her. She'd offered Laura friendship, respect, had even been willing to form a mother-daughter bond. What had she gotten in return? Rejection and hostility. *I will never fit in.*

In anguish, Cherry leaned her hands against the window, and it was then she saw it. Right in the middle of the lawn. She looked again carefully, just to make sure she hadn't made a mistake. It was definitely empty; the pane of glass had gone.

She turned.

"Laura, I'm sorry you still feel that way, but I don't think you understand what I'm trying to say. Daniel and I love each other." Before Laura could expostulate further, Cherry put her hand on the door handle.

"Do you mind if I just get some fresh air? I'm finding this all a little stressful."

She unlocked the bifold door and folded out the first section. Then she took one step onto the patio. It was chilly, but the freshness sharpened her mind further, and there was something about the darkness that made her nerves alive with the moment.

Laura watched warily, her heart hammering against her rib cage. The second she'd finished her tirade, she'd regretted her impulsiveness. Cherry's calmness was disquieting and now she'd gone into the garden. What should Laura do? She weighed the possibility of slamming the door shut and locking it, but Cherry was still too close. Cherry could turn in half a second and put a foot in the door—no, she'd never get it closed in time. She took a step forward, half-thinking that this action might make Cherry move forward too, deeper into the garden and away from the door.

Cherry suddenly turned and slid the door open all the way back to the wall. "Come on, it's a beautifully clear night," she said, and gestured for Laura to step out.

Laura thought for a moment. If she followed Cherry out there and got her far enough into the garden, while maintaining enough distance, she could, maybe, race back into the house and lock her out there. She left the house and went outside, and Cherry started to walk across the lawn.

It's like a miracle, thought Cherry, *as if it was meant to be. That hole, right in the middle of the garden. Laura could make her own accident.*

It was the kind of thing that could easily happen, even if she wasn't there. Cherry knew she had to make Laura angry again, as that was when she got upset, careless.

"What if you were to offer me something to make me stay away?" Cherry made her way a little farther toward the hole in the ground as she spoke. *Not too fast. Little steps, little steps.* She smiled to herself when she heard Laura follow.

"You want money?" said Laura, breathless with outrage. "Money to stay away from Daniel? You must be mad. I pay you off and then you tell him it was all my idea? Do you think I'm stupid?"

No, not stupid, thought Cherry, *just nicely distracted.* She walked a bit farther, as if mulling over what Laura had said. "I wouldn't do that. I'd leave and neither of you would see me again." She'd gotten as near as she dared without making Laura suspicious. Laura was quite close now, only a couple of yards away. She needed to circle her now, get behind her. Then she would run at her so she'd stagger back and have her accident. An unexpected stumble and a tragic fall to the basement below. Then Cherry would just go home, get back into bed. Wake up with Daniel and wait for the news, and she wouldn't have laid a finger on her.

She started to maneuver her way around Laura. "Or I could just tell Daniel that it's not working out, I've met someone else."

Laura's stomach twisted. "Don't. Don't do that. Just leave."

"Let's make it a hundred grand. No, two. That's peanuts to you."

"Please. I'm asking you now. Just get out of my house."

"If I disappeared, that run of bad luck might stop. What's it worth, Laura?"

Laura was shaking now, pleading.

"Leave me alone. You say you want to be friends—that's what I wanted, right at the beginning. That's what I *tried* to do."

Cherry was now almost directly behind Laura. All she had to do was move a tiny bit more toward the house and she'd be in the right position. She couldn't walk it; she had to invisibly shift from one foot to the next as she spoke. Undetectable, minuscule movements. She began to edge backward, giving herself enough of a run up.

54

Saturday, November 7, 11:46 p.m.

DANIEL GROANED IN HIS SLEEP AND TURNED HIS FACE FROM SIDE TO side.

"Go away," he mumbled, but Rufus kept on licking him. Somewhere, deep in his unconsciousness, he knew it was the puppy, but he couldn't seem to wake. He was also very aware of this fact, and it made him want to fight against it, so he mentally forced his way upward through the fog.

Even as he lay on the pillow, blinking in the dark, he wasn't sure if he was dreaming. Rufus was delighted to see him awake, but Daniel's head was pounding. He felt groggy and could feel himself slipping between waking and sleeping. Maybe he was coming down with something, but it didn't feel like that; it felt as if he'd been drugged and he couldn't understand how that could be.

It took him so long to get his mental bearings, and understand he really was awake, he didn't notice Cherry's absence for a good five minutes. Not quite believing it, he switched on the bedside light. Her side was definitely empty. Judging by the smoothness of the quilt and plump pillows, he figured she'd not yet come to bed. He checked the time on the alarm clock: 11:51. God, his head hurt; swinging his feet out of bed, he staggered across to the en suite, pushed a couple of tablets through the blister pack, and swallowed them down with some water. He tried to shake away the fogginess, but that just made it swirl around in his head even more.

He wondered where Cherry was. A light was left on in the hallway, but nothing in the rest of the apartment. Surely, she hadn't gone out, not at this time. Checking all the rooms, with the puppy scampering after him, just in case she'd fallen asleep or something, he started to worry when she wasn't anywhere in the flat. He located his phone and called her, but it went straight to voice mail.

"Cherry, where are you? It's late and I'm worried. Call me as soon as you get this."

He tried to think. Something was most definitely not right, but his brain wasn't letting him work it out. He considered calling the police, but first thought there might be someone else who would know where she was. There was Wendy, but somehow he doubted she'd know. Still, there was no one else, so he picked up his phone again and then he noticed it: an unread text. Thinking it was Cherry, he quickly went into the menu, but it was from his mother: **Great, see you in a few minutes. X**

He didn't know what she meant. It had been sent about forty minutes ago. Daniel struggled to understand. He thought his mum had gone to bed. She hadn't replied to his voice mail. So, why was she seemingly expecting him? Tonight? He called her phone, but it rang out. *Odd. And* where *is Cherry?* None of it made any sense. Who was his mum responding to? In a rush, an answer came to him. He stared at the phone in confusion. *Did Cherry go there?*

Why?

Various unwelcome answers came to him, but none of them were fully formed; all of them were ominous. Quickly he grabbed his jacket and keys and left the apartment.

The chill air was helping, he thought, as he walked rapidly down the street, then felt an urge to run, even though his whole body was leaden with fatigue. His urgency was fueling a growing panic, or was it the other way around? If he could keep up this pace, he'd be there in five minutes. Off the main streets, the sidewalks were empty. Security lights flashed on outside sporadic houses as he raced past them. By the time he got to his parents' house, his limbs were aching and he knew he was under the influence of some sort of soporific drug. There was only one possible explanation as to how he could have ingested it and this realization shocked him. *Cherry did this me.* However, the question that frightened him most, the question that he was now starting to dread, was *Why?*

He turned up the path to number 38 and rang the doorbell. A thread of light was barely visible through the drawn curtains on the hallway window to his right. He stood back and looked up at the upstairs windows, which were dark and lifeless, and then he rang again, but this time didn't wait. Instead he took his keys from his pocket.

Unlocking the door, he stepped inside, listening carefully for sounds of his mother, but it was silent.

"Hello?" he called. "It's me, Daniel."

There was no reply. Slowly he made his way through the house, to the living room first. The TV was on and Moses was half asleep, lying lazily on the sofa. Next he went into the dim kitchen. Almost as soon as he walked in, he felt the cool breeze; and then across the room, he saw the open back doors and through them, in the garden, his mother and Cherry.

At first, he didn't understand what they were doing. Cherry had her back to him, and his mother was upset about something, but although he could hear voices, he couldn't make out exactly what they were saying.

In the soft darkness, with the six-foot-high walls surrounding the garden, Cherry had a sense of privacy, of being cocooned in their own shadowy little bubble. It would be so easy. No one was around. She glanced up at the sky and pretended to admire the moon, clouds scudding across, but really she was checking the windows of the neighboring houses.

"A new moon," she said lightly.

No lights on either side, not for as far as she could see. They were completely alone in a place outside time or space.

It could so easily happen. Laura comes out here to the garden, goes a bit close to the hole, stumbles, slips, and falls. She shuddered. *It really was too dangerous,* she thought disapprovingly.

Cherry ran back through the evidence in her mind. She knew little of crime scenes, and it would've been helpful to research in advance, but she'd seen enough shows to know what to do. Daniel was asleep, so her alibi with him was secure. In the house, she'd touched the doorbell, the inside front-door handle, the fridge door, the juice bottle and glass, the key and the handle on the bi-fold door. That was it.

She remembered it all with the utmost clarity and knew with absolute certainty she could replay every footstep to its exact position if she went back in there. It was as if she had been watching herself move, as if she wasn't really there at all, and that other self would make sure she left safely and without any trace. She glanced up at the windows again. Black sleeping sockets, each and every one, curtains drawn as if to deliberately keep them ignorant. No evil in these high-class streets.

A fox slunk in from the back fence, pushing past one of the panels that looked as if it was broken. For a microsecond she wondered if it was her fox, from Tooting, before realizing that was ridiculous. Before the fox had crossed the garden, Cherry raised her arms and, opening her mouth in a silent roar, ran, like an enraged animal, at Laura, whose face suddenly contorted with stupefied terror as she instinctively staggered back, away from the attack.

"No!" a voice shouted, and Cherry turned in shock to see Daniel bursting through the back door. She lost her balance at the same time Laura flung out her arms in desperation, scrabbling at whatever she could touch.

Laura was screaming now. In fact, the screams kept coming from her throat as she fell to the ground; the plastic barriers flying away from her; she didn't want to die; *she couldn't fail;* she flung her arms violently around, feeling the weight of Cherry against her and she shoved; then, hands and face in the dirt, she tried to crawl toward the house, still screaming in terror; then she heard a strange, distant thud and Daniel had his arms around her and, sobbing, she clung to him, burying herself into him, her mind blank with terror, like an animal or a small child cowering in her son's lap, terrified that Cherry was still coming, but somehow she didn't; and as the seconds passed, she began to understand what the sound had been.

EPILOGUE

*L*AURA WATCHED OUT THE WINDOW AS THE MAN FROM THE REAL ES-
tate agency fixed a FOR SALE sign outside the front of the house.
Not Highsmith and Brown, of course, but there were plenty of
other reputable agents who were anxious to deal expertly with
the disposal of her home. Neither she nor Howard wanted it after
what had happened, and, in fact, Howard hadn't even been down
to the den. He was happy to let the moving guys pack everything
that belonged to him and transport it to his new home. She'd
tried not to watch as his possessions, things that she had lived
around for years, were taken to a house in St. John's Wood, one
he now shared with Marianne.

A few weeks afterward, Daniel had moved into his flat, not the
one he'd lived in with Cherry, but another, without memories.
Something he found himself in a cheaper part of town, rented, and
this time Howard hadn't argued. Laura didn't mind; in fact, she was
moving herself to a mews house near enough to Daniel for them to
meet up regularly, far enough away for them to have their own lives.

It had taken her a while, but Laura had eventually plucked up
the courage to go down there. As she made her way to the basement in the elevator, she couldn't help thinking of the paramedics who'd come down all those weeks ago to take Cherry
away. How she'd looked, what they'd had to do. She'd been dead
when they'd gotten to her. Laura knew this because Daniel had
gone to her straight after the accident, to see if he could help.

Now the area had been cleaned, of course, but the image that came to her was not Cherry lying lifeless on the floor but of her the night of the party, when they'd gone down together, just the two of them, alone, and Laura got a sense of unease, half-expecting to hear Cherry's heels across the floor. The glass window had been fixed and Laura looked up. Suddenly feeling trapped, she had hurried out of there and back up to the house.

The police had interviewed her and Daniel and also the neighbor who had heard her screams and looked out the window from two houses down. Daniel was the key witness as he'd actually seen Cherry fall. He told the police that Cherry had slipped. She'd been trying to cause his mother to fall to her death by running at her; then she'd lost her balance as she'd twisted back round to see him and had fallen herself, crashing into Laura as she did so. Laura had watched him carefully as he'd relayed the course of events in the immediate aftermath and knew that was what he'd seen. His sorrowful report supported what the neighbor had witnessed some distance away from his window. It seemed to be enough for the coroner, who recorded a verdict of accidental death.

No one saw. No one. What a risk—it made her tremble—if it had gone wrong. A moment of madness. Of course, it would almost certainly have been classed as self-defense—Cherry had been trying to kill her, after all. But still, she didn't say anything; she was too frightened. There had been a moment when their eyes had met—a split second—and something primeval had flared up in her. She could have saved Cherry. Maybe. She'd put her arm out. Made contact. But not in order to pull her toward safety. No, to push her toward the dark depths below. It had all been so quick, it would have been hard to see, unless you were right up close. And no one else was.

She had no recollection of making the decision. That's what petrified her. That's what gave her the nightmares. How she'd got to that dark place. Who was that person?

She'd never forget. Maybe, eventually, she'd find a way to live with it.